Chang Ying-Tai is an award-winning Taiwanese novelist and short story writer. She received her PhD in Literature from National Taiwan University, and holds the position of Distinguished Professor at the National Taiwan University of Science and Technology, Taipei.

Over the past decade, she has been the recipient of numerous major awards, including the China Times First Prize for Fiction and Prose; the United Daily Press First Prize for Fiction; the Central Daily News First Prize for Fiction; the Award for Literary Writing from the Taiwanese Ministry of Education; and the Lennox Robinson Award for Distinguished Contribution to the Arts. She has also been a finalist for the Two-Million-Yuan Award for Fiction, one of the largest monetary prizes in Asian literature.

Chang Ying-Tai has written prolifically. Her works been translated into English include the novels: *The Bear Whispers to Me*, *The Zither Player of Angkor Thom*, and *As Flowers Bloom and Wither*.

Florence Woo is a Chinese-to-English translator based in Canada. She holds a PhD in Linguistics from the University of California, Santa Cruz. Her short story translations have appeared in *The Taipei Chinese Pen*, *Chinese Arts and Letters,* and the anthology *Irina's Hat: New Short Stories from China*. *As Flowers Bloom and Wither* is her first full-length novel translation.

CHANG YING-TAI

As Flowers Bloom and Wither

Translated from the Chinese
by Florence Woo

balestierpress

Balestier Press
71-75 Shelton Street, London WC2H 9JQ
www.balestier.com

As Flowers Bloom and Wither
Original title: 花葉如謎
Text and illustration copyright © Chang Ying-Tai, 2017
English translation copyright © Florence Woo, 2017

First published in English by Balestier Press in 2017

ISBN 978 1 911221 04 3

The publisher gratefully acknowledges the support of
the National Museum of Taiwan Literature.

This book is a work of fiction. The literary perceptions and
insights are based on experience, all names, characters, places,
and incidents either are products of the author's imagination
or are used fictitiously.

As Flowers Bloom
and Wither

Dat poenas laudata fides
"My faithfulness, though praised, brings suffering"

— Nicholas Hilliard

Prologue

The story you are about to hear is a historical mystery, told by one who is dying, on behalf of one who is dead. Only here, crouching in my grave, can I write all this down. This memoir is a mere page in a history built with deaths and turmoil—a bit blurry, a bit surreal. Though it may look like a thick volume, it does not even comprise a page, a paragraph, or even a line in the official histories.

This story is an unmarked tomb, just a step up from a mass burial site. It has survived vehement upheavals and has trembled in fear. Only between the covers of this book can it rest in eternal peace. With the turning of each page, it becomes as still as the earth after a snowfall, where all muddledness disappears under a blanket of pure white, not forgotten, but simply blotted out of existence.

These are not meant to be my last words. Neither should I, a breathing soul, speak like one on the verge of death, with light-hearted words belying the utmost gravity. However, before we talk about certain fairly surreal deaths, we should first speak of life.

My life, at the point of my earliest consciousness, was hidden in the attic with the cradle, the basket, and the sloping roof. It was always dark and dank—a musty dankness, a never-ending darkness. Sometimes a ray of light peeped in from a crack somewhere, just a tiny bit. Even if it was just a small sliver of light, I would crane my head towards it with all my strength...

A breeze always accompanied her when she climbed into the attic. With the breeze came a speck of light, and the light revealed a dark shape in my unfocused vision. I yearned for her arrival every day. I could not see her face, but could only sense a big black shape touching me gently. It emanated the faint fragrance of breast-milk, as well as a sickly sweet smell. Only after I had grown up did I realise what it was—floral water.

On the wall opposite the cradle hung a mirror. Whenever the wind rustled the curtains beside it, sunlight peeked through. And if I looked beyond the black shape in front of me, I could see her back, gleaming ever so slightly in the reflection in the mirror. She lifted me up from the cradle, and held me close to her supple bosom. I tugged on her nipple, at which she moved my hand gently aside, and placed her nipple in my mouth. Then I suckled contentedly.

She stayed with me until I started to fall asleep. When she was about to leave, I tried to grab onto her. She patted me and disappeared beyond my world, along with the breeze.

I did not cry. I was already accustomed to staying quiet. Perhaps she had a way for me to get what I needed without crying. Or perhaps it was the realisation that crying was dangerous—something that she made me remember, though I forgot how.

As unwilling as I was, I would sleep out of exhaustion or a desire to please her. I had a pacifier—a button. Holding it comforted me. I had tugged that button off her blouse one day, when I was grasping at her nipple. She gave it to me, and I sucked on it. Immediately, she used her special way to warn me not to swallow it. She pried open my fingers and took the button away; and, before I had a chance to protest, she returned it to me. She had put some uninteresting or unpleasant-tasting substance on it. From then on, I no longer wanted to suck on it, and would be content just holding it.

Aside from the cradle, there was the basket on the pulley. The basket was hoisted into the attic one day. The woman fed me not only with her breast, but also with something that she took out of the basket. After that, I was breastfed less and less, and the basket appeared more and more. However, all that ever reflected in the mirror remained just the woman's back, slightly gleaming, and nothing more.

In the first few years after I had left the cradle, after my memory and vision started to sharpen, I was still kept in the attic. Every day, the maid delivered my meals and snacks with the basket. Around that time I contracted polio. Finding it difficult to walk, I could not be bothered to come down from the attic. Treatment by physicians, Chinese and Western, only relieved my symptoms somewhat, but I still had a limp. Significant improvement only came after the two operations I had right before I started school full time.

I went to school two years later than children of my age. My parents believed that I had refused to go to school because of the polio. I was happy to let them think that way, as long as I could stay home. In reality, the polio did not affect my self-esteem at all. It was just that I disliked moving about in the first place, and would rather observe the world from my perch on my special tree. There were times when I would sit there all day until my legs fell asleep, which paralyzed me more than the polio ever did.

Actually, I had been enrolled in school at the same time as the other children of my age. However, I was in school for just one day (the first of September, 1952, I remember) before I refused to go back. I never told my parents the truth—that I needed help wiping myself after going to the toilet. The teacher wouldn't do it, and called for the janitor. The janitor wouldn't do it either. To make things worse, I had diarrhoea that day, and my behind was soiled all over. As no one would help me, I had no choice but to put my trousers back right on and spend the rest of the day in stench. Even I found myself intolerable. Apart from the period of time around the operations, I quite enjoyed my days staying at home and out of school.

Whenever my older brother was around, we would play War. When I was alone, I would play treasure-hunting by myself. Father had a collection of treasures, a list of which he kept in a record-book. I recognised about half the words on it. Father taught me to read quite early, compared to children of my age. I could read simple books by then, and was able to read and recite some classical poetry too. Some of Father's treasures, I heard, were from the Imperial Palace of the late Qing dynasty. The most valuable ones were normally stored in his treasure-room, and brought out only when important guests were visiting. Those items included "Portrait of a Bodhisattva" by Zhang Sengyao of the Southern Dynasties; "Viewing a Waterfall" by Ma Yuan of the Song Dynasty; "Bamboo in Ink" by Li Heng of the Yuan Dynasty; "Announcement of Spring" by Zou Fulei of the Yuan; "Valley Grove at Mount Yu" by Ni Zan of the Yuan; "Portrait of Li Duanduan" by Tang Yin of the Ming; "Calligraphy and Painting Album" by Dong Qichang of the Ming; "Sunset in the Mountains" by Tang Dai of the Qing; "Bamboo and Rocks on Mount Jiao" by Zheng Banqiao of the Qing... His treasure record also listed the value of some of the paintings in his collection:

Wu Li's "Springtime Lake and Sky", 3000 silver *yuan*
Chen Hongshou's "Plum Blossom", 4000 silver *yuan*
Jin Nong's "Plum Blossom in Ink", 2000 silver *yuan*
Wu Bin's "Thatched Hut on the River", 1500 silver *yuan*
Shen Zhou's "Dawn on an Autumn Mountain", 5000 silver *yuan*
Ni Zan's "Bamboo and Rock", 4800 silver yuan
Shi Tao's "Thatched Hut on Plum Creek", 3000 silver *yuan*
Chou Ying's "Hermit in the Cliff-edge Hut", 4200 silver *yuan*
Yun Xiang's "Landscape Album", 2400 silver *yuan*
Xia Gui's "Landscape Scroll", 5000 silver *yuan*
Ni Qian's "Long Scroll", 500 silver *yuan*
Dai Benxiao's "Brushwork Collection", 6000 silver *yuan*
Zhao Zi'ang's "Preface to the Tripitaka", 10000 silver *yuan*
Wen Zhengming's "Landscape", 8000 silver *yuan*...

These were not terribly interesting to me in and of themselves. But as Father taught me how to critique paintings, I learnt about the pieces to earn his reward. I memorised classical poetry for the same purpose—I was after the reward. Every time I had saved up a sum of money, I would stash it away in a secret location, and draw a treasure map for it. Whenever I was bored, or did not want to spend all day sitting in the tree, I would go on a treasure hunt with my maps, when others were not looking. Once I had found the treasure, I would take it out and hide it somewhere else. I had so many secret treasure hiding-spots that I could not keep track of all of them myself. My treasure maps were full of secret messages and crisscrossed with complicated measurement lines, which actually confused treasure-hunting efforts rather than facilitated them. However, I never tired of the game.

On top of treasure-hunting, I kept my own collection too. Just as Father collected pieces of famous paintings and calligraphy, I collected newspaper clippings, especially those involving taboo subjects, or those that could lead to imprisonment or execution.

One type of clippings were those I called "newspaper puzzles". Every year, around President Chiang's birthday, advertisements for movies in the newspapers would be missing many words, like guess-a-word puzzles. Some such titles included "_____'s Kiss", "Dial M for _____", "An Orphan's _____", "The _____ of the Hunter", and "The _____ with Harry". The grown-ups said that the newspapers had to omit from print any inauspicious-sounding words, such as "killer", "murder", "tragedy", "night", and "trouble". The result was the perfect fill-in-the-blanks puzzles for me. There were so many blanks that it took very much effort to restore them to their original form. Sometimes, though, when I didn't feel like thinking too much, I used my imagination to make stories with them. And if not even that could keep me sufficiently occupied, I would do the reverse, and cut out all the auspicious-sounding words from the newspapers. For example, the congratulatory message "Let the entire nation rejoice and wish him a long and happy life" could become "Let the entire nation _____ and wish him a _____ and _____ life." And then I would have a whole new word puzzle.

Then, there were those deadly typographical errors in the newspapers, such as misprinting "our common leader" as "our commie leader", or "a report to President Chiang" as "a retort to President Chiang", or "the content of the President's instructions" as "the contempt of the President's instructions". Or, those "Happy National Day" announcements printed too early in October (our national day is the tenth of October, while Communist China's national day is the first of the same month). Each word in newspaper-type may be no bigger than an ant, but one slight mistake could cost a few lives. Definitely worth collecting.

There was an even rarer type of treasure, such as this one page in an editorial section that I had reread over a hundred times. On it was an American cartoon titled "Two turtles climbing onto a desert island." I really liked the editor, Uncle Guo. He once gave me a box of delicious butter biscuits. But one day he vanished. He was arrested, and was either sent to prison or shot. According to the grown-ups, the cartoon was seen as a satirical piece, alluding to the President and his son's flight to Taiwan after losing the war on the Mainland. The sunflowers in the foreground (were those the national flower of Communist China?) symbolised that the Communists were about to land on Taiwan... But Father warned me not to tell anyone about that, or I might get taken away just like Uncle Guo.

There was another secret that I knew, one that would get me arrested and shot, too, if it was leaked out. Because of that, I did not even tell Father about it. It was the secret about the Treasure, about the ship full of gold that came with my family to Taiwan. Well, actually, I should put it the other way—my family came to Taiwan on a ship that carried a secret stash of gold. I was just a child then, and the grown-ups had all fallen asleep. A light sleeper, I awoke when the ship was tossed by waves. Or perhaps I woke up because I had to relieve myself. Anyway, I felt my way in the dark to the other side of the boat in order to pee. Suddenly, I caught sight of what was going on. I cowered immediately and covered my head—there were people fighting on the ship, pointing guns at each other.

It started with someone remarking, "The ship isn't heading in the right direction. Why is she going north?" Someone else replied in a low growl, "The captain crossed over to the enemy!" And then all hell broke loose. I hid my head lower and lower. The battlefield gradually shifted to the other side of the ship and began to die down, until some people were bound and thrown into the hold...

"We've been infiltrated by underground Commies!"

"This was supposed to be a two-day voyage. We're already a whole day behind. Who knows how many more days it'll take..."

"There were quite a few battleships that mutinied at the same time, the *Hui'an*, the *Andong*, the *Zhutong*, the *Meisheng*, the *Jiangxi*, the *Ji'an*, the *Lianguang*... Looks like we're next..."

"In that case, do you think we'll get to Taiwan?"

"Hard to say. There are Commie ambushes in these parts of the water..."

"With that gold from the Treasury on board, I doubt they would let us go that easily."

"Keep your lips tight. Don't mention that thing. If they find out we'll lose our heads..."

"We've detoured so far. The food is running low..."

I kept all those whispered words in my heart. They had not noticed me, curled up there so inconspicuously and apparently fast asleep. That was the first time I was exposed to the concepts of danger, and secrets, and treasures—and their paramount importance.

Later, when I played War with my older brother, I was often the pirate, while he was the soldier. We pretended that there was a large stash of national-grade treasures, and we fought for the possession and protection of it.

More often than that, though, we played Real War—War that involved two opposing countries or political groups. Because that kind of war required more manpower, we could only play that when Uncle Yao and Uncle Zhu's children came over to play.

I did not always team up with my brother in those games. Usually, I partnered up with Yao Kunming, and fought against Zhu Xiaokang and my brother. We had military codewords, including pass phrases. Whenever an ally reported at a friendly base, the sentry would converse with him according to a set of watchwords to confirm his identity. For example, if the sentry said "I receive your telegrams often", the other person should reply, "I haven't received a telegram from you in a long time." Or, if the sentry asked, "How do you get to Normandy?" the reply should be, "I don't know. The paratroopers have only just arrived." Or, if the question was "When did you come from the fort?", the reply was, "I came from the fort yesterday". Or, to the statement "The general has moved the encampment," the correct response was, "Rain will hamper our operation."

Our codewords for talking about actual military deployment were mostly found in lists of stationery supplies:

Blue ink: each jar represented a battleship
Fountain pens: each pen represented an armoured vehicle
Pencils: each pencil represented a fighter aircraft
Red ink: each jar represented an artillery gun
Crayons: each crayon represented 100 troops
Drawing paper: each large sheet represented a corps
Construction paper: each stack represented a division
Notebooks: each notebook represented a brigade
Erasers: each eraser represented 100 *yuan* worth of provisions

Just as Father had a record book for keeping track of the value of his collection, we had a stationery list for keeping track of our military strength. The two really had little to do with each other, but I kept feeling that the codewords I devised were inspired by my father's record book. Both appeared to be kept secure in the same way, and both appeared to be covering up something beyond the obvious.

Our battlefield was normally the courtyard of our house. For bigger wars, we extended to the dike behind the house. And for long-distance campaigns, we fought all the way from home to a nearby hill. This was no mere game to us; it was serious. We laid ambushes in narrow alleys, tracked the enemy through thick forests, and set traps in the waist-high grass. Each of us carried heavy equipment, marching forward most carefully to avoid being detected by the enemy. From time to time, the unit leader would lift his binoculars to observe the enemy's movements, check his map, and calculate the unit's distance from the destination.

"We're 400 yards away from the target. Artillery corps, attention!" I issued a command to my unit, "Aim at the enemy target at 30 degrees!" Upon receiving orders, my "unit"—consisting of Yao Kunming, who stood in for a hundred soldiers—launched the bomb (a lump of dirt) in that direction. The enemy returned fire. We dropped to the ground, waiting a while before crawling onward. When the next volley of shells rained down, we dropped to the ground again. Both sides attacked with all their might, the battle-lust burning within, until one side was completely decimated. Sometimes, when we went to occupy an enemy site where there should not have been any survivors, those enemies that should have been "dead" came back to life and attacked. And then, a battle that had already wound down had to be fought all over again.

There was always deceit and broken promises in a war. There was also mistrust of others' promises. I was no exception. All that mattered was avoiding being annihilated. More often than not, the outcome was mutual destruction, and any victory was one accompanied by tragic losses, a victory that deserved no celebration.

Sometimes, though I was not badly "injured", I would suddenly lose all interest in the game and go lie behind a rock, pretending to be gravely hurt. From there, I watched "the soldiers" (Yao Kunming playing multiple roles) dodging left and right to return fire, covering me from enemy fire, and even taking time to bandage my "wounds".

In such times, I would feel an indescribable sense of futility and sadness. I knew that only by suppressing the sudden surfacing of reason and sanity in my head could I continue to fight. But, at the same time, there seemed not to be any convincing reasons to fight anymore. Surrender? No, cowards who surrender were not considered kindly in war: defectors were labelled traitors; not even with death could they redeem their honour. Additionally, captives were not necessarily treated well—there is no shortage of historical tales where prisoners of war were buried alive en masse. As the shells landed, I looked around and surveyed the massacre around me (as we did not have enough actual bodies, we used bundles of grass or sticks to stand in for soldiers—each bundle counted as a unit of 100 men), waiting tiredly for it all to come to an end...

Decades later, I still remember the exhaustion and the waiting.

How should I explain the intensity with which we played that game? At first, we imagined that war was something grand, that we could make ourselves heroes through it. Then, we realised that we were stuck, having no choice but to kill others so that we might live. We rushed forward regardless, madly. The ending was invariably death, the only difference being dying in tragic victory or in tragic defeat. Melancholy permeated everything. However, this melancholy dissipated as soon as the next wave of fury struck. After all, it was so easy to consider others as enemies, to attack them mercilessly. It did not matter that they were not willing participants aware of their actions—when embroiled in an ongoing war, they had no choice but to go with the flow. In death, they joined a list of unfortunate and nameless ones, and history would never know what really happened to them. No one will ever see the stains of their blood, or discover the grief of their past.

The story I am about to tell, though, touches on such bloodstains, such grief. When all fortune and misfortune have passed, there will only remain a tinge of indifference, and perhaps a bit of inconsequential acceptance.

Only one line can be appropriately engraved on their headstones:

He did not matter.

PART I

1
All is covered under rose petals

They naïvely maintain that everything is complicated.
But I, experienced with the world, believe that everything is as simple as could be.

Like the wings of a dragonfly.

The petals of a rose.

I lay out some fragments before them, ones that cannot be put together in meaningful ways.

So they keep trying to make me understand what constitutes useful leads.

Those intricate details I give fail to make them ask for more.

You need to get to the heart of the matter. The heart of the matter is about a plot, about who the enemy is. They want you to tell them things that would entice them to ask for more information.

I know of some heroes who are just like the villains they describe. I don't know who the villains are, but I can probably pass a hero off as one, if only they would listen to me.

I throw more and more random memory fragments at them. The rose petals, scattered in the sky, eventually drift back to earth, burying all underneath them. I, too, am helplessly buried.

They ask me what the enemy said.

I tell them seriously: The Americans have a saying: "The greatest tragedy in human history is not the conflict between morality and corruption, but the conflict between two moralities."

They say, No! We don't want what the Americans said. We want what the enemy said.

So I say, The enemy said, "The greatest tragedy in human history is not the struggle between good and evil, but the struggle between two goods."

They say, No, that doesn't sound like what the enemy would say.

So then I say, I am the enemy. I say, "The greatest tragedy in human history is not the struggle between right and wrong, but the conflict between two wrongs."

2
Of codes, roses, and eggs

Roses

I go to the garden to look for roses—not ones that are blooming in the bush, but those that have been cut off and cast aside. There are roses everywhere. I search among them, one by one, frantically peeling off their petals. Nothing. Nothing. There is nothing here. The ground is blanketed with bits of crimson, scarlet, carmine, vermillion. A gust rises. The petals all shrivel up and crumble into dust. I turn to look at my shadow under the moonlight, but it, too, splinters and fractures at once.

I dreamt of her again last night. It wasn't that I really yearned for her that much. Anyone would do. I was only calling for help, hoping that someone had left a message for me.

Eggs

As soon as I walk into the house, I pick up the hard-boiled eggs in the pot, peeling off their shells one by one, frantically turning them in my hands and examining them. Nothing, nothing. It's all useless. I throw them all out.

I dreamt of her again last night, but she hadn't left any messages for me. I was only calling for help, asking over and over again, "Are there any more hard-boiled eggs?"

* * *

"Roses. Eggs."

The electric current again. A strong zap attacks my heart. They believe that I am lying, and say they will give me one more chance. My hand is connected to the wire again... I did tell them the truth, but they didn't believe me.

A basin of water pours down. I cannot even escape into unconsciousness. Then, they hang me upside-down, sticking my head in half a bucket of water. I gurgle underwater, trying to speak. Someone gives me a yank by the hair and lets my nose leave the water. "Tell us the truth!" I finally understand. What they want me to say is what they want to believe. And so I begin...

"I'm a Communist. My name is Song Chunhuan and I'm a Communist."

This is the first enemy I have named.

"Piece of shit, I already know you're a Commie. Cut the nonsense. Get to the point!"

He presses my head into the water again.

"I passed information to the Communists."

Someone else asks, "How did you communicate with them?"

"I sent coded messages. The code mapped Chinese phonetic spelling into numerals, but with the numbers converted from base-ten into base-three. For example, 100 210 102 121 001 022 112..."

I am released. "Sit still!" The sissy-voiced "Commie Defector" drags me to the desk and throws me onto the chair. I can barely prop myself up with my elbows on the desk. The pen shakes unsteadily in my hand. The lampshade above my head swings around and around... My world has been swinging around and around for three whole days. What do they want me to write?

Write the code

They are all sitting still, at a distance, looking ready to administer another electric shock or water-boarding, or to sit you on a slab of ice and set an electric fan on you. I steady the pen with great effort and demonstrated in earnest:

"Apart from the base-three phonetic code, I sometimes used a type of the Atbash Cipher. The letters abcdefgh... are converted to letters in reverse alphabetical order, zyxwvuts... So, when I write 'urmw z hkb', the meaning is 'find a spy'.

"The other was a Caesar Shift Cipher. Each letter is replaced by the letter a certain number of positions after it, say, three. So, A is D, C is F, K is N, M is P, and T is W. And then the letters are replaced with corresponding numbers, so K=N=11+3=14, M=P=13+3=16, T=W=20+3=23. So, 14-16-23 means KMT, the Kuomintang. However, this cipher is easy to break, so I combined it with the Atbash cipher. The letters KMT, in the reversed alphabet is PNG, and when moved three letters down it becomes SQJ. The equivalent numbers are then 19-17-10, which is the correct code for 'Kuomintang'.

"There's also the Polypius Square, which is also very simple. Put the 26 English letters into a five-by-five square, and label the rows and columns from 1 to 5. Put 'i' and 'j' in the same square, like this:

	1	2	3	4	5
1	a	b	c	d	e
2	f	g	h	i/j	k
3	l	m	n	o	p
4	q	r	s	t	u
5	v	w	x	y	z

"See, 'a' is at the intersection of the number '1' on the left and the number 1 at the top, so its code is '11'. 'h' is at the intersection of the number '2' on the left and '3' at the top, so its code is '23'. 'p' is at the intersection between '3' on the left and '5' on the top, so its code is '35'. In short, each letter has a two-digit code. For example the word 'enemy' translates into the code 1533153254."

They replace their derisive attitude with a more attentive look.

I pull myself together and continue to demonstrate.

"Sometimes, I combined that with roman numerals in order to indicate time. For example, X is the 24th letter of the alphabet, I is the 9th, and V is the 22nd. So, when I send the signal 2422999, it would mean XVIII, which is 18:00... There's another one, where I disguised the message as an arithmetic formula, adding the numerals pair by pair and then converting them into English letters, for example 3+1=6, 4+3=3..."

I lift my head to look at them. A few of them seem to have started to believe. The "Commie Defector", though, is still looking askance at me, as if waiting for me to reveal more.

I ask them for a larger sheet of paper, on which I draw a table of the letters of the alphabet, each row of which is made by shifting the previous row by one.

"This is the Trithemius Cipher. When you want to send a message, such as 'keep silence', you can use this *tabula recta* to encrypt it. Let me demonstrate:

```
a b c d e f g h i j k l m n o p q r s t u v w x y z
b c d e f g h i j k l m n o p q r s t u v w x y z a
c d e f g h i j k l m n o p q r s t u v w x y z a b
d e f g h i j k l m n o p q r s t u v w x y z a b c
e f g h i j k l m n o p q r s t u v w x y z a b c d
f g h i j k l m n o p q r s t u v w x y z a b c d e
g h i j k l m n o p q r s t u v w x y z a b c d e f
h i j k l m n o p q r s t u v w x y z a b c d e f g
i j k l m n o p q r s t u v w x y z a b c d e f g h
j k l m n o p q r s t u v w x y z a b c d e f g h i
k l m n o p q r s t u v w x y z a b c d e f g h i j
l m n o p q r s t u v w x y z a b c d e f g h i j k
m n o p q r s t u v w x y z a b c d e f g h i j k l
n o p q r s t u v w x y z a b c d e f g h i j k l m
o p q r s t u v w x y z a b c d e f g h i j k l m n
p q r s t u v w x y z a b c d e f g h i j k l m n o
q r s t u v w x y z a b c d e f g h i j k l m n o p
r s t u v w x y z a b c d e f g h i j k l m n o p q
s t u v w x y z a b c d e f g h i j k l m n o p q r
t u v w x y z a b c d e f g h i j k l m n o p q r s
u v w x y z a b c d e f g h i j k l m n o p q r s t
v w x y z a b c d e f g h i j k l m n o p q r s t u
w x y z a b c d e f g h i j k l m n o p q r s t u v
x y z a b c d e f g h i j k l m n o p q r s t u v w
y z a b c d e f g h i j k l m n o p q r s t u v w x
z a b c d e f g h i j k l m n o p q r s t u v w x y
```

"In the first row, directly pick the first letter of the plaintext, 'k'. After that, continue to use the top row to look up the remaining letters in the plaintext. When we want to encrypt the second letter, 'e', we find the location of the letter 'e' on the top row and go down to the second row, which is 'f'. To encrypt the third letter, 'e', we also go from the 'e' on the top row down to the third row, which is 'g'. To encrypt the fourth letter, 'p', we go from the location of 'p' on the top row down to the fourth row, which is 's'. To encrypt the fifth letter, 's', we go from the 's' in the top row down to the fifth row, which is 'w'. And so on. So, the ciphertext for 'keep silence' is 'kfgs wnrlvlo'. Even though there are two 'e's in the plaintext, the ciphertext contains no duplicates, thus removing a clue for breaking the code."

"Mm-hmm." Someone hummed lightly. Doesn't sound like an objection.

"Trithemius's Cipher can be strengthened further by adding on a Vigenère Cipher. Which is to add a 'secret key' on top of your plaintext. Agree with the recipient upon a word to use as the keyword, to change the order in which you use the *tabula recta*. Let's say your plaintext is 'they come from the west and attack at dawn', and your keyword is 'decide'. So, use the rows corresponding to 'd', 'e', 'c', 'i', 'd', and 'e' to cross with the letters for 'they come from the west' on the top row. You can repeat the word 'decide' multiple times. Let me demonstrate again:

Plaintext: t h e y c o m e f r o m t h e w e s t a n d a t t a c k a t d a w n
Secret key: d e c i d e d e c i d e d e c i d e d e c i d e d e c i d e d e c i

"The first letter of the plaintext is 't', so we find the 't' on the top row, and follow that downward until the row that starts with the letter 'd', the first letter of the key. At the intersection we get a 'w' as the first letter of the ciphertext. Then, the second letter of the plaintext, 'h', and the second letter of the key, 'e', get you the letter 'l'...

```
a b c d e f g h i j k l m n o p q r s t u v w x y z
b c d e f g h i j k l m n o p q r s t u v w x y z a
c d e f g h i j k l m n o p q r s t u v w x y z a b
d e f g h i j k l m n o p q r s t u v w x y z a b c
e f g h i j k l m n o p q r s t u v w x y z a b c d
f g h i j k l m n o p q r s t u v w x y z a b c d e
g h i j k l m n o p q r s t u v w x y z a b c d e f
h i j k l m n o p q r s t u v w x y z a b c d e f g
i j k l m n o p q r s t u v w x y z a b c d e f g h
```

"And now I finished all the steps and end up with the cipher text wlggfspihzrqwlgziubdrgevbdgnecldaq."

They all come over to look. No one is accusing me of lying anymore.

"What information did you send them?" A stern voice shoots over from the other side of the room.

I tell them an excerpt of the story that I know so very well, but in code, with names of people and places swapped beyond recognition.

They finally let me go back to my cell, and I finally get a good sleep.

* * *

I did know about ciphers. I learnt them on my own, from reading books and historical stories.

I taught myself ciphers solely for fun. However, there was no one to play that game with me.

That's why I preferred roses and eggs.

* * *

I often played this game with her: we would give each other roses, with a secret message etched onto the backs of the petals.

Back then, people often sent flowers to our house. Those flowers rarely made it into our vases, but were more usually thrown out right away. Sometimes, Autumn, our maid, would try to keep a stem or two for herself, but Father would tell her to throw them all out. Later on, whenever flowers were delivered, Autumn would keep them for a while before handing them to Father, who usually took only two stems from the bouquet—the one with the biggest flower and the one with the smallest flower. I had caught him doing so. Originally, whenever Father received a bouquet, he only picked out the largest flower to admire, and threw it out soon after. Eventually, he started to take two flowers, the biggest one and the smallest one. And I came to know that the big one contained a state secret, while the small one contained a personal secret.

The secret hidden in the smallest rose was from Autumn to Father. They had a secret between them, I knew. I, too, guarded all I knew as if it were top secret.

* * *

We imitated the grown-ups in playing this game. Though we had no secrets, we carved words on the petals as if we had one. We competed in carving words as finely and as inconspicuously as we could—perhaps if we could carve words small enough, they would count as a secret.

As for eggs, this is how it worked: Write something on the shell of a raw egg with vinegar, and, after it dries, boil the egg. When it's cooked, there's nothing visible on the shell, but as soon as you shell the egg, you can see that the writing has been etched into the egg white beneath the shell.

I picked up this trick from Mother. One day, from the back of the kitchen, I noticed that she was standing quietly beside the stove, with a couple of eggs on the cutting board next to her. To my bewilderment, she had a fine calligraphy brush in her hand, which she repeatedly dipped in a bowl of vinegar and wrote with it on an egg. Then she put the egg down, picked up another one and wrote on it, until all the eggs had been similarly processed. There was a pot of boiling water on the stove. The eggs were then put in the pot to cook. A few days after that, when Mother and the maid were both away, I tried the same thing—I drew a little turtle on an egg. I cooked the egg, scooped it up and looked. On the outside nothing could be seen, and it was only after it was shelled that the drawing was revealed.

I never told Mother about Father's secret. I did not tell Father about Mother's secret, either. It was just on the days when I was bored that I would teach Floral to play this game with me.

* * *

Floral. The name came from "Star Floral Water," an exceedingly odoriferous perfume that her mother liked. Supposedly of great popularity in Shanghai, it was all the rage among the ladies in Taiwan. The name seemed to be an unintentional and completely harmless joke, but somehow it kept making me want to laugh. From what I remember, she did not smell particularly pleasant. In fact, for a period of time people all said she stank, so much so that my mother would not let her come near our house. It was not that anyone had smelled something bad on her. However, she somehow became vaguely associated with some bad reputation; and, as people had no exact reason for ostracising her, they inexplicably associated her with the word "stench".

3
A secret game of secrets

She enunciates every syllable clearly and with great earnestness, as if she is scared that if she stammered what she says wouldn't count. Her expression is so innocent, so solemn, as if she wants me to think of all the shameful things I did in the past.

She counts off all the things I did. It feels like she has some evidence against me, like I've done something scandalous... I would have forgotten all those things, if she hadn't brought them up.

At the beginning we weren't close friends. However, we had a clear idea of what each other was up to, likely based on those games of secret ciphers to which no one else was privy.

She knows how I forced my pet silkworms to mate. It was a casual game, on a sultry, empty afternoon, when a little boy held two chubby silkworms, forcing them to put their rear ends together, or entwining their bodies together—a game that belonged to adults, when I was still too young to tell male from female.

She also tells about how I dug up worms and stretched them like rubber bands; how I collected ants and cut off their heads to thread into a thin, long "necklace"; how I forced all the little critters I could get my hands on to mate in various ways. On top of that, from my house's rubbish pile she had found an explicit drawing of a man and a woman engaged in intercourse...

I remember drawing something like that, but the rest I had forgotten. How did this picture come about? It was based on what my brother retold of what his friend saw in his parents' bedroom. I once re-enacted the scene, underneath the sheets with the large teddy bear that Mother gave me; later I found out that my brother had also done the same a few times with his little plush dog.

As for my impression of her back then, I still remember a thing or two—how, under the shade of her family's bamboo shed, she lifted up her top, to pull and tug and suck on her own still not fully-developed nipple. Although she could not put her lips around it, she managed to lick it with her tongue. Sometimes, she even stuck her hand under her skirt and rubbed herself, gratification evident on her face. And there's also Fortune's willy, which she could tug and massage until it's a few times bigger than before. Every time a dog's whimper came from next door, I could tell if it was being beaten, or if she was playing with its private parts again...

However, our friendship did not start with those silly antics, of course.

They want her to talk about my secrets, the worse the better. And so this is what she tells them.

They turn around and ask me, "Is she right?" I have no defence. So I say, "Yes." At the same time I make a point of glancing at her with fear and loathing; of course I have stories to tell of her as well, but I will never tell anyone about her masturbating herself or the dog.

"Shameful, aren't you, you little bastard?" The sissy-voiced "Commie Defector", in a rare display of a row of uneven yellow teeth, give a hearty laugh.

When Floral started talking, they all shifted in their chairs, leaning forward towards Floral. But that's all. Floral has nothing else to add. At most, these silly incidents and childish antics would prove that I have had a streak of indecency and violence since childhood, but they are insufficient to incriminate me.

That's it? Sissy-voice stops laughing. Everyone has leaned back into their chairs.

"Take her away!"

I don't know where Floral is being taken.

I'm sure Floral doesn't know what to say in order to prove that I'm an enemy, a Communist. Or maybe, they have already presumed that Floral is my accomplice. I cannot ask her to do anything more for me. That would only bring harm to her. I should not have admitted to being a Communist. They're going to follow this line of inquiry, digging until there is nothing more to be found.

Sissy-voice asks me with a smirk, "You know each other quite well, don't you? She seems to be your type. Remember, tell the truth and we'll be lenient with you. Now, should we have you disclose her past, or have her disclose yours?"

"She doesn't have any past. She's just a dog, a beggar feeding off the swill of my house." I reply snappily, as if he were the dog, the beggar. "Don't make me waste words on this mongrel. And don't you think you can get any information about me from it. What do you want to know? Come on, ask me."

I spurt all of that out and fall silent. Perhaps I should have just endured all the torture from the beginning. Or I should have emulated the ancients, and dashed my brains out against a wall, or bit off my tongue to die by bleeding.

But why should I die? I don't deserve to die. Someone will save me. I cannot disappoint them.

I even put my geography knowledge to use, cobbling together a location that may or may not exist. They appear to be satisfied with my responses.

They want me to name a few more people.

I reply that I have only met them but don't know their names.

They tell me to describe them. I pick out the appearances of my interrogators—Sissy-voice, Fat Chicken, Goldfish-eyes, Baboon-cheeks, Mantis-arms—and mix-and-match them into some characters whose existence is even more dubious.

They finally send me back to the cell. I am too excited and cannot fall asleep. All is dark around me; my watch, glasses, and everything else have been taken away. I wonder what time it is. It doesn't really matter though. I fix my sight on a subdued splotch of light coming through the corridor, imaging that I am in an underground military base, and a secret agent is coming in with a hand-torch, searching for deployment maps... Voilà! Material for tomorrow's confession.

A few dogs bark outside the cell. Someone new is getting locked in here.

Suddenly I remember Anna. Sadness seizes my heart.

Floral. Maybe she is my Anna.

She will be my Anna. That's how I comfort myself in my mind, as I close my eyes and wait for sleep to arrive.

4
It all started with a dog

Floral's surname was Du. The Du family moved into the neighbourhood around the same time we did. I got to know Floral well, and got to know her mother even better.

Autumn isn't a bad person. That's why my brother said then.

Autumn was what Floral's mother was called. That wasn't her real name, just a name my brother picked for her at the spur of the moment. We were the only family in the neighbourhood to call her that.

Most of what I knew at a young age, my big brother taught me. I believed whatever he said. He said if you put cardboard in your mouth and chewed it for over an hour, it would become bubble gum. And so I did chew cardboard for over an hour. He was just telling me things to keep me from bothering him. He told me that Hitler did not die, but was kept hidden by the Soviets. America had already got wind of that. However, as the consequences could be grave—the information could lead to another world war—America decided to operate in secret. Thus I waited patiently year after year—until I went to secondary school. One day in history class I put up my hand to show off what I knew. Only then, after the teacher had made fun of me, did I realise that I had been fooled. So, when my brother told me back then that Autumn wasn't a bad person, I agreed with him without any hesitation.

I agreed that Autumn wasn't a bad person. But she couldn't have been a good person either.

In my eyes, she was more than just a bit odd. She was a bit of a sneak as well. I caught her in the act a couple of times. I did not tell on her, not because I forgave her, but because I did not want to cross my big brother—because he liked her, and I revered him. I only kept on her heels as if she was a spy, not letting her dare to ignore my existence. The first time she gave herself away was when I discovered her peeking through the keyhole of my parents' room. She leaned against the door, looking through the hole, and I came right up behind her. I punished her with a stern glance, and she slunk and fled. Feeling quite proud of myself at that moment, I leaned down and peered into the keyhole as well, wanting to know what Autumn was so curious about and what she saw. That time, through the keyhole I only saw a pair of legs, my mother's legs, resting over the headboard. Father was blowing onto her toe. On her big toe a white rose was painted, the paint still not dry. Not long after, Autumn ran into a puddle of mud when she was trying to catch the dog. She took off her shoes and socks to wash her feet, and I saw that she had roses painted on her toenails as well. I was displeased that she was copying Mother. So, I drew one on Chunhong's big toe as well. See if Autumn can still feel so special, now that everyone's got roses. However, that rose later became one of the reasons why Chunhong was sent packing.

* * *

Autumn's relationship with my family, in my personal belief, started with a dog.

We had had many dogs at home. The first one was not our pet, but belonged to Uncle Zhu.

Uncle Zhu often came to visit in a three-wheeler, carrying Billy with him. I was six at the time. Billy was white and little, smaller than everyone at home. I loved its short, stubby look, and felt that I was its most suitable owner. Every day, the only thing I looked forward to was Uncle Zhu coming over with Billy to visit. Or, if Uncle Zhu was busy, perhaps he could let Billy ride the three-wheeler here itself. Except, too bad dogs couldn't ride three-wheelers on their own.

Sometimes, when Uncle Zhu didn't show up, I'd take my savings jar to the front of the alley, thinking of hailing a three-wheeler to go see Billy myself. But every time Mother managed to catch me and drag me home.

One evening, when Uncle Zhu's three-wheeler was just pulling up to our front door, Billy eagerly jumped out before it stopped—and at the instance right before it was run over by the three-wheeler, I heard it scream—

Maybe I didn't remember clearly. Maybe it was after Billy's scream that Autumn opened the door and came out—that's what my brother claimed. But I kept having the feeling that it was only after Autumn, who lived next to us, swung open her red wooden door, that Billy screamed at the sight of her, which led to it being run over.

I also remember the calm expression on her face at the scene, as if nothing had happened. Standing under the red doorframe of her house, she glanced at the dead dog on the ground, then looked up and down at the panicking grown-ups and children. And then she shut her door unconcernedly. Tears were streaming down my face right then; my eyes were fixated on the dog lying on the ground. I would not have thought to pay any attention to Autumn. However, her frightful countenance that evening, under the gleam of the streetlamps, made her appear to be the cause and culprit of Billy's death.

I don't insist on remembering this episode, and my brother has also provided an explanation regarding Autumn. However, the shadow persisted; as soon as it was about to be forgotten, it would return with a reminder: Billy was not the first dog to die on Autumn's account.

* * *

The second dog was Sisi, a black Dachshund. A dog that only belonged to me, all for me to feed and take care of.

Sisi grew cuter and cuter by the day. That was what everyone said.

One day, my brother suddenly said to me, "Chunhuan, brothers should share all their good stuff, right?"

"Right." I waited for him to bring out the good stuff to share with me.

"So, you should share your dog with me."

I had no grounds on which to refuse him.

"From now on, I'll play with its head, and you'll play with its butt," my brother declared solemnly, a bit pleased with himself.

Although I only got the rear end of the dog, I did not feel particularly short-changed.

Because Sisi was loyal to old friends.

Whenever I petted the dog's behind, he would turn his head around to lick his buttocks and then my hand. And thus I felt victorious, having won the head as well as the tail.

Sisi's expertise was in catching mice. He once caught five mice in a row. As soon as he had killed one, he immediately went after the next, until he had dispatched all five. After our house was clear of rodents, he would go around to rid other houses of their pests. Autumn's house must have received Sisi's services as well. By that time, Autumn had already started working at our house, and I did not fear her anymore. Even though I still remembered the day when Billy died, how Autumn stood under the red doorframe of her house, how eerily black and blue were the lines painted on her face, under the streetlamp—that seemed to be a completely different person now, who had nothing to do with her.

Autumn had a pretty face, with a striking resemblance to the Hong Kong actress Lucilla You. Because of that, my brother, who only listened to classical music, went out and bought a record of Lucilla You's Mandarin songs. The photo on the album cover was almost identical to Autumn. But unlike Lucilla You, Autumn could not sing many songs; she only knew how to sing a song or two that I did not understand. But my brother seemed to understand all of them. He told me that those were songs from her tribe, about the joys of the hunt and the scenery along the way.

My brother did not speak the language of the aborigines, so Autumn must have told him. Autumn was quite good to my brother, and was willing to tell him things she would not tell me. I once heard my brother tell Autumn in private that he would marry her when he was older. Autumn said, "I have a husband already." To which my brother replied, "By the time I'm old enough, your husband will be either old or dead."

It was my brother who gave her the name "Autumn". Supposedly, her original name so vulgar-sounding and difficult to spell that she herself would not mention it.

Before Autumn took up domestic work with us, the children all called her "the Witch" behind her back.

How did that epithet come about? It probably had its roots in the creepy and mysterious ceremonies they performed at home. Everyone was eager to talk about them in graphic detail, but no one had actually witnessed anything. As for me, all I could count was that once when she had black and blue paint on her face. Fortunately, the "witch" never did any harm to anyone, which made her a bit less intimidating. We could not set our minds completely at ease about her, though. Once, it was said, a dog in the neighbourhood crawled into Autumn's house, and was later found hanging on a tree, decayed to the point that only its collar was recognisable. But this could not prove anything; even on the day Billy died, all she did was show her face for a bit.

Autumn was brought in by Jade. Jade was our maid for three years, before a good friend of Mother's asked for her. Before Jade left, out of kindness she got Autumn, who lived next doors, to take over her job. She told my father that she felt sorry for Autumn, as Autumn's family was in need of money. Father did not express any objection; he only said to Mother, "We'll take her in out of charity."

But Autumn was only fit to be the maid's assistant. Mother felt that neither her cooking nor her demeanour was presentable, so she went and hired Chunhong to do Jade's job. Autumn was relegated to be the maid's assistant, and all she did was run errands for Chunhong.

Chunhong wasn't her original name either. She was originally called Lihong. But Mother, apparently in a move to impose a rank system on the domestic help, bestowed our family's name-character upon Lihong. My name is Chunhuan, and my brother's is Chunshao, so Mother renamed Lihong to be Chunhong, to elevate her status over Autumn's.

In 1952, when Chunhong came to us, she was only 20, younger than the 26-year-old Autumn. Mother assigned her to cooking and to looking after my brother and me. Chunhong was definitely competent—she could mind four stoves at the same time, and had no trouble with either Northern or Southern cuisine. She was also well-educated and well-spoken, able to hold a conversation with every guest we had. At that time, Father was the editor-in-chief of a news agency while holding a position in the Kuomintang, and Mother was the deputy director of the Investigation Bureau. There was a steady flow of guests in and out of our house every day, including personages in both the literary and political fields. My brother and I, unable to join in on the grown-ups' conversations, could only hang out in the courtyard doing silly things like chewing on cardboard—and hiding from Chunhong at bath time.

Chunhong bathed us for two full years, until the year of 1954. Even though I was nine and my brother was ten, my mother still treated us like little children. She ordered Chunhong to bathe us every day and dress us fastidiously, like a palace maid serving on the emperor.

But the whole bathing business was really awkward, especially for my brother, who by that time felt he was almost an adult.

I heard him protest to Mother. Mother said, "This is a maid's duty to her masters. It is befitting of her position." And so we could only let Chunhong continue to wait on us. But my brother's uneasiness made Chunhong uncomfortable, too. Then, he thought of a solution—he had Chunhong wait outside the shower curtain and just pass us our clothes. We were finally able to bathe ourselves. My brother was fast at washing himself, and I was slow, so after he was done he rubbed my back as well. In reality, my brother was not opposed to have people serve him; once he asked Mother to have Autumn, whom he fancied, to come help us take baths, but Mother did not consent to it.

Perhaps taking in Autumn was an act of charity, but Mother never fully trusted her. Chunhong, on the other hand, was only hired after Mother had a thorough background check done on her and ascertained that she was above all suspicion—in particular, suspicion of being a rebel spy. However, I felt that Mother had an ulterior motive. She wanted to have the two maids watch each other and keep each other honest. After all, Chunhong was overqualified to be a serving-maid, while Autumn, though fitting the description of an ordinary maid, had too complicated of a background. In short, to Mother, both of them were not quite right—but then again in her eyes no one was ever all right.

My brother told me that those black and blue lines that Autumn had painted on her face were for curing her husband's illness. It was a treatment passed down in her tribe, an aborigine ceremony. She was not a witch. He showed me a few of the tricks he had learnt from her; but, as I was not sick, their efficacy could not be determined.

Autumn's family was so poor that all they had to eat at home every day was an egg each. Her husband was a carpenter, but as he had been sick, he had not worked for several years. She could no longer afford a doctor, and thus she turned to her own methods. By the time she came to work for us, Autumn was barely able to pay the rent. They lived in a small lean-to shed put up by the people next doors, a small abode squeezed in between two houses. It was narrow and dilapidated, looking more like a shack than a house. Jade knew the landlord of the house next doors well, and that was how she got Autumn in with us.

Our family's house occupied the largest plot of land in the neighbourhood. It was a government-allocated house, with only a few other houses nearby. Its former occupants were all high-ranking Japanese military officers. Although I was not sure what was so special about my father's status, by looking at the crumbling tile-roofed houses next to ours I could tell that my family was very different to everyone else's. Before moving in, Father had hired workers to spend four months renovating it into his ideal mansion. Along the wall separating the front door from the street, there was a row of orchids and osmanthuses, pines and firs, and an immense Queen-of-the-Night that could produce forty-eight blossoms in one night. Within the courtyard, different flowers were planted according to the colours of the season, and dotted among them were a few stone lanterns, which lent the yard a sense of elegance during the day, and, when lit at night, meditative serenity. On one side of the courtyard was laid a small pebblestone path, lined with bamboo, skirting the living room and leading into the backyard. In the backyard was built a greenhouse, which, besides an assortment of exotic plants, had a large container of water in which were grown rare species of water-lilies. Outside the greenhouse was a 66-square-metre fish pond. Beneath a magnolia beside the fishpond my beloved Billy was buried. The end of the fishpond marked the boundary of our property; beyond that was a dense bamboo grove, and beyond the grove was the river bank.

Once we reached the river bank, no one could see us from inside the house. We played like feral children, forgetting all the rules Mother had taught us. Chunhong would be too busy in the kitchen to worry about us; as for Autumn, since she was not even qualified to serve us, she was even less qualified to mind us.

But if Chunhong told Autumn, Autumn would come get us, bringing Sisi along to lead the way. Sisi had a keen sense of smell and never failed to find us.

Sometimes, my brother took Sisi with us to eliminate that possibility. But Autumn could still find us. She was nimble and agile; she would climb up the magnolia tree to get onto the rooftop, and from that vantage point nothing could escape her vision.

But Autumn really did not care to go catch children. That was not her duty. Besides, she knew clearly that there was no point in upsetting us. She would rather loiter outside the living room, listening to Father chat with the guests, and then come retell a thing or two to us.

Obviously Father did not discuss confidential matters in the living room. What the maid could overhear were all old anecdotes. Like the one during the Anti-Japanese War, when the Communist Party of China allied with the Soviets, and a Soviet envoy flew to Chongqing to meet with Zhou Enlai. The newspaper headline ran: "Zhou Enlai extends a worm welcome to the Soviet envoy". "Worm" was naturally a misprint of "warm". Then, when news came of the victory by Zhang Fakui of the Nationalist Army, the newspaper in Guangxi ran this headline: "The government praises the bravery of Zhang Fakui's genetals"—obviously not meaning "genitals", but "generals". There's also that one about Gu Zhenglun, an ultra-right wing Kuomintang member known as "The Executioner" on the Mainland. On the day he became Provincial Chairman of Gansu, the *Gansu Daily* announced in large characters: "Gu Zhenglun steals the appointment of Provincial Chairman". "Seals" was misprinted as "steals". The editor, Guan Jiyu, packed up and fled as soon as he saw the prints. Gu Zhenglun ordered for the editor to be executed, but they could not find him despite a long manhunt...

Of course those were not intentional mistakes. However, it was true that there were many rebel spies back then, many of whom had wormed their way into the newspaper agencies. Some people did indeed misprint on purpose to irritate the authorities. So, it did not matter if they were really rebel spies—it was always shoot first, ask later. There was one newspaper which accidentally printed "A warning against the Committees' atrocities" instead of "A warning against the Commies' atrocities", and the editor-in-chief was so scared that he took his own life.

Whenever Autumn retold these stories, her voice would be calm but betraying a bit of smugness, as if what she knew was top secret. Or as if she shared in her master's glory and held some special privilege. She was generally taciturn, working quietly, making it impossible to know what she was thinking. But the expression on her face made us felt that she was never focusing on the work at hand. Whenever she called my brother directly by his name, Chunshao, or when she told him what Father and his guests talked about, she felt like an older sister, or a close friend of our age, sharing a special toy.

While she recounted those stories offhandedly, I was getting goosebumps all over. What if Father's newspaper made a typo one day and our whole family was to be executed? Because of that, I deliberated with my brother quite a few times on what to do if we had to be on the run. We only had one three-wheeler. Who and what should we cram into it? Chunhong, Autumn, and the dog probably wouldn't get a seat. I said I would hold the dog on my lap. My brother said he would hold Autumn on his. And Chunhong? Perhaps she would have to sit on the top of the car. I wouldn't be strong enough to carry her.

I liked Chunhong. My brother liked Autumn. To each his own. Chunhong was hospitable, generous and easy-going. When guests wanted to come over to play cards, all they had to do was telephone and confirm with Chunhong. She would make sure to keep the food and drinks flowing. Even when the master of the house was not in, everyone would be made to feel completely at home.

Chunhong treated the friends of the equally hospitable Sisi in the same way. Whenever Sisi brought home a group of doggie friends from outside, Chunhong would cook a large pot of delicious-smelling doggie meal for them, making Sisi look good before his friends. And Sisi, like a dog from a proud family, made sure his friends all had enough to eat before he would take a few bites.

What a gentlepuppy. That's how Chunhong described my Sisi. After every meal, Chunhong would brush Sisi's teeth tenderly, carry him to bed, and sing him a lullaby. I looked contentedly at my excellent dog and my excellent maid, feeling that life could not be better.

For many years, I could not imagine Chunhong being Sisi's murderer. Even though that's what Mother told me, I would rather not believe it. I could not think of any reason why Chunhong would want to kill Sisi. Perhaps Chunhong was framed. Or perhaps the culprit was Autumn. But my brother would never believe that it was Autumn. Though, if it wasn't Autumn, who else would let Sisi starve to death?

It was probably my prejudice that led me to suspect Autumn. I had no evidence at all. It was just that I did not want to believe what Mother said. That year, 1956, our whole family went to the Alishan Mountains on vacation for three days. Upon our return, we found that Sisi had disappeared. I howled and threw fits, demanding for Sisi to come back.

Mother said to me, "Sisi ran away." Even Father, normally stoic and stern, tried to console me. I made him hurry to post notices on the streets for the lost dog, and even insisted that Mother send the agents from the Investigative Bureau to go look for him.

They both agreed, but Sisi never returned. I cried for a month. And then I lost hope that Sisi would ever return. Besides, I was tired from all the crying, and had no more strength to cry and insist on looking for the dog.

It was only much later that Mother told me that Sisi did not run away. Sisi died of starvation.

"He starved to death in the cage." She interrogated Chunhong, and she interrogated Autumn. But she did not tell me why.

* * *

Mother only revealed this a few years after Chunhong left: "During the three days we were at Alishan, Chunhong fed Sisi nothing, neither food nor water... It wasn't that she really wanted to starve Sisi to death. She said to me afterward, crying, that every time she fed the dog she thought about how it had better food to eat than her whole family, and how hard it was for her to accept that. And so, when we were out, she stopped feeding the dog. And that's how Sisi died."

Mother spoke in a calm and even tone, as if she was worried about stirring up grief again in my heart, but also as if she had thought that I had already got over the pain of losing the dog. Or perhaps she was just trying to make me stop thinking about Chunhong.

I really did miss Chunhong. She cooked delicious meals, was kind to me and Sisi, and served all our guests well. She was famous near and far as the most cultured maid imaginable. After sending home her remittance every month, she spent the rest of her wages on books and records. She had also read all the works of our literary guests. All the Western music I knew I heard from her room. And so, even though I did not study English, I understood more of it than my brother did.

The night before Chunhong left, she carried me to her room, where we held each other and cried through the night.

She was so loath to leave me. How could she have starved my Sisi to death?

I felt that Mother's words should have come from Autumn. I felt that Mother had suspected that Chunhong had designs on Father, that she was displeased that Father allowed Chunhong to receive guests like the mistress of the house, that she had wanted to send Chunhong away long ago. And here was a convenient opportunity both to use her as a scapegoat and to get rid of her. During those three days, Chunhong would have been busy looking after visitors; since her arrival, we had had visitors every day. She really should have let someone else take over feeding the dog...

Did Chunhong not defend herself? No. She was very clever. She would have understood Mother's intention, and nothing she said would have helped. Besides, I knew that she indeed loved Father, though she would never dream of doing anything improper with him.

Autumn, on the other hand—I felt she was the one who had designs on Father. But Mother would not listen to me. She doted on my brother, and he wanted to keep Autumn. He said she was all right, and Mother believed him. He reported on the rose on Chunhong's big toe, and Mother took that to heart... I no longer believed my brother that easily anymore, except for the business with Hitler—I still resolutely waited for the Americans to find him and uncover the Soviet ploy. I did not need to grow up before realising that the other things he had told me, like chewing on cardboard or eating spiders (he said they tasted like chocolate), were lies, that he was just playing pranks on me. Not only did he play pranks on me, he also joined hands with Mother to get rid of Autumn's archenemy—my Chunhong.

After Chunhong had left, Autumn was officially promoted to maid status, and was an errant girl no longer. She took charge of everything in the kitchen as well as taking care of my brother and me. After apprenticing under Chunhong for two years, she was able to manage one stove, even though four was still beyond her.

Autumn was not as warm toward me as Chunhong was. By then, my brother did not play with me very much, as he had friends of his own. I could only turn to Autumn when I was bored. She had a trick or two up her sleeves to help me kill time, such as roasting sausages—

Once, she tossed me a sausage, started a charcoal stove in the courtyard, and had me roast it myself. I stared at the sausage, feeling utterly wretched: that's all I had to kill the entire afternoon with. So, picking it up with the roasting fork, I set it to roast far away from the fire. An hour later, the sausage was only lukewarm. Two hours later, the fire was about to go out, but the sausage remained the same. I went to the living room, and picked out a few patriotic, anti-Communist novels from the shelf. Those books were not in short supply at home, being gifted to us by visiting writers. I made a point to choose books by authors whom I disliked to feed the fire. Thus I roasted the sausage for a whole afternoon. When it was finally cooked, it was beautifully and evenly roasted all around, without a single burnt bit.

There's another time when she handed me a few peanuts, a bit of glutinous rice flour, and a mortar and pestle. I ground the peanuts into bits, added a bit of sugar, rice flour, and water, and rolled them into a little ball. Then, I rolled the ball in a thin coat of rice flour, sprayed water on it, sprinkled more rice flour on it, sprayed more water... I did that repeatedly for two hours, and ended up with the perfect rice dumpling. All Autumn did for me was to cook this dumpling for me as a snack.

All in all, she only ever let me play alone, and never cared about whether I was having fun or enjoying myself.

Autumn had two children. One was Floral, and the other was called

Daoxiong. Once in a while I would see them climb to the top of the wall and peer into our house, but Autumn never allowed them to come in.

Floral was about my age. Her name amused me, reminding me of the "Star Floral Water", which you could catch a whiff of anywhere in town. Daoxiong was two years her junior, and his name was much more proper. His old man actually went to a bookstore and consulted a dictionary to find the characters for the name, copying them down reverentially on paper.

Before I turned eleven, the only contact I had with Floral was on the way to school. On a few occasions, Floral did not have time to walk to school, and Autumn picked her up and let her get a ride with me in the three-wheeler to school.

At first, Floral did not speak, but looked me up and down like a dog. Finally she initiated the conversation. "Let's play a game!" She spoke Mandarin with a stammer, and her pronunciation was not entirely standard. Even though I did not want to play with her, I had no reason to refuse.

It was a bizarre kind of game. She was the princess, and I was the king. The script was identical every time.

She would say, "I do not want to live anymore. Please grant me death, my lord."

And I would say, "How would you like to die?"

And she would say, "Please prepare a brazier and start a fire in it, so that I may fall into it and burn to death."

Thus, on several occasions, on the way to school, she had me help her act out all kinds of corny methods of dying.

Later on, Mother forbade Autumn from putting her daughter into our three-wheeler, and thus the story of the King and the Princess came to an end. Floral returned to observing me secretively like a dog, or poking her head over the walls of our house.

Sometimes, I thought up some original ways of dying, but without Floral there to act along, I had look for other targets.

Ants, for one. I sprinkled white sugar along the path the ants were bound to take, to lure out a troop of ants. Then I picked out the worker ants with larger heads, stuck their heads through thorns of roses, and watched them writhe and wriggle. Or I might pluck off their heads and collect them in a glass jar; once I had enough, I'd string them into a necklace and hang them around a doll's neck. Also, inspired by my textbook, I would cut earthworms in half and wait for them to grow new tails, or try to grow pearls in ordinary clams, taking them to be pearl oysters—I stuck a bead in each of the clams, and waited for them to secrete mucus and turn the bead into a pearl... But things never worked the way I wanted them to. The worms never grew new tails, nor did the clams make pearls. They just all died.

After that, I invited a "method of living". I made myself "God"; I drew a pretty landscape in the interior of a matchbox, filled it with sugar, and chose a lucky ant to live in the matchbox. Then I buried the matchbox into the ground and let the ant live in peace and plenty in "Heaven". However, the ant always escaped, no matter how deeply I buried the matchbox. Even when I set the matchbox to float in a vat of water, or however hard I tried to cut it off from the rest of the world, the ant would still try to escape by any means. Sometimes it even gathered a group of friends to carry away my gifts. So, at the end, my "methods of living" were turned into massacres. It was death to all the ants who destroyed Heaven or who escaped from it.

It was not until the third dog came to our family that I put an end to those silly games.

The third dog was called Anna.

5
I once thought that was the sea

In my family photo album, there was a photo, on the back of which my brother wrote this line: "My most faithful Anna and my most faithful little brother".

Once, he asked me, "If Anna and I fell into the water at the same time, who would you save first?"

I replied, "Anna would push you onto the shore first, no matter what, even if it means her death."

"And you won't go in to save her?"

"No, that would make things worse. She would also do everything to push me ashore, even if it means she'd be too tired to swim to the shore herself."

"Then what if... it's Father and me?"

I stared at him, feeling torn for the first time in my life. "I will push both of you ashore no matter what."

"Even if you'll die?"

"Yes, even if I'll die. But," I glanced at Anna, curled up beside my feet napping, "I know that if Anna is nearby, she will hurry over to save me, so I will hold out until the very last moment."

My brother threw his arms around Anna and me.

"I won't let you die, never!"

Anna woke up with a start, whimpered into the air, then eagerly licked my brother's face and mine.

My brother and I looked at each other, across Anna, and then all of a sudden we both burst out wailing.

Neither of us knew what it was that caused that storm of feelings. "Destiny"? That word is too distant, too immaterial. But we were just that sentimental, until our sentiments became presentiments.

* * *

Before we had presentiments of anything, we were just idling around, using sentiment as entertainment, as a way to pass the time.

Besides those repeated scripts we acted out on the "battlefield"—for example, the disingenuous grief when a brother-in-arms fell in battle, or the regret-tinted excitement when an enemy was wounded—we also played tricks on Anna, though her loyalty made us feel guilty and remorseful for teasing her.

Anna was a good dog, the best I had ever seen. Unlike the adorable Sisi, whom it was impossible not to pet, to love, Anna was not our plaything. She was our guardian angel, a member of our family, our best friend.

Anna was just a puppy when she came to us. My brother and I had each fed her milk several times. Anna was one who treasured old friendships. From the day she arrived at our house until she was fully-grown, she would stay only with the people and things from her puppyhood. Unlike Sisi, she was not keen to travel around or make friends from all over. When we tried to entice her with novelties or bring her to new places to play, she would at most come along only to not spoil our enthusiasm. She never actively sought new things. It was as if in her past life she was a traveller who had seen so much of the world that nothing surprised her anymore, that she had no desire to leave home in this life, that there was nothing more that was worth seeking out and exploring.

When she was still little, we often carried her to the river bank beyond the bamboo grove to wash her. And sometimes, for fun, we would put her in a grass basket and let her drift on the river, listening to her whimper, plucking her out unhurriedly only when the water was about to go over her head.

But she tolerated all that and always forgave us. Her tolerance came from her absolute faithfulness. If anyone else had done the same to her, she would not have let them off easily. But in reality we did not do this to her very often, because she quickly learnt to swim, and became our guide on our trips.

That river was quite wide on the surface, and at parts was so heavily covered by reeds that the water could not be seen. I once thought that was the sea. When I was a small child, such wide waters scared me. But it was really just a small stream.

My brother and I were still in primary school then. Every evening, we took Anna and ran straight toward this stream that I took for the sea. Anna preferred not to leave the house, but for us—her family—she would go anywhere. There were some dirt paths along the river bank where the reeds grew thickly. If we wanted to discover new ways and hidden places, we would let the dog go ahead for a bit and check if the path was fine—for example, there were no snakes—before following behind her.

After every little stretch, Anna would turn around and give us a look to let us know whether or not to follow her. Once, my brother and I went hiding on purpose in the reeds by the path. When Anna turned around and could not see us, she ran back worriedly to look for us. And as she caught the scent of our hiding spot, she barked and barked at us, as if she was scolding her own unruly children, scolding us for not keeping close to her. She was just a little thing then. Although we were ten times bigger than she was, we dared not talk back at her. She was so worried, so disappointed, that we could not help but feel guilty. Yet, that did not stop us from playing tricks on her, such as coming up with new ways to test her, waiting to see her alarmed reaction, seeing if she would come look for us, or if she'd just take off, knowing that we had tricked her.

And there was one time when we went overboard in our game. We hid too deeply in the reeds and fell off solid ground into the water. The reeds blocked the line of our sight. We yelled and yelled for help, and heard Anna barking in reply. She was searching for us, but could not come to our aid. In her cry we heard a mad howl of distress and desperation...

* * *

I had known that feeling of desperation before. I still remembered that night of my childhood when I was on that ship, the ship with the secret golden cargo. It was one night after the captain's defection was taken care of. Completely out of the blue, I heard a loud noise, and my body instantly tilted to one side along with the deck. And then, everything shook fiercely, amidst the screeching noises of metal and wood scraping against each other. People were running around helter-skelter, pushing each other, yelling. Seawater splashed onto me, covered my feet. I was picked up by my father, who went hither and thither along with the crowds. People looked like they were being tossed up by the waves and caught again by the deck. Within earshot were loud booms, the sound of cannon fire mixed in with the roar of the storm. Even though I was in my father's arms, I felt the weightlessness of one on the verge of expiring, as if my body was being yanked away from this world by some centrifugal force. More distressingly, even the arms that were holding me tight felt as if they were being torn away by some powerful menace. I despaired at the thought of losing this person, this embrace, the anchor of my life. And then I burst into tears. Although I had been accustomed to staying quiet from infancy, to not crying in the face of danger, I howled my heart out then...

When I was eight, I asked my parents what happened then. They told me that the ship had run into a heavy storm on the sea. But I knew there was more. The first loud boom clearly came with a strong smell of gunpowder. Perhaps they didn't want to tell me more. Chunshao, on the other hand, remembered nothing. I lost my only source of corroboration. It was not until fifty years later, when the historical records were declassified, that I found out the truth: In 1949, after the captain had defected, we ran into a storm and a Communist attack on the sea. On that secret voyage away from the Mainland, we were twice in grave danger, and only escaped safely by good fortune.

Apart from experiencing my first feeling of fear amidst the stifling atmosphere, I thought that the voyage was fairly calm. I remember that, after the commotion, most people were crouching on the dripping deck, panting; Father set me in a washbasin so that I could sit down comfortably. My gaze swept lightly past the crowd's blanched faces, and as I lifted up my head, I saw a silver-white sliver of the moon high in the sky, surrounded by a few twinkling stars. Sparse specks of lamplight shone from the little islands dotting the sea. The boat was sitting in the dark water, set in the equally black sky.

* * *

Anna's barking was out of earshot. My brother and I had also stopped yelling for help. We were apparently drawn into an eddy. I struggled and struggled, trying to move my head out of the water. In a fleeting moment, my mind was filled with just one thought:

Anna! She stopped barking! Please, don't let her come and try to save me. She must save herself! An icy feeling gripped my heart.

My head finally emerged out of the water.

Through the water dripping into my eyes, I saw something floating my way.

It was coming closer and closer.

A wooden bucket! I held on to it tightly.

At that moment, Anna's head popped out of the water.

Ah! It was Anna who pushed the bucket over! Good girl, Anna!

I held onto the bucket and paddled it to where my brother was flailing, a short distance away, and yanked him out of the water.

Anna piloted our vessel. At long last we were back on solid land.

"Anna went to save you first," my brother said to me with a laugh afterwards. "From now on, you can pet her head. She likes you better."

"No, she pushed the bucket to me just because I was closer."

"You don't have to explain. Like I said, I won't let you die. Never ever. I won't be sad because she didn't come to save me. She saved you, after all."

"She saved me in order to save you. Because I'd definitely save you."

I threw my arms around my brother and Anna. Anna woke up with a start, whimpered into the air just as she did before, then eagerly licked my brother's face and mine. My brother and I looked at each other, across Anna, and then all of a sudden we both burst out laughing.

From that day on, my brother let me call him directly by his name, Chunshao, instead of addressing him properly as "elder brother". "This signifies that we are equals, that it doesn't matter who's older or younger." He sounded so noble when he said that, a proper, chivalrous gentleman. He had long been famous for being a gracious, well-bred boy. Though still young, he bore himself with grace and dignity, like an aristocrat, a prince. It made me proud to have the privilege of addressing him directly by name. At least, it meant I was no longer obliged to give him precedence. I still did, though, out of habit. After all, he was three years ahead of me in school. Although we were born only one year apart, I went to school two years late, as a result of which he knew a lot more than I did. I was still convinced by anything he told me, except for pranks like chewing cardboard or eating spiders.

But I still ceded the dog's head to Chunshao, out of courtesy, and stuck with petting the dog's behind.

Whenever I petted the Anna's behind, she would turn her head around to lick her buttocks and then my hand, just like Sisi did. And so I felt victorious, having won the head as well as and the tail.

There was probably another person who felt the same satisfaction— Floral Du, who was always snooping about from the top of the wall.

Floral Du had a dog too. It was originally my dog, a soft toy. It was torn and dirty, so I threw it into the rubbish. And she picked it out and kept it. I saw her, but I never told her.

In my eyes she was like a dog herself, a dirty stray who fed on bones people tossed away, all the while watching about herself in case someone threw a stone at her.

Back then, I really did have the urge to throw stones at her. Just her scabby head with the uneven hair was repugnant enough. Rumour had it that she had a case of head lice, so she had her head shaved and medication applied. Autumn must have been quite inept with scissors, judging by how badly she cut her daughter's hair.

Of course it wasn't just her hair. There were numerous other reasons.

Like how she pulled on our clothesline until it broke, causing my mother's favourite dress to fall onto the ground.

Like how she spat out her gum on the street, causing my shoes to be soiled as I stepped out of the house.

And there's also that time when she had the nerve to spit her gum onto my mother's wig. I saw it with my own two eyes. But I didn't give her away, because Mother was just about to take me to the cinema. Mother would not set foot out the door without her wig. And if she had to clear the gum off her wig, we would probably miss the movie I wanted to watch... So, all I could do was give Floral a stern look as she peered over the wall, warning her that I saw what she did. There was another reason why I let the matter slide. I felt sorry for her, knowing that she had only recently been beaten harshly. That time, she was squatting in the rubbish heap, digging here and there, until she dug out a small toy that we had thrown out. As she did so, she looked up and caught sight of me. Laying down the newly-discovered loot, visibly reluctantly, she hung her head and ran off. After that incident, Autumn gave her a sound beating. Not for digging for rubbish, or so I heard, but for stealing money from Autumn to buy a toy—a toy that resembled the one in the rubbish. Autumn took the toy that Floral bought, stomped all over it, and threw it into the rubbish as well.

For some reason, I felt I owed her. Although I did not stop her from taking a toy I discarded, she must have been afraid, afraid that I would tattle on her to her mother or mine. But what else was mixed in with her reluctant, wary, expression? I had better things to do than to tell on her, so why did she need to steal her mother's money and get beaten for it?

Besides, she had a strange sense of integrity. Once when she was walking by my house, she saw a five-*yuan* coin by the door. She halted for two seconds, checking her urge to pick it up. Later, Daoxiong picked up the coin, and Floral had a fight with him (the whole process was audible from the other side of the low wall). She insisted that he put the coin back to where it was. That's right—she would rather get beaten for stealing her own family's money, than to pick up a coin lying in front of my house. And yet, as soon as we threw out a torn plush dog, she came right away when nobody was watching to dig through the rubbish and take it away.

Although I did not know why she was afraid of me, I could tell that she liked Chunshao. Whenever Chunshao was around—be it a chance encounter, or on the way to school, or when she spotted our three-wheeler from afar—she would stop in her tracks, squat down, and clumsily pretend to tie her shoelaces. Only when the three-wheeler was near would she stand up and take a glimpse at Chunshao, sitting inside the car—

Even when she was looking at Chunshao, she resembled a dog. Like one who was looking cravingly at a delicious bone beyond its reach, all the while looking around itself nervously, then running away in shame before people came to shoo it away.

Once, the idea came into my head that Floral did not pick up our toys only because she liked toys. Perhaps there was an element of imitation there; perhaps she was imitating Chunshao and me. The way she played with the stuffed dog was exactly the same as how we played with Anna. Her breaking our clothesline or spitting gum in my mother's wig were not necessarily solely for getting even with my mother for not letting her ride in our car, either. What else could be her motive?

Being instigated by Autumn, perhaps?

Otherwise, why would Floral, the timid little dog that she was, dare to go look for trouble? Besides, she liked Chunshao, and there was no reason for her to make herself despicable in his eyes.

I held no prejudice against Autumn. It was just that I wondered what she etched in the roses that she gave to my father. Those must have been secrets that she dared not let Mother know. The reason I did not tell on her was that I was loyal to my father, and this was an act sanctioned by him. I could not tell on anything that he did. At the same time, Autumn was engaged in disloyalty towards my mother, by passing secret messages to my father. And my mother had held her in disdain all along. She knew that, and would not intentionally do anything more to worsen my mother's opinion of her. But she could easily command a dog that was already filthy to go do things that a filthy dog would do—she could tell Floral to play a petty trick here and there. Though not sophisticated, it was a type of revenge in its own right.

My mother once said I was of the crafty sort. I was only ten at that time. I didn't know how she came to that conclusion, but I took that to be a reason for her favouring Chunshao over me. In reality, though, Mother was very good to me. It was just that she was more austere towards me, and not as affectionate as she was towards Chunshao. I felt I was not really that crafty. It was just that I had nothing better to do than to look for convoluted explanations for everything happening around me. It was just for fun. All my hypotheses about what Autumn, Floral, or my parents were thinking were just a game. I did not take it seriously.

* * *

Long before I started to build up a real friendship with Floral, an investigator working for my mother had already performed a thorough background check on Autumn and Floral. The check was thorough enough, but it had a tinge of incredibility to it. To me, the squeaky-voiced, shifty-eyed, affectedly coy investigator sounded exactly like the eunuch Li Lianying in the movies, the one who was Empress Dowager Cixi's favourite attendant. He was likely reading out a story that he cobbled together himself, weaving unconnected bits of information into a coherent whole. It wasn't like it was important intelligence anyway, just an errand for the boss. No need to be completely serious. Anyway, this is Autumn's story, according to the report I heard:

Autumn, originally named Toway Minrakes Fasay, was from a Highland tribe around Nanzhuang Township in Miaoli County. Her parents' names were unknown. Her grandfather, Elas Fasay, was conscripted to serve in the South Pacific when Taiwan was under Japanese rule. After being discharged, he idled around at home, humming Japanese songs, and became not quite all there. One day he raped an older woman and was almost beaten to death by her son. A year later, someone dropped off an infant girl at his house, saying that it was his daughter. Not knowing how to explain the matter, the bewildered old man started looking after the baby. He told others that he was her grandfather (of course, he could very well be her father as well, if that older lady did indeed give birth to a girl—or he could be neither). When the girl was thirteen, her "grandfather" married her off to an amputee veteran, for such a paltry bride price that he might as well have given her away for free. Not wanting to babysit a young girl all day, the veteran let her go off to play on her own. The girl became with child. Only by the time she was in her sixth month did her tummy bulge up to the size of a fist. The veteran, busy working to make ends meet, did not notice that. The girl continued to go out and play. In her eighth month, the veteran finally saw that something was going on. But he thought that she was early in her pregnancy with *his* child, and he even stole a chicken to make a tonic for her. Soon after, the girl had a bit too much fun with a boy in the neighbourhood. They went off miles away from home and spent the last of their money. The boy took her to a restaurant and gave her the slip without paying the bill. The girl, not having the means to pay for the meal, managed to chat up the man sitting at the next table over and have him pay. And she followed him home. Although the man had a lung condition, his job as a carpenter was sufficient to feed the two of them. Not long after, the girl popped out an infant daughter, and the man, without knowing how himself, became the father. The baby took the surname Du after the man, and was named Floral. Floral Du and Autumn (who hitherto had no Chinese name) went to register their residence on the same day. Autumn made up a Chinese name for herself on the spot, and claimed to be a few years older than she actually was, to make her motherhood claim more credible...

The name that Autumn made up really did sound like something crass, so it shall be omitted here. Her real name, however, deserves further investigation. My own research showed that Fasay was not a clan name used by the Highland tribes around Nanchuang Township in Miaoli, but by another Highland people from far away. So, this report only served to explain why Autumn looked much younger than her reported age (the one in her residence registration record)—Autumn did in fact look so youthful that she had been mistaken to be our older sister. Or something else to Chunshao, as he grew up.

Chunshao grew up fast. By the time he was twelve or thirteen, he was already as tall as a grown man, and taller than Autumn. Sometimes after school he would tell me historical anecdotes he learnt from class or political gossip he picked up from the grapevine. Sometimes he was eager to teach Autumn how to read and write. He did not run with me to the river every day anymore. On the occasions when he was too busy, and Zhu Xiaokang and Yao Kunming could not come over to play either, I had one just one playmate, a devoted dog that stayed with me—Anna. But Anna could not talk or do things that humans could. So, I still needed a "dog" that was more human.

Floral.

Floral started becoming my friend when we were in Primary 3. She was in my class.

At first, we sat far apart and did not interact much. None of the other pupils interacted much with Floral either. For some unknown reason, Autumn disliked her daughter, and allowed her to be filthy and unkempt like a dog thrown out the door by its master, a dog whose looks were ravaged by wind and rain, who cowered and grovelled before people lest they kick it aside. In the first term, I barely spoke to Floral at all. In the second term, we had a new teacher for our class. Mother did not know about it ahead of time, so of course she did not manage to forewarn him, and of course the teacher would not have known about my problems—

I had only learnt to tie my own shoelaces when I was in Primary 2. A year after that I was still unable to wipe myself. At home, it used to be Chunhong who did it, and after she left, Autumn took over. At school, I had to ask the teacher for assistance every time before I went to the toilet. As my arms had not fully recovered from the polio, I had difficulty reaching behind my back to wipe myself. So, when I felt the call of nature on the first day of school that term, I asked the new teacher to help me wipe myself, just like I did before. Upon hearing the request, the teacher, far from agreeing to help, glared at me harshly and said, "Song Chunhuan! Are you still a baby?!" I held it for the first class. After the second class, I made the same request. The teacher ignored me again, and told me that I was being ridiculous. He did not know who my parents were, so no wonder he dared to be so rude. I was red in the face with anger, and as I returned to my seat I started sobbing quietly, not daring to make a noise, until my tears and nose drippings streamed onto the book opened on my desk, resulting in a large, wet, sticky patch. Derisive looks from my classmates shot over constantly. Full of shame, I shut the mucus-filled book. When we broke after the third class, I asked again with more urgency. This time, the teacher let disdain show on his face, saying, "At your age you ought to be taking care of your own hygiene. Have some self-respect!" I could not hold it any longer. I burst out crying all of a sudden. My bowels were about to burst open as well.

At this moment, from the other side of the room, Floral raised her hand. She spoke softly, but her words were clear.

"I will help him."

The teacher looked at her from head to toe, apparently a bit stunned. I stopped crying as loudly, but was uncertain if I should stop altogether. A moment later, the teacher composed himself, and, flinging his arm as if tossing away a hot potato, agreed for her to take me to the toilet. That day, under full view, Floral ran with me to the toilet. And wiped me after I did my business.

Just a note—when I went to the toilet at school, I was given the privilege to lock the front door so that no one else could come in. Because of that, no one else saw her wipe me.

* * *

By this time, besides wiping behinds, Floral also knew a few fun tricks. When I taught her the game of roses and eggs, she taught me another way for passing secret messages.

For example, a piece of clear sticky tape on the top portion of the wire pole (head-height) outside my front door meant that the meeting place was in front of a certain church.

A piece of tape on the middle portion of the pole (shoulder-height) meant in front of a certain restaurant.

A piece of tape on the bottom portion (belly-height) meant in front of a certain cinema.

If there were a big strip and a little strip making an "X", it meant to meet inside the indicated location.

But if the two strips did not cross, it meant to meet at the back door of that location.

The angle of the larger strip (or the sole strip) indicated the time of the meeting, like the hour hand of a clock.

When you see the message, you tear off the tape to indicate that you've got the message. But, to hide our tracks, we might change our plans, in which case we would stick on an extra piece of tape to mean "here is new information".

We could have met without making these covert plans every day. It was just for fun. And she did not invent the game on her own; she had seen it from somewhere.

I found that she had inherited her mother's worst trait—or maybe her best—that of liking to observe people in secret and learning from them quickly. Not only did she snoop on us from the top of the wall, she also watched the people who came to visit. She giggled and said she learnt the game from us. I demanded to know who it was that she learnt it from, and who she was stalking. She resolutely refused to tell. I think I probably forgot to make it obvious that I was teasing her, and my expression scared her from telling. Later on, she said that she forgot, because there were too many people going in and out of my house. She returned to her old way of looking like a cowering dog, preparing for me to kick her any time. Likely she was worried that I would tell my parents, who would send her far, far away, or that Autumn would give her a good spanking. Anyway, I went and examined all the wire poles, fences, and pillars of buildings near my house. Once or twice I'd find a bit of sticky tape or something equally inconspicuous on them, and some of them had appeared and disappeared. Those could be the game of any child, and one could not read too deeply into them; however, soon after Floral and I started playing the sticky tape game, I never saw the other ones anymore.

PART II

6
The bottomless treasure box

On the wall of the living room at home was hung a piece of calligraphy in dancing cursive characters. It was hung there originally, before our family had moved into the house. Father had said that the writing was a poem called "Jiawu", by the Qing-dynasty scholar Liang Qichao. Over the years, we had put up many new decorations in the house, but we never removed this piece.

A thousand-gold sword,
Ten thousand words of learning—
Both have I squandered.
Drunk, I hurl my soliloquy at the wall;
Waking, I find myself in tears.
Be it that my years have fled!
I only mourn that my youthful ambitions
Have mootly faded away.
Still, may I carry the trials of all people
And bring them, bowing, before the divine.

Because the script was difficult to decipher, I once had Father read it out to me twice, and wrote it down carefully in my notebook in neat print hand. Once I had it memorised, I could ask him for more prize money. By that time, I had already memorised all the poetry I could find in my books, and I had to develop new sources of income. The memorisation of this particular poem netted me two whole *yuan*.

This kind of Chinese calligraphy did not seem like a collection item favoured by Japanese military officers. Supposedly, after the Japanese troops had moved out, the first person to move into this mansion was a high-ranking Kuomintang general. However, in less than half a year's time, he was executed on presidential order. Only after that was this property reassigned to Father. So, the calligraphy piece could have been left behind by the general who was shot. The piece was not signed, and it was unclear whose work it was. Father kept it, probably due to his hobby of collecting calligraphy pieces and paintings.

The guests who usually came to visit, in particular my father's closest friends, also had interest in art collections and poetry. When they came over to drink and play cards, Father would also bring out pieces of art for everyone to assess. They would, in turn, bring their own collections for Father to appraise.

These cultural gatherings were also my sources of income. Once the guests had been gathered, Father would summon me, point to a few pieces and test the art appreciation skills that I studied on a daily basis. The first time I was put in the spotlight, the piece that Father took out from his collection to hang in the middle of the living room was Tang Yin's "Portrait of a Tang Dynasty-style Lady". Like a little academic, with the calm and composure befitting of a son of the Song family, I began to analyse it before Father's friends:

"This painting was created approximately between mid-15th Century and the early 16th, during the Ming Dynasty, and was inspired by the story of Li Duanduan, a famous Tang Dynasty courtesan, who went to demand justice from the poet Zhang You. It started when Zhang You wrote a poem mocking Li Duanduan as a 'prostitute of disrepute'. To clear her name, Li Duanduan bravely went to Zhang You to demand fairer treatment.

"Please take a look at white peony in the hands of the lady in the painting, standing before the screen here. This is an important symbol Li Duanduan used to represent her character. At the same time, the poet, Zhang You, is sitting on the couch, with an expression that seems to say that he was about to explain his earlier words to her. On the top right corner of the painting, Tang Yin wrote:

'Li Duanduan of Xianhe Hall—
Fair peony, pure, she walks the earth.
But in gilded Yangzhou, where pleasures call,
Bookworms dull rule the lady's worth.'

The poem not only described Li Duanduan, but also was Tang Yin's way of self-deriding.

"On one hand, Li Duanduan was using the white peony to demonstrate her pure and noble character; on the other, by taking the initiative to go reason with a man, she had violated the code of conduct for women of that time. This signifies that, despite being a courtesan, Li Duanduan had the courage to challenge tradition, to claim the moral high ground; this is also an act of surpassing tradition, through the conflicts between different understandings of tradition. Therefore, in depicting the lady in this painting, Tang Yin abandoned the soft, feminine lines popular in the Ming Dynasty. Instead, he employed a steady and deliberate style to emphasise the independence and uniqueness of this woman. At the same time, Tang Yin was using Li Duanduan's story as an analogy for his behaviour and mind-set as one unwilling to be constrained by the rules of propriety."

The guests all nodded. "Jiafu, what a son you've got." "He's just a young boy, but what he said was spot-on..." "If the younger son is so capable, shouldn't we ask the elder to give us one as well?" Hearing that, Chunshao shook his head, and went to hide behind the grown-ups, grinning. Chunshao was capable of many things, but as a rule he had little patience for these things. He would never admit it; he only put on the airs of a proud big brother, saying that he wouldn't compete against his little brother for prize money. In reality, though, he would rather go play outside or hang out with Autumn, instead of wasting time with these ancient artefacts. However, with his perfect auditory memory, he knew quite a bit by rote. He had once recounted to me what Father told him about Zeng Gong's famous letter "Jushi Tie" and

Zhao Zhiqian's "Commentary on the Water Classic", and it was no different to what Father would have said himself. It was impossible to tell that he was a layman. On a previous occasion, Uncle Yao came to visit, and Mother made Chunshao come out and talk about Qi Baishi's painting "Bamboo in Wind". All he did was recite what Father had told us once, but no one could tell; they all thought he was well-versed in the subject all along. His looks, his bearing, and his silver voice made him doubly more convincing, and made Mother feel that it would be a sin to not make this son of hers demonstrate his God-given talents. But Chunshao was only willing to demonstrate once or twice, as if his knowledge was something to be jealously guarded. He would rather have me take his place in the spotlight, saying "like elder brother, like younger brother". And, obviously, after seeing my performance, all that people would say was, "like younger brother, like elder brother".

Politely, I retreated to one side, waiting for someone to correct me. The exegesis of this painting would probably earn me a prize of ten *yuan*; however, I must not display any sign of being proud of myself, else it would appear trite of me, unbefitting of a Song family upbringing.

Father did not dismiss me. This meant the guests had not had their fill yet, and were in the mood for another one. Indeed, Father pointed to another painting. In the picture were only two branches of plum blossoms. On top of a lack of personages or anecdotes to recount, the image was too minimalist. This was a true test of skill for the explainer.

"In this painting, 'The Herald of Spring'..." I paused stylistically, to buy some time to think about what to say next, "the key feature is the technique of the lines... that is also the technique for conveying mood. With just a few strokes, the artist was able to outline the moods corresponding to solidness and hollowness, fecundity and demise.

"What's special about this painting is that it's not a 'drawing' of plum blossom, but a 'writing' of plum blossom. The lines outlining the flowers obviously betray calligraphy techniques. That's why I said it's a 'writing' of plum blossom. Using writing instead of drawing techniques makes this stand out from the pedestrian.

"The branches of the plant here illustrate another calligraphic technique. Look at this old branch here. It was done by swiping the side of the brush in one continuous stroke. There is tremendous power and forcefulness in the stroke, but the branch, though sturdy, is old. Hence demise in apparent solidness. Then, here is a young branch with a slight curve in it. It soars all the way to the top in a hollow stroke made by a half-dry brush, and looks like it is piercing through the heavens. It is a new branch, delicate, and yet full of life. That's what I meant by fecundity in hollowness.

"Then take a look at these ethereal blossoms in the snow. Instead of outlining them in the traditional way, the artist chose to represent them by dots of very diluted ink. This makes the petals appear illusory, though they are actually there. Here is a dreamy, otherworldly scene, hinting at a faint fragrance, a misty vision. And, overall, the painting presents a figure that is leaning over to one side, like a celestial being peering over and down at the earthly realm."

Analysing this piece brought together everything I had ever learnt from studying poetry and art. I estimated that it would earn me twenty *yuan*. The guests exclaimed in admiration, as if I should have been older than I was. I, though, dared not be too pleased with myself; after all, this was the result of eight or nine years of hard work.

Father pointed at another few pieces of calligraphy. This was my weakest subject. The abstractness of calligraphy made it many times more difficult to understand than paintings of concrete objects. Although I was able to write a few characters in imitation of the historical masters, and speak a bit to the style and origins of those works, I was unable to analyse the abstract lines in any rational manner.

So, I told a few relevant anecdotes, then brought out the stash of phrases I had prepared for such an occasion, critiquing the pieces purely by visual impression. I pointed at one and said "the strokes are smooth and fluid, the characters lively as if in flight, graceful and inviting". Then, on another piece, I said "elegant in structure, tastefully using the edge stroke for finesse, resulting in openness and spaciousness". Yet another piece: "whimsical and spirited brushwork in a free and easy structure, like unfurling wisps of clouds, evoking the playfulness of nature". When I saw a piece in running script, I'd say it "flows like drifting clouds and running water, with sure and confident lines"; if the lines were thicker, I'd say "vigorous and robust, demonstrating a powerful hand". And for pieces in the full cursive script, the messier ones I would describe as "capricious and unfettered, like horses running freely over the plains", while the tidier ones were "examples of a brush wielded with facility and deliberation, where the evoked mood leaps out from the lines". In this way, I was able to hit the right answer occasionally and not be too far off the mark.

"All right, that's good for now." Father seemed to be satisfied with my performance. I did not look at the guests' expression, but only looked for Father's approval. Father pointed over to where Chunshao, Zhu Xiaokang, and Yao Kunming were, and had me go play with them. I breathed a sigh of relief, and retreated to the background. However, I was reluctant to go too far away—I was only responsible for the prelude; the main event, Father and the guests' discussion time, was only just starting. When it came to those ancient toys, that was where my true interest lay.

On this day, Uncle Zhu Anqiao brought along an inkstone featuring two dragons gazing at the moon. Everyone stood around this piece, supposedly a rare find from the Qianlong period, entranced as if it had whisked them to another time and place. Someone stroked the stone gently, speaking of the slightly cracked, greyish-blue surface as "an expanse of blue ice with ripples frozen within, like reflections of clouds cast by broken rays of sunlight". Someone else poetically described the carving on the inkstone as "twin dragons glide through the heavens, as the moon peers out from the canopy of clouds; the frolicking dragons turn around, and lo! They spot the radiance of the moonshine and marvel". Yet another person, studying the decorative pattern on the side of the stone, said it was like wisps of clouds, layer upon layer, extending into infinity...

Uncle Huang Yingbi, whom I was meeting for the first time, brought a set of multi-coloured inksticks. The set was kept in a lacquered case with a dragon-and-phoenix design in gold. When the box was opened, we saw that in the centre of the lid, in vermillion ink-paste, were imprinted the words "Studio of Antiquities" in the ancient Seal Script. The case itself, lined with richly-decorated brocade, held ten inksticks of different colours arrayed as the Yin-Yang symbol and the Eight Trigrams. On the tops of each inkstick was carved the dragon-and-phoenix of good fortune, and the corresponding Daoist symbol.

Uncle Huang ran an art gallery specialising in paintings and calligraphy. He was also well-versed in all kinds of antiques. He began to explain to us, "The two in the Yin-Yang symbol in the centre are Pure Yellow and Earth Brown, colours corresponding to Earth, the element of the centre. The eight encircling them are respectively Pure Red, Pure Blue, Pure White, Pure Black, Scarlet, Jade, Violet, and Slate, colours corresponding to the element of each direction." He lay a silk handkerchief on his hand and took out the coloured inksticks one by one, showing everyone the words carved on the back. On each inkstick was a line of neat and dignified Clerical Script characters in gold inlay. Uncle Huang read out each line to us: "Daybreak glow", "Curtains of rain", "Mountaintop mist", "Springtime river", "Underwater blossoms", "Frost-dusted peaks", "Cliffs of verdure", "Moon after storm", "Gleam of steel", "Riverside incense"...

I quietly committed all that to memory, thinking that one day I could recite them back to Father. Father praised them as skilfully made, with bright and lively tones and an exquisite fragrance, demonstrating the luxuriousness and sophistication befitting of inksticks made by the imperial palace.

Then Uncle Yao Tiepeng opened up a brocade box that he brought with him, and from it he took out a tiny white Buddhist statue with gold inlay, just six or seven centimetres tall. "Jiafu, take a look at this tridacna shell Tara Bodhisattva statue. It's from the Qianlong period, isn't it?"

Father took a magnifying glass and inspected this miniature statue carefully, turning it over and over in his hand. After a long while, he said, "Tiepeng, it is indeed a Qianlong piece, and an exemplary piece at that. However, it seems that we're missing an exquisite Ghau, a Tibetan prayer box, to keep her in. This is an amulet that should come in a set with a little shrine."

"Now that you mention it, I've been thinking all along that it didn't seem right for a Bodhisattva statue to be kept in a brocade box. So it is a homeless Bodhisattva," Uncle Yao nodded and said, while looking regretfully at this piece that seemed to have lost some of its collection value.

Father pointed at a spot on the bottom plate and continued, "Look at these words here, 'Awangbanzhuer Khutuktu'. Once, when I was visiting a former Qing dynasty nobleman, I saw an amulet statue that was extremely similar to this one in style and workmanship. On the back of its shrine were engraved words in Chinese, Manchurian, Mongolian, and Tibetan. I actually copied down the Chinese lines... I think they said, 'By imperial order, Awangbanzhuer Khutuku adjudged this shrine of the tridacna statue of the Saviouress White Tara, on the 7th day of the 8th month of the 24th year of the Qianlong reign.' To 'adjudge' in this case means to determine the religious value of an object and to bless it. The choice of the person doing the 'adjudging' crucially depends on the nature and rank of the deity. Awangbanzhuer Khutuktu was the *tulku* most respected by Emperor Qianlong. He presided over many major Buddhist religious events. His lineage began around the time of Emperor Kangxi, and reached the height of his influence several reincarnations later in the Qianlong period.... This White Tara statue is quite similar to that one, so it is likely made around the same time. So, I infer that it was created during Emperor Qianlong's time, but not after the 32nd year of his reign, because there was a major change in style after that year.

"Then let's turn to this White Tara statue. She is, in common parlance, the Seven-Eyed Lady, with eyes on her hands, her feet, her forehead, and her face. White Tara is one of the three Deities of Long Life in Tibetan Buddhism. Her eyes symbolise her ability to perceive the suffering of all living beings. Even though this is a very small statue, it is richly decorated, the workmanship is superb, and the features are perfect and complete. This is far superior to most Tara statues. See how her face is smooth and gentle, her eyes lifelike, her expression serene, and her appearance elegant and dignified. The main body of the statue uses the tridacna skilfully to show flowing clothing on a still figure. And her crown, earrings, necklace, shawl, and armlet—all these delicate parts are inlaid with hammered-in gold. They are also decorated with turquoise inlays in just the right places. Under her seat of lotus is a discreet compartment for keeping a relic. Even the bottom plate is engraved with the Double Vajra symbol and the Ashtamangala, the Eight Auspicious Signs... On the whole, the workmanship is very sophisticated and the material is also top-notch. I think this is of a quality reserved only for the imperial house. My guess is that this was an amulet that the emperor carried with him..." Father explained, as he pointed out the details of the statue to the group.

This day's topic appeared to be Emperor Qianlong of the last imperial dynasty. Everything the guests brought had to do with the Qianlong period. We also looked at a brush container carved of bamboo and a snuff bottle. But at the end, Father brought out a jade pendant in the shape of a dancing maiden. This was the first time I cast my eyes on this item. It was not a Qianlong period piece. It was from the Han dynasty.

"Let's start with the material. The texture of this jade is smooth and even. It has a high degree of translucence, and there is a thin sheen all over its surface. Its tone is saturated throughout, balanced and elegant. It's the highest quality Hotan jade." Uncle Huang was the first to speak.

"Then let's look at the form," Uncle Zhu joined in, "The dancing figure has one arm throwing a long sleeve over her head, and her other arm is bent and held out at her waist. Both sleeves are flying in a semi-circle arc. See how elegantly she's dancing. At first sight, this almost looks like a jade pendant with a swirling cloud design."

"That's right, this is the popular 'Long Sleeve Dance' of the Han Dynasty," Father said. "The workmanship of this piece is quite sophisticated in comparison to the average jade dancer figurines from the same period. See how there's a swirl hair bun on her head and a half-moon pendant on her dress. There's a wave pattern on her belt and intricate folds in her dress. It's very time-consuming to produce such a piece." Then Uncle Yao added, "Furthermore, her facial expression is quite lifelike. Her eyes are gazing at something, and her lips are pursed slightly, as if she's thinking about something or signalling something..."

"Jade dancer figurines from the Han Dynasty vary in their level of detail," Father continued explaining. "They can generally be put into three categories. First is the abstract design, where only the basic contours are carved, and the rest—face, eyes, nose, mouth, waist, body, sleeves—are represented by engraved lines. The next is the regular design. The work is finer in detail, using a combination of engraving and openwork techniques. The features of the figurine are easily distinguished. Finally, there's the intricate design. These come in various forms, flat, three-dimensional, or kneeling. Some have jade pendants on the figurines, some have hair buns, cloth folds, or belt pendants. This one figurine I have is an example of an extremely intricate model..."

Besides this jade figure, Father had a number of other items listed his collection registry but which I had never seen. Among them were some Qianlong period pieces, including a white jade ewer with a carved dragon holding a pearl, a *famille-rose* porcelain brush-holder, an underglaze red porcelain "fruits and flowers" urn, a purple glazed plate with a dragon design, a pair of gilt bronze connected vases with a dragon and a phoenix; and some Yongzheng period pieces, including a lotus-shaped yellow glazed plate and a dragon-and-phoenix inkstone of *songhua* stone. When I asked Father about them, he said he had given them away, or traded them for something else. He bade me not to look through his registries. I obediently agreed. But though I stopped looking through them when he was around, I still pored over them when he was not looking. Sometimes he would catch me red-handed, and would tell me off. However, he never scolded me harshly for it, so I kept repeating the offence, scanning through of his collection registry like it was one of my treasure-hunting experiences. I did keep mum about it, though. I never told Chunshao, but just kept it all to myself.

Father had a huge art collection. I had seen most of it, and knew where the rest was stored. The only exception was a nondescript wooden box. Father did not stash it anywhere special, just leaving it in a corner of the bookcase. But he forbade me from touching it.

To stop me from touching that box, he gave me a beautiful curio box as a present. It was a cube, tightly sealed, painted with shiny red lacquer on the outside. On each side were leaves and branches inlaid in gold threads, forming the background for inlays of flowers and fruits made of coral, jade, turquoise, and ivory. It was like a little magic box from a fairy tale.

On the surface the curio box was a seamless whole. There were no gaps or joints to be seen anywhere. Inside it were many interconnected pieces and compartments. Without a single lock or clasp, it nevertheless contained many mechanisms and could be opened in many different ways. It was impossible to discover all its secrets without quite a bit of dedication in taking it apart. For example, a round jade knob on the top of the box was one of the opening mechanisms. You had to rotate the jade until the mouth of the bat engraved on it was lined up with a particular leaf inlaid in gold, in order to loosen the lid of the box. After loosening the lid, you could swivel the four corners of the box outward to reveal four fan-shaped drawers. Each drawer contained miniature compartments of different sizes and shapes. In each compartment was a Lilliputian treasure, such as miniature vases, miniature plates, miniature combs, miniature jade goblets, miniature jade bowls, miniature ivory balls, miniature gold dogs, miniature wooden figurines... Furthermore, each drawer was put together in differently intricate ways, some obvious, some not. Once you had lifted out the four screens covering the fan-shaped drawers, you could see little window-holes in the shapes of peaches, gourds, plum blossoms, and clouds. In the centre of the windows was another area for exploration, with more hidden compartments put together in various ways. Then, when you had finally removed every layer, and lifted out the board at the bottom, the square box would turn into a large round dish. It was like playing hide-and-seek to find all the different methods of opening the box, enough to keep one occupied for a good few days.

But that was only enough for a few days' worth of exploration. Even though the curio box kept its hold on my interest, I was still curious about the forbidden wooden box. Until I finally had a chance to open it—

In the wooden box was only a yellowed sheet of lined paper, with a recipe of chicken essence written with an ink brush: "Take a young hen weighing about a *jin*, preferably wild. After butchering, remove its head, feet, guts, and skin. Place in a jar without water. Steam over a pot of water for four to five hours. This makes one bowl of chicken essence. Add a few peppercorns."

In my memory, we did make chicken essence at home at one point. That was to help me recover after my leg operation in my childhood. The maid kept watch over the earthenware jar, fanning and fanning the little stove under it. It was very work-intensive. Accompanying the chicken essence was another memory, an extremely unpleasant one— that of bird's nests. They made bird's nest soup for me at that time too. Originally I had believed that bird's nest was only made of the saliva of swiftlets. But later on, I found out that what they made for me at home were "red blood nests", the most prized variety of bird's nests. One day, Jade told me that, after a swiftlet's nest was taken away, it had to build a new one, or its babies would have nowhere to stay when they hatch. And when it had made another nest just to see it taken away again, it could only keep secreting saliva in a rush to make another nest. After its saliva had dried up, it would still attempt to spit, until it coughed up the blood of its chest. And so the pale red bird's nest made this way was called "red blood nest". This would be the bird's final nest, made with its most precious blood. But even as it was finished, the nest was still taken away... After listening to that, I wailed, overwhelmed with sadness, refusing to eat bird's nest ever again. So, after that, my recovery tonics were replaced by chicken essence. True, that also involved the killing of an animal, but I did not shed a single tear for the chickens, because the maid would not tell me how they died...

I carefully examined the wooden box with the lined paper in it, inside and out. I could not find anything special about it, and so I never touched it again.

On the other hand, I became increasingly interested in the curio box. I even created new mechanisms for opening it, and not even when Chunshao, Yao Kunming, and Zhu Xiaokang put their heads together could they figure them out. That stoked my sense of pride for quite a while.

Just as the grown-ups visited each other over antiques and artwork, we children visited each other over toys. For a period of time, figuring out the curio box was the most entertaining game we had. Beating out Chunshao's robot, Yao Kunming's toy train set, and Zhu Xiaokang's army playset, the curio box became the most popular toy.

The curio box was so popular that, for an extra half a day's time to play with it, Yao Kunming brought over his father's classified material in exchange.

One day, he brought over a roll of ink ribbon, saying that it's a typewriter ribbon that his father had brought home. They did not have a typewriter at home, but had a few of these spools, all of which had been used. He suspected that his father took them from the typewriter at work. I unrolled a little bit of it and read the strike marks against the sunlight. Immediately I gave the roll back to him, and told him to replace it without his father noticing. He knew that I liked collecting or creating secrets; however, the secrets of the adult world were too much for me, even if they involved words that piqued my interest.

Missiles, fighter planes... I wanted to tell my father what I saw—So that he could be wary of Uncle Yao? That thought was in my mind, though I dared not think it. At the end I did not say anything. For some reason, it seemed to me that the grown-ups were also wary of me, wary of their own child. Some formless force stopped me from speaking out. Maybe I was just too sensitive, but my sensitivity was like a dog with its ears always perked up, howling at the slightest indication of trouble.

* * *

The curio box was great fun. I gradually added a variety of curios to it, mostly little pieces of handicrafts. I had another treasure box too, one that required no additions.

One day, Floral asked me this:

"If you could choose from the Flying Carpet, the Crystal Ball, and the Magic Apple, which would you pick?"

This conversation came about after I had told her stories from the Arabian Nights. The Flying Carpet could take you anywhere you wish to go; the Crystal Ball let you see anything that was happening anywhere; and the Magic Apple could save the life of any dying soul. I did not have to think about the answer, as there were treasures even more fantastic than those in the stories. So I replied,

"I'd pick... a bottomless treasure box, one with a servant inside who would serve me forever."

Floral likely did not understand what I meant, but the treasure box I mentioned was actually her.

By that time, I no longer needed Floral to wipe me. At the start, the teacher moved Floral's seat to be next to mine, so that I could easily ask for her help. Oddly enough, a few times after Floral helped me, I figured out how to turn my wrist and fingers the right way, and after a bit of practice, I was able to wipe myself.

But I still needed her. I was even willing to play the silly "King and the Princess" game with her, or have silly, childish conversations with her about "flying in an aeroplane to take all the clouds home" or "I wonder how much cloud you need to have a person float in the sky" (in front of the grown-ups, though, I still said educated, grown-up things, because I had to). All so that she would lead my way home.

I was afraid of getting lost. This was a secret I was reluctant to tell anyone.

After Chunshao had moved on to the junior high division of our school, his classes finished much later in the day, and he was unable to walk home with me. I was not used to walking alone. I had to have Floral lead the way. It was not that I did not know the way home, but that, if I left the only route I knew in order to go play as I was wont to, I would have been completely lost. Floral accompanied me all the way, letting me wander off the main street, waiting for me to move the parched snails off the road, to pet the sick puppy, to catch a rare dragonfly, to feed a hungry kitten... before guiding me back to the right way. With her taking me home, I could go wherever I liked without fear of getting lost. Also, on sunny afternoons, I would feel much more secure if she walked me into the black hole that was my front door, into the large, empty house (even if Autumn and Anna were home, they could be in any room, in the backyard, or out in the bamboo grove).

I was not afraid of burglars or ghosts. But if I had arrived home alone after school, I would wait outside the door, and go in only when I had ascertained that someone was walking inside, or when Autumn came back with her shopping.

That's just how I was. I did not like walking alone into an empty house, returning to an empty home.

I did not need Floral following me all the time, or insist that she played with me. All I wanted was for there to be another child in the house. Her presence was enough.

Floral. She was my Anna. The Anna who was human.

I had that thought often, but I never told her.

Floral led my way, just like Anna. Whenever I said that to myself in my heart, a smile would reflexively appear on my face.

We would always be running around in the labyrinthine alleys after school. On the way, Floral would touch and sniff everything curiously, like a dog, feeling everything in the environment. She had her own idea of fun. Once in a while she would end up somewhere away from me, but she never once left without me.

Floral was indeed just like Anna. More than once that thought brought a smile to my face. How cute she was, walking along, turning around every now and then to give me a look to let me know whether or not to follow her. Perhaps she was used to doing that, or perhaps it was her instinct. Either way, she was Anna, as I reaffirmed to myself now and again.

Once in a while, when the mood struck, I would intentionally hide behind the trees or bushes by the roadside, waiting for Floral to turn around, waiting for her to not see me, waiting for her to turn back and look for me, waiting for her confounded expression. I wanted to know if she would give up the search, or if she would leave angrily, once she realised she had been had.

I liked to test her in various ways, longing for her to bellow and shriek at me when she found me, as if she were scolding an unruly child, scolding me for not following her closely.

But she never bellowed or shrieked at me. Whenever she found my hiding spot, she would only squat down nearby, waiting for me to be tired of playing (she'd think I was playing inside) and come out on my own.

Conversely, sometimes she wanted to play with me as well, and hide so well that I could not find her, until I was running around madly, howling of distress and desperation...

I did not admit that I was dependent on Floral, nor did I admit that I gave her gifts to obtain her favour. I mean, I could have generously let her choose from all my toys, or I could have told her, "This toy is for you. I don't want it anymore." I did not do it on purpose; I was just being generous with my devoted servant, as I ought to. Just like how my Anna ought to receive a delicious bone every day. And when I searched for her, called for her, it was not because I was afraid of losing her. I was merely carrying out my part as a master, supervising a devoted servant. That was what I told myself. And I believed myself, as if I managed to convince myself.

I did not neglect my duty in "supervising" Anna because of Floral. I only just give her a day off now and then, giving her the freedom to chase butterflies and lizards, or pursue her never-ending task of sniffing and feeling everything.

Floral did not replace Anna, nor did Anna fall out of my favour because of Floral. When grown-ups were asked if they had a favourite among their children, they would often say things like, "They are both my precious darlings." I could use the same line regarding Anna and Floral, except that was not entirely appropriate as they were not my children. Besides, I had to remember that my status was their master. So, perhaps, "my vassals" would be a more appropriate way to describe them, though that feels too distant. Or maybe I could use a term I heard in period dramas: "my beloved ministers". That was what emperors called their closest assistants. Though, obviously, the most perfect term would still be "my faithful servants".

Anna and Floral became friends quickly. In my mind, they became more and more similar: the dog taught the girl to become Anna, and the girl guided the dog to become Floral. The two were perfect together, like two avatars of the same being. "My faithful servants," I named them in my heart. Though that may just be just wishful thinking, I was convinced, and I believed, that it would become reality.

But before becoming my faithful servant, Floral probably only wanted to be Chunshao's faithful servant.

She often gave me little gifts that she had made herself. Not for me, of course. "Could you please give this to Chunshao?" she would tell me straightaway. Plus, she called my brother directly by his name, just like I did, as if they had been close acquaintances already.

"It's not for me? Why aren't you giving me one as well?" I asked her, feigning innocence, the first time it happened.

"There's only this one. I don't have one for you." She serenely threw cold water on me, as if she did not know this would hurt my feelings.

"Then, maybe next time... maybe next time you could give me one as well?"

"You have many fun toys already. You don't need anything from me."

That was the reason she provided, which did not sound entirely reasonable. "So you mean Chunshao's toys are not fun?" I retorted.

"Chunshao never gave me his toys, so I don't know if they're fun or not."

Her expression was completely unaffected when she said that, with neither flattery nor hypocrisy. She was unaware that, at the same time she praised my toys, she snubbed me.

She was not like this with Chunshao, though. She was neither serene nor unaffected. In fact, she could be downright annoying.

For example, when she saw that Chunshao was collecting aeroplane stickers, she would blurt out some random questions such as "Why do some planes have propellers, and some planes only have fixed wings? Which one is faster... So if the propeller planes are slower than the ones with wings, then why did they bother with the propellers? Why don't they replace them with wings instead? Wouldn't planes go faster if they have more wings..." Or, when a baseball match was on the radio, she would improvise an ignorant opinion, "How many strikes do you need for a home run? Why do you get a base from balls? Shouldn't the pitcher get a prize for three strikes?"

It seemed as if Floral turned into a chatterbox whenever she saw Chunshao, asking this and that while knowing nothing herself. It was unbearable. The first time I heard her talk like that, a tragic image appeared in my mind, that of a frightened little bird throwing herself this way and that in a cage.

I believed that it was not because she loved to chat. It was because she was afraid Chunshao would be silent to her.

And Chunshao was such a considerate boy. He would not give Floral many such opportunities to be frightened. Consciously or not, he often gave little favours to Floral, such as giving her whatever he was holding at the time, or giving her food that he could not finish. Even though he did not like having Floral follow him everywhere, he would think of ways to leave her without hurting her feelings; he might ask her to go do something for him, and disappear before she returned.

In reality, though, Floral was only following Chunshao at a distance, as if she was not serious about him, as if she was just an unconcerned individual.

That distance spoke of a desire to watch over him without getting too involved, to let him be while absorbing a sense of security and happiness from his presence.

Perhaps Chunshao was too sensitive. Or perhaps he knew too well? His intentions were probably above Floral's head. To requite those little favours, Floral could only send presents to him indirectly through me. Perhaps she was afraid that she would start blabbering uncontrollably when she came before him. Seeing her flap her wings in a panic was more pitiable than seeing her silence.

That's how she was, simple, dogged, possessing a subtle nature that was a bit gentle, a bit foolish, and a bit vulnerable; this stirred up something deep in my heart.

Only many years later did I realise that she and I were like twins. She was the part of me that I was ashamed of showing in public, a part that was furtive and reticent... When she was sniffing about like a dog on our way home from school, she always seemed so serious, even though she was driven by emptiness and boredom. From her, I saw sacred solitude, the immense solitude one experiences when immersed in fantasising, worry, or pleasure. Even though her sniffing about was based on emptiness, there was a sense of anticipation in it, a sense that she was focusing on the advent of something.

How empty would the world be without this kind of focus?

A hazy sense of foreboding started making waves on my overflowing sense of emptiness.

7
When the grown-ups were away

Floral's father did not often show his face outside the house. He gave the impression of a listless, fragile man, like one whose insides had been sucked out of him, of whom only an empty shell remained.

I remember when I saw him for the last time, it was a bright and sunny day. A Sunday. He was sitting under the eaves of his house, taking in the sunlight through the sparse foliage. He was wearing an old undershirt that was threadbare from washing, two stick-like legs stretching out before him. The features of his face were jagged, skeletal. The sun cast trembling shadowy spots on his face, adding a bit of expression to his expressionless countenance. A breeze picked up. He broke out coughing, as the wind chimes hanging from the eaves began ringing. He leaned forward slightly, making gurgling noises in his throat, his sunken eyes appearing to be in danger of falling out of their sockets. He expelled a large glob of phlegm on the ground. It was so viscous that I could see a thread of yellow phlegm stuck to his teeth in his slightly opened mouth. He heaved few dry coughs, then spat forcefully at the ground. A long thread of phlegm shot far away from him, as if his life was shooting away along with it.

I thought, Chunshao may get his dream a few decades early now. Autumn's husband did not have long to live. He seemed to be just waiting for death, just waiting for the grave to be built. Autumn herself had stopped trying to keep her man alive as well. As if she had already come to terms with the situation, or was secretly hoping for something, there was not a trace of worry on her face; as if, once the time came, he would return naturally to the earth, while she still had a future to look forward to.

Around that time, my game with Floral transformed from the King executing the Princess to the Immortal saving the Princess.

She would say, "I don't want to die. Please save me, Lord Immortal!"

And I would say, "How would you like me to save you?"

She would say, "I want to live forever. Please grant me one of the immortality pills in your alchemy furnace."

I was playing a game of alchemy with Floral. We were making immortality pills, according to a 3rd Century method documented in an ancient manual. I went and bought a full set of equipment, including a tiny mortar and pestle, a distiller, a sublimator, and a custom-made stove that functioned as our alchemy furnace. On this, I spent all the money I had earned from reciting poetry and critiquing paintings. All of this was to satisfy our spirit of experimentation, and also to answer Floral's question about "Immortality Pills".

We collected all the ingredients indicated in the ancient method: the "four metals" in alchemy—gold, mercury, lead, and copper—and the "eight minerals"—cinnabar, sal ammoniac, borax, chalcanthite, realgar, orpiment, arsenolite, halitum, saltpetre, and aluminite. For more potency, we supplemented all that with some Chinese herbs such as ginseng, ganoderma, honeysuckle flowers, millettia, and poria mushroom, along with animal bones and blood.

I played the role of the immortal, while Floral played two roles— the princess seeking the elixir, and the apprentice running errands for the immortal. Though this was a game, neither of us treated it as one. With the significant gaps in the procedure described in the historical text, I had to research numerous scientific books before we were able to implement the ancient method.

The complex procedure involved the Fire Method (solidifying the ingredients in dry heat) and the Water Method (dissolving the solid material and extracting it in crystalised form). When the first pill was completed, I granted it to Floral. Deep inside, though, I was more wishing to dig Sisi out of the earth under the magnolia tree, and feed the pill into his mouth.

Floral did not take the pill. She said, "I'll wait till I'm about to die. It'd be a waste to take it now." What she meant to say was, "I can't tell if it works if I take it now. I can only tell if it's an immortality pill if I take it when I'm almost dead." Nonetheless, she received the pill gladly, without saying a word of doubt regarding its efficacy. I did doubt its efficacy, though. All I did was prove that the ingredients and the method could indeed produce a solid pill; I could not guarantee that it granted immortality.

Later, I heard that Floral gave the immortality pill to her father. This was no surprise. She had always prayed for her father to return to health, and the efficacy of the immortality pill would be most readily demonstrated on a dying man. Her father put the pill in his mouth and sucked on it for a bit, but, suddenly, he felt an itch in his nose and broke out in a coughing fit. The pill, carried by the sputum, flew into the ditch before her front door. Floral took a nylon net and fished for it in the ditch for a long while before she recovered it. She washed it, dried it in the sun, and placed it at the feet of the icon of the Bodhisattva in her household shrine.

Naturally, her father refused to put something in his mouth that was scooped out from the ditch. And Floral stood by what she said to me before: "I'll wait till I'm about to die. It'd be a waste to take it now."

After the alchemy equipment served its purpose, it was left to the elements in the backyard. Autumn found it a waste of space and a breeding ground for mosquitoes. One day, when the junk collector passed by our house, Autumn took it all out and sold the set for five *yuan*. She looked quite pleased with herself when she came back, saying that she had got a really good deal on it.

* * *

Autumn was always a bit careless with me. She was neither as attentive as Father or Chunshao, nor as vigilant as Mother. But she still held some reverence towards me. She seemed to understand that I knew what she was up to. Besides, her culinary skills came mostly from me.

"For braised meatballs, you have to use pork rib meat with 70-30 fat. Don't use anything too lean. Not this piece... the meat has to be chopped finer, right, chop it all into rice-sized bits like this.... Wait!

Add another two tablespoons of crab powder and give it a stir... turn the heat down. Meatballs have to be braised on low heat... 45 minutes is enough. They don't benefit from overcooking..."

"For shredded beancurd salad, boil a pot of broth and put the beancurd shreds in when it's come to a rolling boil. Shred the dried scallops and daylily flowers, and mince the dried shrimps... Right, pour all that into the broth. Add a bit of Shaoxing wine. Turn up the heat and let it come to a boil... Good, turn it down and let it simmer for an hour for the flavours to be absorbed..."

"This is noodle sauce? That's not it! It's not enough to just put in diced meat, diced dried beancurd, and chopped fried gluten... Go chop up some shrimp and bamboo shoots as well. And add some garlic paste. Yeah, much better. Mix all that into the sweet soybean sauce and simmer it over low heat... Let me see. Ah, the oil is starting to separate now. Turn the stove off."

"To make stir-fried bamboo shoots, use just the centre portion of the shoots. That's the most tender part. Discard the rest... Don't cut them too thin; about two inches long is good... There! Now heat the wok and add the oil... when the oil is hot, put the dried shrimp, Sichuan peppercorns, Goji berries, and ginger slices in and stir-fry those for a bit first... Now put the bamboo shoots in. Just a few stirs is enough. All right, you can take it out now..."

All this culinary knowledge I learnt from Mother. Mother was a gifted chef; no matter how complicated a dish was, she only needed a bite of it to figure out how it was made. At home, Father taught me poetry and art, and Mother taught me gastronomy and cinema. It was as if I was obliged to know all forms of entertainment and pleasure of the privileged class, and to be graceful in the knowledge. Chunshao did too, but he did not have the same quickness and intuition in learning as I did. That was the reason why Mother spent more time teaching me—so that I could supervise Autumn on her behalf. Thus, I tragically inherited a gift I did not want. Mother was generally busy, and so I became the manager of the kitchen, looking over four stoves at the same time. With great effort, I was able to train Autumn to do seventy percent of what Chunhong could do. It was only seventy percent, though, not a hundred; the remaining thirty were dishes that I liked or recipes that I invented. Chunhong's dishes were too authentic. I liked having my own opinions and tastes.

But my opinions were not met with Mother's approval. Whenever she had time, or was in the mood, she would go to the kitchen and wrangle back her thirty percent of lost art.

One day, Mother was in the kitchen directing Autumn's cooking. With nothing better to do, I wandered by Father's study. The door was closed. Soft lamplight radiated into the corridor from the frosted window. I knew Father was inside. As usual, I went up and turned the doorknob. Normally, Father did not mind me opening his study door without knocking, so I was not worried about upsetting him. However, I did not want to disturb him either; I just wanted to poke my head in and say hello.

As gently as possible, I turned the doorknob, just to find that the door was bolted from the inside. I did not knock. I was about to shrug it off. But after walking a few steps away, I stopped, thought, and turned around.

An unusual force drew me back to the study. Because it was unusual for Father to lock the door.

Through the frosted glass, only the lamplight, as well as one or two pieces of furniture close to the window, was visible. Nothing beyond that could be discerned. I felt the rough surface of the glass with my hand, remembering that it was not rough on both sides; the smooth side was on the inside. Only this side was translucent.... An idea came to me. I licked my finger, and, copying an old trick in period dramas, wet the glass with my saliva as if it were window paper. I did it just for fun, not expecting anything to happen.

Although it was impossible to poke a hole in glass like one could with window paper, the bit of moistened frosted glass, just like a hole in window paper, became almost transparent.

I was terrified. I did not intend to commit a crime, but unintentionally I committed the worst crime of all. Though, to be completely honest, it was not a completely innocent act, but something in the grey area between unintentional and premeditated.

Snooping was a crime. Snooping on my father's secrets was an even more serious crime. Temporarily pushing my conscience aside, I quickly pressed my eye against this newly-created peephole.

In the study, Father was leaning over a spread-out sheet of rice paper. Using a writing implement that was not an ink brush, dipping it in a liquid that was not ink, he drew something on the paper. I could not see what he was drawing. Not because the transparent hole in the glass was too small, but, really, the paper remained completely blank.

He drew thus for a while before stopping, then packed up the brush and the unknown liquid. He waited for a few moments, then straightened out the rice paper, and, picking up the ink stone and the inkstick from the table, he ground some fresh black ink. He took an ink brush from the brush stand, dipped it in the ink, and started writing on the paper anew. It was far from a meticulous piece of calligraphy, though, but just a few lines of careless scribbles. He put down the brush. Then he put the paper aside, as if he was waiting for the ink to dry.

A few moments later, the jingling of a bell came from outside. I could tell that it was the old junk collector passing by our front door, pushing his cart and ringing his handbell.

Suddenly, Father picked up that sheet of what seemed to be a bad calligraphy draft, crumpled it up, and threw it into a battered cardboard box along with some scrap paper and old newspapers.

He stood up and went to open the door. I hurried to hide in a corner.

"Autumn! Autumn!" Father opened the door and called for the maid.

"Take this box of scrap paper and give it to the junk collector outside."

Autumn wiped her hands on her apron and took the box from him, looking meaningfully at Father for over two seconds. Then, without a word, she turned around and went downstairs.

On this day I learned a new skill: "Secret writing".

There were a few methods for "secret writing". The most basic way was writing with rice broth, which dried clear and could only be revealed by heating over a fire. Lemon juice or milk could also do the job—while the former was also revealed through heat, writing done with the latter could only be read when one rubbed a dark powder, such as ground-up lead from a pencil, over the paper. To be more sophisticated, one could write with eye drops or invisible ink; the reader would then need to soak the sheet of paper in some special solution in order to read the writing. Of course, a sheet of blank paper was always suspicious. So, it's always best to write some innocuous content over the secret writing in coloured ink, and pass it as a regular letter, note, or scrap paper for calligraphy practice...

I taught Floral the game of secret writing. Our code name for it was "God's Decree".

The other game did not involve paper, but rather using acetic acid to write on eggshells. This game of hard-boiled eggs we secretly referred to as "Baseball".

Chunshao and I also played a game when the grown-ups were not watching. This also came from observing the grown-ups. Chunshao called it "Chipper". Whenever he said "Let's go chipper" or "Do you wanna chipper?", it felt like he was telling me to chew cardboard into gum, or continue to wait for the Americans to find Hitler. It was not necessarily fun. But I was accustomed to concurring with whatever my big brother said. And if he said he wanted to play "chipper", I naturally agreed without the slightest hesitation.

The time when we "chippered" was usually after dinner. If our parents had gone out, and Autumn had gone home next door, my brother and I would climb into the closet for a game of exploration. The closet, not being very big, meant that our range of exploration was limited to each other's body. Through rows and rows of clothes, we reached out to feel out each other. We would touch, and we would try to undress the other person. Sometimes this kind of touching stimulated a physical reaction. It was purely a reaction, without any sense of sexual excitement.

Once we were both naked, we would move towards the other in the dark, moving aside the rows of clothes, and start caressing each other at close distance... The first few times, Chunshao and I were just rubbing our bodies against each other; later on, Chunshao taught me to put my hand around his penis and stroke it. He did the same to me, until we were both drenched with sweat.

With no one else in the house, we did not have to worry about being discovered. However, we seemed to have a tacit agreement that this game could only be played inside the closet. The act of hiding in the closet itself was already suggestive of a forbidden act.

Even though Chunshao never told me, I knew that it was Autumn who taught him this game. It was as if she was grooming her future husband, helping him grow up faster.

She had been tempting him for a long time. For example, she knew that Chunshao peeped when she was changing. And so she would intentionally undress when he was looking.

But I knew that there was more than adolescent desires and urges to Chunshao's peeping at her. He truly loved her.

It seemed to me that Chunshao's first crush was like the kind of mismatched love in one of those banal dramas, where parents opposed the relationship of two star-crossed lovers. The anticipation of hindrance added a sense of indescribable futility to the whole thing. So, he could only look at her in secret, or do things that could only be done when no one else was watching.

Did Autumn love Chunshao or did she love my father? It was probably both. However, she might have loved Father a bit more, because the obstacle that was my mother would have given her a sense of tragic hopelessness. As for Chunshao, even if she was just using him, she did care for him; it was entirely possible for care to turn into love. Besides, Chunshao was still a child, and it would have been a few years before the "mismatched love" would become a problem.

And myself? My feelings towards Floral were obviously not simply the appreciation a master had for his faithful servant. I felt we were more like two young children, playing innocently in the bathtub, having no indecent thoughts even as their bodies touched each other in the water. Or, we were like twins, or bosom friends. My heart yearned for that kind of friendship, that epitome of friendship. It was possible that it would not stay at that level for very long, or maybe I would start having other thoughts—not indecent ones, just ones out of impulsion...

That day, for example, when Floral fled towards the river in order to avoid being beaten by Autumn. I was soaking in the water; it was a hot day and I had taken off my clothes to cool off. Suddenly I caught sight of Floral running at me.

"Chunhuan!" She called my name as she leapt into the water.

At that moment, I reflexively put my arms around her. And as we sank, I kissed her.

Why did I do that? I could not explain it. All I could say was that it was an impulsion.

That day, when Autumn followed Floral's tracks to the river bank, when she looked around and called Floral's name, the wind lifted up her skirt. Looking up from the water, I saw her panties, and a red birthmark on her thigh. A certain thought came up in my mind, one that I knew was beyond an impulse—it was also impure…

Once I was quarrelling with Chunshao and he had the upper hand. I suddenly declared that I had slept with Autumn.

Chunshao fell silent and stared at me, transfixed. Emboldened, I stated, "Autumn has a red birthmark on her thigh."

The colour left Chunshao's face. In that moment, I turned the tables on him. But there was no pride in that. I had destroyed his dream.

Autumn was definitely very dear to Chunshao's heart. Now that I had put a stain on her purity, he would never ever forgive me.

Would he really suspect Autumn to have done the deed? No, Autumn, in his mind, was above all suspicion. I was certain of that.

For the rest of that day, Chunshao did not speak a single word more to me. I did not apologize to him, but I did not say anything else either, even though I regretted what I did. However, I was certain that although he would not forgive me for saying that I had slept with Autumn, in his mind I was still a dear brother to him, one above all suspicion.

8
The one who mattered

Since childhood, Chunshao had held social formalities in contempt, holding himself to be above the common crowd. Even though he was courteous to all, it was merely etiquette that came with his upbringing. He maintained his dignity, and nothing more. However, as soon as he saw someone be nice to me—such as giving me a seat on the bus, or giving me a candy—he would bow to that person in the most deferential, most obsequious manner, to show gratitude for the smallest favour given to me. So, I had never doubted that in his heart I was his dearest little brother, since he was willing to bend his principles for my sake.

With such a good big brother, I naturally had a price to pay. Especially to those who held Chunshao in contempt.

"This is for what your big brother owed me. Hah, hah, 'a brother pays a brother's debt', as the saying goes." When they saw that I was alone on the road, they would suddenly tackle me or push me down, and, taking my cap, badge, or toy, swagger away.

And those were the nicer ones. Some others would block my way, making it clear that I was not to pass; sometimes they dumped the contents of my satchel on the ground, and sometimes they pushed me around roughly. In all fairness, they were not as rough on me as they could have been. They knew, after all, that my parents were not nobodies. However, my parents were not particularly special somebodies, either, in comparison with their parents. Most of my school consisted of the offspring of officials, Floral being an exception. That was a benefit Father had granted to Autumn, extending wardship of a servant to her children. On the surface this seemed to be an act of kindness; however, putting Floral in such a school for the privileged made her look as absurd as a pig kept in a cage for exotic birds. (As for Daoxiong, he went to our school along with Floral at the beginning, but before the term was over he was already fussing about not wanting to go anymore. So, Autumn transferred him to a normal school.)

I did not tell Chunshao about getting picked on. I dealt with it all by myself, feeling that by suffering all this, I was standing up for him, courageously repaying his "debts". Or perhaps, I did not want to let him know that, without him by my side, I was no more than a lamb waiting to be slaughtered.

Chunshao was too well-known throughout the school. I was hoping that, even if those who were too timid to challenge him, who could only stomp their feet behind him knowing that they were inferior to him—even if they managed to beat a lamb, it would only prove that they were only strong enough to deal with sheep.

Among these bullies was one Pan Baojiang. His father was quite a powerful figure—the deputy director of some intelligence agency. My mother had warned me to avoid mentioning the name of that agency, else we might get into trouble. So, all I could reveal is that his agency and the Investigation Bureau, where my mother worked, were rivals. Pan Baojiang had a lot of novel toys at home, all imports, but none of them bought from abroad. They were all foreign goods confiscated from the well-heeled rebel spies his father had arrested. Back then, the property of all arrested spies was confiscated, supposedly by the state, but some items ended up in private hands as well. I thought, his father must be doing a much better job than my mother was. At least, Mother never had any foreign toys to give me.

Pan Baojiang's report cards were unimpressive. He kept a crew of flunkies, but they were no geniuses themselves either. The lackeys helped him cheat, but never once got him an award. On the contrary, Chunshao was a solitary knight, keeping no retinue, though he had admirers who voluntarily followed him around. Once, Pan Baojiang went to Chunshao with an alliance proposal, but Chunshao's response was simply, "I dare not aspire to that honour." On another occasion, Pan Baojiang challenged Chunshao to a duel, and Chunshao completely

ignored him. Even if Pan Baojiang managed to rough me up, I felt that
it was unnecessary to trouble Chunshao.

I was capable of managing Pan Baojiang on my own, thanks to two
weapons. The first of those was the "rocket sprocket": I took the rear
sprocket off a bicycle and held it between my fingers, thus making my
punches unblockable. The second was the "steel-wire whip", which
was made by wrapping metal wire tightly around a few electric cables,
creating a flexible whip useful for both attack and defence. These were
all ideas from *wuxia* martial arts novels, adapted to modern materials.

Of course, it would be silly of me to try to fight them all on my
own. I also had Floral, who would lie in ambush somewhere, ready
for my orders. All I had to do was whistle, and Floral would dash over
with Anna. Anna specialized in biting legs, while Floral specialized in
throttling people from behind or smearing dog poop on their faces.
She kept a full bag of dog droppings in her satchel for this purpose.
She had the fortunate characteristic of being smelly to start off with,
and did not mind the stench. Those sons of high officials, never having
encountered stench before, fled upon her approach. The three of us
formed the perfect team. Not even five Pan Baojiangs together could
withstand us.

All those scoundrels, including Pan Baojiang and those who wanted
me to "pay my brother's debt", were all vanquished by the summer
of 1957, and gave me no more trouble. In September of that year,
Chunshao began junior high school. Those quiet alleyways, no longer
the territory of those who harassed us after school, became the private
playground of Floral and me.

Sometimes Yao Kunming and Zhu Xiaokang came to play guerrilla
battles with us, and I would have Floral join us. There was not much
she could do; most of the time she played the role of the fallen,
dying now in this camp, now in another, dying over and over again.
We really needed someone to die in our "battles", but we could not
sacrifice the commanders. In either camp, the final survivor must be
the commander. Going by this logic, the battle dead actually served
quite a useful purpose...

Dying in battle was naturally included in the "King and the Princess"
repertoire, since it was a method of dying. As for the pill of immortality,

Floral still had no intention of taking it. She kept saying that she would wait until she was about to die.

* * *

There are many kinds of death. How many, you ask? I'd say, "Too many to count." But it really boils down to just two kinds, good deaths and bad deaths. At most you could also include normal deaths, or, deaths that do not matter.

Normal deaths generally do not matter. In the category of the good and bad deaths, though, some do not matter, while others matter greatly.

The first time I learnt about the difference between deaths that mattered and those that didn't, it was from a movie.

One day Mother took my brother and me to go watch *The Teahouse of the August Moon*. It was basically a comedy: Marlon Brando, playing an Okinawan, had dark makeup on and said silly things, which made a great impression on a young mind. Beyond that I remembered nothing about the plot, or particularly liking or disliking it. However, there was one particular line that Chunshao explained to me afterwards, which me feel truly afraid.

That line was uttered by an American colonel. He was under orders to bring democracy to the islanders: "My job is to teach these natives the meaning of democracy, and they're going to learn democracy, if I have to shoot every one of them."

I asked my brother, "What did he mean by 'democracy'?"

He replied, "He meant, someone said everyone could do whatever they wanted, but in practice only a selected few could actually do whatever they wanted."

I asked again, "Why would it be all right to kill everyone, just so that some people could do whatever they wanted?"

He said, "Because they wouldn't be obeying their overlord."

I asked, "What's an overlord?"

He replied, "A man who takes himself to be God. Everyone has to obey him. Because he thinks he is the only one who is right."

Something clicked in place in my mind. Imitating his tone of voice, I said, "Right, just like someone who took himself to be an overlord, to be God, who locked up the obedient ants in a matchbox full of sugar, and beheaded all the disobedient ones..." For some reason, I shuddered at the memory of a certain game that I had played for fun.

The analogy of the ants was a bit tangential, but the main point Chunshao made stuck in my mind: To realize a certain goal, an overlord may kill everyone, because their lives did not matter. From this was formed my rudimentary understanding: For the sake of democracy, or any pretext, it does not matter how many people a man kills--if that's what it takes—because their deaths would not matter.

This understanding chilled me to the bones. I asked my brother, "What if the goal of a man who thinks he's right is different to the goal of another man who also thinks he's right? Meaning, what if there are two opposing goals?"

He said, "Then they'll have a war. Fight to the death. Whoever wins can realize his goal."

"Then, it wouldn't matter to the winner to kill everyone that was spared by the war, if it helps him realise his goals?"

"Yeah," Chunshao paused for a moment, probably tired from all my questions. "Something like that. There's a line in the movie, let me think... I think it goes like this, 'Life itself is a battlefield with its own obscure heroes.' That's what it is.... but..." Chunshao thought for a bit, and continued, "If he kills everyone, who will help him realize his goal? After going to the trouble of killing each other... what goal is he left with?"

The next time was when I watched the Julius Caesar movie. I teared up at the death of Caesar, but then Brutus, the one who killed Caesar, came out to the crowd and said: "not that I loved Caesar less, but that I loved Rome more. Had you rather Caesar were living and die all slaves, than that Caesar were dead, to live all free men? As Caesar loved me, I weep for him. As he was fortunate, I rejoice at it. As he was valiant, I honour him. But, as he was ambitious, I slew him. There is tears for his love, joy for his fortune, honour for his valour, and death for his ambition."

I asked Chunshao, "Did he have to kill Caesar? Did Caesar have to die?"

Chunshao said, "That's because to Brutus, Caesar's life or death was the one thing that mattered the most. In other words, Caesar's death was so crucial because so much rested on him. If there is a man whose life or death causes everyone else's life and destiny to be changed drastically, you can call this man's life consequential. His life will be elevated to extreme heights, whether he is a hero or a demon..."

When Chunshao said that, the name of a certain someone came into my mind.

There was one man on whose pleasure and displeasure hung many lives. However, I had still not imagined how he would be significant to me.

From about the year 1953 onward, occasionally someone would come to our house bearing gifts, all of them lavish. Take, for example, the orchid called "Spring Dream" that Mother kept in the greenhouse. That was worth twenty thousand *yuan*. A 200-square metre mansion in the city also cost twenty thousand. Some pieces in Father's antique collection were also gifts. Those people ingratiated themselves not only to my parents, but to us as well. Chunshao's robot set, tank and cannon set, and my chemistry set were all bonus presents that came with the primary gifts.

Why did they have to give us such extravagant gifts? This would not have been a question—it was not out of the ordinary for a family like ours to receive expensive gifts every now and then—if Chunshao had not overheard a rumour from an officer from Mother's bureau.

"They're under suspicion of being rebel spies, so they are hoping for Mother's mercy, or for Father to put in a good word for them before Old Papa." Chunshao's eyes darted around surreptitiously as he said that. He was not given to acting furtive. "Old Papa" was how my parents referred to the President in private conversations. My brother and I followed suit when we spoke together, as if it was a great honour to be able to use the term.

It was also said that all officials holding different views from those of Old Papa all had files on them, that they were all under surveillance and investigation.

Even Old Papa's own son, the one whom my parents called "the Crown Prince" in private, was being monitored by a group of agents, and his telephone line was wiretapped. Every day, the agents recorded everyone who visited the Crown Prince, and everyone whom the Crown Prince recommended to Old Papa, and all their backgrounds and possible motives. Some of the agents were disguised as junk collectors, shoe polishers, cycle-rickshaw drivers, or hawkers peddling noodles or tofu snacks; some used the residents nearby as informers, keeping a 24-hour watch, letting nothing slip through.

They called it "protective surveillance".

Once, unable to deflect Chunshao's constant pestering, Mother took us outside, and, under the magnolia tree, told us about the situation the Crown Prince was in. Her aim was to caution us to speak carefully and not to ask too many questions. By that time, Father had stopped chatting about those anecdotes about misprints, but he continued to have guests over for cards, poetry, wine, and antiques. In those days, the power would occasionally go off in the neighbourhood. The police would occasionally come check our residency papers, and technicians would come fix the water or power—even if we just had everything checked and fixed. "It's the MND doing signals monitoring. They picked up some abnormal wavelength nearby, and had people go look for hidden transmitters. Then, Mother's Bureau was also ordered to join the investigation. In a ramshackle straw hut by the river they dug up a table, and in one of its legs was concealed a powerful receiver. What a close shave! Who'd have thought that there were rebel spies lurking around these parts?" Chunshao told me in a hush-hush way, after he got the details out of one of Mother's subordinates.

As a matter of fact, we were also subject to the same surveillance. In 1956, Autumn accidentally discovered a wire hidden behind the wallpaper and running under the flooring. She told Chunshao. But my parents never said anything, as if they already knew it.

"Even the officials that are close to the President are under surveillance. You can be proud and successful one day and locked up the next," Little Wang, a photographer from Father's news agency, told us.

"The President believes that the Mainland fell to the Communists because he was betrayed by the many rebel spies who have infiltrated the Party and the military. That's why he has special agents for catching the spies, and that's why everyone is asked to report on spies...

"They've got many agencies for arresting people and detaining people. Besides your mother's Investigation Bureau, there's also the Military Police, the Criminal Investigation Bureau HQ, the Department of Security, the Intelligence Bureau, the Combined Logistics Command, and the HQ of the Army, Navy and Air Force...

"Some of these offices fight amongst themselves too. For example, people from your mother's Investigation Bureau and a certain Mr. Zheng's intelligence agency really don't get along. Once in a while, they'd make up some evidence and report someone from the other group as rebel spies to get them executed..."

Like unravelling a yarn, Little Wang gradually revealed more and more inside information to Chunshao and me. Fortunately, Mother had already prepared us for this kind of information. So, while we were shocked, we were not entirely dumbfounded. Really, though, Little Wang should not have revealed such things. It was only to curry favour with his boss's sons, given my father's position. Whenever he told us such confidential information, he would always look a little smug, as if knowing such information made him someone of importance.

Little Wang was often sent to photograph executions. At that time I had started Primary 3. Whenever Chunshao and I had nothing to do after school, we might, on a whim, drop by Father's newspaper office to look at photographs. Little Wang's photos interested us the most. Those were pictures to be shown to Old Papa, and we got the preview.

Naturally they didn't have such photographs all the time. Sometimes the newspaper would announce that a rebel spy would be executed on a certain date, and that was when Little Wang had to go and take pictures. Our parents forbade us from going to such things. If nothing else, at the execution grounds there was always a large crowd of onlookers who heard the news and came; they'd jostle to get a better view, but none would ever get close enough to see the faces of the condemned. Only Little Wang had the privilege to go up as closely as he liked—

"Supposedly, they don't have such professional photography equipment at the Bureau, and that's why they ask us to go take the photographs. But I've got a different theory. Our news agency is the one the President trusts most. After all, it's the Party's newspaper, and you can only trust your own folk. You know, the President reads it every day.

"It's the President himself who convicts each of the condemned. He can only rest his mind when he's seen them shot dead. Since there are some high-ranking officials among the rebel spies, he can't trust the soldiers at the execution grounds. What if the army was being partial, or if they took bribes and found someone else to sub in for the convict? So, the President has to send the most reliable person from his own newspaper agency to take photos of the dead. Only when he has seen the faces of the dead traitors can he be sure that they're dead.

"Before the execution, I first have to take a photo of each of them. Then, they take turns to sign their confession and have their identity verified. After that, the military police in the steel helmets parade them through the streets. Each of the condemned has a large strip of paper pinned on his chest and one on his back, with his name written on them. They walk and walk until they get to the execution grounds. They take their places, then the military police kick them from behind and push them down into a kneeling position. The military police point their guns at their backs. The commander reads out the names of the condemned and the sentence, pauses, then, suddenly he barks out the order. A shot in the back, a shot in the neck, and down the criminals go. After the execution, the commander will go up and take a look, and if he's not satisfied, he'd tell the military police to give this or that person an extra bullet.

"After the commander is satisfied that they're all dead, it's my turn to go up and photograph them. What a chore! Even though the commander tells the police to come over and hold up the bodies for me, it's not an easy job at all. I have to squat down before the body, use one hand to hoist up the head by the hair, and with the other hand— yeah, I only have one hand free to steady the camera and aim it at the face... Ah, you wouldn't know, but some of the police only have the guts to shoot someone but not to touch the dead body. They'd grab onto the shoulders of the corpse, and they'd be shaking like there's no tomorrow."

We relished Little Wang's tales about the rebel spies he photographed, and about how they behaved before the execution. This was even more exciting than watching war movies. Little Wang said, some people walked the whole way with their heads down and their mouths shut, and some others fervidly cried out "The Chinese are innocent" and "Long live Communism". Some looked towards their family with tears in their eyes, and some smiled and waved at familiar faces while being paraded... Among them, there was an official, a Mr. Chen who used to visit us. Little Wang said, the President was so angry at this man that he was not satisfied with just a picture of his face after the execution. Little Wang also had to take a picture of the bullet hole in his chest, which looked like a flower bursting open in bloom, with blood spurting out like a fountain...

I was scared to tears when I heard that. Uncle Chen once gave me a toy machine gun as a present. I never would have imaged that he would be killed by a real gun. I kept the newspaper clipping about his execution, as a way to commemorate an old friend. However, I never had the courage to look at it again—the head of the corpse, in the newspaper photograph, was swollen, hideous, and terrifying, not at all resembling Uncle Chen's kindly and genial look in life.

Another time, Little Wang recounted to us the scene of a child being executed. The child was so little, looking no more than two years old. He was too short when he knelt. So, a military police held him up midair, while another police shot him.

"If he's so little, how could he have been a rebel spy?" asked Chunshao.

"I don't know either. Perhaps his parents were rebel spies, so he got executed along with them," answered Little Wang.

The night after I heard that story, I wet my bed.

I had always thought that the children of rebel spies would at most end up as beggars. I never thought they'd be shot. Once Chunshao and I saw a little beggar on the street. I thought he looked familiar, but Chunshao grabbed my arm and hurried me along, saying, "Don't get close to a rebel spy's kid." Chunshao did not say that out of scorn for the child, but out of fear that there were plainclothes around. If we made contact with the child we would be implicated as well. I then remembered that the child's father was called Guo Tingliang, and was a subordinate of General Sun Liren. The Guos and General Sun were in occasional contact with my father. In 1955, Guo Tingliang's rebellion conspiracy was all over the papers. General Sun was implicated; he lost his job and was placed under house arrest. With a copy of the paper in hand, I went up to Father to ask if it was true, but Mother tore the newspaper out of my hand and tossed it away. She gave me a stern look, as if telling me that I had forgotten her earlier exhortations. Later on, Chunshao told me that Mother had originally been involved in investigating Uncle Guo, but was soon relieved of the file. All I could think of at that time, though, was the telegraph transmitter dug up beside the river. If a rebel spy had wanted to frame us, or if...

"Exterminate the rebel spies! O countrymen, beware
Your friend, your kin, no matter who; no effort should you spare.
Observe his speech, observe his deed, if fishy, go report indeed,
Together we'll catch all of them, for a homeland safe and fair..."

"Report the leading spies, for glory and a prize.
What's the award, you ask? Six thousand for the task!
But if you let them be, they'll harm your family..."

Children often walked by our house while singing such songs that they were taught at school. Now, I could not listen to them without feeling nervous.

On the wire poles and the walls of the school, painted in large, red characters, were slogans such as "Conceal our secrets; reveal the spies" or "Spies could be right beside you". Those words that I had seen every day, to which I had been desensitized, suddenly popped into my mind, stirring up unease.

"Don't worry, even if there are rebel spies everywhere, the Communists can't do anything to us. The Americans sent the Seventh Fleet to protect us. The Taiwan Strait is crawling with their battleships. The Communists can't get here," Chunshao consoled me one day, when I asked him if Taiwan was full of spies sent by the Communists.

But I had another unspoken worry. Perhaps it was Uncle Chen or the Crown Prince, or perhaps it was because others had...

Chunshao told me, "The secret police arrest people first before collecting evidence. They don't need to have evidence first. They'll get it once they've tortured and interrogated the suspect. That's how all the rebel spies get convicted." He got that from a subordinate of Mother's. Seeing my anxiety, he added, "It's all right. The police don't arrest people for nothing. You'll be fine as long as you don't have any strange ideas, and don't blab or ask questions so that they have cause for prosecuting you."

Although I still believed Chunshao, I did not believe him completely. Chewing cardboard could not turn it into gum, and spiders didn't taste like chocolate; it was still possible that he was just saying things to shut me up for a bit so that I would not go bother him and Autumn.

Partly due to a sense of danger, and partly for fun, I started to read about ciphers. There were always a few books about ciphers on Mother's bookshelf. At first I only peeked into them when no one was around. But when I found out that Mother had no intention of stopping me, I pursued my studies openly.

From Morse Code, the Atbash Cipher, the Caesar Shift, the Route Cipher, the Trithemius Cipher, the Vigenère Cipher, to composite ciphers—once I had learned the basics of one I would make up new ways of using them. When I had no one to use them on, I would play two roles by myself, sending encrypted messages to myself, or embedding encrypted instructions in my treasure maps, to make treasure hunting feel like a more serious task.

There was a simple cipher language that I taught to Floral. We then made "cipher songs" to sing to each other. This involved mapping the letters of the alphabet to their corresponding numbers, then, mapping the digits 1 through 7 to "*do*" through "*ti*" on the solfege music scale; the numbers 8, 9, and 0 were mapped to the notes "*do*", "*re*", and "*mi*", an octave higher.

Take, for example, "I love Floral":
First map each letter to its corresponding number:
I (9) L(12) O(15) V(22) E(5) F(6) L(12) O(15) R(18) A(1) L(12)
Then, turn that into solfege notation: *re' | do re do sol re re sol | la do re do sol do do' do do re*

Armed with ciphers for communication, my sense of unease was slightly assuaged—even though we had no secrets to communicate, and played this just as a game.

"Rebel spy" remained the phrase that instilled the greatest fear in me. According to Zhu Xiaokang, because the Mainland called our President Chiang the "Rebel Chiang", the President was obliged to label them rebels as well. Or maybe it went the other way. Regardless, we each called the other side "rebels".

*　*　*

Old Papa killed Uncle Chen. That horrified me. But he looked even more kindly and genial than Uncle Chen had been.

"He's the most generous man ever," declared Floral.

"Whenever he goes out to tour the city, everything becomes cheap. Like, once he went into a shop and picked up an egg and asked the shopkeeper 'how much is it for one?' And immediately the shopkeeper said, 'twenty cents.' But normally they are fifty cents each! And the same with sugar, rice, noodles, fruit... whatever the President touches, it becomes super cheap," Floral waved her hands excitedly as she spoke, as if she could not wait for the President to touch everything in the world.

A photo was printed in the newspapers around that time—

The President, on a tour of the city, holding Floral's hand.

Floral was the scruffiest kid on the street that day. She was ogling at the malt candy in the shop. In front of all the reporters, the President picked her out to pose with for a photograph. He also gave her a large stick of malt candy, one with a sour plum inside.

In the scene captured by the photograph, the President appeared to be a man of the people, a man for the people. Floral appeared to be engaged in conversation with the leader of the nation.

I asked her, "What did you talk to the President about?"

Floral answered, "I saw he had a little red bump on the back of his hand, so I said, Grandpapa, I'll go catch you two dragonflies. If you put them inside your mosquito net when you sleep, they'll eat the mosquitoes, and the mosquitoes won't bite you."

In the photograph, Floral was neither smelly nor dirty. The grime on her, after being printed into a black-and-white newspaper picture, was indiscernible, rendered invisible.

That was the most glorious moment in her life, being able to take a photograph with Old Papa.

That day, she even went to the President's home.

Old Papa let her ride in a stylish black limousine and took her on a tour of his residence. When she came back, she had her hands cupped together carrying something. Carefully opening up her fingers, she presented me with a dragonfly from the President's garden, for me to keep in the birdcage.

"I caught him a dozen dragonflies and put them in the birdcage. When he's ready to sleep, he can just take a few out. That should be enough."

"He's really going to put dragonflies inside his mosquito net?" I was incredulous.

"Yeah. The mosquitoes are bothering him and keeping him from sleeping, and he doesn't like the smell of mosquito coils or sprays. So I told him, the dragonflies will do the trick. He was really happy about it, and gave me a big apple too," Floral said, evidently pleased with herself. "The table at the President's house had a bowl of apples on it. He asked me if I wanted another one. I thought it would be rude to take another one, so I only ate one. But I was full from just one anyway. It was so delicious and so crisp..."

I knew this was likely the first apple Floral had had in her life. An apple of the size she described would cost at least 30 *yuan*.

"The President... was he not mean at all? You weren't afraid of him at all?" I blurted out a question that had long sat in my mind.

"No, not at all. He was so nice to everyone. I wasn't afraid of him." Floral looked at me, "Why did you ask me that? Are you afraid of him?"

"I don't know. But many people are."

"Why would they be? He's a kind old grandpapa. He told me I could go play at his house again. Next time, I'm going to ask him if the dragonflies managed to eat all the mosquitoes..."

Listening to Floral, my fear of Old Papa decreased quite a bit. Or should I say, was pushed aside quite a bit. I had never thought that mosquitoes would bite the President, or that the President wouldn't be immune to mosquito bites. In my mind, Old Papa had been taken off his pedestal and placed back into the realm of mortals—though not all the way to the realm of the common man.

I did not know for certain if dragonflies only ate mosquitoes. But we did not have any mosquitoes at home, as Autumn had exterminated them with insecticides.

The dragonfly from the President's house was kept in my birdcage like an exotic pet. I admired it for three days. I did not feed it. When I saw that it was on the verge of death, I let it go. The next day, I saw it, dead, at the foot of a bamboo. I could not tell if it died of starvation or if it was killed by insecticide.

Floral and I buried the dragonfly, beneath the same magnolia tree where Sisi lay. Rain had just fallen. A toad was chirping on a tree. Floral sprinkled the last handful of dirt over the dragonfly's burial mound, lifted her head, and gazed at something.

"What are you looking at?"

"The toad. The toad is chirping at this height." Floral stood up, indicating a position on the tree with her hand. The toad immediately hopped away. "If there's ever a flood, the water will come up to here."

"How's that possible? That's is so high. And how do you know there'll be a flood anyway?" I asked.

"My mum told me. She said, toads don't climb trees, and if they do, there will be a flood."

Floral gazed into the distance. "If it comes up this high, my dad's grave will be underwater."

I looked in the direction of her gaze. The evening glow blended into the distant horizon. I could not see the grave she referred to.

Floral's father was buried at the bottom of a nearby hill. It was not long after I had crafted the pill of immortality. One day, he coughed and coughed and coughed. Bright red blood came up. Then he died.

After her husband died, Autumn buried him casually, without keeping vigil, without a funeral. She continued to keep herself busy working at our house. Instead of making good her promise in marrying Chunshao, she soon married an idler, who supposedly gambled. Sometimes, when she was looking at us, we could see a tinge of bitterness in her eyes, as if she was saying we owed her, or that we should rescue her.

Why didn't she marry better? Was it intentional, so that people would pity her, would feel sorry for her? Or was it to increase my mother's guilt?

"Mother wanted Autumn to be married. In order to stay with us, Autumn had to find someone to marry as soon as possible." Thus said Chunshao.

"Don't blame Mother," I countered. "Autumn isn't that dumb. She could've chosen to take him or not. She did it on purpose." However, in Chunshao's heart there was only pity for Autumn, sorrow for Autumn, and no room for my words. Even though Mother had always been partial to him, always loved him more dearly than anybody else, when faced with such a situation he still did not hold Mother as dear as he did Autumn. And so Autumn was married. It was too bad that Chunshao had not grown up yet; he still had a long wait ahead of him.

The gambler did not treat Autumn badly, but he did not treat her well either. He was mostly like a traveller—he came home to sleep at night, but no one knew where he went off to gamble during the day. One day, he came home declaring that he had owed a huge sum of money and was thinking of selling Floral to repay it. Autumn slapped him twice across the face and threw him out the door. When my father heard about it, he gave Autumn a sum of money for the divorce.

Not long after, Autumn remarried again. But this time she married an honest man. According to Father, he was the President's attendant, whose job was to bathe the President and cut his nails.

Naturally it was my father who found this husband for her. Autumn probably figured that Father could not remain on the side-lines forever, and that's why she gave herself leave to do what she did, and gave the gambler leave to do what he did, until Father intervened. That's right, Father would definitely have a plan for her. But did she truly need this kind of plan? She knew what she wanted. And she could not get it.

With a new father, Floral's wish became true. She could go to the President's residence again—though not at the President's invitation. Old Papa seemed to have already forgotten his promise to Floral. He did not recognise her anymore. "I waved to him, in front of his black limo. His guards shooed me aside. He saw me, but he acted like he didn't," Floral said with regret. But, undefeated, she and Daoxiong went back to their old trick of climbing up walls and trees, peering this way and that, and, before the guards detected them, scurrying back to their stepfather's breakroom.

"He was also acting secretively in his garden, like they're talking about something important," Floral told me.

Floral used to snoop on people in my family having secret conversations in our backyard. It had not crossed my mind that even Old Papa had to be wary of something as well.

Floral also told me that her stepfather told her that the President rarely discussed matters of importance indoors. The attendants guarding the door could all hear what went on inside the room. Sometimes, the President would take someone into a car and speak with the windows rolled up, or he might take someone into a hidden corner of the garden; that signified that he did not want anyone else to overhear something important.

What secrets did Old Papa have, that he feared others would find out? I demanded Floral to provide me with more detailed inside information, without considering that it might get her in trouble. I was only selfishly demanding from her, taking from her. And, like a loyal dog, Floral braved all dangers to accomplish her mission, climbing up to even more treacherous places to scout around for her master.

"He recited some lines of poetry when he was taking a walk," Floral reported one time.

"How do you know it's poetry?" This was not anything top secret, but it piqued my interest.

"I overheard a line or two that sounded like the sentences you often recite..."

The fact that he liked reciting poetry was a surprise. It almost made me forget the terrible bullet hole in Uncle Chen's chest.

"He has a yellow dog called Whitey, Whitey..." Floral said, while gesturing with her hands.

"During Christmas, they dressed Whitey up with a red hat and a red coat, like Santa Claus..."

"Whenever he's feeding fish in the pond, he's always mumbling something like he's talking to the fish..."

"Once, his false teeth fell out when he sneezed. A monkey jumped down from the tree and ran off with it. The attendant ran after the monkey and fired at it..."

Floral did not know if the shot hit the monkey, because the gunshot gave her such a fright that she fell off the wall and twisted her ankle.

Another time, Old Papa and his wife went for a picnic on the hillside behind their house. Floral and Daoxiong spied on them from a tree nearby. Old Papa's dog discovered them, and started barking beneath the tree. Seeing that it was two children, Old Papa waved at them, and invited them over for a snack.

"Even though he didn't remember my name, like I said, he still remembered me. He was kind to me like before. When they left, their attendants didn't shoo us away either. And he even turned around to wave to me and Daoxiong," Floral beamed.

"Did you ask him about the mosquitoes?" I was still curious about that.

"I did, but he just smiled at me. The lady said they didn't have mosquitoes at home. So I didn't bring it up again."

From the bits of news that Floral passed along, Old Papa did not seem as frightening as I had imagined.

But one day, Floral said Whitey died. Her stepfather told her that Old Papa, while quarrelling with his wife, shot the dog, who was wagging its tail by his feet. His wife had brought the dog back from America. It was her favourite dog.

Though I did not witness Whitey's death, it hit me hard. The bullet hole in Uncle Chen's chest returned to my memory, and seared its mark into it.

I stopped telling Floral to snoop on the President. It was too dangerous. But Floral told me about the last strange thing she discovered: "They have secret passages at home. I saw him and two men wearing black suits walk under a dark shadow under a tree. They stooped down, parted a bush, and disappeared."

This wasn't news to me. I must have had heard about it from Chunshao or someone else. Supposedly, in each of the President's residences there were secret passages, some leading to the airport, some to the sea port, some to underground military commands, surrounded by bullet-proof fortifications outside. Maybe I still fantasised about fighting battles in those secret passages and forts, alongside Chunshao, Zhu Xiaokang, and Yao Kunming, with real weapons. But, once I got over this inborn battle-lust, more than anything I just wanted to sit on the rooftop with Floral, looking at other people's houses and the laundry hanging in their courtyards; the flowerbeds, fish ponds, and trees in the neighbourhood; the bamboo grove beyond those; and the stream appearing in and out of the reeds in the distance.

Those were the happiest times we had together. We hummed our cipher songs, and exchanged pieces of paper with secret writings, which we heated under the sizzling sun to coax out the contents. To change things up, we might exchange flowers with secret messages etched in them, or eggs with turtles or bunnies drawn with vinegar.

Floral and I climbed along the rooftop like cats, played hide-and-seek in the backyard, and explored every nook and cranny. When we got tired, we would lie beneath the magnolia tree, listening to the insects chirping in the trees, listening to the fish blowing bubbles on the surface of the fish pond. Floral had a smell that made me happy to fall sleep with my head cradled in her arm. Under her arms there was a grassy smell that was mixed with the fragrance of cream and the odour of sweat. On top of all that were a few drops of floral water that her mother sprinkled on her clothes (for neutralising the wet dog smell), sweet-smelling but cloyingly so. It was a familiar smell—the smell that came up close to me in the darkness, when I was still in the cradle. I did not remember Mother wearing that fragrance after that time, nor did she smell of sweat tinged with the fragrance of breast milk. Occasionally, I missed the gentle, supple breast that leaned toward my cradle in the attic, feeling that part of my memory had been covered up or erased. That which is covered up tends to cause curiosity; that which has been erased becomes forever unrecoverable in the abyss of regret.

Time stirred up a certain feeling in me. I started to find myself caring or worrying about something. But when Floral was by my side, time became stationary; both the past and the future stayed still beside us...

9
Neither peace nor prosperity

Central Daily News
20 September, 46th year of the Republic

MND capture rebel guerrilla base
Rebels led by Zheng Jinfu netted

The Military Police Corp of the Ministry of National Defence recently captured an armed guerrilla base in the Xindian hills. The rebel leader, Zheng Jinfu, along with his accomplices Lin Shengbiao, Liu Yuzhi, Huang Awan, Su Quanxing, Wu Chamou, and Xu Shunde, had established a secret armed organisation in the hills under the pretence of opening up farmland. The group stockpiled weapons and ammunition, and lured soldiers from local regiments to bring their weapons and defect to them.

The hillside stronghold comprised a watchpost at the front, for spying on military and police investigations, and a workhouse at the rear where they billeted rebel spies from the plains who had been exposed. Investigation reveals that Zheng not only snooped on the laying of military telephone lines and the building of bridges and tunnels, but also planned to sabotage electrical substations and raid armouries. His goal was to reduce the strength of the Nationalist Army in case of a Communist invasion.

The furtive behaviour of Zheng and his associates led a villager to become suspicious and report them covertly to the security agencies.

Deputy squad leader Zhu Anqiao of the Military Police Corp led an
operational team to assault the base, killing seven rebels, wounding
twelve, and uncovering 28 guns and 54 hand grenades.

Minister of Defence Yu Dawei expressed that even though the rebel
organisation was crushed, Communist rebels will not relent in plotting
to invade Taiwan by force. He also expressed that, as the time for our
counteroffensive of the Mainland is nigh, we must tighten our homeland
security in order to thwart all enemy plans for invading Taiwan;
furthermore, we must remain vigilant in our investigative work and in
restricting access to rural areas.

Yesterday, the operational team was awarded a monetary reward. The
informant was awarded 20,000 yuan. (Reporter: Zhang Hongzhan)

Uncle Zhu was over for a visit. We children sat in a circle around
him, pressing him to tell us how he cracked the case.

Uncle Zhu, cigarette in mouth, took a sip of tea, gracefully leaning
sideways into the rattan armchair. Sitting under a trellis full of wisteria
in bloom, gazing at the fishpond and the magnolia tree before him, he
graciously acceded to our request.

"Well... we actually received a tip long ago, about how there were
suspicious characters going about that area. We observed them
covertly for a while. With the information provided by the villager,
we ascertained that they were rebel elements. So we decided to take
action. That day, we first went to the village that was close to the armed
base. We disguised ourselves as villagers to avoid alerting the rebels.
We walked towards the hill, everyone wearing a bamboo hat, a ratty old
singlet, and carrying either a hoe or bamboo basket on a pole. When we
got to the hill, we found a concealed watchpost among the trees in the
front, a 200-square metre workhouse in the back, and a few abandoned
mines and caves further in. We split up into three groups. We had
four men guarding the front, and everyone else closed in from either
side, to cut off the path between the workhouse and the mines. We
first looked for something to conceal ourselves while we observed the
workhouse for any signs of activity, then we closed in slowly. Suddenly,
two grenades were thrown out from inside the house, and scores of
rifles and handguns started shooting at us. We had anticipated that,

so we retreated outside completely, and waited for them to lower their guard before charging in again. The first few rebels who resisted were shot dead, but the rest were still fighting like cornered rats. It was only when the floor was covered with casualties, and their leader, Zheng Jinfu, was injured and captured, that they dropped their weapons and surrendered..."

"It wasn't just guns and grenades. The mines contained barrels and barrels of explosives. Later on, the military also found out that the rebels had more than this base in the hills. They also encouraged grassroots organisations along the coast. Then, they planned to establish communication stations on the plains, and where the coast, the plains, and the hills meet, to coordinate forces all the way from the sea to the hills, and to provide support for the Communist armies when they land. Besides sabotaging bridges, highways, and wiring equipment along the way, and raiding military supplies, their one most terrifying plot was to destroy the fuel depot at the military airport..." Where Uncle Zhu had omitted details, Zhu Xiaokang filled us in, in private. It wasn't every day that he could show off with the exclusive scoop. We were all blown away by the story.

Chunshao suggested, "Let's go check out the base Zhu Xiaokang mentioned."

That was exactly what Zhu Xiaokang had in mind. From his face we could tell that he couldn't wait to lead everyone on a genuine base-capturing expedition.

But where was the base?

Zhu Xiaokang spent half a day trying to wheedle the information out of his father, but only managed get a rough idea. "My dad said this was a military secret and he couldn't reveal too much."

But he still pieced together a route on a map. One early Sunday morning, we marched off on our mission.

"176th Infantry Regiment to HQ, enemy artillery company spotted ahead..."

"HQ to front, that artillery company shouldn't be in the battle zone... The commander thinks they were left behind from our previous engagement. They have at least 50 armoured vehicles and 120 guns.

You are to maintain original plans. Be careful out there..."

"We're 300 yards away from the target. Artillery troops, aim at 45 degrees and ready to fire!"

"Medic! Bring the stretcher over! Pass me the first aid kit..."

"Report to HQ at once that we need more ammo..."

"Reporting to HQ: the enemy countered our attack and are less than 200 yards away from our trench..."

Like going on a regular outdoor excursion, we started playing a serious game of War again, improvising as we went along.

Once I captured Zhu Xiaokang but did not kill him. He turned around and squeezed my neck, saying, "To be kind to your enemy is to be cruel to yourself." I swung my arm around in a stabbing motion. Zhu Xiaokang rolled his eyes and pretended to fall onto the ground—

"Shhh!" Yao Kunming, who had been leading the way, turned around and signalled for us to be quiet. Together we looked towards the saddle of the hill that he was pointing at.

One military vehicle after another drove up to a platform built over there. We each found a tree to hide in, and looked down excitedly.

The military police removed the tailboard from the backs of the vehicles, and brought down a flock of convict-looking people, who had their hands tied behind them and were tied together two by two with a rope around their waists. The group at the front was herded towards a narrow set of railway tracks, and loaded four by four into wooden pushcarts. Every time a cart was filled, a policeman gave it a hard push, and the cart, with the convicts in it, rolled down the tracks into somewhere invisible deep in the hills. Seeing that, the convicts in the back, who had not been loaded into the carts yet, fussed and looked like they were trying to escape. The military police clobbered about a dozen of them with the butts of their rifles, and the convicts quieted down. After that, they resumed being loaded four by four into the carts, like fowl being sent to the market, and pushed down the hill.

Carefully we shifted to a position where we could watch from a different angle. With a better line of sight, we saw that there was a tunnel at the bottom of the hill where the carts rolled down, and the convicts were carried into the tunnel...

We rushed to take up position further down the hill, and saw that,

NEITHER PEACE NOR PROSPERITY

after the carts had passed through the tunnel, they stopped by a place that looked like an abandoned quarry. By now, the military police had unloaded all the convicts, and brought them before a large trench. Once the trench was lined densely with kneeling convicts, the policemen took up position behind them. A barrage of gunshots was heard. The convicts dropped into the trench one by one. There were some who fell backward and not into the trench; they were shoved in with metal shovels. Then, the military police started shovelling dirt, covering the bodies with one shovel of dirt after another. The wide-open, glaring eyes, those mouths gaping with terror, those horribly contorted faces—they were being swallowed by the earth, bit by bit, until they were completely buried.

At the sight, Yao Kunming could not stop his tears from rolling down. His face was white as a sheet. Zhu Xiaokang, seeming to have forgotten the reason why he brought us out here, bolted off. My legs were weak with terror; Chunshao had to drag me along to keep up with Zhu Xiaokang and Yao Kunming.

They were silent all the way, running helter-skelter, as if they were looking for shortcuts, or they had forgotten the original path. Sometimes we moved in different directions.

Suddenly, Yao Kunming knelt down, and vomited all over the ground. His tears and snot flowed onto the ground as well.

Zhu Xiaokang, on the other hand, looked like he was infuriated with someone. He looked around madly for something, like an angry little beast, unable to leave its cage, wanting to chew through the bars and make a hole from which to escape.

Chunshao and I, barely able to hold ourselves together, followed Zhu Xiaokang in his search, either subconsciously or due to a lack of choice. We almost forgot that Yao Kunming was still behind us, vomiting and crying. No one turned around to look at him.

Soon, Zhu Xiaokang found an old rubber tyre hanging from a tree by a hemp rope. He went up to it, looked through the round hole in the tyre towards the bottom of the hill. There was flat land at the bottom not that far away. It really did not look that far. But our hearts did not feel like they could sustain us for the remainder of the distance.

Swiftly, Zhu Xiaokang untied the tyre, bent over to curl up inside it, and rolled straight down the hill.

It took a moment for Chunshao to realise what happened. He ran anxiously after the tyre, yelling, "Xiaokang! Xiaokang!" But, less than a hundred paces away, he stopped.

Chunshao fell heavily onto his buttocks. He had skinned his foot and twisted his ankle. He looked at me apologetically, helplessly, as if he could no longer fulfil his duty as an older brother in protecting his little brother. His expression seemed to say that I was his only worry, and perhaps his burden as well.

I stood over him, not knowing what to do. The wind continued to screech and howl in my ears, giving me goosebumps all over. "Chunshao!" I called his name, as if to remind him of something; then, gritting my teeth, I bent down and hauled him onto my back. Then, I sprinted forward, and ran as if the devil was at my heels.

I waded through mires, made my way through tall grass, not knowing why I still had energy or if I could keep it up for very long, not knowing which way to go, knowing only to run and run with all I had. I heard my own heavy panting and Chunshao's shallow breathing. And Yao Kunming's mournful wails, which, piercing through the wind and the woods, bore into my eardrums.

* * *

There was flat land at the bottom of the hill, not that far away. It really did not look that far. But I could not reach it. We were freezing in our own sweat. I dragged my feet along despairingly. Chunshao weighed heavily on my back and I had difficulty carrying him. The autumnal hills were a vast expanse of whiteness, a large swath of silvergrass blocked my vision. There was no path, no roadsign. All I could be sure of was that I was going downhill.

The slope became steeper and steeper, and shapes of houses appeared vaguely in the distance. I found a shortcut, I thought. Chunshao asked me to put him down. I said it was fine, we were almost there. The wild grass was tall, reaching past my knees. My feet trudged along, making cracking noises, feeling like I was stepping on stones or branches or something. I concentrated on steadying my pace and holding onto Chunshao on my back. We both saw that, around the corner downhill beyond the silvergrass, there was a well-marked trail.

I headed towards the path. Suddenly, I stubbed my toe on something. I lost my balance, and we both rolled into a ditch. The ditch was full of hard, sharp—

Only now could we see that those weren't branches. They were human bones! A ditch, a valley full of human bones!

A few round skulls rolled away from us. We struggled to climb back onto our feet, but our limbs seemed to be weighed down by more round skulls, as well as various hard and sharp shinbones and ribs. Panicking, we pushed them all away, while bursting into tears.

A long, long time passed. I still do not know how we climbed out of the ditch.

We sat down side by side, exhausted. There were some bone fragments scattered about the grass. By then, we were no longer scared, just tired.

"They killed people and buried them here too. Later on, when the rain washed away the earth, the bones were uncovered," said Chunshao.

"Who's 'they'? Where did they get these people that they killed?" I was just talking to myself, not expecting to get an answer.

"It doesn't matter who they were or where they came from. Just know this: Some people are killed like this. Some people die like this," stated Chunshao.

"Then what?"

"Then avoid getting killed. Avoid dying like this," Chunshao replied.

At that moment, we seemed to have grown up instantaneously. Or perhaps I should say, we became more worldly-wise, more vigilant.

We had both known that there were some things that we would come to understand, without having to ask or talk about it. But, under the protective wings of our parents, we had passed a happy childhood as an unconcerned party. Even if we had noticed that something was wrong, we did not pay heed to it, or we waved it off. Because it had not seemed to matter.

"There are some things, we can't pretend to be none of our business anymore, and turn a blind eye to them," Chunshao continued.

"You're talking about danger awareness?" A strand of unease stirred in my mind.

"Yeah, it's time we have a sense of danger awareness. It has come to us naturally, expectedly. We did not generate it intentionally or suddenly."

"I have felt disquiet for a long time. Does that count?"

"Yes," Chunshao looked a bit depressed. "This is a world of neither peace nor prosperity."

Silently, we watched dusk descend upon the earth. A tree in bloom, covered in bright red flowers, took our breath away with its beauty in the glow of the setting sun. It looked like a newly-excavated piece of ancient art, with flowers red like rubies, leaves green like celadon, branches glowing like amber. It was so pretty, so pretty. And behind the prettiness were hidden events from a long time ago, secrets, massacres.

Helping Chunshao to his feet, I supported him down the hill, slowly, one step at a time.

Dense branches covered half the sky with their darkness. A light fog flooded in around us. The moon, floating out from behind a black cloud, hung high up on a branch. In the distance, besides the dark silhouette of the distant hills, there was nothing to be seen except the fog; nearby, there were just quavering shadows of trees and of us, and bumps and ditches on the path; bits of the trail turned silver-white in the moonshine, as if covered with a sprinkling of frost. Some nameless flowers were exuding a strong fragrance, and the moss beneath our feet was wet and slippery. A large boulder lay on the path right in front of us. Grabbing onto some drooping branches, we skimmed around the boulder along a narrow sliver of dirt. After this patch of landslide, we returned to an open path.

The breeze in the hills was most chilling. We were cold. But we had worked up a bit of sweat, too. When the cool wind touched our sweat, our body temperature began to dissipate.

Somewhere, there was the sound of someone moving bamboo stalks aside and walking towards us.

Rain started spitting down at us. We felt a bit annoyed.

A cluster of faint dots of light appeared mid-air and was approaching us.

A waft of dense fog floated by. The light disappeared.

The fog dissipated. The faint cluster of light started bobbing up and down in the darkness once more.

It was near. Human noises, the sound of footsteps. We stopped walking and waited for it to come closer.

The cluster of light became clearer and clearer in the darkness, distinct dots that appeared and disappeared.

The specks of light encircled a face. The face floated towards us in the air.

Fear seized our chests. Our hearts stopped. We could not move. We could only stare at the pale green face in front of us.

"Chunshao, Chunhuan, there you are!"

That person finally arrived.

We saw Floral, with fireflies stuck all over her hair. Her face was dappled with splotches of light and darkness, appearing terrifying and comical at the same time.

"You sure gave us a fright!" I said.

"Just one? Not many frights? All right, have another one." Floral playfully made a scary face at us.

Having just heaved a sigh of relief, and seeing the arrival of help, our hearts gladdened instantly and we burst out laughing.

Floral knew about our plan. Before our departure, we had refused to let her come with us. She was left home to wait for us to return and tell her about our adventure. But she grew impatient and came looking for us by herself.

"I spent the good part of the day looking for you," said Floral. Unable to find us, she started amusing herself along the hillside. When it became dark, she caught a bunch of fireflies to light the way.

She studied the frenzied look on Chunshao's face and mine. She seemed to have understood, and asked no questions. We did not ask her either whether she saw anything, not wanting to mention or recall those scenes.

Floral walked over. She and I supported Chunshao on either side, and together we walked down the hill. Before going home, we went to the park and found a tap to wash the grime off ourselves. And then, we sauntered into the house, humming a song, as if nothing had happened.

10
As flowers bloom and wither

There was a poem that I loved. It evoked an inexplicable sense of loneliness in me. Father had marked this page in the anthology with a dried leaf:

Aspens rustling in the wind,
Aspens rustling in the calm,
Beyond the rustling nothing more is heard;
Wildflowers blooming in silence,
Wildflowers withering in silence,
Beyond the silence the garden is empty.
—Zhu Xiang, "The deserted garden"

It felt like when, in the chill of autumn, those mossy lanes, those wandering footsteps fade away in time; it felt like when, at the end of a calligraphy stroke, the faint traces of ink linger beyond the character's completion.

I was looking over a folding paper fan in Father's collection. On the fan was written a poem, signed by one "Hermit Woodcutter":

Snow settles on the old bridge
Like powder on your radiant face
As it does every year, before
melting and joining the springtime river
carrying it far, far away.

The wildflowers in the courtyard, who
saw the wind whisk away your shadow,
remain, to lament with my memories
of you, who once stood here.

The writing on the fan was faded and the ink faint, like wisps of smoke, reminiscent of the lines in "The deserted garden"—there was nothing more beyond the rustling, nothing more beyond the silence. Perhaps the melancholy experienced by the poet was already a thing of the past. But now, his fan had found its way into the hands of a stranger, who held it, admired it, and mused over feelings evoked by some unknown person or situation... There was a certain hypnotic sense of fascination that could not be described.

But even though it invited one to muse over it, it was just a way to pass idle time, with a thought as ephemeral as the sound of a babbling brook.

On drowsy, languid afternoons, I would go to Father's room and sneak into this modest little chamber, to escape from the overly expansive emptiness of the outside world, to enjoy being enclosed in this tiny sliver of solitude.

I liked to trace my finger along the characters on a calligraphy piece hanging by the southern window of Father's room. As my finger, in the air, flew along with the soaring lines, I would gaze at the changing shadows cast on the paper by the westering sun. This was a time when I would feel my finger transform into something celestial, leading me into another place, another time—

A solitary lamp burning on, beyond sun and moon
Shining on my cares, nor sleep will find
Here, lying between life and death
On what should I rest my mind?

The handwriting was Father's own, but I did not know who authored the poem. Father only said those were lines composed by a poet in the Ming or Qing dynasty, and told me to research them myself. However, despite having pored through all the poetry anthologies at home, I could not find the source. In 1963, as I was entering adulthood, I saw from this dappled scroll a vague sense of grief or bleakness. It brought anxiety to my heart, at the same time it drew me closer to it.

The banquets at home still went on in those glorious springtime evenings. Chunshao and I were no longer pages ushering in the evening with art critiques. Our parents allowed us a seat among the guests, as if they were wanting to acclimatise us to the social functions of the adult world.

On the very last banquet in the spring of 1963—as Chunshao and I still remember—the Queen-of-the-Night produced forty-nine blossoms all at once. After supper, Father and Mother had the dining table moved to the courtyard, and had the maid light the candles in the stone lanterns. In this elegant atmosphere of a bygone era, we enjoyed dainty desserts while sipping tea.

One of the guests remarked, "This tea tastes a bit different. Did you put in new tea leaves?"

"The tea leaves are the same as what you just had, but we did use different water. This is better water," Father said. "Actually, good tea depends crucially on good water." He refilled the guests' teacups, and, picking up a cup of Dragonwell tea, continued, "In the old days, Lu Yu, who was revered as the God of Tea, was very particular in choosing water for tea-brewing, and had many insights on the subject. During his lifetime, he travelled all over China in search of the best water, and found twenty sources of it. In the Tang Dynasty, Zhang Youxin recorded Lu Yu's list in his work, 'Notes on Water for Tea-Brewing'..." He then indicated for Chunshao to continue. Poised and confident, Chunshao spoke:

"Among the top twenty sources of water in China, the best is from the waterfall in Kangwang Valley of Lushan Mountain. Spring water from Huishan Temple in Wuxi ranks second; underground water of the Lanxi Stream at Jizhou ranks third; fourth is water from the springs at Toad Rock at Xia Prefecture's Fan Mountain; spring water of Huqiu Temple in Suzhou ranks fifth; sixth is the water beneath the stone bridge at Zhaoxian Temple at Mount Lu; water from Nanling of the Yangtze River ranks seventh; water from the Xidong Falls of the West

Hills in Hongzhou ranks eighth; ninth is the water from the source of the Huai River in Baiyan County in Tangzhou; tenth is the water from the ridges of Longchi in Luzhou; water from the Guanyin Temple of Danyang County ranks eleventh; water from the Daming Temple of Yangzhou ranks twelfth; water from Zhongling, in the upper reaches of the Hanjiang River in Jinzhou ranks thirteenth; water from Fragrant Stream below the Yuxu Caves in Guizhou ranks fourteenth; Luo River water west of Wuguan Pass in Shangzhou ranks fifteenth; water from Wusongjiang ranks sixteenth; water from the Great Waterfall of the southwestern peak of Tiantai Mountain ranks seventeenth; Yuanquan Spring water of Liuzhou ranks eighteenth; water from Yanlingtan Shores of Tonglu ranks nineteenth; snow-water ranks twentieth."

Uncle Zhu laughed and said, "Jiafu, how would we get our hands on any of the waters your son mentioned anyway? Clearly this was just a demonstration of your children's erudition." He then held up a cup of tea, sniffed it, and said, "Since you are so sophisticated in your choice of water for tea, do tell, what water was used in this cup of tea?"

"Anqiao, of course I couldn't have brewed with any of those twenty water sources of renown. But I did send someone to fetch this water from the hills. Have you heard about the Springs of Bodhisattva Hill? It is a bit off the beaten path. Not many people know about it. But the water there is just fabulous! It is mild and not harsh, sweet yet not heavy, clear and pure. It really is choice water for making tea..."

Uncle Huang Yingbi examined the tea-bowl in his hand, as if admiring a piece of art. "Jiafu, I see. Let me try. Not only are you discerning in your choice of water for brewing tea, but I think even this tea-bowl of yours is no ordinary ware. Looks like it's got a story behind it too." Besides running an art gallery, Uncle Huang was the First Lady's private tutor since 1960. He was driven in a black limousine to the Presidential Palace to give art lessons to the First Lady every week. Father was in fairly frequent contact with Uncle Huang as well. Whenever he was in need of gifts for social obligations, he would go to Uncle Huang's shop to buy a painting or two. Sometimes the two of them traded collection items as well. As soon as Uncle Huang finished speaking, Father gave him a look of praise.

"Not bad, Yingbi. You sure have sharp eyes." said Mother.

"Li Juan, what kind of tea-bowls do you use here? Tell us a bit about them," said Uncle Yao.

"Tiepeng, this tea-bowl is Yue porcelain," said Mother.

"Yue porcelain? What's special about it?" asked Uncle Yao.

Father replied, "Yue porcelain has the texture of jade and the colour of ice. Tea held in such a vessel appears particularly delightfully verdant. Being discerning of tea vessels is about considering the colour that the tea appears in the vessel, whether or not the colour of the vessel and the tea complement each other, for creating the greatest sensory pleasure when enjoying tea. Of course, there is a ranking for tea vessels as well, dividing them into six grades by the colour and texture of the porcelain. Chunhuan, tell our guests a bit about it."

I said, "The top ceramic ware comes from Yue. Second to it is porcelain from Dingzhou, followed by that from Wuzhou, Yuehzhou, Shouzhou, and Hongzhou. What's so special about Yue ware? In the Tang dynasty, the poet Lu Guimeng wrote thus in a poem called 'Yue ware of the Secret Colour':

Born of the Yue kilns
Clear dew of high autumn
In which gleams the verdure of springtime hills

The poet Xu Yin of the late Tang also wrote a poem called 'The Imperial Tribute Teacup', which has the these lines:

A fine-carved moon washing the floods of spring;
A sheet of delicate ice holding turquoise cloud;
An ancient mirror, moss-covered, leaning by the wall;
A dew-topped leaf of lotus along the river's shroud.

Both pieces describe the outstanding texture and colour of Yue ware. Despite being a ceramic, Yue ware is as bright and smooth as jade, as clear and light as ice. It is indeed of superior quality in the realm of ceramic ware."

"You've got to say they are well-versed in the subject. Jiafu, Li Juan, though the two fine young men of your household are not very old, they are certainly worthy to be our teachers. We are nowhere as discriminating when we take tea. Perhaps, instead, they could have a glass or two of wine with us and join us in our drinking game?" said Uncle Yao.

Chunshao and I took a look at our parents, who did not show any objection. Then we asked if Zhu Xiaokang and Yao Kunming could stay behind and join the game too. The grown-ups had a special game for drinking, involving poetry and versifying. My parents considered it a form of refined entertainment. Mother called for the maid to clear the table and bring out another two bottles of wine.

Uncle Yao declared the rules for the first game. "Let's start with the word 'spring'. The two young gentlemen of this household both have the character *chun*, or 'spring', in their names, and we are also here together on this beautiful spring evening. Thus, we shall use the theme of 'spring' to mark the occasion. Beginning with myself, each person shall recite a line from a classical poem. The first person shall recite a line that has 'spring' as the first syllable, the second person shall recite a line that has 'spring' as the second syllable, and so on and so forth. After we've had 'spring' as the seventh syllable, we shall start from the beginning again. Whoever fails to come up with a line shall take a drink."

He then begins: "**Spring** winds announce the colours of the fields."

Uncle Zhu was next: "New **spring** knows not the wand'rer's secret thoughts."

Uncle Huang had the third syllable: "Fall moons, **spring** days I lived, but cherished not."

Father, fourth, recited, "The trees know **spring**, ere long, will fade away."

Mother followed with the fifth syllable: "A flower whom **spring** rain has bathed—she wept."

Chunshao recited for the sixth syllable: "The passions, love, of **spring**time dreams fulfilled."

Yao Kunming paused and thought. I whispered a hint to him. For the seventh syllable, he said, " A carefree boat along **spring** rivers drifts."

I was up next, and we were back to the first syllable: "**Spring** blossoms fill the air throughout the land."

Zhu Xiaokang took the second syllable: "With **spring** as my companion, I return."

It was back to Uncle Yao for the third syllable: "A bird's **spring** song laments the ancient king."

Uncle Zhu on the fourth syllable: "I lie, in **spring**, alone in a light robe."

Following him, Uncle Huang recited, "And overnight, **spring** winds have breathed new life."

Father had the sixth syllable: "My house, with streams of **spring**time girdled round."

Mother, on the seventh syllable, said, "Their clothes adorned as late **spring**'s brilliant days."

And then it was Chunshao's turn, and back to the first syllable: "**Spring** floods emboldened by the evening rain."

Yao Kunming could not think of the next line, and was made to drink a glass as forfeit.

I followed with "Winds of **Spring**! Bring my thoughts to lands afar."

Zhu Xiaokang thought hard, but only came up with "Canst repay the warmth of spring's mild sun?" However, the word was not in the correct place, and he drank a glass in forfeit.

Having finished two rounds of the "spring" theme, Uncle Zhu announced a new round on the theme "autumn". The rules were to be the same as the previous rounds, except the requirement on word position was removed.

Uncle Zhu started with, "The season when leaves fall with autumn rain."

Uncle Huang then recited, "Frontier autumn—a sole wild goose cries."

Father continued with "Autumnal dusk; a candle; painted screens."

Then Mother said, "The autumn scene—my endless banishment."

Chunshao, following her, recited, "A solitary sail on autumn's tides."

I had to give Yao Kunming a hint again. Then he said, "With curtains drawn, to touch the autumn stars."

At my turn, I said, "At their ruins, wild grass stir in autumn winds."

Zhu Xiaokang recited, "Where autumn waters blend into the sky."

Uncle Yao followed with, "A full moon shines in the autumnal sky."

After a round of "autumn", Father declared a round with new rules, with "flower" as the keyword. Everyone, in turn, should recite two lines of a classical poem, one of which must contain the word "flower", and one of which must rhyme with a line recited by the previous person. Whoever failed to produce the appropriate lines would drink a glass as forfeit.

So he began: "Dayglow fades; light haze settles on the flowers; / The silken moon looks on the sleepless night."

Mother followed with: "No flower blooms beyond a week, and yet / the *yueji* rose, year-round, beams equally bright."

Chunshao continued: "An unswept path, flower-lined, never walked; / The grass-weave door today will first see light."

I was next: "Can loyal hearts not weep for this their plight? / Can stream-borne flowers halt their ceaseless flight?"

Yao Kunming recited: "The catkins sway like flowers in the wind, / but who shall care when they fall to the earth?" But it did not rhyme with the previous lines, so he took a glass in forfeit.

Zhu Xiaokang said: "On Xunyang's banks, the sending-off at night / as grey reeds rustle in the autumn wind". "Reeds" was not a flower, so he had to drink a glass in forfeit.

Uncle Yao recited: "Take that branch while the flower's blooming bright! / Ere long it'll fade, leaving a naked stick."

Uncle Zhu followed with: "Last year you left during the springtime's height / The flowers bloom again—a year has passed."

Uncle Huang started: "Wild flowers bloom along the Zhuque Bridge...". But the following line would not fit the rhyme, so he drank a glass.

Father then declared a game of "change-a-word". Each person was to recite a line of classical poetry, but change the last word of the line to another word, then create a new line in the same rhyme and meter to explain the change. If either the explanation was inadequate, or if the line was not in the right form, a glass of wine would be the penalty.

Father began with, "'In springtime laugh the blossoms of the chives.' It should have been 'plums', not 'chives', but... The plums were picked clean by the farmers' wives."

Mother pondered for a while, and was made to drink a glass in forfeit.

Uncle Zhu grinned and said, "'To the halls I go, riding on my dog.' It should have been 'horse', not 'dog', but... My horse I'd tied too tightly to a log."

Chunshao followed up with, "'We drink, and laugh, and break a branch of rose.' It should have been 'bloom', not 'rose', but... It's been so cold that all the flowers froze."

Uncle Huang paused a moment in thought, then recited, "'On a winter's morn stood a watchful wren.' It should have been 'crane', not 'wren', but... The crane was gone, and never seen again."

Uncle Yao did not even pause to think, but drank the forfeit straight away. Yao Kunming and Zhu Xiaokang in turn took a glass each. I went bright red in the face, and with great difficulty, said, "My line is: 'A cold night's guest—the host brings out the tea.' It should have been 'wine', not 'tea', but... I drank too much, and now I have to pee."

At that, everyone broke into guffaws. I said I'd had too much tea earlier and really had to go. Then I ran off to the toilet.

The drinking over, the tables were cleared away for the next activity. Mother had the maid prepare a candle for each of us, each held in a clay cup. Carrying the candles, we wandered among the shrubbery, enjoying the landscaping of the garden, while rhyming off couplets on the spot as inspired by the scenery.

In the quivering candlelight, faint silhouettes meandered throughout the garden, creating an almost phantasmal picture of a night-time ramble. Chunshao and I were walking beside Father. Before us, amid an expense of tree-shadows, were several dim green specks, the glow of fireflies. At that, Father uttered, "About the willow-boughs fireflies wound." A few moments later, Chunshao followed up with, "Amid the peach blossoms swifts fly round." I took a look at Anna, lying by a tree and dozing off, and continued with "Atop the fragrant grass rests the hound."

We walked along the pebblestone path, the bamboo leaves rustling and murmuring in our ears. Uncle Zhu stopped and said, "Jade-green bamboos, emerald pines." As Father caught up with him, he matched that with "Snow-white cloud puffs, yellowing vines." Uncle Zhu looked at him, smiled, and continued his line, "Jade-green bamboos, emerald pines, casting shadows on the wall." Then Father said, "Snow-white cloud puffs, yellowing vines, swaying in the winds of fall." Mother, who was standing beside him and looking at the flowers, started a new line, "Flowers bloom sparse beyond the weeds." Uncle Yao thought for a moment and responded with "Wood-flute trills clear beside the reeds." A while later, Mother continued her line, "Flowers bloom sparse beyond the weeds; their scent pure and fairy," to which Uncle Yao answered, "Wood-flute trills clear beside the reeds; here must dwell a fairy."

We arrived at the backyard and crossed the greenhouse. Uncle Huang stood over the graceful lilies in the pond and muttered, "A profusion of lilies in the pond." Chunshao, gazing into the same waters, did not take long to reply with "A solitary moon in the sky beyond." Uncle Huang then extended his line to "A profusion of lilies in the pond, where the lotus grows," and Chunshao came back with "A solitary moon in the sky beyond, where their perfume blows."

Then we walked around the magnolia tree and arrived by the fishpond. Zhu Xiaokang was chewing on a candy. He folded the candy-wrapper into a little boat and placed it on the water. Seeing that, Father declared, "In a springtime pond, a swaying boat sails in the sky," and Uncle Huang, stepping forward, matched that with "On the autumnal hill, silent crickets in the painting lie." Yao Kunming reached into the pond mischievously and stirred the water, breaking up the reflection of the moon. Uncle Zhu saw that, thought for a while, and said, "Up and down, around the shadows, moonbeams dance as stillness breaks." Father followed with "To and fro, over the water, reflections cross the terrace in the lakes." Uncle Zhu laughed and said, "You have neither bridge nor terrace over this water." Father answered, "Not a problem. I'll have them built straight away." As he said that, he broke off a twig and put it on the water to be a bridge, and over that he balanced a matchbox to serve as a terrace. I stared and stared into the water, and only came up with "The sparkling moonshine imprints on the living tides," which Chunshao matched with "An ancient mirror shines beyond its crystal sides."

Right then, a frog hopped onto the coral rockery in the centre of the pond, and disappeared into one of its dark holes. Someone came up with the line "In the dark, the caves join the sky where the sky meets the caves," and someone else in the distance answered in a clear voice, "At duskfall, the waves churn the sea as the sea lifts the waves." Then the first person announced another line: "The delight of watching the fish, as the fish delights in the stream," which the second person matched with "The realisation when contemplating life, that life is a realisation of a dream."

Wisps of clouds floated across the firmament. There remained only one snowy-white puff of a cloud in the jet-black sky. In the gleam of the moon the cloud appeared extraordinary clean and bright. A few black specks dotted the cloud, possibly a few geese flying past. The night deepened. Some of the candles had burnt out. Before we called it a night, Uncle Yao suggested, "Why don't we compose a couplet together on the scene before us? We can then write it out and hang it up at the gazebo to commemorate this evening."

The suggestion was met with enthusiasm. At once, the garden became a hub of activity, with everyone going to and fro conferring with each other. Before the last candle went out, we finally came to a pair of lines:

Guilelessly white clouds float
While birds flit hither and fro, fro and hither

Silently clear brooks flow
As flowers wither and bloom, bloom and wither

* * *

The card tables had been set up in the drawing room. We went back inside. Everyone was in high spirits, with no sign of fatigue.

Uncle Yao sat down in his usual spot. The other grown-ups took their seats one after another. Then, Uncle Yao smiled and waved at me, saying, "Young Master Song, do you know this game?"

Of course I do! When I was as young as six, Father taught my brother and me how to play mah-jong. At eight I learnt dominoes and poker. Father used to say, "If you let kids learn to gamble when they're little, they'd be tired of it when they grow up, and it won't be a novelty to them anymore." It remained to be seen if he was right or not, but at least at this time I was eager to play.

I looked towards my parents for approval. Mother said, "Chunhuan, see how perceptive your Uncle Yao is? All right, come over and play a few hands with Uncle Yao." I took a look at Father, who also nodded. Happily, I walked over and took the last seat. Hanging right next to this seat was a piece of calligraphy signed by Chunshao:

> O'er moonlit mountains shines a beaming shaft;
> On placid waters sails the lonely craft.

Chunshao was the author, but I was the scribe. Father never found out about that. One day, Father gave us each an exercise of composing a couplet and writing it out in calligraphic form. Chunshao was afraid of being scolded, because he had not been diligent in his calligraphy practice, and so I wrote it for him. We were both trained in the script style of Wang Xizhi, the Jin Dynasty calligrapher revered as the Sage of Calligraphy. Even though the handwriting we turned in were similar to each other's, as the lines were different, no one was the wiser. My lines were:

> A hermit amongst crowds, in markets and squares;
> A retreat amidst the din, but far from worldly cares.

The meter and the parallelism were not exactly right. Chunshao's lines were much better. Because of that, Mother had Chunshao's work mounted solemnly and hung in the drawing room. Every time she had a chance to, she would remind guests to take a look at it. "Such a great imitation of Wang Xizhi's form!" everyone would say.

Today's game was Five-card Stud. I knew long ago that Uncle Yao was a master of the game, but I had not been defeated either. This was a fantastic opportunity for me to test my skills against a master. It was, however, only ten minutes in when I started to feel the pressure. I felt as if everything in my mind had been laid bare before Uncle Yao, as if was impossible to hide from him what card I wanted, or what card I had concealed.

I could not beat him. That was clear. But I could not let myself be eliminated this quickly.

Since he had seen through all my thoughts, I thought I might as well not look at my face-down card. If not even I knew what my hole card was, there should be no way for him to discern anything from my facial expression, right?

With butterflies in my stomach, I waited for the cards to be dealt. When the final card was dealt, I had an open-ended straight showing, while Uncle Yao had three-of-a-kind...

"My dear Chunhuan, may I suggest that you look at your hole card before deciding if you want to continue."

"I'm not folding," I said, almost sulkily. Without thinking—and without anything to think about—I bet the rest of my money. That was the pocket money I had saved up over the course of half a year, two thousand *yuan*, approximately a month's salary of a high-ranking official. "Uncle Yao, let's see your cards."

Uncle Yao's expression remained calm as before, but there was now a stiffness in it. He waited for a moment, without blinking once, then said suddenly,

"Chunhuan, you're good."

"Tiepeng, it's just a game. Don't get serious with the kids," Father attempted to resolve the tension.

"Jiafu, I lost to your son. A bet's a bet. I'll pay up," Uncle Yao said with a smile on his face.

With this hand, I won over nine thousand *yuan*.

I looked at my hole card. It was a straight. Uncle Yao did not show his card.

As Uncle Yao left, he patted me on the shoulder in the same gallant manner, and said he'd come play again another time. He turned and waved goodbye to my parents. Following his father's lead, Yao Kunming also waved goodbye to Chunshao and me. As we stepped out of the living room together, Yao Kunming turned around once more, taking a good look at Chunshao, me, and everything around the room.

Afterwards, Father scolded me for being competitive before my elders, telling me that it was very impolite not to know when to stop. I was regretful about the matter too, but the damage had been done, and time could not be turned back.

* * *

In the summer of 1963, I was ready to move up to my first year of senior secondary school. And, after the summer holidays were over, Chunshao became a university student. He had truly grown up, and could justly declare himself an adult. He had not forgotten his childhood promise, either—to marry Autumn. Even though Autumn had already left us.

Autumn left us in 1962. That was the year her husband died. Perhaps more accurately, he went missing. According to Chunshao, Old Papa was suffering from digestive problems, and was unable to have bowel movements. Every day, he needed an attendant to reach into his rectum and scoop out his faecal matter bit by bit. One day, Autumn's husband accidentally perforated Old Papa's anus. Old Papa, in a fit of rage, had her husband locked up. Whether or not he was shot, though, was unknown even to Autumn.

But why did she have to leave us? Although Mother had said in private that Autumn was a cursed woman, Autumn had not brought misfortune to our family—with the exception of Billy and Sisi—the shadow from my childhood occasionally passed through my mind. However, over all these years, she had done everything she could for Father and Chunshao, and was at least respectful in serving Mother and me... But when this happened, she left. Father did not try to keep her, nor did he find her another husband.

I remember that, about a fortnight before she left, one day she entered Father's study and stayed there for a long time.

Mother and Chunshao were out that day. Using my old trick, I moistened the window with a bit of saliva. A transparent peep-hole appeared in the frosted glass, and I peeped through it.

"Is it... is it not possible for us to be together at all?" Autumn said, almost pleadingly.

"It is not," Father replied with an even tone.

"You care that much for Li Juan? It's obvious that you..."

In the room was playing Father's favourite piece, Tchaikovsky's Nocturne Opus 19, Number 4. A passage of high violins covered over

Autumn's words.

Father replied, "It's not as you think... Autumn, you have to find your own happiness, but not from me."

He added, "I cannot be where you want me to be. It's completely out of the question... I don't disregard your feelings, but I cannot love you."

"You're too cautious. You're always holding yourself back. You don't want to commit because you're trying to hold on to your exclusive claim to always being right. You're afraid of losing something."

Father's facial expression was serene, every bit looking as if he had nothing to hide. He said nothing more.

Seeing that he would not respond to her declaration of love, Autumn sighed. "Song Jiafu, you have no heart. Not even your wife ever had your heart. Li Juan—I bet she never ever truly had your heart."

Autumn fixed her gaze on him. He did not avoid it, but met this expression of adoration with his eyes.

I did not know what Father was thinking. But his silence, his refusal was a trap, leading Autumn to fantasise, in spite of herself, about waiting for him. Many years later, I was still convinced that the reason why she had forged ahead in spite of the obstacles of reality was because she felt her efforts would not be in vain. She wanted to change the fate of the two of them, all by herself. He, however, did not lift a finger to help her. But his just being a bystander was enough to make her jump into the trap. This heartlessness was the ultimate reason for her striving and fighting all her life.

After that day, Father told us that Autumn was going to leave us. He did not say why. According to Chunshao, it was because Mother could not suffer her presence, because Autumn was too beautiful. I was silent when I heard him, not knowing what to say. But, unable to let the matter slide, I asked Mother about it. She said she let Autumn go, because Autumn didn't want to work here anymore, and Mother had been thinking of getting a new maid anyway. The reason seemed simple, but I knew Chunshao would not believe it.

On the day Autumn left, Chunshao ran out to see her off. They held each other under an out-of-order street lamp and cried. They cried for a long time.

Earlier that afternoon, I saw her alone with Chunshao in a hidden corner of the greenhouse in the backyard.

Chunshao asked her to do one last thing for him.

She asked him, "What do you want me to do for you?"

"Anything, as long as you are willing."

Autumn, smiling, nodded her head, and asked him to sit by a bed of primroses. She went to fetch a basin from a corner, and from the large container for the lotuses, she scooped a few ladles of water into the basin. She carried the water basin to Chunshao, knelt by his feet, and placed them in the water.

Then, she put her hands into the water and bathed his feet slowly, washing them gently, reverently, washing them tenderly, adoringly. A few tears fell into the water. She blinked with her long and dark eyelashes, and continued washing his feet with a smile.

I believe that her smile was genuine. At that moment, she must have felt bliss, because Chunshao had accepted her.

Finally, she undid her braid, letting her beautiful hair fall to one side. With her hair, she dried Chunshao's feet...

Suddenly, my heart ached. Back on that day in the study, Autumn had implored Father, "Let me do something for you. Even if you don't want me to stay, please let me do one last thing for you." All Father did was refuse, telling her that there was no need. But when she was before Chunshao, her every action pleased him and attracted him. I thought, this must be love. Chunshao truly loved her. When she wiped his feet with her hair, his tears also fell in her hair. He must be wanting to let her know how much he loved her.

Chunshao said, "Autumn, wait for me. I must marry you."

Autumn only shook her head, "No, that would only hurt you."

But I knew full well that Autumn's words only served to strengthen Chunshao's resolve.

Chunshao's resolve was real. After Autumn left, he became even more diligent in reading the newspaper, sometimes even scrutinizing the advertisements and the classifieds.

In the past, whenever he read the papers, he did not pay much attention to the advertisements, let alone the tiny print of the classified section. But his habits changed. It was barely noticeable, but the change was definitely there, even if he was just taking a quick glance or two at those sections. Mother had remarked rightly that I was a crafty one—I was adept at finding small changes in behaviour. I did not do it intentionally, but it was just that I perceived details more keenly than most. When Chunshao concentrated on reading a particular part of the paper, I would remember where his eyes landed. Later on I would study the area of the classified ads he was focusing on. As expected, there would always be a few lines, hidden in the inch-sized square, which did not seem to be an advertisement of any sort. Even if that little square was wedged among many other similarly-sized squares, I always found it. They were using ciphers, numbers, apparently to communicate through an agreed-upon way.

Decoding took a long time, but I worked out a few lines.

He was chatting with Autumn. Back and forth, through the newspaper, covertly, yet for the world to see.

An extended conversation.

—Despite not being able to evade the surveillance of the Investigation Bureau runners under Mother's command, despite not ever deviating from his route to school or going home late.

And now, Chunshao finally started university. This meant he now had some freedom to make decisions for himself. Of course, this did not include marrying Autumn. But I knew that he became bolder and often slipped off to a tryst with her.

Autumn became a prostitute, a celebrated one, at a well-known café called the Blue Lamp. When she first started, she did not even count as a bargirl, nor was she admitted to the Blue Lamp. She could only stand on the street corner, passively waiting for prey to come to her. It was Mother who helped her out.

Mother sent someone to pay passers-by, sort of like a prepayment (in the words of the eunuch-like investigator), and tell them where Autumn was so that they could go obtain her services. In that way, she supplied Autumn with a steady flow of business, and kept her in the trade.

Why did mother help her in this fashion? I could not help but suspect that she so despised Autumn that she wanted her to fall even faster, so fast that she would have no more hope of being worthy of Chunshao, or worthy of dreaming about Father.

Once during that period I ran into Autumn. She carried herself very differently. Gone was the deferential, submissive look, replaced by the pride of being well-off for the first time, of having self-esteem for the first time. Rumour had it that she had the skill to make a man lose his inhibitions in no time and feel like he's in heaven. Many men adored her and requested her—among them were businessmen, political figures, and special agents from intelligence agencies as well. Chunshao watched those men, and found out that the establishment, though called a café, was in fact a house of debauchery. "What corruption!" Chunshao decried the establishment in private, gnashing his teeth. I knew that it was only because he felt bad for Autumn.

However, I did wonder if Father visited such establishments; and if he did encounter Autumn at the Blue Lamp, what would they do? I also wondered, if Autumn were to marry Chunshao right away, could Chunshao truly give her happiness? Even though Chunshao was now eighteen and counted as an adult, he was still a long way off from being a real grown-up. Chunshao was used to being waited on. He could keep a maid, but not a wife.

In the summer of 1963, Zhu Xiaokang and Yao Kunming had time to come play again. Zhu Xiaokang and Chunshao were both heading to university. Yao Kunming was a year younger than me but a year my senior in school, heading on to his second year of senior secondary. Our games not only involved increasingly realistic battles, but also the trade of increasingly realistic arms. Zhu Xiaokang, for example, had a toy Uzi that could pass for the real article—its bullets were not lethal, but the rest of it was just like a real Uzi. Chunshao had a hand grenade. It had the body of a real grenade, and was filled with a small amount of explosives that I put together. Although it was not high-powered stuff, once detonated it would not be something to be scoffed at. Naturally Chunshao could not bear to actually throw the grenade; he had spent no little effort in getting the grenade body from an American soldier. Normally we would only fill tin-cans with explosives and use them as grenades in our games. As for Yao Kunming, he only had a bayonet, one taken from a real rifle. However, without the attached gun, it was fairly useless, like a head without a body.

Yao Kunming came up with a plan: he traded information that we were interested in for our second-tier weapons. Soon, his battle outfit became quite respectable as well. Most of what he knew had to do with the missiles that the Americans had sold us. His father was in the missile defence unit of the army, and so he held the most authoritative information in our circle of friends.

—Taiwan has two missile defence systems, a long-range one and a short-range one. Let's say a plane from the Mainland is flying over here. If we are able to detect by mid-Strait that they mean to attack us, we'll use the long-range missile—the Nike—to repel it. That's why Nike bases are usually built on the coast or on top of mountains, to make it easier for the radars to detect enemy aircrafts. When a Nike is launched it can reach the Taiwan Strait, or even somewhere close to the Mainland. And if the Nike doesn't hit and the plane continues flying our way, we have a short-range missile system called the Hawk...

— The Americans are selling us the second generation Nikes, the Nike-Hercules missiles, also known as MIM-14. Supposedly they cost eighty thousand American dollars each. The Nike-Hercules looks like a rocket, 12 metres long and 800 millimetres wide, and has a semi-ballistic trajectory. It has a range of over 154 kilometres and can intercept a target at 3,487 metres. It is launched almost vertically, at an 85 degree angle, and reaches a flight speed that is twice to thrice the speed of sound. The booster at the bottom of the missile sends the missile body high up into the sky. And, after it reaches the highest point and the fuel is depleted, the booster separates from the missile, and the second stage turns downward. In the front section of the missile there are explosives and a radar guidance system, which can calculate the point of interception with the enemy aircraft and explode over the plane. Obviously it has to fly higher than the plane in order to hit it. If the plane can fly above the missile, it won't get hit. So, if the Nike misses and the enemy plane continues to fly, we'll attack with short-range missiles. The Hawk system consists of a triple-missile launcher, and the three missiles are launched one at a time at a lower angle, directly at the enemy aircraft. But if not even this stops the enemy plane, we'll have to send the air force to fight it.

—The Nike-Hercules unit is divided into three battalions. Their commanders are all graduates of the Military Academy. There are two platoons in each missile unit, because there are two systems involved in a missile, the radar system and the control system. The launch control team is on the top of the hill, and the launch team is at the bottom of the hill. Because of how far the missile goes, the two teams must be at least three to five kilometres apart, in case the missile explodes and takes out the system on the other side. After the launch team launches the missile, they must monitor radar signals from the control team. The Nike-Hercules has three kinds of radars. One is called the low power acquisition radar, or LOPAR. When the enemy aircraft approaches, the LOPAR finds the position of the plane through electromagnetic waves, and then the Target Tracking Radar, or TTR, continues to track it. Then, the Missile Tracking Radar, or MTR, tracks the signal emitted by the missile and guides it. After the radars lock on to the target, they will automatically calculate the intercept point and guide the missile to intercept the enemy aircraft. On top of all that, there are two control vans, the battery control van, or BCV, and the radar control van, or RCV. They've got vacuum tubes inside and are really hot... Normally, the launch team is responsible for the maintenance of the missile, and the control team on the top of the hill is responsible for the maintenance of the radar systems. Once a Mainland plane crosses the Meridian, we have to be ready to defend against it. The Nike-Hercules missiles are raised and readied for launching. But the Mainland is usually just testing us intentionally.

—The troops are on four-week rotations, some in Readiness Condition One, some in Readiness Condition Two. One of the companies must be ready for imminent action. The other company is on Readiness Condition Two. In case the enemy is sending more planes over than one company can handle, the second one will join the fight as well. Then there's also Readiness Conditions Three and Four...

These wondrous American missiles fascinated us immensely. Someone in the group wanted to go see the base. Yao Kunming was not that bold as to take us there, though he knew the layout of the base like the back of his hand.

—The base is located in a very secluded spot, protected by wire fences. In the front is the living area, in the middle is the main camp, and the back is the missile area. The missile area is entirely surrounded by earth walls, and there is an underground storage chamber that they can move the missiles into. When the missiles are underground, they can't be picked up by overhead surveillance. Each platoon has 30 to 40 people, divided into five groups: three launch units, one launch control trailer, or LCT unit, and one guard unit. There are two layers of guard patrols, the first one at the entrance to the base, and the second at the entrance to the camp. Family and visitors can enter the first area, but most people are not allowed in the second. The three launching sections are about nine hundred metres apart.

—All I know is, Group A consists of four launchers surrounded by an earth wall. The missile has to be pushed out to the launcher before it's raised. In normal times, the missile is kept in an underground magazine. There are tracks in the magazine leading to the launcher outside. In preparation for launching, the missile is pushed out horizontally along the tracks from the magazine to the launcher, then raised with the help of a hydraulic system to an 85 degree angle. When on defence readiness, one of the missiles on the four launchers must be on fifteen-minute standby. Two other launchers are on half-hour standby, and the fourth one is on one-hour standby.

—The first control system for the missile is with the company commander. He goes, 5, 4, 3, 2, 1, fire! Then he lifts up the red cover and flicks up the launch switch. Then the missile gets launched. The company commander and the platoon commander each has one such switch. The platoon commander's is in the LCT, just in case the wiring between the launch team and the guidance team gets destroyed. Because the two teams are so far apart, if the cables between them gets damaged by enemies and the company commander can't launch the missile from where he is, the platoon commander can activate the switch from the LCT. The LCT is usually set up near the front of the second wire fence. In case the LCT and the cables inside are destroyed, there's also a control panel in the underground bunker for Groups A, B, and C, which can be used for launching. As soon as the missile is raised, everyone in the launch team has to go hide in the underground bunker. That's because the booster at the bottom of the missile sends out huge flames, and anyone in the vicinity would be burnt to death. But in case even the underground bunker has been destroyed by enemies, there is still one last control panel over at the launch site with a switch for launching the missile. It's just that as soon as the missile launches, the whole site would be covered in flames, and the person activating the switch would certainly die in his mission...

How did Yao Kunming know this much? Did his father leak information to him? Yao Kunming claimed that he got all this from bribing one of his father's subordinates. I personally suspected that he had secretly looked at the ink ribbons his father collected. Chunshao warned him to be careful, else his father would find out and skin him. Zhu Xiaokang, though, said if that subordinate could be bribed that easily, he could come under suspicion of being a rebel spy, and what if one day he leaks secrets to someone else... Regardless, we were all Yao Kunming's accomplices, at the same time warning him and condoning his continuing to leak secrets to us.

Those days, whenever we played War, Chunshao normally played the Nationalist Army, the easy side. He got Zhu Xiaokang to be on his team, leaving me and Yao Kunming to play the Communist side. They launched pebbles and bamboo sticks at our rubber band aeroplane. I kept prodding Yao Kunming, the one with the stronger arms, to wind up the aeroplane ever tighter and throw it ever higher; but no matter how high he threw the plane, it was no match for the attack of Chunshao and Xiaokang's "Nike-Hercules Missiles".

One day, Yao Kunming brought over a remote control plane. That was the first time we had seen one. Furthermore, it was a military aircraft, not like our wind-up propeller plane with zero attack power. The appearance and the structure of the plane was just like the real thing; it also boasted two shiny black machine guns. With the press of a button on the remote controller, the plane could continuously fire (plastic) bullets while in the air.

We had no experience with "air battles", and in our hearts we all longed to see a re-enactment of the air battles in the movies, with fighter planes chasing each other and exchanging fire in the air. That was so much more mesmerising than "land battles" and "sea battles". We only had one aeroplane, though, and could not play "air-to-air" combat; however, "surface-to-air" combat or just having the plane patrol solo in the air was enough to entertain us.

That day, Zhu Xiaokang and I got to be the Nationalist Army. We launched fierce volleys of paper balls with our slingshots (we didn't use pebbles or bamboo sticks for fear of damaging the plane), saying that we were launching Nike-Hercules missiles. We were hit quite a few times by the plane's plastic bullets, but our Nikes never hit the plane, because it always flew higher. Higher and higher.

I will never forget how, when the plane flew over the backyard, over the greenhouse, over the horizon of the bamboo grove... Yao Kunming, Zhu Xiaokang, and Chunshao glowed radiantly with joy, and how even Anna was yelping excitedly, running in circles around everyone. Forgetting whether we were Nationalists or Communists, we grabbed the remote controller from each other, tussling for a turn to press the buttons, transforming the remote control flying into a dream of elusive freedom...

I still remember that last time when Chunshao pressed the button. It's flying so high! So far!

Everyone ran desperately after it. We ran and ran.

I felt as if a balloon had suddenly inflated in my chest, stopping me from breathing.

The plane flew very high. And then, from the heights of the skies, it started falling down in a parabolic curve.

Yao Kunming's jaw dropped. He jumped up with all his might. But everyone knew that was in vain—the plane did not turn around in time, and, like a kite on a broken string, fell into the river far, far away.

Our minds were all in disarray. After a rainstorm a few days ago, the waters were high and the current was swift. No one dared to get in the river.

"Anna, Anna, go fetch it!"

Chunshao turned around and ordered Anna, who was following him all this time. Obediently, Anna jumped into the water, and swam as hard as she could towards the distant target.

The current was very swift. The water was a yellow and murky from the mud. Watching Anna bob up and down in the water, now above water, now under, I was so worried that I was on the verge of tears.

How could he sacrifice Anna for the plane? Anna! Anna! I shouted in my heart, starting to hate Chunshao for what he did.

Fortunately, Anna returned, barely alive from the trial. She was out of breath, but was still holding tightly onto the wing of the plane with her mouth. She was very clever: after she had reached the plane, she knew that she would not be able to swim back against the current. So she strove to swim to the closest land first, then ran back along the bank.

"What a good dog. 'Atta girl." Chunshao stooped down to pet Anna's head. With an aching heart, I was left to pet her behind.

But the plane flew no more. We watched Zhu Xiaokang, the most machine-savvy of our bunch, turn the plane over and over, trying to find a way to save it. But ultimately he failed.

Yao Kunming's face turned ghastly white. He shot a dark look at Chunshao, but Chunshao evaded it, pretending that nothing was the matter.

Perhaps Chunshao was very sorry, but there was nothing he could do. The plane was from the U.S. It was not available in Taiwan. And even if we were willing to pay, there was nowhere to get it fixed.

Only later did Yao Kunming reveal that the plane was on loan. From Pan Baojiang.

He did not tell Chunshao or Zhu Xiaokang, nor did he tell his father. His father had recently lost a few months' salary; he was not so dull as to not know how to read his father's mood. But how was he going to pay for the plane? No one knew. Later on, we often saw him hanging out with Pan Baojiang, doing whatever Pan Baojiang told him to do. He became Pan Baojiang's dog. I kept feeling that I was in his debt; I should have returned the nine thousand *yuan* to him. But that was no longer the issue. The milk had been spilt. No matter how you tried to clean it up, there would be a stain. Besides, there was just no way to clean up this mess.

Yao Kunming did not come visit us very much anymore. But he still took me to be a friend. Once, Pan Baojiang told him to block my way on the street. But he only made a feint, signalling to me to hurry and go. As I rubbed my nose and retreated from their turf, pretending to have been hit, I turned around subconsciously, and saw the indignation on Yao Kunming's face. It was as if he did not want anyone to see him standing subserviently next to Pan Baojiang, as if some injustice had forced him to sell himself into bondage. I felt downcast, wishing that he had actually beaten me up so that he could report success to Pan Baojiang. But all I could do was to scurry away, fleeing from his discomfort of being seen.

The last time Yao Kunming hung out with me, he told me news about the Nike missiles. The information was a free gift; he did not want a single penny from me. That was also the last time I heard about the missiles.

According to him, one day the soldiers on duty were going through the regular readiness preparations. After the missiles had been raised, a missile from Group C launched for no reason. As we all knew, the control system was located where the commanders were. One must be very cautious about pressing the launch button. And so there was a small red lid installed over the button, just in case. They were just going through readiness preparations that day. And the missile suddenly flew up; the booster fell off by the seaside, the missile continued on its way towards the Taiwan Strait, and, somewhere beyond radar range, it exploded. Everyone suspected that the commanders were too nervous and hit the button by mistake. But that seemed unlikely.

Because of this, HQ sent several teams over to investigate.

Neither the company commander nor the platoon commander had any reason to make this mistake. As for someone intentionally trying to get them in trouble... That would also be improbable. The company commander had other staff with him, and the platoon commander was in the LCT, along with three or four soldiers on the control systems. It would be hard for them to try anything funny... Or, perhaps, the staff intentionally omitted discharging the static electricity during regular maintenance. The missile system was controlled by electronic equipment, which generated static and required discharging at regular intervals. There was weekly, monthly, and seasonal maintenance. It would be possible for someone not to have discharged the static during one of these maintenance cycles, thus intentionally creating an accident... But then there was more than one person on the maintenance staff. The investigations yielded no concrete details.

Afterwards, the army announced generically that the accident was caused by mechanical reasons. Mechanical reasons could include static.

Having confidentially shared this information, we seemed to have returned to the happy days of the past.

"What amperage of static do you need for the missile to launch on its own?"

Yao Kunming asked this question before he left. But I never had the chance to figure out the answer.

Because some situations were changed. Some people were changed.

One day, when both my parents were out, I was in the kitchen showing the maid my new spaghetti sauce recipe:

"Cut up a stalk of celery into two-inch pieces. Chop up a third of an onion. Take two cloves of garlic, four cinnamon leaves, four sprigs of parsley, six basil leaves, and four sprigs of thyme; crush and add salt and pepper. Grind four nutmeg seeds and add five tablespoons of olive oil. Slice seven tomatoes..."

A cacophony of barking rose up outside. Several unfamiliar men, dressed in black, came crashing into the house.

"Which one of you is Song Chunshao?"

As soon as they had stepped inside, the leader of the group waved an identification document from an intelligence agency, demanding to take Chunshao away.

"What did I do? What right do you have to arrest me?" yelled Chunshao.

They pointed at the calligraphy on the wall and said, "That's your writing, isn't it?"

"What about it?"

"We'll discuss that at the Bureau. Get going!"

I stepped forward and interrupted, "That's not his writing. That's mine. Tell me, what's wrong with it?"

"That's yours? What's your name?" The leader looked me up and down, warily and cryptically.

"Song Chunhuan," I replied.

"The signature on the scroll says Song Chunshao."

"I wrote it for him. What's the problem with that?"

"Bring them both back to the Bureau."

"No, you can't take us away without a good reason," I protested.

"Very well. You may each provide a writing sample right here," said the leader.

"Who are you to tell us what to do?" Chunshao was still trying to object, but his voice became noticeably feeble. Feigning calmness, he pushed my hand down, "Chunhuan, don't do it. Don't fall for their trap. Let's see what they can do to us when Dad and Mum get home."

"If you refuse, we'll take you both away." One of the men in black was about to lay his hands on us.

Chunshao fell silent. He was standing by the table, evidently wanting to escape. But there was no way out. The telephone wire was cut. We had no recourse for help.

I called for the maid to grind some ink for us. Her hand kept trembling; a few drops of ink flew out of the inkstone and splattered over our beautiful dining napkins. I gave Chunshao a look, "Let's do it."

Chunshao and I each wrote a sheet of brush calligraphy. To be precise, I filled a whole sheet without interruption, but Chunshao could only produce one line. Because he was unable to finish, he had his ears boxed.

They looked at the two sheets of writing, pointed at me, and said, "You, come with us."

I did not resist. Because I knew that even if I resisted I would still receive the same fate, plus a beating to boot.

Behind us, Chunshao yelled, "Chunhuan, we'll come save you! We'll save you!"

As they dragged me out of the living room, I turned around to look at Chunshao and the maid one last time. Suddenly, Chunshao's words came to mind: The secret police always arrest first and collect evidence after. Evidence would always be revealed through interrogation and torture... But if I had nothing to hide...

A feeling of hopelessness seized my heart. I felt that Chunshao's promise to save me was just to console me or to console himself. He was still shouting about that behind us, but Anna had already dashed up, circling us and barking.

"Anna, sit! Be quiet." I said.

Anna obediently stayed still for two seconds, then, feeling something was wrong again, started barking at us once more. One of the men in black suits kicked her. She was about to leap at him, when I ordered her to sit again.

Right when she sat down, she saw that I was being dragged out the door, so she ran up to us.

Several of the men kicked her away even more forcefully, and hurriedly shoved me into a car.

The engine started, and immediately the car drove away from our front door. I saw Anna running madly behind us, once managing to jump onto the car but was thrown off right away. There was blood at the corner of her mouth, and yet she picked herself up and continued the pursuit. Her front paws managed to touch the car a few times, but she had no more strength to jump.

The man in the front seat whispered something into the driver's ear. The driver suddenly put the car in reverse—

—and sped ahead again.

I cried Anna's name hysterically. They punched me and told me to shut up.

I kept looking out the rear window, my heart broken, my face covered with tears. The night was dark. I could not see Anna.

Anna!

PART III

11
The white rose in the crack in the wall

The mess cook opened the flap at the bottom of the cell door, and pushed in an aluminium plate with food in it. The hole closed. I glanced at the aluminium plate. A few pieces of pickled cabbage and two chunks of salty fermented beancurd lay on top of some rice. I had not eaten in a long time, but I had no appetite at all.

This cramped cell was less than nine feet long, and about four and a half feet wide. The cell door was also only four and a half feet tall. When they pushed me through the door, I did not duck in time, and my head hit the wall, making a loud thud.

Above the door, on the wall about six feet from the floor, was a small window a square foot in size, fitted with iron bars. I lifted my head towards the window, and, with the dim light filtering through from the corridor, looked around me. All four walls were stained with grime, and carved into them were phrases like "death before dishonour" and "cruel and unusual punishment". Reading the messages from those who came before me, I felt my mind go completely blank. With nothing else to do, I resorted to lying down.

The floor under me was covered with wooden slats. They were chipped in places, forming holes of various sizes. I picked the area where the holes were smaller and lay down on my side. At first, I used a forearm as a pillow, but soon it started to go numb. I turned over and lay my head on the other arm. Soon, that arm also went numb. I pulled my arm back down, and tried to sleep on my back. But without a pillow in the cell, I could not fall asleep either on my side or on my back. So, I got up, took off my trousers, and rolled them up into a bolster and put it under my head. I closed my eyes and tried to sleep as best as I could. I could not tell how much time passed. Suddenly I felt very cold. Without any choice, I put my trousers back on, and used my slippers to be a pillow instead. From the corridor occasionally footsteps were heard. But I fell asleep, as if noise could not wake me up anymore. I was truly exhausted.

Dreams whisked through my mind one after another. There was chasing. There was killing. There were also many Annas, big and small, many Annas licking me.

I felt something crawl into my clothes. Not only that, it started wriggling all about me...

I woke up with a start. Lifting my hand, I snatched at something on my body. I did not catch anything, but saw a mouse poke out from underneath my collar. I broke out in cold sweat. On a more careful look, there were other furtive-looking creatures between the cracks in the floor, now popping out, now hiding back, disappearing along with the mouse that was just on me. I could sleep no more, feeling as if there were mice hiding in every crack underneath me, ready to crawl on me any moment. I straightened up and lay flat against the floor, wishing I could cover all the cracks with my body. I was so tired. I had to sleep.

This was the second day of my detention. The first night I did not sleep, nor was I allowed to rest. They interrogated me for the entire day, with three groups of people taking turns to get a confession out of me. They asked the same questions over and over again—

What organisation did you join?

Who else were in that organisation?

What else did you conspire to do?

How did you carry out your anti-government activities?

Do you know how generous the government is to you? Do you know the government has established a confession program?

If you make an honest confession, the government will be lenient to you. Your case isn't serious.

People like you who confessed to joining that organisation usually only get a few months in the penal colony. The sooner you confess, the sooner you're released...

The sooner you confess, the sooner you're released...

In my ear, the squeaking of mice became louder and louder. But I was so tired I could not even open my eyes.

Throughout the 24-hour interrogation, there was nothing but squeaks in my mind. When I spoke of something that interested them and they leaned forward to listen more closely, their chairs squeaked. The squeaking never stopped, haunting my day, my night, my sleep.

Confess and we will be lenient. Confess and everything will be all right...

The interrogators were still trying to convince me, but I had run out of things to say.

For a full 24 hours, they had just as well been talking to themselves, repeating the same content like a broken record. At the end, they told me to sign my statement. They had me remove my watch and my belt, and hand those over along with my fountain pen, and all cash and belongings for safekeeping. Then they sent me back to the cell.

On the third day, on this third day of the similarly-dim light through the metal-barred window, of a time that could be either morning or evening, a jail guard opened the flap at the bottom of the cell door, and passed in a cup of water. Only then did I know that this was the beginning of a day. That cup of water was for washing my face, brushing my teeth, and bathing myself. With no toothbrush, I wet a finger in the water and scrubbed my teeth with it. Then I poured a bit of water in my palm and splashed that on my face. The remaining I used for my "shower".

On the third day, they only told me to do one thing: write my confession. Write down everything about myself, from my birth to my schooling, and everything about my entire family. Whenever they thought it was not detailed enough, they had me rewrite it. Rewrite it, over and over again.

The fourth day also began with a cup of water passed in through the hole. After I brushed and washed, I sat for a full day in boredom. They only fed me one meal at some point, also plain rice with a few pieces of pickled cabbage and two chunks of fermented beancurd. I shifted to sit in another position. When I was tired of sitting, I had no choice but to pick a spot, somewhere where the cracks in the floor were not too big, to lie down on my side, trusting to luck that there would be no mice.

Without a watch, I could not tell the time. Perhaps it was night-time. Anyway, it was after I fell asleep. The cell door suddenly opened. Two men brought me out. The lamps in the corridor were not particularly bright, but the sudden light blinded my eyes.

For many days after that, they came to fetch me for "night-time interrogations" right when I was about to fall asleep. It was always the same questions, repeated in barrages over and over. Apart from preventing me from sleeping, they would, at my hungriest moment, give me a bowl of noodles covered in salt and force me to eat it. And if I still did not give them an answer, they would attach my hands and feet to electrical wires and send shocks, or remove my clothes and throw ice-cold water on me then put me in front of an electrical fan until I was covered in goosebumps. Or else, they would hang me upside-down, stick my head into a bucket of water, then come up to me and ask the same questions in my ear...

I became better at it. I worked hard at thinking up answers. The more moving and curious the account was, they more they wanted to listen to it. During these days, Floral was also brought in for cross-examination, though my answers always managed to leave her completely out of the picture.

On the thirteenth day, they finally revealed to me the reason for my imprisonment.

It was because my handwriting, the handwriting that too closely imitated that of the Sage of Calligraphy.

"Someone found an anti-government pamphlet outside Song Chunshao's school, written in brush calligraphy. We collected the calligraphy exercise books of all the students in the school for comparison. The handwriting on the pamphlet matched that in Song Chunshao's book. But since Song Chunshao's calligraphy was all done by you, and since on-site investigation showed that Song Chunshao's writing did not match indeed, we determined that you were the true culprit."

Seeing the alleged anti-government pamphlet that they threw onto the table, I flew into a rage:

"No, that's not the way I write! This was traced then filled in, merely a technique for imitating a calligraphic style, whereas I write mine in one pass."

"Tracing or no tracing, the handwriting is the same! The evidence is right in front of your eyes!"

Their expressions, just softened a moment ago, turned menacing at once. I took a glance at the yet-unused torture instruments next to me, and argued no more.

After the interrogation concluded on the fourteenth day, I was moved to a larger cell. It was not really that large, only about the size of six sleeping mats, with over a dozen people crammed in there. No one could lie flat. Everyone either sat or stood; the stifling, foul air and the odour of sweat permeated the cell.

I had nowhere to sit, and could only stand leaning against the wall, next to the nightstool in the corner, trying to breathe in the other direction. Seeing a newcomer, everyone became curious and began to ask me question after question. I briefly described my case and the torture I suffered. They looked me up and down, remarking, "Not too bad. You look pretty intact."

One man held up his hands to me, saying, "At first, they threaded wires through my fingernails. But that's not all. Eventually they tore all my nails off." The others all came over to show me the injuries on their bodies, and, pointing to the few men lying on the floor, said,

"This man was put on the 'tiger bench'. You know, the 'tiger bench' is about making you sit on a special bench, with your head and upper body tied to a rack standing on one end of the bench. Your legs are stretched out straight, and they tie your thighs and knees to the bench with belts. When they're extracting information from you, they force bricks in between your ankles and the bench. As you know, human knees can only bend backward, not forward. So they keep elevating your leg from the ankle, forcing your leg to bend forward against the direction of the knee joint. Your leg tendons are in a lot of pain from the tension. If one brick isn't enough, they'll add another one, or two. This is no easy task, since your knee is tied tightly to the bench. So they have to put a stick in under your calves, and have two men, one on each side, push the stick upward. That way they can lift your legs up enough to put more bricks in. After three bricks, you'd pass out from the pain. At the fourth, at most, your knees will break. If you still do not confess, they'll hit your legs with a large wooden hammer. It's not just a whack or two. They torture you slowly, hitting you over the course of a few hours. Look at him now. His legs are completely black and he can't walk anymore. With great difficulty he can crawl around with his hands, but his lower body is basically paralysed. We have to hold him up if he wants to go to the toilet. It's quite a chore, actually."

"That one over there, he got the 'aeroplane' treatment on top of that," the speaker gestured with his hands. "The 'aeroplane' is the next level of service after the 'tiger bench'. After his legs got beaten, he's suspended mid-air along with the bench that's tied to him. The suspension rope is of course tied to his arms and not the bench. Now, both his arms and both his legs are maimed. When he eats, he has to lie on his stomach, moving his mouth to the bowl in order to feed himself. To go to the toilet he needs us to lift him—no, not lift, carry him. He has to be carried everywhere. He doesn't even have the strength to squeeze out a drop of piss on his own."

"Don't spook him. New kid's gonna wet his bed," said an old man.

"We're educating him, letting him know life's rough. Let him know how evil those bastards are," the other man continued, apparently displeased at being interrupted.

"And there's that one there. They took his willy out and scrubbed it hard with a toothbrush, then sprinkled salt on the wounds on his bellend. Now, he can't piss even if someone's helping him."

Finally, there was one curled up in a ball on the floor. They said he was just waiting to die. "This one had flames held up to him to burn. They tied him up, then burnt him here and there, eyebrows, chin, arms, legs, crotch... until he had blisters all over. Not only that, they also put fire inside his mouth. Now he can't lie down or eat nor sleep all day. Even crying is too painful for him."

"Ugh, this is what they call a democracy," said the man whose fingernails were torn out.

"Democracy? That's just what they tell the Americans. Who really gives you democracy?" said another man, whose eyes were beaten black and blue.

"Hey, new kid, give us some news from the outside. We haven't read a newspaper in months. We have no idea what's going on out there," requested a man seated on the floor with his legs curled up. Everyone else concurred.

I was just about to speak when they suddenly motioned for me to be quiet. The man who stood closest to the door was the first to hear footsteps in the corridor. After the footsteps passed, someone said whispered, "In this place, even the guards are intelligence agents."

I told them the recent news of some armed guerrilla base being captured. One of my listeners flew in a rage. "Lies! Those are just farmers' huts, and they falsely accuse them of being an armed base. It's just the dogs from some intelligence organisation trying to get ahead by framing innocent people. How can a few ramshackle huts count as a rebel base? Total bullshit!" Someone whispered in my ear, "He's one who put up a straw hut and had someone labelled it an armed rebel base, and then he got locked up in here for no good reason at all."

Early the next morning, the guards let us go out to wash our face, brush our teeth, and shower. We all crowded in the yard, with one hose for every few people. A hose was much more effective than a cup of water. We jostled for the hose for washing ourselves, and dipped our fingers in salt to scrub our teeth...

"Be discreet when you speak. Beware of spies in the cell," a skinny old man with a few missing teeth came over, offered me a few words hurriedly, before going off to mingle with another crowd.

Two minutes later, we were herded back to the cell, beginning a whole day of listless sitting and idle talk. I kept an eye on the old man with the missing teeth. He did not speak much. There were a few others who were taciturn like him, while another one or two were particularly fond of voicing their opinions. They were always criticising politics, speaking forcefully and authoritatively, attempt to solicit general agreement. One day, the old man whispered to me again, "They plant spies among us to get inside information about certain people in here, or they'd intentionally spread false rumours to mislead us. There are also some who were arrested just like we did, but are wanting to play snitch in exchange for leniency."

Only a while later did I discover that Mother was also in the jail.

One morning, we were let out to wash ourselves. Avoiding the crowds going for the shower, I went to brush my teeth with salt, crouching by the wall of the yard along with a few others. There were some noises from the other side of the wall. Out of curiosity, I peeked through a crack in the wall. I saw a pair of female feet, wearing slippers, walking past. Following that were a few more pairs of female feet in slippers going back and forth. It was then that I realized that the female inmates were on the other side. One of those pairs of feet belonged to Mother. I recognised them. On one of her big toe toenails, painted red, she had drawn a white rose. A white rose on red, so familiar from my childhood.

A warm feeling rose in my heart. I felt so excited, but I could not call out to her. Absolutely not.

The next few mornings when I went to brush my teeth by the wall, I paid attention to those feet, that white rose. I held a leaf in my hand in which I had etched a few words. Cautiously I waited, waited...

Until the most suitable moment arrived.

One day, I flicked the leaf over, and it fell right on top of the toenail with the white rose. The toe's owner bent down and picked up the leaf with a hand. And then nothing.

At noon that day, just as I was eating, from above the ceiling came the sound of someone striking a rice-bowl. It was soft but clear. Someone was sounding out a question to me in simple Morse code.

I struck an answer back.

And the reply came, stating who she was.

It turned out that Mother had been kept on the floor just above mine. She had been in here for some time as well. On that leaf I had etched my name (in code) and the cell number; with the cell number she was able to figure out the approximate location of my cell.

After that, every day at lunch time we would communicate by striking our bowls. But we could only do it sparingly, exchanging at most a sentence or a few words every day.

And the white rose in the crack in the wall still flashed by every morning, amongst the shapes of many feet.

* * *

I did not know what crime my mother committed—

—Until they showed me Mother's confession statement and demanded that I divulge information beyond what she had confessed to. They were also suspecting Father... But I could not make up evidence against my parents. I read the confession line by line, from her childhood, education, and marriage, through to her employment. But there was not a single word in there about me or Chunshao.

Those interrogators began another round of "attack by exhaustion", and once again denied me sleep for 24 hours.

"You should know best. What rebellious activities did Li Juan participate in?"

"Just say it. Li Juan isn't your mother. You have nothing to worry about. She has confessed to everything. Remember, honesty means leniency. If you tell us about her crimes, we can commute your sentence."

"You'd better believe it. We figured out your year of birth. Before she came to Taiwan, someone had met her on the Mainland. They were on stage together. At the time when you and your brother would have been born, she had not been pregnant."

My memory fell into an abyss of helplessness. To which year could my memory reliably reach? The breast which I saw against the light from the cradle; the woman who held my hand on that boat laden with gold—was that not Mother? My mother was Li Juan, I could remember that much.

I had nothing to say. No matter what they tried, they could not get anything else from me.

And then I was moved to another cell, and heard the sound of the bowl no more.

One day, the jail guard opened the cells one by one and read out names. Those whose names were called were all brought to the admission desk to retrieve the articles taken away when we were taken into custody. Then we were handcuffed, and herded into a prison van.

The inside of the van was windowless. We could not see where the van was going. A few cellmates whom I knew discussed our situation in a low voice. An "old hand", who had been arrested twice before, threw in a few words in a whisper:

"We're going to the Military Judiciary Division."

Upon arrival at the Military Judiciary Division, we once again handed all our personal belongings to the warden to register and to keep. Empty-handed, we prepared to be conducted to the cell.

Before that, someone from the jail came to take photographs of each of us. Besides front-view and a side-view mugshots, close-ups of each person's unusual facial and physical features were also taken.

"This is for identification purposes when you're taken to be executed in the future," revealed the photographer secretly.

That's right, and then after the execution another close-up photograph had to be taken, to verify that the body belonged to the same person. I looked at this man, the man I used to pester all the time in my childhood, asking him for secret tales from the execution grounds. I sneaked in a greeting, "Uncle Wang, haven't seen you for a few years. How did you end up working in here?"

"I got arrested for something. Fortunately the sentence was light. I served a few years, and they kept me here to do my old job," Little Wang said very softly.

"What did you do?" I asked even more softly.

"I don't know. They found some book in my house. They took me here, gave me a few beatings, and I confessed to everything. They said I violated the 'Statute for the Finding and Purging of Spies during the Period of Communist Rebellion'..." Little Wang looked around him surreptitiously, and, using the cover of taking a close-up of my ear, whispered softly to me, "Your mum came through here earlier. Had photos taken. Not sure where she's locked up now."

It was the next person's turn for photographs. Little Wang and I exchanged a farewell look, and I was conducted straight to my cell.

The new cell was twice as big as the previous one, but was even more crowded. Over twenty of us were stuffed in there.

I knew the rules. As soon as I entered the cell, I went to stand next to the nightstool in the corner, an unpopular spot. This time no one asked me about my case. By the time a new inmate walked through the door, almost everyone in the cell knew the details of his background. It was as if they had been tipped off ahead of time. They also commented on the newcomers one by one, discussing if he was trustworthy, or if he was a spy. I also quickly gained an idea about my cellmates, who included hairdressers, farmers, post office workers, railroad workers, and union officials. Among them were also a few with impressive backgrounds: A Mr. Ding, who was the Chief Aide to the President and who served the President for fifteen years; one Deputy Director Li of the Intelligence Department of the Air Force HQ, who once directed the collection of air defence-related intelligence against the Mainland; one Director Wu of the Investigation Bureau, who had received a medal from the President; and a Mr. You, manager of a printing plant, who printed the newspaper ran by my father—the official newspaper of the Kuomintang. Someone said, "One day, a worker printed 'the mighty Republic of China' as 'the nighty Republic of China', and then the manager went to jail." Mr. You did not speak much to anyone; hearing others discussion himself, all he did was lift his head and take a look at the speaker, with an expressionless face, then looked down again to continue cleaning his fingernails with a broken end of a toothpick. I asked Chief Aide Ding about Autumn's husband. He laughed at my question, "Tore the President's anus? He's dead for sure." The hairdresser, Mr. Lu, who was standing opposite him, said, "I heard about the case. The attendant who tore the President's anus apparently was sent to the penal colony on Green Island."

The first night I slept next to the nightstool.

It was too crowded in the cell. I could only sleep sitting down. In the middle of the night, I was woken up by a warm splash. Opening my eyes, I saw that it was Director Wu of the Investigation Bureau; he had not aimed well at the nightstool when urinating, and splashed everywhere. I wiped off the urine from my face. Seeing that he was looking a bit apologetic, I said hello to him.

I then asked him in whisper if he knew where my mother was.

"Li Juan? She's in here too? I haven't seen her yet."

"What case is my mother involved in? Is it the same as yours?"

"I don't know. They did bring up Li Juan when they interrogated me. But all I know is that both the director and the deputy director of her section were taken into custody. I'm not clear about the details."

Director Wu did not know where his own charges came from either.

He only knew that two directors and three deputy directors from the Bureau were arrested.

The squad leader on duty began his patrol. Director Wu and I stopped our conversation, and went back to sleep.

With the cell being overcrowded, no one could lie flat normally. Everyone lay on his side; when one person turned to the other side, everyone else had to turn over as well. The first few nights I could only sleep by the nightstool. After that, they made a bit of space, and I could finally lie down on my side to sleep.

The cell was surrounded by solid walls on three sides. The fourth side, facing the corridor, consisted of a frame of thick planks of wood and the cell door. Air could not circulate with so many people in the cell. Sometimes, when it became too hot and none of us could sleep, we would throw a blanket over the ceiling beam, and tie a rope on each of the hanging ends. Two of us would stand on either side, pulling the blanket back and forth. Fanning thus, circulation came to the stagnant air, and we would finally be able to sleep, for a while.

We divided a day into several shifts and took turns fanning. Sometimes I was partnered with Director Wu, and sometimes with the farmer, Mr. Su. Besides fanning the blanket, every morning we also had to send one person in turn to take the nightstool outside for the jail guards to clean.

One day, when I was in queue outside the cell door carrying the nightstool, the man on nightstool duty from the next cell over turned around and saw me. I recognised him immediately. "Uncle Zhu," I called to him softly. We exchanged a look, as we were not allowed to talk.

After the nightstools were emptied, We returned to our cells, waiting to be let out in turn to wash our faces, wash our clothes, and bathe. Farmer Su tugged at the corner of my shirt and asked me, "You know him?" He was referring to Uncle Zhu.

I replied, "He's my dad's friend, a family friend since I was a kid."

"It was him who arrested me. Never would've guessed that he'd end up here as well," said the farmer. "Bah, just a few worksheds and they call it an armed rebel base. What a bunch of crooks!"

Once, when I was allowed to go out to wash my face, I ran into Uncle

Zhu. I took the opportunity to ask about the case. He admitted that he had made the arrest by mistake; he said that the head of that village had, for the sake of a reward, falsely compiled a list of rebellious villagers. "There was actually no armed rebel base. But once someone made a report, we had to go make an arrest." Uncle Zhu's face was pale and swollen. He hurriedly soaked the shirt he was holding in water, wrung it dry, and left. Watching him walk away, I felt something collapse in my heart, crashing with a loud boom.

"That kind of thing is much too common." Director Wu knew about Farmer Su's case. He continued, "The government runs a training course on 'rebel behaviour research', specifically for training special agents. Some students, upon completion of the course, have no work to do. So, to contribute to the cause, they pretend to be Mainlanders, first travelling to Hong Kong and then returning 'in search of freedom'. In this way, they get to create news items, and receive a cash reward to boot. As for rebel spies, if our superiors tell us to go arrest some, we'd have to go arrest some. And if there isn't any, we'd fabricate a list of names and arrest some random people so that we can say we've accomplished the mission. If you work for the government, you always have to have an answer for your superiors." Then, pointing at a man called Liu, who was crouching against the wall, he added, "He was one of the special agent training graduates who was a phoney Mainlander 'in search of freedom'. But his supervisor did not help him straighten out his identity afterwards. Later on, some people started suspecting that those Mainlanders who came 'in search of freedom' were really infiltrators, and blacklisted them as rebel spies. And so he was arrested as one."

The man called Liu apparently confessed under torture. He spent his days mumbling to himself, saying Chairman Mao this, Chairman Mao that. "If I don't admit to being a Communist, they'd beat me. So I have to say I'm a Communist, every day, so that they'd just go and sentence me and spare me the torture."

"They make a big hullabaloo about Communists every day, and yet they keep a whole horde of Communists on the payroll in the intelligence agencies," the phoney Commie confided to me one day. "Sometimes, when a KMT agent arrests a real Communist and the real Communist surrenders, he's kept in the intelligence agency to work for them, to help them catch other Communist elements. You know that sissy-voiced investigator with the baboon cheeks, the one who's especially vicious and cruel during interrogations? He is one of them Commie defectors. Also..." he pointed at Director Wu, "that one was also a real Communist. When he got caught by the KMT, he surrendered without a fight, and ended up specialising in catching Communists for them. Who'd have thought that he'd end up in here as well... They're really a heartless bunch. For example, that hairdresser Mr. Lu, all he did was attend a wedding. Afterwards, the bridesmaid was accused of being a rebel spy, and so everyone who attended the wedding was arrested on the charge of 'being a member of a rebel organisation'. And there's that railway worker, Mr. Xu, who was listening to the radio and accidentally tuned in to the broadcast of a Mainland station. Someone informed on him, and he was framed for 'disseminating Communist propaganda'."

But, in turn, Liu the Phoney Commie was suspected by others of being a spy bought off by the jailers.

"Don't talk to him too much. Some people want their sentence commuted, so they befriend you and try to get you to tell them things, so that they can snitch on you. Watch out you don't get betrayed," Farmer Su warned me when we were let out to wash our faces.

* * *

"You really were a Communist defector?" I secretly asked Director Wu during our short time outside.

"Yes," Director Wu nodded, "I couldn't get away, so I had to accept their conditions."

"They really have deals with the Communists?"

"Yeah. Sometimes the enemy is your best helper. They know how to use the enemy and how to buy off the enemy."

"How did you get caught?" I pressed him for more details, after looking around me carefully and ensuring that we were not being watched.

"At that time, the upper echelon of my organisation fell apart. The higher-ups believed the government's amnesty in exchange for surrender, and gave away the mid-level cadres in order to save their own hides. In turn, the mid-level cadres were tricked into giving away the frontline staff. And so the whole organisation collapsed. Some tried to flee, but they could not hide for long, and had to turn themselves in eventually. Those who turned themselves in, just like those who were caught, had to reveal information about the organisation in order to save themselves. However, each person had limited knowledge, and, fearing that they'd be persecuted for providing insufficient information anyway, everyone revealed every detail that he knew, and not without embellishment. I was given away by one of my comrades."

"Under the threat of death, they had no choice but to betray you..."

"I don't blame them for betraying me. They all had their own reasons that were beyond their control. It's true, that they tried their best to limit the damage, when they gave away my name, but once you're implicated in this kind of thing, even a petty offence becomes a major felony. And then it's running away, endlessly running away. But you can't be on the lam forever. Surrender is the only option."

"And then you betrayed others as well?"

"Yes. For survival. Others informed on you to exchange for leniency. You in turn have to inform on others to redeem yourself. The snowball rolls bigger and bigger. Thousands, tens of thousands of people get dragged into the net... All I can say is, the special agents are wolves. There is no single wolf in the world that does not eat meat. So, no matter how the government threatens you, entices you, you must not waver. Once you provide them with a speck of information, they will keep pressuring you, until they have squeezed you dry."

"Have you been squeezed dry? They promised to let you redeem yourself?"

"I don't know. At least... I'm still alive now. In the future? I don't know. I don't trust them to honour their promises. Only a few cadres, those of a certain status in the organisation, were granted commutation on their sentences, because they were believed to be useful still. Everyone else, after revealing everything honestly, may still not avoid death..."

As Director Wu spoke, his eyes betrayed an expression of dejection. He saw that someone was looking our way. Hurriedly he concluded the tooth-brushing motion that he had been carrying on for far too long, walked up to the tap, and hastily rinsed his hair and face.

As I watched him walk away, my mind was completely blank for a few moments. Then, I recalled the massacre and the burial that I witnessed on the hill many years ago, the dead bodies in the ditch appearing to number in the thousands, tens of thousands.

At ten o'clock, the jail guard brought the first meal of the day. He doled out each portion of onto aluminium trays and passed them into the cell one by one. Those who stood near the cell door passed the meals to the people in the back. We only received two meals a day, at ten in the morning and four in the afternoon respectively. Each meal was the same, consisting of a bowl of salty soup with just a few bits of greens and turnip slices floating on it, accompanied by a bowl of gritty rice. Many people suffered from swollen faces and legs due to malnutrition from this poor diet. I opened up the tins of meat that my family sent me, and we each had a bite. They did not show any gratitude, but only swallowed their piece quickly and greedily eyed someone else's piece. But there was nothing else to share. In the last few days, no one else had received food packages from their families, apart from me; ten tins of meat were quickly finished over the course of two meals. As for when would be the next time a care package would be sent, no one knew.

Here, care packages from the families were delivered indirectly by the jail guards. Inmates could not receive them in person, nor did they have a way of communicating with their families. Only after the sentencing could they meet with their loved ones.

"Some people get the death sentence or are sentenced to Green Island, to be carried out immediately. They don't get the chance to see their families for one last time," Hairdresser Lu told me.

Plant Manager You's sentence came through. Fifteen years, not a short time, but not a long time either. But when he met with his family, he urged his wife to remarry, and to send their child away to be fostered. "Who knows what will happen in 15 years? Who knows if I can hold out for 15 years?" Saying that, he lowered his swollen eyes, and sat down leaning against the wall, with his swollen legs drawn against his chest. After that day, he spoke no more. Farmer Su whispered to everyone in private that, given how swollen he was, he did not have many more years, or even months, to live.

One night, when the jail warden came to do his rounds, he flashed his hand-torch around us. The light finally settled someone and stayed there for a few seconds. The hand-torch was switched off. And then the strong beam of light swept through the next cell...

What could that mean? We did not dare to ponder the answer.

The following morning, the warden appeared before each of the cells, announcing an inmate's name, the verdict, and the sentence. When Liu, the phoney Commie, heard that he was sentenced to death, he bellowed, "You lied! Liars! You said you'd let me live. You lied..." He had diarrhoea for a full four days after that. Before his sentence was carried out, he breathed his last.

Everyone said he was scared to death. We looked at the space he left behind. No matter how crowded it was when we slept at night, no one dared to lie in his spot.

The second one was Director Wu. That night, the light of the hand-torch fell on him and stayed there for a few seconds. At dawn the next morning he hurried to write his last will to his family. But before he finished, several burly men came to drag him away. With no time to spare, he stripped off all his clothing, and threw them to an old man who always shivered from the cold at night.

"Put them on. I have no more use for them." Those were his last words.

We all stood right against the wooden frame, with our sight following this pale figure in nothing but underpants until he disappeared serenely around the corner of the corridor.

Not long after, I received a woollen cardigan. I was told that my mother had knitted it while incarcerated, and before her execution she asked the jail guards to deliver it to me.

Tears covering my face, I stood against the wooden frame, gazing towards the end of the corridor where Mother's silhouette could not be seen.

The third one was Chief Aide Ding. When they dragged him out, he let loose a torrent of curses against the President and the Kuomintang. One of the guards struck his mouth squarely with the butt of his rifle, until his mouth was full of blood and broken teeth.

The fourth one was Director Li from the Air Force Intelligence

Department. This time, to prevent the condemned man from yelling and cursing, the prison guards came in at midnight, dragged him up and bound him. They stuffed a ball of rags in his mouth and carried him out like that. He looked back towards us, over the policeman's arm, with no fear in his eyes, and only a grim smile. As previously pledged, we sang a farewell song for him softly, as he was taken away. Right before his body left our line of vision, I saw him close his eyes.

The fifth one was Farmer Su. Before the guards came up to him to tie him up, he brought out a hidden piece of rock and hurled it at them. One of the guards was hit and started bleeding profusely. The other guards quickly surrounded the farmer, fitted bayonets onto their rifles and stabbed him until his innards fell out through his abdomen. With bulging eyes, he was carried out, and died with wrath written on his face.

The sixth one was me.

That morning, there was no announcement of the sentence, no forewarning of any kind. Two jail guards sudden burst in and yanked me out. Several other condemned prisoners and I were handcuffed together in a row, and marched into a truck.

Arriving at the execution grounds, we were pushed off the truck. Behind us stood a full row of military police, rifles in hand. The one who escorted me kicked me from behind and made me kneel down. The commander stepped forward and read out our names one by one—

It was just like how Little Wang described it before. My mind was in turmoil. All those details we listened to and relished before, the standard procedure of taking one photograph before death and one after...

There was no time to ruminate on that. The commander issued the order. The military police fired.

Those around me fell, one by one. I was shot too.

I heard it very clearly, the sound of a bullet searing through a chest.

One in the back, one in the neck, they fell beside me, eyes bulging, mouth open wide, two large bloody holes behind them.

But a few did not fall, a few were still breathing.

The military police put those of us still alive in handcuffs once more, left hand connected to another person's right hand, and in a row we were pushed back into the truck and driven back to the jail.

"This is called being the 'accompaniment'. They only shoot a few dead. The ones who didn't die were shot with blanks. It's for intimidating you, making sure you obey their every word, confessing whatever you should be confessing," a seasoned cellmate told me.

When I was sent back to my cell that day, I was trembling all over, my mind filled with the terrible countenances of men executed by firing squad.

"The bodies of those executed by firing squad are left there at the execution grounds for the undertakers to bring back to the mortuary. Families have to pay large fees to claim the bodies. Some families who could not afford the fee or who were afraid of being implicated left the bodies unclaimed. Once I was under orders to go take a photograph of a body in the mortuary. I saw a huge pile of dead bodies soaking in a pond of formalin. When they had verified the one I had to photograph, they just scooped the body out from the pond. It was really creepy! Some of them had bullet holes that look like something exploded, huge bloody holes." Little Wang had told Chunshao and me when we were little.

I could imagine the bullet holes in the chests of Chief Aide Ding, Director Wu, and Deputy Director Li, as well as their grisly countenances at death.

But did Little Wang photograph my mother?

I wanted to ask him, but I did not have the courage to do so. I did not run into him either.

Would they have put the post-execution photo of Mother in the newspaper?

If so, then Chunshao and Father would have seen it. Would they have saved a copy for me?

I could not think about it anymore.

Some daily essentials and food sent from home on several occasions were passed on to me, as well as a short letter that passed inspection. I found out that Father and Chunshao were all right. I only found out a bit about everything else after my sentencing, when Autumn and Floral brought me supplies.

The first visit was under close watch by the guards. Through the small window covered by wire mesh, Autumn and Floral said nothing.

The second time, Floral came alone. I asked her many questions, but she only revealed news about Anna.

Recounting a witness's testimony, she said that on the day I was taken away, Anna ran after the prison van and was run over when the driver put the van in reverse. She lay in a puddle of blood but did not die. They brought her home and saved her. But Anna appeared to have been traumatised by the incident. She was clumsy when she ate. If she left the house, she would forget how to go home, and would look for the way in a panicked manner until someone went out and found her and brought her back...

I recalled the scene that day, when she chased after the prison van, jumping repeatedly onto the vehicle and being thrown off repeatedly... But now, she was no longer the quick and wise Anna who watched over us. Having been incapacitated, she was just a pile of old bones waiting for the arrival of death. She had lost all her abilities, forgotten how to do everything. But did she forget her master?

Suddenly a million regrets surfaced in my heart. How I wished Anna was not a loyal dog, just an ordinary, death-fearing dog. An urge rose in me and I cried out to the heavens:

I don't want a loyal dog anymore!

I just want Anna to be well and alive!

I just want Anna to be the same as before...

* * *

The length of my sentence was announced. Six years. Upon reading the sentencing statement, I finally understood the crime I was convicted of: "Participating in rebel organisations, expanding the scope of anti-government propaganda, disseminating toxic Communist ideology in bulk, conspiring to sow discord between the populace and the government, designing to instigate riots..." I knew very well that my family worked really hard on this. Although Autumn and Floral did not tell me anything about it, I knew that Father and Chunshao, though unable to speak up on my behalf, must have been implicated in this affair too.

I removed the wrappers from the food my family sent me. I glued the colourful cellophane paper and the aluminium foil onto stiff cardboard, and carved out the faces of Father, Chunshao, and Floral. Two pieces of cardboard I cut into the shape of Anna. These were the only mementos I could leave my family with.

The last time Floral came to visit me at the Military Judiciary Division, I gave her these papercrafts to deliver for me. Floral looked at them, fell silent for a while, then said, "Anna died."

She told me that Anna was having more and more mobility problems. Every day, Chunshao brought Anna outdoors for exercise to aid in her recovery. One day, he ran into Autumn on the street, with a client. The two men started an altercation over Autumn. The other man struck Chunshao. Anna leapt up to bite him, but he grabbed hold of her limp back leg, with which he flung her onto the ground. He flung her on the ground hard. Again and again. Anna screamed a few times, and breathed her last.

Floral stared at the Anna on the cardboard. She paused, the continued, "Anna looked horrible when she died. She was bleeding from her mouth, from the corner of her eye. One of her eyeballs was hurled out of its socket, and the other one was still staring at Chunshao..."

I held back my tears. Everything before me appeared blank.

"Would you be my Anna?"

I finally mustered up the courage to plead with Floral.

"I have lost Anna. I cannot lose you as well. Would you be my Anna?" I repeated.

Floral looked at me with astonishment. I knew that my request was completely irrational: how could she be Anna? But she should know what I meant. Anna was my dearest, dearest friend. I was willing to be devoted to her, just as she was devoted to me.

Floral must have understood what I meant. She smiled at me, and, airily, started to hum an unfamiliar tune.

It was a cipher song. I figured it out. She was humming:

"I would love to... be your Sisi."

I hummed a coded phrase back at her: "Be my Anna."

She continued to hum mischievously, "Be your Sisi."

* * *

If Autumn was a cursed woman—I remember Mother saying that.

I do not know why, but I kept blaming Autumn for Anna's death, in spite of myself.

Chunshao. He did not protect Anna. But I had said that Anna would protect us, no matter what.

But Chunshao should not have neglected Anna for the sake of Autumn.

Chunshao really only treated Anna as a dog. A loyal dog, and nothing else.

I hated Autumn with an unreasonable passion. Billy, Sisi, and Anna all died because of her.

After all, they were not just the first dog, the second dog, the third dog to die on account of Autumn. There would be many, many dogs... I cried. I could not keep my own dogs safe, and all I could do was blame others.

What about Floral, then?

If Autumn was a cursed woman, then Floral would be a veritably pitiable creature.

Autumn never really cared much for Floral. Sometimes, Floral was less than a dog, especially the dogs at our house.

Autumn did not let Floral continue her schooling, but had her go sing in the cabaret. For some inexplicable reason, Autumn would rather Floral be like her and be drooled over by men.

And Floral actually adopted "Anna" as her stage name. She told me that, on the day of her last visit at the Military Judiciary Division.

She had kept her promise.

She had promised me long ago.

I lay in the crammed hold of the boat, smiling. On this boat carrying convicts to the outlying islands, I thought of her, I thought of the expression on her face when she hummed a cipher song. It was so innocent, and a bit foolish. But when she laughed, she was like a broken butterfly, whose wings were no match against the wind. I imagined that I heard the fragile sound of them snapping in the wind.

I will protect my last Anna.

Even though I was an inmate with no control over my fate, I made this vow in my heart.

The winds and waves were rough outside. At night, the hold was cold and wet. Some inmates curled up out of the cold. I draped the cardigan over myself, and immediately felt much warmer.

The night shook and roiled. Around us, on top of the sounds of people vomiting from seasickness, people breathing unevenly from nervousness, there was an atmosphere of morbid despair. God and Heaven were very far away. All I could do was caress the fine knit pattern on the cardigan, intently humming to myself the new cipher song I made—this was the coded message Mother wove, with her hair, into the inner side of the cardigan:

Stay alive. I love you.

12
The crimson volcanic isle

After the sentencing from the Judicial Division was finalised, I was transferred to a cell on another floor, joining several others who had been sentenced. One midnight, a flurry of footsteps in military boots tore the silence asunder. It sounded like a few dozen people were approaching. The lamps in the corridor lit up all at once, followed by a cacophony of keys clanging, cell doors opening. Very soon, our cell was opened as well. An officer, with four military police in tow, entered, stooping, and hurried us out of bed. The policemen checked our names and numbers against a list. As they called out each name, they tossed over a uniform with our new numbers sewn on. "Change into that. Make it quick!" the officer yelled. With two inmates still not finished changing, he was already impatiently barking out the next order: "Everyone face the wall. Stand straight and still!"

We lined up right against the wall. The four policemen immediately stepped forward and handcuffed us together two by two, wrist to wrist, ankle to ankle. In turn, we each picked up our personal belongings, which had been packed up for us in advance, and were led to the corridor to queue up along with the inmates from the other cells, also cuffed together two by two. Together, we were marched to the courtyard, and the military police marched us into the trucks.

Cuffed together, the inmates could only move in unison, climbing clumsily over the high door sill. Some pairs who were not matched in height had difficulty coordinating their movements, and tripped and fell badly. We were put twenty-four in a truck, sitting in two rows facing each other. Two policemen with ropes in hand first called roll, then tied us up twelve at a time, tightly against the benches. When everything was ready, each truck was assigned a sergeant and five officers for supervision. The windows, tightly-closed, were covered with opaque dark green canvas curtains; similar curtains enclosed the rear of the trucks.

As soon as day broke, the caravan started on its way. After driving for a while, two loud blasts for a whistle sounded ahead of us. The truck suddenly came to a halt.

The curtain at the rear of the truck was rolled back. Several policemen walked up from either side of the caravan, looked in and asked us loudly,

"Who picked it up?"

No one spoke.

"Own up! Don't make us use force!"

"What on earth are you referring to?" Someone asked.

The speaker was slapped across his face, perhaps as a lesson for asking the obvious, or perhaps he was misheard as asking the police "What on earth are you?"

"The things float— ing— out— side—" The policeman who hit the man blared.

"That'd take some skill. See how we're tied up. How can we reach outside to pick up anything? And floating things too! It's not like we're snakes or lizards, with tongues long enough to reach outside." A man who did not mind being hit mocked the policeman, and, as expected, received two slaps across his face as an answer.

Undeterred, the policemen outside continued questioning each of the trucks. The sergeant responsible for monitoring each vehicle ordered us to sit still, and meticulously examined each inmate's hands, feet, shirts, and trousers.

At the sound of a long whistle blast outside, all the policemen in the trucks alighted.

An inmate who sat close to the end of the truck took the opportunity to poke his head outside.

"There really are things floating around outside!" he said.

What is it? Everyone wanted to go look, but no one could move.

"Pieces of paper. There are words on them... Also, there are some toiletries dropped on the ground." The man at the rear whispered in a low voice to his neighbour, who in turn told it in a hush-hush tone to the man next to him, until the message had passed all the way around: "Airdropped by the CCP."

"Why didn't they send some helicopters to take us away instead?" someone joked.

"Interesting that they chose this time of all times to airdrop stuff."

"How thoughtful of them. Besides distributing pamphlets, they somehow knew we're in need of toiletries..."

"See how nervous the police are!"

The man at the rear of the truck poked his head out again. He said, the policemen outside were all crouching down, like they were trying to clean up everything on the ground.

After a while, the policemen monitoring the trucks hopped back up, and the long, snaking caravan started off again.

Before we were put in the prison trucks, we had witnessed the line-up of the convoy. At the very front were a few military vehicles full of weapons and soldiers. There was also one such vehicle between every three trucks. Besides that, there were military police on motorcycles flanking the caravan as escort, and at every few paces along the road stood armed guards. After the caravan got on its way, we even heard the buzz of helicopters above us. I could not figure out how the CCP managed to airdrop anything here. But one inmate, who had experience picking up airdropped items, whispered to us that the items were floated in by hot air balloons...

The military vehicles took us all the way to Keelung Pier. The police loosened the ropes tying us to the benches, and hurried us off. The inmates, still bound wrist to wrist, ankle to ankle, and now with luggage in their hands, stumbled and bumped into each other as they walked.

A few landing crafts were docked at the pier. Some other inmates, delivered even earlier from other prisons, were already queued up by the boats.

We could barely withstand the wind, blowing relentlessly from the sea. We were hungry and cold. The plank to the belly to the boat was finally lowered. The military police pushed us on either side as we walked into the hold of the boat. We boarded gradually. Once all the inmates had entered the hold, the cover above us was thrown shut. The tiny bit of light that had streamed in from the deck was cut off.

The hold of the boat was dark as could be. The boat stayed put for a long time. There seemed to be people still moving things about above us. Someone said they were moving food and supplies, while others conjectured that it was arms and ammo. Half a day passed before we felt the boat set sail. It was terribly shaky in the hold. We lay on the bone-breakingly hard hull, shoulder against shoulder, arms and legs crossed over each other or wedged amongst the cargo, like piles of rubbish left to rot.

Even though we were given neither food nor water before boarding the boat, some people got sick. The sounds of vomiting rose and fall, permeating the air with the thick, acrid smell of stomach fluids, making it impossible to fall asleep. Occasionally, someone would step over your head and your body in order to go to the toilet at the stern of the boat. In the entire boat there was only one toilet, located at the stern. I thought, those who went to the toilet must have been desperate; once you got up, there would be nowhere for you to lie back down.

As for me, I could put up with the hunger, the urge to urinate, the acrid smell and the stench, because my entire body was drained. I was completely empty inside, with nothing to feel hunger, nothing to urinate, nothing to vomit. The only things looping in my mind were a few cipher songs, the one that Floral hummed, the one that Mother knitted in the cardigan, as well as the rhythmic melody of people urinating—

That counted as a code as well. You could translate it into words, into strings of ridiculous gibberish.

A long, rambling nonsensical speech, lasting sixteen hours. The trapdoor to the deck finally opened, and a tiny bit of light was let through.

Stopping my song-composing and code-deciphering, I stood up together with the person shackled to me. We all climbed up to the deck, and took in the sight of this crimson volcanic isle, rising above a bed of white sand.

Green Island. That was its name. But at this time when autumn was giving way to winter, there was no sign of greenery on the island. The wind from the sea brought too much salt with it, withering all plant life; from afar the land looked as if it had been scorched.

We landed at the pier. In groups of twenty we were placed in a military truck and driven to the prison.

The prison was built against the hill, facing the sea. On the outside were at least a dozen guard posts and towers. There were dense barbed wires on top of the walls. The inmates were sent through the gates in groups. Each man was carefully searched before being sent to an isolation room awaiting team assignment. All the inmates were divided into three brigades based on the nature of their crime. Each brigade was divided into four squadrons, each squadron was divided into two sections, and each section consisted of three teams. I was assigned to the 10th Squadron of the 3rd Brigade. The 3rd Brigade consisted of the 9th, 10th, 11th, and 12th Squadrons, all of which were political prisoners.

After the team assignment, each team was taken in turn to their quarters. At the entrance of the barracks was a long corridor, with four dormitory rooms on either side for the officers stationed there. We passed through the corridor and entered through a metal gate. Inside the gate were rows of bunk beds facing each other across the corridor; the 1st, 3rd, and 5th teams were on one side, the 2nd, 4th, and 6th on the other.

After the teams took their places, the team supervisor began to assign sleeping areas.

The so-called sleeping areas were just double bunks constructed of wooden planks, with an upper and a lower bunk. The area that we each got measured no more than six feet by two feet. Cramped into such a narrow bunk, we were unable to sleep on our backs as our shoulders would overlap another man's. Some people ended up sleeping head-to-toe with their bunkmate.

The supervisor was around my height, so we shared a bunk.

The first night, I breathed in the odour of his feet until daybreak.

The second night, he seemed to be taking advantage of me, taking up enough space to lie flat on his back. I could only lie on my side all night.

The third day, he went one step further, leaving me no room to even lie on my side. I had to crouch until morning.

On the fourth day, I held my ground. Neither of us yielded, and neither of us got any sleep. He went and told on me to his superiors, and thus I was sent to disciplinary confinement for the first time. After my release, I quarrelled with the supervisor again on several occasions. Both the sergeant and the captain took the supervisor's side, and I was labelled a trouble-maker and subject to much punishment.

The director and the deputy director were in charge of both the administration and political management of the prison. On the administration side, below the director there were the commanders of each brigade, captains of each squadron, sergeants of each section, and their deputies. All of them were military officers. The team supervisors alone were chosen from the inmates. Each brigade and squadron had a political management adviser. Teams paired up into crews, each with a political officer and a crew chief. Except for the crew chiefs, who were inmates, all the advisers and political officers were officials. I belonged to Team 3 of the 1st Section of the 10th Squadron. The team supervisor was a former military officer in the Nationalist Army, and it was unknown what he did to end up in here. He spent his days ordering others about, as if he had forgotten that he was also a prisoner. But as he was birds of a feather with the more senior staff, no one dared to challenge him.

My stubbornness and insubordination must have annoyed him. They kicked me out of the 10th Squadron and put me in the 9th. Word had it that this squadron were for the more recalcitrant inmates.

My new team was Team 6 of the 2nd Section of the 9th Squadron. On the very first day, the squadron captain showed me who was boss. Captain Tian was short a finger on his right hand. Someone in the squadron told me that he was formerly BIS—the Bureau of Investigation and Statistics—and would not think twice before killing someone. True enough, under his tender care, I almost had all of my fingers cut off.

Happily, though, I got along with the new team supervisor. Supervisor Ma was an "anti-Communist volunteer". During the Korean War, he answered the government's call and defected to Taiwan, becoming the favourite poster-boy for the anti-Communist effort. However, when he established a "Patriotic Alliance" in order to coordinate with others who came to the Taiwan for the same reason, he was accused of running a conspiratory organisation. And that was how he got in here. Supervisor Ma had had his share of suffering during his interrogation; he was a veteran of everything from electric shocks to denailing, tiger benches, and aeroplanes. As if trying to avoid getting into any further trouble, he was extremely courteous to all of us.

Also, to my surprise, Zhu Xiaokang and Du Daoxiong were locked up in here as well, in the same unit as myself.

"I saw your dad at the Military Judicial Division. He was in the cell next to mine. I wonder what happened to him at the end?"

It was inconvenient to talk inside the cell. Once we were sent on work detail to the production base, I took the opportunity to ask Zhu Xiaokang about Uncle Zhu.

Zhu Xiaokang's expression grew grim. He shook his head, "My father is still in Taiwan. They were originally going to sentence him to death, but they didn't. He wasn't sent to the Outlying Islands either. His sentence is shorter than ours, and should be free before we are."

"What happened? What did they convict you of?"

Zhu Xiaokang glared at me, "What did they convict me of? Would you believe it if I said I'm innocent? And what are you convicted of anyway? Do you really think you can take their verdicts seriously? The verdicts are all arbitrary."

"It's true. It's all arbitrary. It's like, my mother worked for them, and they took her too," I said.

"Your mother was arrested? What happened?"

"I don't know why or what they convicted her of. Anyway, she was executed..."

"They've gone completely insane." Zhu Xiaokang forcefully hurled a handful of gravel at the pigs he was feeding. A commotion broke out in the pigsty. Everyone around turned their attention to us.

We hastily lowered our heads and went about our work, cutting short our conversation.

"My nine-year-old baby brother was spared, but both my parents are locked up."

Zhu Xiaokang finally told me one day what happened to his family. "They used my baby brother as a hostage and threatened my mother to reveal my father's crimes. My mother refused, and they beat my brother. My father didn't want to see my mother and my brother suffer, so he confessed... There was one particularly brazen special agent. The bastard tried to get my mother to divorce my father and remarry him. My mother pleaded to the bastard and asked him to promise to have mercy on me and my father. The bastard told her that she could only choose between me and my father. She had no choice, and picked my father. As soon as she married this special agent, my father's sentence was commuted. My brother, on the other hand, was sent to an orphanage... From what I heard, we have nothing left. Our house and all our possessions were confiscated..."

* * *

"Yes, your family home was confiscated," Autumn told me.

On the other side of the window of the visiting room, Autumn appeared weary and careworn. Having expected some woe to have befallen my family, I actually felt relieved at this news. "Apart from the house being confiscated, are Dad and Chunshao all right?"

"Yes, they're fine," replied Autumn.

On that visit, Autumn brought me a full sack of clothes, food, and pocket money. I could tell that it took her much effort to get to Green Island. I asked her how she came. She said, "Starting from Taipei, I took the train to Su'ao, then took a bus to Hualien. I stayed overnight in Hualien. The next day I took the light rail to Taitung, and transferred to a bus to go to Fugang. I stayed overnight at Fugang. The day after I took a small boat from Fugang to Nan-liao Harbour. It took about half a day. After getting off the boat, I took a bus..."

I was grateful to her, even though I knew that she did not do this for me, but for Father and Chunshao.

"You know what? Yao Tiepeng moved into your house." Autumn looked at me, wanting to add something, but stopping herself before speaking further.

Upon hearing that, my mind was thrown in disarray, but not without a sense of relief at the revelation of an answer. I knew that the property of those reported as rebel spies was confiscated by the government, who awarded a portion of it to the informer. Furthermore, the reward for informers under the "Statute for the Finding and Purging of Spies" had been increased to 200,000 *yuan*. An average citizen's monthly salary was only about 300 *yuan*. This of course was hugely enticing.

I paused for a while, and finally said, "It's the Yaos who informed on us? Is that what you wanted to say?"

"Yeah, they're saying it's the boy, Yao Kunming, who went to inform on you with a pamphlet written in brush calligraphy."

I remembered that Yao Kunming came to visit us in the spring. The calligraphy piece in Wang Xizhi's style, which Mother praised, must have made an impression on him.

"What about my mother? How did she get implicated? Why did she die?"

"Chunhuan, I don't know."

"Did Uncle Zhu's family get dragged in because of us? I saw Uncle Zhu at the Military Judiciary Division, and even Zhu Xiaokang is locked up in here."

"The Zhu family seemed to be involved in something else. I'm not sure if it has anything to do with your family..."

A prison guard was watching us. We had to stop talking about sensitive topics.

"Right, I'm in the same dorm and section as Daoxiong, if you didn't know already."

"Daoxiong told me. Please take care of him." For the very first time, Autumn gave me an imploring look.

I promised her to take care of Daoxiong. At that moment, I began to realize that Autumn had almost spent all her money because of my family and Daoxiong. The cafe where she used to work no longer employed her. She probably had Floral quit school and sing at a cabaret because she was desperate for money.

Daoxiong's incarceration was probably the most baffling of all. He had nothing to do with my family. It was just that one time when a special agent went to Autumn's house to ask about us, Daoxiong naively bragged that he went to the hill with us to look for the armed base. He described himself as a hero, but that led to him being arrested. As a matter of fact, he had never even once played War with us, let alone going with us to look for the base all those years ago. Most likely, he heard Floral talk about it, and, envious of our adventure, he made up his own version of the story. But at the end that led to a false charge made up against him.

Compared to us, Daoxiong was still a boy, a silly boy with no real world experience and no opinion of his own. Whenever there was menial work to be done, the officer on duty would always assign it to him first. And he, unwilling but with no idea how to get out of it, would always end up taking it on.

Daoxiong, Xiaokang, and I belonged to the same production team. Daoxiong was responsible for growing vegetables on the hill; Xiaokang was responsible for feeding the pigs, and I was responsible for keeping turkeys.

Both the pigsty and the turkey coop were on the hillside right behind the dormitory, but the vegetable garden was farther away on the top of the hill. Early every morning, Daoxiong had to go collect a full bucket of night soil. Then, carrying this fertiliser, as well as farming tools and some rice for cooking for lunch, he would trudge up the hill. Being so far away in the hill, he was not able to return to camp for lunch but had to cook his own, using scavenged brushwood for fuel. Xiaokang's job involved either carrying a large bucket of rancid-smelling swill or going to a nearby garden to pick sweet potato leaves to feed the pigs.

My job was the easiest of all. I only had to bring onion greens and rice bran to go feed the turkeys assigned to me. Once I arrived at the turkey coop, I would chop up the onion greens and mix them in with the bran to make turkey feed. Then, I would check the baby turkeys' heads to see if they had been bitten by mosquitoes. Turkeys were susceptible to mosquito bites, and this was an area infested with large mosquitoes. Even though there was mosquito netting around the coops, the net always had a tear here or there, and the turkeys nearest the edges were bound to be bitten. Mosquito bites in the eye area, especially in young poults, would cause rapidly-swelling blisters around the eye, leading to death. As a way to pass the time, I whittled slivers of bamboo, punctured the blisters, drained them, and applied anti-inflammatory ointment. After performing such dermatological treatments, I would take a long bamboo pole to herd the turkeys outside for exercise, letting them roam and feed freely. And, if I finished ahead of schedule and had no more work to do, I would go visit Xiaokang at the pigsty. There was a shed built of coral and silvergrass next to the pigsty, for us to rest and get out of the sun.

This was where we kept our secret. Here circulated some banned books and newspaper cuttings scavenged by the team. Together, we copied out passages and quoted excerpts of their content into notebooks, for ease of reading. We kept the notebooks wrapped in waterproof cloth and hid them inside the thatching of the roof. As I found out, there were a few who kept their own private collections buried by the pigsty or in the vegetable patches nearby, digging them up to read only when there was nobody around.

We had few books there. Books sent to us from outside had to be inspected and stamped as approved before they passed through. Newspapers were forbidden to us. Whenever someone managed to smuggle in a banned book or two, it would necessarily become the most popular item in here. And as for newspapers, while the convicts were not allowed to read them, the officers were; the newspapers that the officers forgot to put away or accidentally tossed into the bin became gold to us. Even though the officers only read the Party papers, reporting filtered through political lenses, being able to find out about a thing or two that happened in the outside world was precious to us, like catching a whiff of the air of freedom.

We were like soulless bodies, having lost our own time, thought, and will. Life each day was crammed full with mandatory lessons or labour.

Before daybreak, we rose from our beds in the starlight. First came the morning roll-call, the slogan-chanting, the national anthem, and the small group meetings where we criticised the Communist Party. After that we could finally catch our breaths and gather around on the ground to have breakfast. After breakfast, we were called by a whistle blast to assemble in sections and be led off to either lessons or labour, depending on which day it was in the schedule. If it was lesson day, we would spend all day in the classroom listening to "Teachings of

Sun Yat-sen" and "Quotes by the President", or "The Crimes of Mao Zedong" and "The History of Soviet Invasions of China". After the lessons there were tests and the students were even ranked by their marks. But if it was a work day, the sergeant on duty would assign tasks to everyone and the whole section would go out and labour all day, returning only at nightfall to bathe in the stream by the dormitory. We had a short time for supper, after which we assembled again for anti-Communist plays or other group activities. Not before we were exhausted and our minds drained of energy was the bedtime bugle sounded. But before going to bed, we still had the evening roll-call and the sergeant's address. Finally, with singing and chanting patriotic slogans, we finished another day.

"There's no time to do anything all day except an afternoon nap."

At noon, a man walked into at the work shed grumbling. Not in the mood to chat, he lay down on the ground right away, pulled up his undershirt to cover his face, and got ready to sleep.

The flies dancing about him ignored his face, but rested on his belly, which was drenched with sweat. The skin of his belly was covered with fly droppings. A prankster placed a few white pebbles on his belly, saying that he was playing checkers against the black pieces.

"Bugger off! Let me have a snooze!" This old campaigner, Shi Baixing, nicknamed Shit Boxing, was on guard duty last night. After the early morning labour he was completely exhausted.

"Get up, Shit Boxing, tell us another story about our 'leader'," several people around him pestered him to get up. There having been a recent shortage of newspaper and books, Shi Baixing's insider anecdotes were our preferred antidote for boredom.

"Help me shoo away the flies. I'll tell one when I've had my sleep."

A few people really got working on shooing away flies for him. The flies flew all about; as soon as they had shooed the flies away from his belly, the flies landed on their own faces. They had to fan Shi Baixing's belly with one hand and fan their own faces with the other. They worked up quite a sweat from this labour.

The noon break was not a long time. Taking advantage of this rare occasion of leisure, everyone found something to do even if there was nothing to chatter about. Some took a piece of scavenged old cable, cut open the plastic covering, and used the copper wires inside to make a sewing needle. Some used a stone to grind a tin can top into a razor. And some others unrolled scavenged cigarette butts to reroll the tobacco into a thin new smoke...

Before it was time to start our afternoon chores, Shi Baixing was true to his word and "woke up" as promised.

He stretched and yawned, and started to tell two historical anecdotes. The year was 1949. Before the Kuomintang army retreated to Taiwan, the Director-General (now President) of the Kuomintang presided over the last military parade at the Whampoa Military Academy.

"At that time, the Communists had seized more than half of China. The Kuomintang retreated and took up position in the southwest. As you know, even the southwest was about to fall. I remember that day, our President came to Chengdu in an aeroplane and visited our Academy. He rallied the thousands of cadets below the podium with a passionate speech, saying, Do not fear the Communist rebels, as the Nationalist army will surely counterattack successfully and recover our lost land... As he spoke, his expression grew gloomy, and then he said, someone in our Academy betrayed the Party, giving the Communist rebels an opportunity to strike against us...

"He didn't finish that sentence. Guess what happened? Something white suddenly fell out of his mouth. His false teeth! Yeah, false teeth! His set of false teeth fell out just like that, fell onto the yellow sand on the field. His son—we call him the 'Crown Prince'—the Crown Prince was standing next to the President. In a moment of panic, he took a step forward. But, as soon as his first foot stepped up, he regained his composure and stepped back into his spot. He glanced towards the bottom of the podium. I happened to be standing the closest to the podium, so I went to pick up the false teeth, and even considerately wiped them clean on my uniform..."

"Did our leader put them back on?" Someone asked anxiously.

"How could he have opened his mouth wide in public to stick his teeth back in? Of course he acted as if nothing happened. He just casually put them in his pocket."

"Shit Boxing, did he reward you for that?" Someone else interjected.

"Uh-huh, of course. When he left on the aeroplane, he let me go with him."

Everyone made a long ooooh sound.

"You might not know, but planes can't always take off whenever you want them to. It was really cold back then, so cold your jaw could freeze straight off. The pilots were ordered to guard the planes all day, and no one was allowed to sleep. They put coal stoves around the fuselage and under the wings, to keep the plane warm around the clock. So, no matter how cold it got, if the enemy was close in pursuit, once the President boarded the plane it would be ready for take-off immediately...

"Also, when the plane got in the air and you look back down, you could see the most magnificent sight ever. On the ground were all the cadets from the Academy, staying there to stand between him and the Communists' gunfire..."

"You were on the same flight as him? That's quite something. If it wasn't for such a glorious reward, you wouldn't have had the chance to come to Taiwan, which means you wouldn't have been invited here to Green Island..." someone teased Shi Baixing for bragging, and got conked on the head for it.

"Hey, stop interrupting! It's almost time to start work again. Shit Boxing, hurry up and give us another one!" Everyone else told the interrupters to settle down, and pressed Shi Baixing to continue.

Pleased with himself, Shi Baixing pursed his lips, swallowed, and continued, "Let's stay with the parade. On the same day. After the President put his false teeth into his pocket, he did not speak anymore. You know, without teeth, you can't speak very clearly, so you might as well not speak. The commander on the stage ordered for the parade to begin, and the military band started the marching music. First, the infantry marched by in neat formation, saluted to the President, and the President saluted back graciously. Next, it was the field guns. They were driving along, all powerful and majestic-sounding, and the President beamed at the sight... until one of the field guns started charging at the stage!"

"Oh no! Who would dare to do that?" Someone gasped.

"Yeah, that'd be pretty bold. In an instance, all the guards rushed up to the President and formed a tight circle around him in protection. A few dozen armed soldiers rushed up to stop the field gun—but there was no need. It stopped right in front of the stage, and wouldn't move anymore."

"What happened?"

"It broke down," replied Shi Baixing. "It happened to break down, just in front of the President, and no one could get it to budge. The entire artillery unit was held up behind this gun, and it was a complete mess. And so, the parade was over."

Break time was also over. Someone who hadn't had enough asked Shi Baixing to tell another story. Shi Baixing turned around, put on a grave expression, and did an impression of the President giving a speech: "You lot can't tell where the enemy is. Careful the rebel spies are right beside you."

Everyone burst out laughing. But, seeing the sergeant coming towards us, we quickly dispersed.

Although he didn't know what we were laughing about, the sergeant saw us and made a note of it. Before the end of the day, several of us were listed as trouble-makers, charged with "illegal assembly" in the work shed, and assigned to new tasks. My turkeys were given to someone else to keep. With Shi Baixing and some others, I was to go help Daoxiong with the vegetables on the hill.

Growing vegetables on the hill was a chore. Every morning, after collecting the night soil, we each had to carry a heavy bucket of it from the bottom of the hill to the top, the stench following us the entire way. And, no matter how we watered and fertilised the vegetables, they would not grow; the wind from the sea was too heavy with salt and the vegetables would wither before they were fully grown. We shook our heads as we examined the yellowed stems and leaves—what a waste of effort it was to keep a garden on this kind of hill! But, later on, we figured out a way. We went into the forest to gather branches, silvergrass, and shellflower leaves, and wove them into screens for blocking out the wind. We placed them around the seedlings. It worked. We overcame the wind and the salt, and the vegetable garden flourished.

As the vegetable garden expanded, more and more branches, leaves, and silvergrass were needed, and our workload increased. We had to go into the forest more frequently to harvest the material. Under the supervision of the sergeant, we dared not slack off; he demanded that each of us do the same amount of work. But we figured out that he could not be bothered to monitor us every time we went in and out of the forest. As long as we came back with the required amount of material by the given time, all was well. So, after deliberating among ourselves, we would send a few people in turn into the forest to gather enough material to meet everyone's quota, while the rest of us would go for a swim in the sea.

As we became more and more accurate in timing our activities, we had more and more free time.

Some swam closer to the shore, some swam farther out. Some, like me, liked to dive deep into places where no one else could see.

Using a large rock as a landmark, I followed the undulating seagrass down to the bottom of the sea. Then, from the turquoise shallows, I gradually made my way into a patch of dark blue waters.

In the dark blue waters grew coral of every fascinating shape and colour: they grew like spirals, like trees, like fingers, like umbrellas; they were resplendent with orange, indigo, yellow, and pink... On several taller columns were attached bright-coloured sea anemones and slender sea whips. On the tallest of the coral columns grew the rare black coral and pearl oysters as big as one's hand...

Following some butterflyfish, I wove in and out of the bright blue light. Every now and then, I saw a few small red fish bouncing playfully in the blue, like little balls of fire. Sometimes it was a purple tropical fish with delightful pale yellow dots, turning slowly towards me, drawing a semicircle in the water. There were also jellyfish, gently glowing, floating by in a pulsating motion. That was the most elegant movement in all my memory.

I swayed my body in the rhythm of the waves. A school of fish slipped past me on either side, then forming a sinuous silver ribbon once more behind me.

As I swam around a beam of sunlight shining into the water, I was bathing within a halo of light. I flittered up and down inside the halo, happy and carefree, feeling that I had become one with an eternal, boundless pulse of life.

Sometimes, here in this boundlessness I would run into an old friend. I called it "Mr. Phantom".

The first time I saw him, he was just a large, nebulous dark shadow, quavering at a distance, stirring up the mud in the water around him.

The second time, he came up close to me. I saw a phantom-like face—with an enormous, speckled forehead, lips curving downward, bulging eyes—staring at me. Startled, I flapped my arms and legs about. That seemed to have scared him, and he swam away immediately, his splashing tail swirling up a series of whirls in the water.

The next few times I met him, I stayed still. He did not swim away from me anymore. We just looked at each other in silence.

One day, I finally reached out and petted him.

He did not flee. In fact, he actually turned around in the water, and again, and in different directions, as if he was frolicking blithely. From that moment on, I became his friend. Whenever he gave me a head-bump with his enormous forehead, I knew that it was a friendly hello, that he was desiring my touch.

* * *

When the afternoon sun began to subside, the swimmers and the woodcutters met up at a pre-arranged spot. Here, we divided up the brushwood, shellflower leaves, and silvergrass collected by the group, and carried them back to the vegetable patch.

On the way back, as we stood on the hillside path and gazed into the distance, the island of Taiwan across the channel seemed so near. But when the weather was inclement and the sea was covered with waves, that vision would be taken away from us.

We could see that, a few low-lying hills away, the sergeant had arrived at another hilltop waiting for us to return to camp. He did not look like he was out to catch slackers; he just looked eager to return to camp.

I did not think that he was as cold and cruel as he looked. He was just an old wolf tired of hunting; when he extended his claws and posed to strike, he was only asserting his status as a wolf. But he must be afraid of us seeing through that.

"Actually, the officers supervising us are no freer than we are. They're stuck guarding this lonely island. They can't go back to Taiwan, can't be discharged, can't get married, can't hope for a transfer. A lifetime of military service is no different to a life sentence," Shi Baixing remarked one day plaintively, while watching the sergeant smoking and pacing on the hilltop.

"Yeah, and they can only take it out on us inmates. It's like we're the culprits who prevented them from going home, like the Mainland fell because of us," a man called Wu Yaobang burst out.

Shi Baixing continued, "They resent us, because they don't dare to resent those who they truly resent. So they take out their anger on us. Even the commanders and captains who swagger about all the time, they got sent to this island only because they were unsuccessful and underperforming on Taiwan. What else could they do on here, besides roughing us up and yelling at us? They can't do anything if they go back either. They're treated as useless people there."

"Yeah, they're useless men who can't do anything. You have no idea how bored they get," A short fellow called Jian Liangnan, who always had cigarettes to smoke, said with an entre-nous look. "No women, no entertainment, all they get to do is keep watch over us blokes with shaved heads. Of course they'd lose it. You know how I get these cigs? They give them to me. I trade for them. I draw a naked woman, as sizzling hot as you like, and give it to them. And they give me cigs to smoke. But this is a secret..." Right after revealing the secret to us, he begged us not to let it get out, else that would be the end of his source for smokes.

Joyful singing voices were heard from afar. We turned our heads towards the sound.

On a dirt path at the bottom of the slope, a row of local women were walking along, carrying farm tools. Some had baskets on their backs, some carried hoes on their shoulders; some were leading oxen, some were pulling handcarts behind them. They had just finished the day's work in the fields, and were going home with the newly-harvested peanuts, sweet potatoes, and black-eyed peas. We slowed down to watch this group of aborigine women. We watched their tanned faces gleaming in the sunlight, sweat drops glistening on their foreheads; we watched their ordinary, easy looks and relaxed footsteps, looking like they came from another world on this island.

The flat shoreland below the hills was dotted with stone-slab houses and thatch houses, the homes of these aborigines. They let pandan trees grow around their houses, forming natural fences. Inside the fences they kept pigs, chickens, ducks, and deer, or there could be yards covered with shredded sweet potato, drying in the sun. Every day, the men went out to sea to fish, and the women farmed along the shore or in the hills. The men wore nothing but a loincloth, and even the women were mostly bare-backed. They were so tanned from the sun that their bodies had a rosy glow; their mouths, from the habit of chewing betel, appeared especially bright red.

Jian Liangnan pointed at a girl in a stylish dress, and said that Sergeant Hu liked her. "Her name is Miko. The dress she's wearing is a present from Sergeant Hu. See, the officers have a lot more freedom in going after girls. They have the money and the time. Plus, they get to keep their hair, and don't have to have ugly shaves like us." As he said, he gave Shi Baixing a sidelong glance, then added, "If we go after women, we'd be in deep trouble."

However, not long after, we all found out that Jian Liangnan was courting Miss Miko. Before coming to Green Island, he was a billboard designer. After coming to Green Island, he became responsible for all the sets for the squadron's evening shows. At that time, we had just added some Taiwanese operas to our repertoire of anti-Communist plays. Apart from drawing backcloths, Jian Liangnan was occasionally assigned by the sergeant to the stage. Although the plot was always the same bland anti-Communist humdrum and we all dreaded having to act, the shows were an attraction for the local islanders. Not having other forms of entertainment, they could only go watch the inmates' plays as a way to pass the time. Besides, Jian Liangnan did a good job with the backcloths. Even if the they found the shows unbearable, they could at least enjoy looking at the backcloths.

Sergeant Hu always saved a front row seat for Miko. Whenever she was in the audience, Jian Liangnan put his heart and soul in his acting, as if he was doing it just for her. All the other inmates hated performing; when they were assigned a role on stage, they would just muddle through it. But Jian Liangnan always gave an expressive and moving performance.

He made many pretty trinkets to please Miko. The masterpiece he was most proud of was a portrait of Miss Miko, made with shells and sand glued on paper. In addition, he was a diligent letter-writer, always sending her philosophical quotes from books or lines of poetry. A notebook hidden on the roof of the work shed was his source of inspiration.

"What are changes of empires, the wreck of dynasties, to life? What are the revolutions of the globe which we inhabit, and the operations of the elements of which it is composed, compared with life?"
— Percy Bysshe Shelly

"You smiled and talked to me of nothing and I felt that for this I had been waiting long."
— Rabindranath Tagore

"There are two tragedies in life. One is to lose your heart's desire. The other is to gain it."
— George Bernard Shaw

Before this letter was sent, it was discovered by Sergeant Hu. Sergeant Hu reported the matter to his superior, Captain Tian.

Jiang Liangnan was hung up next to the dungeon by the sea and beaten, with Captain Tian interrogating him. After the beating, he was locked into the dungeon, and brought back out two days later for another round of interrogation and beating. And again and again.

One day, as soon as the beating was over and the guard let him down, he made a dash for the sea and leapt into the water.

Everyone knew that he couldn't swim. His sole purpose was to die. But the sea kept pushing him out of the water; Jian Liangnan could not sink, and thus could not die either.

Captain Tian ordered a guard to jump in and bring him back to shore, put him on the ground, and push on his abdomen until he had heaved up all the sea water in him. Before he had a chance to catch his breath, they hung him up again and resumed beating him.

Jian Liangnan finally disclosed the location of the banned books and the notebooks. Fortunately, Shi Baixing and Zhu Xiaokang had already shrewdly moved the books to the pigsty and buried them.

Since there were no books there, he must have had accomplices. Captain Tian ordered a full search in the section's dormitory. He had everyone strip naked so the guards could search us from head to toe, looking even inside our buttocks.

Besides a tiny scrap of toilet paper found stuck in someone's back end, they could not find anything either.

For a few months after that, every move of every man in the section was kept under close watch. We were forbidden from communicating with the outside world and from meeting our families. A result of that was that our precious source of outside food and pocket money was also cut off.

This gave the section a sense of unity from having a common enemy, but at the same time there was a overwhelming tension that felt like it would tear the group asunder. It started when someone proposed pooling all resources inside, food or otherwise, for communal use. We had already been willingly sharing some of our possessions with those who needed them, to whatever extend we could; but now, some people wanted to make it compulsory for everyone to share everything equally, including vitamins, anti-inflammatory pills, and stomach medicine. Not even shoes, socks, and undergarments could be owned privately.

The chief proponent of sharing everything equally was Wu Yaobang. Jian Liangnan, Zhu Xiaokang, and Du Daoxiong all supported him. Some of those who normally had no opinions of their own also concurred with the majority opinion without asking questions. As for Supervisor Ma, he had always been congenial, offending none, agreeing with whatever anyone said.

"This is the fairest way to treat those who have nobody to send them stuff from outside. We can't be selfish and hoard things for personal use," said Wu Yaobang, like the embodiment of justice, a hero for the deliverance of all. Many people nodded in agreement.

Standing against the popular opinion, I said, "This is not about selfishness. It's about each person's own situation. Some things could be really important to some individuals, like, the sick and weak will have a particular need for nutritious food and medicine. The elderly with missing teeth also need special kinds of food. If their families send them these items, it's because they're needed. If the rest of us normal folk get a share of the things that they need, it'd be pointless for us and a deprivation for them. You're promoting false equality by forcing everyone to share all personal items without considering each person's need. It's also unreasonable."

Some gave me looks of agreement, but they all seemed to want to stay on the side-lines. No one spoke up in support of me.

"Who's sick? Who's weak? Someone tell me?" Wu Yaobang bellowed at the crowd. No one answered.

"Hong Yucheng, what do you think?" Wu Yaobang named an anaemic inmate who was sick at the time. All he did was stare at Wu Yaobang with large, innocent eyes, and shook his head. Wu Yaobang then asked several old men. No one said anything. Wu Yaobang continued, "Those whose families are poor and those who have no family don't get material assistance. Only people with wealthy families, only rich boys like you get this much material help. But it's not like you earned all that money from hard work. How many ordinary men did you step on, how much class inequality did you exploit, to enjoy all this wealth?"

"You can say my background is based on inequality, but you have no right to judge me. I won't resent sharing my things. I'm just warning you, this kind of blind equality will create another form of inequality. It is also an irrational form of totalitarianism," I responded, while Shi Baixing nodded along.

"That's exactly what we're doing. It's a revolution of the proletariat against totalitarianism. Don't twist the truth and label people."

"Oh, Wu Yaobang," Shi Baixing finally spoke up, "You're all brave and bright young men, but you're too presumptuous for your own good. Wouldn't you just be publicly implementing Communism by doing this? I'm not opposed to your Communism—after all, we're only here because they thought we're Communists. But they're watching us really closely now. If you promote Communism in such a big way, you'd just be flaunting the fact that you're opposing those in power. You're going to get in big trouble."

"You know nothing, Shit Boxing! The KMT is holding secret discussions with the CCP. The anti-Communism movement is just for show now. The Communists are coming, very soon. We won't have to be afraid of the KMT anymore..." Jian Liangnan sudden revealed a piece of inside information. Someone asked him how he found out about that. He said in a hush-hush tone that he heard it when he passed by the captain's office.

"Then wait till the Communists are actually here. Now, it's more important to stay alive. If you're too obvious about it, we'll all get shot before anything happens. This isn't the time for heroics and playing tough. You don't have the right to drag everyone to their deaths," Shi Baixing spoke again.

"Don't join if you're afraid to die. I'm not forcing you guys. People who don't want to share will continue to eat what they have and use what they have," Wu Yaobang declared finally. Following that, Zhu Xiaokang stood up and said, "This system is probably the best for all of us at this point. Some of you might not be used to it, but we need to make it a priority to help the majority. It's fair and reasonable to sacrifice a few people's rights for the sake of the many." After saying that, he looked expectantly at me. I nodded at him.

Some people called Wu Yaobang and Zhu Xiaokang's group the "Communist Alliance", in private. Shi Baixing and I both brought out all our belongings to share with everyone else; those who were sympathetic to our opinion but who did not want to upset group harmony also cooperated. Although the "Communist Alliance" held us to be different-minded, negative, and conservative, those personal differences did not affect our unity on the surface.

We implemented our Communist system very thoroughly. But goods that were distributed evenly, especially food, ran out quickly. Our meals every day became even blander than before. All there was to go with rice were peanuts and dried radishes.

Although we grew vegetables and kept pigs and poultry, those were not for us to eat. The prison required us to purchase them with our own money. Without money, we could only look helplessly as lush fresh greens were picked, chopped, and fed to the animals. The animals grew fatter and fatter, and were bought up by the other sections. We never got a taste of them.

Since we could not get any meat, we tried to get some seafood.

There were lobsters in the sea. But, when we worked on the hill, the sergeant kept too close a watch on us, and we could not find enough opportunities to go down to the sea. Occasionally, we'd cover one or two people to go down to the water and catch lobsters. They might find two or three, which would be no more than a bite for each man. Once, Daoxiong discovered a cave filled with lobsters, and reached in to catch them. It just happened that the tide was coming in and the strong inflow suctioned him against the cave. Struggled as he could, he couldn't free himself. Wu Yaobang rushed down to save him. As he yanked him out, he slipped and fell against a coral reef. Although the reef was covered with soft coral polyps, the reef itself was sharp as a knife. As the tide came in, Wu Yaobang was hurled by a wave onto the reef, which cut a deep wound in his arm.

For the next while, Wu Yaobang's arm was basically incapacitated, and he could not do his normal chores. Only because other teammates covered for him did he avoid getting into trouble. Zhu Xiaokang took over as the leader of the group. Once in a while, he would manage to get a sharp bamboo pole from the islanders, sneak down to the water and spear a few squids so that Wu Yaobang could get some nutrition in his meals.

One day, when the sergeant was not looking, Xiaokang took a few of us to the seashore and dug up a pile of pig innards.

"These were newly buried," said Zhu Xiaokang. "I fed hot, cooked sweet potatoes to a pig, so that it would get a stomach-ache and stop eating regular feed. A veterinarian was sent over to look at it, so I bribed him to declare the stomach pain to be swine fever. With that, the pig couldn't be kept in the sty anymore. The captain and the other officers slaughtered it and ate it, but they didn't dare to touch the innards of a sick pig. So they had the offal buried by the sea, and now we get to feast on it."

We cooked the offal by the sea, and smuggled it back to the base and shared it with everyone. Wu Yaobang ate the most out of everyone; he'd grab the next piece before swallowing the piece in his mouth, as if someone was going to snatch it from him.

13
The remaining few

A book on socialism that the "Communist Alliance" kept in secret was found and taken away by the officers. Most of us in the section were to be investigated. Upon that, the Alliance held an emergency meeting and decided to have Jian Liangnan volunteer to the sergeant that the book belonged to Daoxiong. They also agreed to have Daoxiong take on all the consequences.

For revealing that, Jian Liangnan was treated well by the officers and given a few days off work. On the other hand, Daoxiong was hauled out several nights in a row to be interrogated. When he was sent back to the dormitory at midnight, he was always trembling and wetting himself.

"Xiaokang, you're going to get Daoxiong killed," I protested to Zhu Xiaokang in a low voice.

Zhu Xiaokang kept a dignified look as he repeated himself, "We have no choice but to sacrifice one person for everyone. It's about damage control."

Shi Baixing leant over and interjected, "This is irresponsible talk. You are the ones who want to be heroes. So why, when you mess things up, you send a minion to die in your stead? Weren't you so adamant at the outset about not joining if you're afraid to die?"

At that moment, the whole corridor reverberated with Daoxiong's painful howls. Every night, when he was hung up by the toilet at the end of the corridor and interrogated, we could hear clearly the sound of the cane on his flesh.

"It's our fault. Let me think of a solution," said Xiaokang.

I didn't know what solution Xiaokang came up with. Later, I heard that Xiaokang had to bring out his gold watch, a memento from his mother, to trade for Daoxiong's life.

But this might not have been all.

Once when we were bathing in the creek, he took a long step over a large rock, half crouching. As he bent over to pick up the towel that had slid off, I vaguely saw his anus. It was severely red and swollen.

Daoxiong was in tears when I questioned him. Steadying his trembling voice, he told me, "They told Xiaokang to crouch down and suck them off one by one. And then they had Xiaokang turn around and let them take turns penetrating him."

"In front of you?"

"Yeah. I was hanging mid-air and watching. They ordered me to keep my eyes open," Daoxiong said, fear in his face, "Don't ever let Xiaokang find out that you know."

"He warned me that if this got out, he'd kill me." Daoxiong began weeping again.

Soon, Zhu Xiaokang and I were appointed to the meals committee. Zhu Xiaokang was elected by the group; I got my post by writing for the senior officers, things like "reflections on 'The Precepts for Soldiers'", various essays and reports, and all kinds of congratulatory messages on the President's birthday.

The meals committee was responsible for purchasing fresh foods for the squadron's meals.

Xiaokang and I most often bought fish. Every day, we went to the seaside to wait for the fishing boats to return, and from the fishermen we bought freshly-caught fish, such as swordfish, flying fish, rudderfish, skipjack, batfish, whitebait, tuna, grouper, sailfish, yellowfin, and mahi-mahi. Everything was 1.5 *yuan* for a kilogram, a superb bargain. Every squadron's meals committee members pretty much all waited by the sea at the same time, ready to spring on the bargains. Occasionally we also bought beef, mutton, venison, and pork, or farm produce such as peanuts and sweet potatoes; even though we grew our own vegetables and kept our own pigs, there weren't enough for all of us.

If the goods were wrapped in old newspaper, Xiaokang would ask the hawkers to wrap them in a few more layers. On the way back, we would pore over the newspaper-wrappers and memorise a few important news items, to pass along to our teammates either orally or in writing. Sometimes in the rubbish pile by the sea there were also newspapers that had been thrown out; we watched out for those and collected them as well.

Buying farm produce took a different route to buying fish. Every so often, at daybreak, we would have to go along the stream on the east side of the camp up to the flat fields on top of the hill.

It was a beautiful trail, one rarely used. The light mist of the morning veiled us. Wild grasses and trees, covered in dew, sparkled in the morning light. Strands of silver light danced upon the jade-green sea. The line where the sea met the rising sun continued onward into a long strip of fields and clouds. We breathed in the delightful fresh air, running joyfully through this open land.

After passing through a stalactite cave, we came to the path turning uphill towards the hilltop. We climbed to the highest point. From there, we could see Orchid Island, forty nautical miles away. Sometimes, we looked towards the bottom of the hill, watching the waves crashing against strange rock formations. The sharks swimming around the current looked like tiny specks.

I asked, "Can you swim back to Taiwan from here?"

Xiaokang answered, "Not sure."

I asked again, "Can you swim to Orchid Island?"

Xiaokang said, "Let's try it."

We never did. We just thought about it, talked about it all the time.

Walking downhill from the highest point southward down to the seaside, one would pass by a hot springs village. It was not a place that inmates could normally visit; we were privileged to do so. But we had no time to soak in the hot springs—we quickly bought a hog, then worked on carrying this hundred-and-eighty-pound animal over the hill and back to the camp.

There were many ways to cook pork: red-cooked, braised, steamed with rice flour, stewed as meatballs, stir-fried with spring onions, minced and steamed with chopped pickles, sliced and served with mashed garlic... Besides shopping for the ingredients, I also often went to the kitchen to direct or take the place of the mess cooks. The fruits of my labour first went to the senior officers. Once they got addicted, we would have more opportunities to go out and buy meat to supplement everyone else's meals.

* * *

In the height of summer, the heat was unbearable. There were flies everywhere, in the kitchen, in the dormitory, more numerous than in any other season. One day, Captain Tian found a fly in his food. He summoned the mess cook and questioned him over it. The mess cook replied, "There are just too many flies. They're all buzzing and flying above the woks. Probably one of them accidentally fell into the hot oil, got fried and couldn't fly out."

From that day on, the squad was put on a "fly-swatting exercise". Every one of us had to turn in a hundred flies every day.

But besides swatting flies, we also had to keep up with our regular labour. No one wanted the extra work, so someone put out a dead rat to attract flies. However, the stink of the rotting rat drove us all mad. Another person had the idea of rolling grains of rice into small balls, then dyeing them black and sticking them in with the real flies to make up the number. But the inspectors were shrewd enough to pick up the flies one by one to smell. In this way they caught quite a few phoney flies. Xiaokang and I, on the other hand, took advantage of our shopping duties. We detoured to the rubbish collection site by the sea and collected the dead flies we had dumped there the previous day. We reused these flies for our quota, and if we had any extras, we shared them with everyone. From collecting flies and newspaper articles, Xiaokang and I became well-respected individuals in the squadron.

Autumn had not visited in a long time. I had to rely on everyone else for spending money and daily essentials. Xiaokang's mother had only visited once; after giving up the gold watch for redeeming Daoxiong, Xiaokang had nothing more either. We could only get by through keeping the peace in the unity of the group.

But the peace did not last very long. We only had a short breathing space before a new wave of trouble arose. This time, it was beyond anybody's power to stem it.

It was about Supervisor Ma. He disappeared. At the evening count, the captain questioned us one by one, but no one knew where he went.

That evening, all the officers and all the inmates of the Third Brigade were assembled urgently.

The commander ordered, "You must find him, even if it means turning the island upside-down!"

Even the ordinary people on the island were mobilised to aid in the search.

Someone reported seeing a man by the seaside acting furtively, like he was going to steal a boat.

An islander reported to an officer that he lost a small sampan.

We each had a torch in hand. The entire island was lit up brightly. But our search turned up nothing.

The next day, a secret tunnel was discovered. Near the chicken coop where Supervisor Ma worked, concealed in a gap in the hillside, a tunnel was dug into the dirt. The captain sent someone down. It led to a rock cave by the shore.

"And the anti-Communist volunteer goes back to the Communists," Shi Baixing scoffed, with a forlorn expression on his face, while whittling a toothpick with a piece of metal from a tin-can. He stuck the newly-crafted toothpick in his mouth and dug around. "So, we're now all his accomplices, guilty of not having kept a close watch on the anti-Communist volunteer."

Very soon, the piece of tin-can that Shi Baixing was using to shave and to whittle toothpicks was confiscated. All our other make-shift supplies—such as the sewing needles made of copper thread, hooks made of bent wire, ear-picks carved out of pieces of bamboo, ropes woven from the fibres of shellflower leaves—were all discovered and taken away. The section's dormitory was searched thoroughly. They also encouraged the inmates to inform on each other; else, the entire group would be punished for being accomplices of anyone who was found to be hiding prohibited items, or for withholding information.

There were always a few in the section who were weak-willed or who only cared about self-preservation. They most readily complied with this new policy. After Supervisor Ma's escape, the strength in solidarity of the "Communist Alliance" disintegrated. The officers only had to warn everyone that this was a serious investigation and everyone would think of only saving themselves. No one could spare a thought for solidarity. Inevitably, such a situation created informants. Some did it out of hope of a commutation of their sentence; others were loyal to the Kuomintang in the first place, and though they were incarcerated for trumped-up charges, they hoped to regain the trust of the party by informing. They might not have intended to harm others, but as soon as you informed on someone, you had to tell a complete story, even if you only knew a few bits and pieces. Embellishments were unavoidable. And the extent that embellishments went was beyond anyone's control.

"We have to be careful. There could be snitches in here."

Zhu Xiaokang and Shi Baixing already started to be vigilant. During the raid on the dormitory, Jian Liangnan hid a newspaper that we had been circulating underneath a bed on the other side of the room, when the soldiers were looking the other way. Zhu Xiaokang noticed that another inmate was watching Jian Liangnan's every move. Right away he took a swipe at him.

That strike served its purpose of intimidation. No one told on anyone to the sergeant. However, for hitting the sneak, Xiaokang was made to wear handcuffs and shackles for three months. Every day in those three months, he could only walk with his back bent over; he could not stand up straight.

No one knew how Supervisor Ma managed to dig the tunnel. The teammates on his work team were interrogated individually; some were hung up by the toilet and beaten. But not even with several days of beatings did any answer emerge.

"It's too uncanny. If there's only a whiff of a clue, we could at least make up a story to dupe them, and not get beaten so badly," people said. Such a long tunnel was not just two or three days' of digging. But no one had seen him dig. And even if he had an hour or so of time alone on a daily basis, there was no way he could dig this fast.

The investigation never got anywhere, and the production team's tools for daily farm work became strictly-controlled items as well. We had no way of even digging a small hole in the ground.

A discovery was finally made when I switched to Supervisor Ma's bunk.

It was the bed board. One of the planks was not nailed down, and could be lifted up from beneath. I supposed that he was crawling under the bed to look for something or to put something away, when he hit the board with his head and felt it move. Perhaps he looked up from the dark space beneath the bed, or perhaps he just took out the board in order to fix it—either way, that was how he saw the words on the bottom side of the board.

Words written in blood. A few dozen signatures followed.

The content was basically this: Angry at their wrongful conviction, they dug a tunnel together at a certain hidden spot, intending to use it to escape. However, before they had the chance to use the tunnel, they were suddenly notified that they were drafted into a task force sent to fight the CCP at some outlying island. After the notification, they were given only a little time to pack their things before they were to be sent away. Not expecting to survive the mission, they hurriedly removed the bedboard, bit their fingertips to draw blood and with it drew the location of the tunnel they so painstakingly made, to be left as a gift to future inmates.

I recognised one of the names. It was Autumn's husband, the attendant who tore the President's anus.

I did not reveal the matter underneath the bedboard to anyone, in case it would cause another raid on our room.

* * *

Xiaokang revealed to me that his father was a real Communist. His father built a secret armed base.

"My father was originally going to lead a unit to go destroy the KMT's armoury. They shut the water gate at the head of the canal, then everyone advanced stealthily along the dried waterway, planning to attack under the cover of the night. Unfortunately, the reinforcement supposed to meet up with them chickened out at the last minute, and even informed on them. So, their plan was exposed..." Xiaokang's handcuffs and shackles were removed that day. The officer warned him that if he repeated the offence the punishment would be doubled. Xiaokang stretched out his back, watched the officer walk away, then suddenly told me in a proud voice that the Communists would liberate Taiwan very soon, and his father could claim most of the credit.

"I thought... your family was framed, like us..."

"Framed? What's wrong with being a Communist? I don't accept their trumped-up charges. Only a totalitarian nation would deny its citizens the freedom to join other political parties." Xiaokang looked at me, and chuckled mysteriously, "My dad is a Communist. Maybe yours is too. The only difference lies in whether or not you have the balls to admit it."

Xiaokang originally had no idea that his father was a Communist. His mother only told him before she remarried. At first, he had been proud of his father's rank and achievements in the Kuomintang, and was full of resentment at his family's arrest. Discovering that his father was a Communist actually took away his sense of indignation and guilt. "There's no need to be loyal to this kind of party. The Kuomintang deserves to be beaten! My dad was right."

Xiaokang's optimism was either excessive or premature. Occasionally he got too flippant for his own good, which inevitably led the prison guards to teach him another lesson. Once, a prison officer came to inspect the rooms. As soon as he turned around, someone suddenly blew a raspberry behind him. The officer turned around and demanded, "Who was that? Step up!" No one admitted to it. Right then, Xiaokang was on his bunk and getting ready to sleep. Although he did not knew who did it, he did not keep his mouth shut either. When the officer came up to question him, he chuckled and said, "What's wrong with that?"

This time, they pushed Xiaokang face down onto the floor, and, holding him down, grabbed his hands and feet together, and wrapped a rope around his wrists and ankles several times. They tied the rope tightly, and under the knot they inserted a pole. Two guards lifted the pole from either end and carried Xiaokang into the corridor. In the middle of the corridor stood the officer. He pushed Xiaokang back and forth like a swing. Xiaokang was facing down, hogtied and held up with just a single knot. He swung and swung like an overladen basket;

his face was puffed and fire-red, and his eyes were bulging so much they looked like they would burst out from their sockets. They swung him in this manner for another half an hour before releasing him. Then, they put a few sets of handcuffs and shackles on him, hung a few rounds of heavy chains around his neck. They paraded him around the prison with this set of equipment weighing a few stones.

Only a few months later was Xiaokang relieved of his "heavy equipment". He was seriously ill then, and had appendicitis. There were no medical supplies in the team. Seeing that Xiaokang's was on the verge of death, a cellmate who had been a veterinarian before his incarceration mobilised everybody in the room to manufacture surgical equipment.

Scalpels made of sharpening pieces of a tin can.

Cotton thread unravelled from a shirt.

Needles made from the copper wires in a cable.

Xiaokang kept his life. He recovered slowly, and became taciturn. One day, we passed by a mass grave by a ravine. That was where the inmates who died on the island were buried. He pointed at a hillock off to the other side, and proclaimed suddenly,

"If I die, I don't want to be buried with those people. You must dig me up and bury me on the other side. From over there I will be able to see home."

I patted him on the shoulder, "Don't give up. Rather than being buried here, we should just go home. We will definitely be able to go home." But when I said that, I was not certain in the least if I could leave this volcanic isle as a living man. I even picked out another hillock and secretly told Shi Baixing,

"If I die, bury me over there. From there I can see my home."

Not long after, on a grey and rainy day, Captain Tian suddenly came with his troops and herded us to the base of the hill at the end of the beach. There was a cave there, with a narrow entrance. We were forced to enter the cave, one by one; those who were not moving fast enough were pushed along harshly by the barrel of a rifle.

We crammed inside the pitch-black cave, our hair standing on end. Only when our eyes grew accustomed to the darkness did we realise that the cave was very spacious inside, able to accommodate hundreds of people. We huddled inside, shoulder against shoulder, back against back, occasionally feeling the chilly and bitter wind blowing in from the sea.

A group of armed guards stood outside the cave, not letting us out.

"What are they going to do?"

A secret massacre, kill us in one fell swoop?

Mow us down with gunfire? Release poison gas?

Burning is faster.

Everyone suggested their conjectures, helplessly waiting for them to act. My only regret was that, if I were to die in this cave, I would never see my home again.

From dawn to dusk, nothing stirred outside.

The guards, blocking the entrance of the cave with their rifles pointed in, were completely stationary.

Some of us could hold it no more, and relieved themselves right where they stood. This meant our death would be even less dignified, as our bodies would start to stink even earlier—I had already given up on the illusion of dying intact. I also urinated where I stood. Better to die in my own urine than to soak in someone else's.

We felt a whole day had passed.

We couldn't keep standing anymore, but there was no place to sit down either. So we stood leaning against one another, the anxious torture of waiting for death apparently relieved by commiseration and mutual support.

Some noise came from outside. The guards suddenly raised their rifles and pointed them at us.

"Go! Hurry up!"

The few men closest to the entrance of the cave walked out, with the guards' rifles pushing at them.

The guards waved their rifles impatiently, continuing to rush the people inside to move faster.

"Hurry up and go out. Don't make a noise!"

We filed out of the cave, and followed the military police down the dark path in the night, our hearts in our mouths, our minds full of questions.

Where are we going? No one knew.

Until we caught sight of a few flickers of lamplight not far away. We then passed by the guard posts, and entered through the familiar metal gates.

We arrived at our quarters. We had not had a bite for the whole day, but no one dared to ask for a meal. All we could do was to go to bed, hungry but full of misgivings.

It was only a few days later when someone picked up a newspaper from the rubbish pile by the sea that we found out what happened. American journalists had come to report on the prison. The prison kept the healthy and obedient inmates behind for show, and the rest, people who looked like they could be trouble, were herded to the cave and hidden, to be let out only after the Americans had left.

"If I ever get out, I'll let the Americans know the truth."

"Don't be silly. The Americans are in cahoots with the KMT. Probably someone got out and complained, and so they sent someone here to poke their head in and remind the KMT not to be an embarrassment to them."

"America is enemies with the Soviets, and the Soviets are in cahoots with the CCP. If it weren't for the Korean War, why would America bother with sending troops to protect Taiwan..."

"Careful. Don't say too much." Shi Baixing waved his hand in disapproval, in a rare moment of seriousness. "No matter what, we must pass through this period of time safely, even if it means we have to be forever silent."

Everyone fell quiet.

* * *

In April 1965 came a sudden summons, listing a few dozen names, instructing us to pack up our belongings immediately. We looked at each other knowingly; there was no mistake about what was going on.

Before we were due to depart, at my suggestion the group pried loose a bed board together. We bit our fingertips and with the blood we wrote down our last words and our names on the back of the board. Before dawn broke, we waved goodbye to the sick and weak left behind, and were escorted to the shore and onto a landing craft

Upon reaching the Zuoying Naval Base in Kaohsiung, we were

assigned to the naval special operations unit, where we underwent intense military training.

On 30 July, the vessels *Taikang* and *Zhangjiang* arrived in the port. However, upon inspection, the *Taikang's* sonar capsule was found to be damaged from a previous mission, and it was deemed impossible to repair it in time. On 3 August, the *Jianmen* arrived to replace the *Taikang*.

At 0000 hours on 5 August, all personnel were ordered to board the *Jianmen* (PCE-65) and the *Zhangjiang* (PC-118) and prepare for departure. At 0600, the ships left Zuoying Pier and sailed towards Dongshan Island. Most of those from the 9th Squadron of the 3rd Brigade, including Zhu Xiaokang, Shi Baixing, Du Daoxiong, Jian Liangnan, and myself, were assigned to the larger ship, the *Jianmen*, while Wu Yaobang, Hong Yucheng, and some others were assigned to the *Zhangjiang*, the smaller vessel.

This mission was codenamed "Tsunami Number One". We found out much later that our mission was to carry out a special operation under the direction of the Intelligence Bureau of the Ministry of National Defence, as part of Project National Glory, a secret government project. We were to transport special forces to Dongshan Island to gather intelligence, and to destroy Communist radars and capture PLA soldiers if the opportunity arose.

On the *Jianmen* was the commander of this operation, Rear Admiral Hu Jiaheng of the 2nd Fleet of the Naval Defence Command. The vessel was captained by Commander Wang Yunshan. I was assigned to serve in the telecommunications room because of my knowledge of Morse. At 1513, the battle supervisory team suddenly contacted the commander with the message that the Zuoying Naval Communications Station had just intercepted a report from a Communist radar station. They had already discovered unspecified targets on the ocean, which they conjectured to be American ships.

Admiral Hu pondered for a moment after hearing that.

By 2300, we were approaching Mainland waters. We stayed on a south-westerly course. At this time, the radar showed that an uncommonly large number of fishing boats were gathering between Dongshan Island and Nan'ao Island.

The captain conferred quietly with the admiral. The only words we heard from the admiral: Proceed as planned.

At 0000 hours on 6 August, we changed course for due north. When we were 3.5 nautical miles southeast of Xiongdi Island, the captain ordered the vessel to decrease speed and for the rubber boat to be readied. Seven commandos in PLA disguise were lowered onto the water in a M-2 rubber boat.

At 0029, the supervisory team sent another message regarding the information the Naval Communications Station intercepted from the Communist radar station. The enemy had already identified the unknown targets as Taiwanese vessels the *Jianmen* and the *Zhangjiang*. They had discovered our tracks. The admiral looked grim and did not reply. He only ordered the *Jianmen* to stay on alert, and the *Zhangjiang* to prepare for battle. By now, it was visible on the radar that among the slower-moving fishing boats were some faster vessels. They were closing in on us.

At 0148, the two sides exchanged fire. Communist torpedo boats advanced towards us rapidly. When we were less than 300 metres away from them, several personnel on the bridge and the battle stations were shot.

They first concentrated their attack on the *Zhangjiang*, the smaller vessel. The *Zhangjiang* was under fire from six torpedo boats.

The *Jianmen* rushed to the rescue, fending off the torpedo boats with her 3" guns.

Round one. The Communist attack failed.

But it did not take long for them to regroup and come within a hundred metres of us. The *Zhangjiang* suddenly about-turned into a collision course with the Communist corvette. Apparently they tried to sink the smaller ship by ramming into it. However, the corvette was small and agile, and dodged the attack.

Immediately, four other corvettes closed in and fired at the *Zhangjiang*. Their shots all hit the *Zhangjiang* below the waterline. The *Jianmen*, upon receiving the alert signal from the *Zhangjiang*, sped away eastward into a safer area.

Messages came in one after another through the wireless. The *Zhangjiang* was hit and caught fire. As she was retreating, a few torpedo boats caught her up and engaged her at close range. The *Zhangjiang* was hit over and over again...

At 0310, we lost contact completely with the *Zhangjiang*.

The admiral ordered the Jianmen to search for her immediately.

However, it was pitch black over the ocean, and the *Zhangjiang* was nowhere to be found.

At 0336, the radar showed that six enemy gunboats were advancing rapidly towards us. Three other gunboats were approaching us from another direction.

When we were 11,000 metres apart, the admiral ordered us to snipe them with the 3" guns.

Very soon, we hit one of the targets.

When we were at 7,200 metres, the admiral ordered the 20mm guns and the 40mm guns to join the attack. At once, gunshots resonated in the sky, covering it in a wide net of fire.

But the enemy boats did not return fire at all. Instead, the radar showed that they increased their speed.

Report: "Ammo at 50 percent."

"Keep firing. We can't let them get close!"

The admiral had HQ telegraphed for further instruction, while ordering all ships to employ evasive manoeuvre and to increase the distance from the enemy. Larger naval vessels were better suited for mid- and long-range fighting, and were severely handicapped in close-quarter battle.

"This is unusual. So many torpedo boats swarming at us," remarked Captain Wang.

"The *Zhangjiang* was lost in duty," Rear Admiral Hu suddenly stated gravely.

"Should we withdraw?" asked the staff officer standing beside him.

"General Staff HQ will reply soon. There'll still be time to leave then..."

The admiral ordered another urgent message to be sent to HQ.

At 0420, there was still no response from HQ. Enemy vessels were less than 180 metres away and began firing all guns at us. We did our best to fight back.

But the *Jianmen*'s gunwales were too high. Once the enemy torpedo boats came right up next to us, they would hide in the blindspot of our guns. Troops on the deck were being gunned down mercilessly. Our casualties were mounting rapidly. The *Jianmen* began to evade eastward at full speed while returning fire. One of the bright dots on the radar vanished. We hit another target. But the other dots only kept closer on us.

Report: "Fifteen percent ammo remaining."

"We're running out of ammo. Can't we make the decision ourselves to withdraw?" the staff officer asked in an agitated tone.

"We fight to the last moment. This is the duty of a soldier. We cannot retreat," said the admiral.

"You're planning to sacrifice the whole ship," the staff officer became even more agitated.

"We're almost out of ammo. We can't outrun the torpedo boats. It's all or nothing now," said Captain Wang.

At 0457, three torpedo boats, covered by corvettes, kept on the *Jianmen*'s heels. The telegraph room intercepted a message from an enemy ship: "25 cases of 25 mm ammo fired". Before I managed to report this to the admiral, the spare ammo box at the battle station in front of the bridge was hit. There came a huge *boom*. Then I saw Admiral Hu, a mess of blood and flesh, dead. Captain Wang was also covered in blood from the explosion, his entrails sliding out from his torn abdomen.

Captain Wang ordered someone to help him back on the bridge, and continued to direct the battle.

At 0521, the radar showed five torpedo boats joining the battle area. I only remember the last message we intercepted in the telegraph room: "The torpedo boats shot ten torpedoes in total, three hit the stern of the *Jianmen*."

Amidst a chain of explosions, the Jianmen began tilting to one side.

I caught on fire, and barely managed to dive into the sea before an even bigger explosion.

A great ball of flames lit up upon the sea, now littered with numerous corpses and bits of corpses.

I saw Captain Wang and the staff officer floating nearby. Captain Wang appeared to be unconscious. His safety vest had been blown to pieces, and his guts had drifted out of his abdomen and were floating on the water. A seaman was trying hard to prop up the captain's head and neck, to prevent water from going into his nose. Apart from them, there were at least fifty or sixty other survivors bobbing about on the open sea.

The Communist speedboat was nearing us. I swam away with all my might, and soon came across Zhu Xiaokang. Holding onto a plank that he had retrieved from the ship, we swam and swam eastward. A fishing vessel was coming our way on a rescue mission. We gritted our teeth and kept swimming, as if all Hell was behind us. When we turned around to look, we saw the soldiers who were bobbing about scooped out of the water one by one by the Communists...

The *Jianmen* was sunk. A blazing ball of fire, it was swallowed by the sea. Captain Wang and other wounded men who fell into the sea were captured by the Communists, and only eleven—including Zhu Xiaokang and myself—were rescued.

I remember lying immobile in the fishing boat. As day broke, we saw four white lines in the skies. They said that our Air Force sent four F-100s to the waters around Dongshan Island on a rescue mission... But by this time, there was only a frightful mess on the surface of the sea; only half-burnt bits of flotsam remained.

We were unconscious for most of the day. That evening, the radio on the fishing boat picked up a news broadcast from the Mainland: "The PLA's Shantou-South China Sea Fleet mobilised yesterday evening and intercepted Taiwanese vessels raiding under the cover of the night, in the waters between Dongshan Island and Nan'ao Island. The fleet sank two Taiwanese submarine chasers, the *Zhangjiang* and the *Jianmen*, respectively at 24.7 and 38 nautical miles southeast of Dongshan Island. The fleet also shot dead 357 enemy personnel, including Rear Admiral Hu Jiaheng, commander of the Taiwanese naval fleet, and Lieutenant-Commander Li Zhun, captain of the *Zhangjiang*. Thirty-four officers, including Commander Wang Yunshan, captain of the *Jianmen*, were taken captive. Another 170 men are still unaccounted for. On our side, only two torpedo boats were hit. Sources indicate that Taiwan was attempting to deploy seven commandos via Dongshan Island to the Mainland. The *Jianmen* was the flagship of this convoy.

As a deceptive manoeuvre, the Taiwanese flotilla sailed on a detour via the commercial shipping route to Hong Kong. However, before they even crossed the Taiwan Strait Meridian, they were discovered by the PLA's radar station at Qingshan..."

The Naval Battle of August 6th, the battle on which was hung the nation's leaders' hope for recovering our lost land, was a very short one, lasting all of three hours and forty-three minutes. For the next three days, there was nothing else on the front pages of every Taiwanese newspaper. The boatman showed us a newspaper article. It wrote, "The fleet fought valiantly and killed numerous enemy combatants in the battle. Unfortunately, our ships were hit by enemy guns and torpedoes, and almost a thousand troops gave their lives in the line of duty. Only five men survived and were rescued from the battle. The Minister of National Defence announced that all soldiers who fell in battle will be honoured in the National War Memorial..."

The official list of survivors did not include Zhu Xiaokang or me.

"Officers only. No convicts." Zhu Xiaokang scanned through the newspaper carefully, and confirmed that our names were not in there. "Hah, hah, after all, it's too much for them to admit to having us political prisoners accused of being Communists, help them fight the Communists."

"But they did count all the convicts in among those who 'gave their lives in the line of duty.'" I said.

"Even if you count in all the convicts, the number is still inflated. Doubled, in fact," Xiaokang snickered. "Perhaps they thought the massacre wasn't bloody enough? A thousand troops dying for their nation? How terribly epic."

Soon after that, Zhu Xiaokang, myself, and a group of newly-arrived prisoners were sent to a nearby island to boost the defences there. For a few days in a row, we heard gunshots from the direction of the beach. One day, while it was our turn on patrol, Zhu Xiaokang and I sensed something moving on the sea. The squad leader lifted his gun and took aim at a few black figures.

"Don't shoot! We're escapees! We're not the enemy!" One of the figures yelled.

I saw them clearly. It was Jian Liangnan speaking, and with him were a few others from the *Jianmen*. Jian Liangnan, who did not know how to swim, had draped himself over a bloated corpse for floatation, and was paddling hard with his hands.

Those in the front came ashore and lay on the beach, gasping for breath. One of them waved to us, beckoning to us to go over and help. The squad leader walked over and shot one of them without uttering a word.

"No! We really are from the *Jianmen*! We swam for a long time and..." And the second one was shot.

Zhu Xiaokang and I rushed forward to stop him. His gun was pointed at Jian Liangnan. The rest of those who were coming ashore were all held at gunpoint by the guards. "They're really our own guys who made it back..." Before Zhu Xiaokang had finished, the squad leader fired.

He turned around and pressed his gun against Zhu Xiaokang. "Finish off the remaining few, or I'll be finishing you off. And the same to you—" He turned and pointed his gun at me, urging me to shoot.

"Why?" Zhu Xiaokang grunted.

"They've been sent to the War Memorial already. How can they be alive?" The squad leader said with disdain.

"They were either captured or just missing in action. They didn't die..."

"Nobody said anyone was captured, or anyone went missing, or anyone escaped. Except for the few who were rescued, they all 'gave their lives in the line of duty'. Shoot now!"

A few gunshots resounded over the ocean.

Daoxiong was swimming up last. As soon as he lifted his head out of the water—as soon as he recognised me and smiled—a bullet shot out from Zhu Xiaokang's gun.

* * *

"... The *Jianmen* was originally an Auk-class minesweeper in the U.S. Navy. The U.S. gave her to us, and our navy refitted her to be a gunboat. She's 222 feet long, with a beam of 32.2 feet and a displacement of 890 long tons. At full load she's 1,250 tons. Dual-shaft diesel engine, running a maximum of 3,530 horsepower and a top speed of 14 knots. She's fitted with top-notch armaments: two 3"/50 calibre guns, two 40mm guns, and two 20mm guns. In terms of anti-submarine weaponry, she's got a Hedgehog, two K-guns, a three-tube torpedo launcher, two depth charge tracks, a radar...

"The *Zhangjiang* was also originally an American submarine chaser. She's got a displacement of 280 long tons, 450 long tons at full capacity. Max speed 20 knots. She's got five 20mm guns, one 40mm gun, one 76.2mm gun, four depth charge tracks, a 76.2mm rocket, and a radar... The Mainland's torpedo boats are P-4s and P-6s from Russia, 63.3 feet long, with a beam of 12.1 feet. Each boat is fitted with two twin-mounted 37mm guns, two twin-mounted 25mm guns, and has a max speed of 55 knots. Then there's the Type 062 gunboat..."

Back on Green Island, Zhu Xiaokang and I, along with an assortment of personnel from other brigades, were put together in one dormitory. Everyone sat around Zhu Xiaokang and me, wanting to hear about the Naval Battle of August 6th, about the specs of the military vessels. Zhu Xiaokang tried to satisfy them by briefly talking about the event, and describing some of the basic naval knowledge we got from our training. I, on the other hand, did not feel like saying anything.

They must have understood that Zhu Xiaokang and I were hiding something. At the very least, the newspapers picked up by the seaside did not mention our survival. Unwilling to let the matter rest, the crowd kept asking questions.

"Just be glad that they got back alive. They'd get in trouble for saying too much..."

This cellmate, nicknamed Black Pine, who had participated in a naval exercise four years ago, spoke up on our behalf, beseeching everyone else to stop pressing us. He himself, though, shared his experience in the "Success 1" exercise of 1961.

"I remember it was the 24th of June that year. I was in the Marine Corps, and we held a landing drill at Taoziyuan near Zuoying. We knew that the President was coming to watch us, so we all took the drill seriously. No one dared slack off. That day, the waves were abnormally high. But no matter how strong the winds and the waves were, our amphibious landing crafts were ordered to launch, one by one. Five in a row went on the water and capsized in the waves. But the President was watching us from the platform. As long as he said nothing, no one dared to stop the drill. Seeing that the next boat, and each boat after it, would be sent to the same fate, an officer from the American advisory group stepped forward. He yelled something at my commanding officer. I didn't understand English, but then I saw him suddenly jump into the sea. The American was trying the best he could to keep swimming, to save our guys. And so we were forced to cut short the drill. Almost everyone in the five landing crafts died. I was a soldier in the sixth craft, getting ready to launch into the water...'

Black Pine sighed, "There are many things that you can't talk about because they'd damage the national image. Isn't that so, kiddos?" Saying that, he patted Zhu Xiaokang and me on our shoulders.

On 15 November, we secretly circulated half a sheet of newspaper that we found by the sea. It said that there was another naval battle on the 14th. The Nationalist Army sent the *Shanhai* and the *Linhuai* from Magong towards Wuqiu; the *Linhuai* was sunk by twelve CCP speedboats; in the heroic battle, all hands were lost.

On 22 November, the newspaper reported that the navy had a 10,000-strong welcoming party at the Zuoying base the previous day, to celebrate the glorious return of the heroes of the naval battle. Mai Bingkun of the *Linhuai* and leader of the Southern Patrol, and Zhu Puhua of the *Shanhai* were cheered on by the crowds on either side of the road.

A few days later, Zhu Xiaokang was sent to buy sweet potatoes and peanuts from the village. He overheard a Communist broadcast on the radio from a villager's house: In Taiwan, Captain Mai Bingkun of the *Linhuai* and Commander Zhu Puhua of the *Shanhai* were court-martialled by the Kuomintang for their losses in the naval battle.

Zhu Xiaokang threw away the two old newspaper pages that were still being passed around.

"Ridiculous". That was how he described to me how he felt about it.

And a few more days later, another teammate heard the news when he went to the seaside to buy a hog—the CCP had released all the officers and soldiers captured from the *Jianmen*, and all who wished to return could do so. The Ministry of National Defence had already sent boats to the territorial waters in the Kinmin area to pick them up... Yet another teammate, who, when queuing up to buy fish, heard Shi Baixing in a Mainland broadcast announcing to the Taiwanese people that he was treated well by the CCP when he was captured, and that after he recovered from his injuries he decided to stay on the Mainland willingly, and that Taiwanese people should let go of their preconceived notions...

* * *

Before the end of 1965, the political prisoners in the three divisions on Green Island were transferred gradually to the newly-built Taiyuan Prison in Taitung, back on Taiwan. The exceptions were inmates who had completed their terms but lacked a guarantor, or who, supposedly, were denied transfer to other facilities due to their special political backgrounds. And there some who were not given a clear reason. Zhu Xiaokang and myself, for example, were kept behind in order to "provide administrative assistance".

The abandoned barracks were gradually occupied by thugs deported from Taiwan. In this new environment, the political prisoners, who were the original inhabitants, became a minority group, like a school of little fish watching each other's backs in a muddy puddle, huddling close together.

In September of 1966, there were some unusual interactions among the political prisoners. They communicated more and more frequently, such as by passing notes with contact information, folded up so small that they could be swallowed easily once discovered...

However, note-passing was risky, and there was always the danger of leaving evidence behind. Thus, an alternative way was devised for passing information too complex to be communicated through passing notes. For instance, when the ringleaders needed to discuss something in detail, they would bury the information outdoors, and indicate its location with a code system. A white string, for example, represented an agreed-upon pigsty, while a black string meant a certain vegetable patch. One knot on a white string meant under the first fence pole at the pigsty, and two meant the second pole; one knot on a piece of black string meant the first patch in the field, two knots meant the second patch, and so on. If, while in the washing room in the morning, one saw that there was a white string hung on the left-hand side of some agreed-upon nook, it meant that a large amount of information was buried at the pigsty. He would then move the string to the right, to show that he received the information.

At the same time, Zhu Xiaokang asked me to teach Morse Code to everyone in the prison, so as to communicate messages converted into a phonetic spelling. Those whose bunks were on either side of the corridor could simply move their fingers along their bed-posts in short or long strokes, and the person on the opposite side could read his meaning. I also designed hidden compartments under their bed boards, and even inside the bed-posts I made for them turning drawers that were invisible from the outside. Those secret compartments were inspired by my curio box from all those years ago; things could be hidden inside them.

The group also found a way to help teammates who were handcuffed. All it took was a thin sliver of bamboo, a flat piece of aluminium, or a straightened paperclip—insert it into the keyhole, feel for the pins and push them up, turn and press, and the handcuff was off.

On top of that, someone wrote to his family asking for a simple sketching kit—including rubber erasers.

The chief organizer of all this was Zhu Xiaokang, and among the assistant organizers were Fat Cat, Black Pine, Lucky, Flathead, and Lizard. Though I had some misgivings about this attempt and did not want to be a full participant, I volunteered to provide support as needed.

Obviously, they were planning an escape!

Once, while passing through the metal gate to go outside for an activity, a few of them created a diversion. When the guard was distracted, one of them pressed a mould of the lock with the rubber eraser, so they could create a key later... I knew, too, that they had a boat hidden in a ditch by the beach.

One midnight, after the guards had gone to sleep, they made their move.

Some went in the front, and some were to stay behind. Some were responsible for carrying blankets and quilts, while others were to bring rope...

Once the gate was opened, they filed out quietly.

The group in the front doubled over and headed out first.

Another group, who had made ropes with peach tree leaves, began tying together the door handles of the officers' dorm rooms. They tied each door to the door opposite to it in the corridor, so that the officers could not open them (the doors opened inward). Then they proceeded to the exit, which they stuffed with blankets and quilts, on which they sprinkled the explosives that I had taught them to make.

The rest of them went to the entrances of the other dormitories, and packed them with blankets and explosives as well...

After that, the first group stole towards the wall.

The sentries on duty discovered them. The sirens rang loudly.

Upon hearing the sirens, the officers sprung to action. However, the officers in Dormitory 3, where we were kept, were unable to open their doors. The officers in the other dormitories were having difficulty coming out as well. All the exits were blocked with fire set by the inmates who were staying behind. The blankets caught on fire rapidly, and all the dormitories were filled with smoke. In the fray, someone managed to snatch a weapon. Some others made a dash to the wall, threw blankets and quilts over the barbed wires and quickly scaled it...

In the midst of the commotion, there came the loud roar of a

propeller. A few fighter planes were approaching. That would be the anti-riot unit...

It emerged from later accounts that only two men managed to climb over the wall. One injured his foot while he was scaling the wall, by catching it on a part of the barbed wires that was not completely covered by the blankets. Although he was able to leave the compound, the guards found him by following his trail of blood. The other one managed to escape farther. He ran to the edge of the cliff, hung a string of beer bottles around himself as a floatation device, and jumped into the sea. However, he did not drift far before the waves washed him back to the foot of the hill. The officers sent someone to go down to retrieve him. After the two escapees were brought back to jail, they were given a heavy flogging. Then they were given shovels and ordered to dig a hole. After that, they were shot on the spot, and their bodies were thrown straight into the hole. As for the rest of the escapees, the troops arrived just in time to drag them down the wall before they managed to scale over it.

Seeing that things were not going well, I ran back to my room during the confusion, and pretended to be asleep. By then, the inmates who were not part of the escape were all running out to see what the commotion was about. Shots were heard outside. I imagined that the guards had already surrounded the escapees. It would not be reasonable for me to keep pretending to be asleep in such a time.

Just as I was heading back out to join the on-lookers, Zhu Xiaokang came running in, a rock in his hands. He wanted me to hit him with it.

"Hurry and do it!" he urged me.

I couldn't.

Suddenly, he lifted the rock and knocked it against my forehead. And then, with all the strength he had, he hit his left arm with it—

My injury was not serious. With some ointment and bandaging, it would heal in a fortnight. Zhu Xiaokang, though, was in critical condition. With a bone fracture and a badly mangled wound, he had to be sent to a medical facility immediately. The vet who treated him last time had already finished serving his time and had been transferred. This time, the officers did not ignore his injuries, since we all testified that he was hit while attempting to stop his fellow inmates from escaping.

Zhu Xiaokang had always been generous to everyone around him, and as a result everyone confirmed his statement. Even those not involved in the escape would not think of contradicting his testimony. As for me, the wound on my forehead saved me from a worse fate: those who were arrested during the escape had their arms and legs tied up, their eyes blindfolded, and were taken to the dark ocean by helicopter. Those who were told on after the incident, as well as those who came under suspicion, were put in shackles and locked up in the dungeon by the sea.

Early the next morning, Zhu Xiaokang was sent back to Taiwan to be hospitalised.

There was one thing that he forgot to destroy or take away with him. Anticipating thorough searches in the days to come, I took care of it for him. It was a newspaper clipping from over two months ago, folded into a tiny square. From the flecks of salt on the clipping, it seemed that it was picked up by the seaside. The headline was eye-catching:

Former spy turns bank robber

According to the article, *a robbery case that happened at the Bank of Taiwan a few days ago had been cracked, with the suspect, Zhu Anqiao, arrested. The police, with the help of a lead, found most of the loot in sacks hidden under the bed in the house he was renting. The remaining money had been spent in the purchase of an electric kettle and a rice cooker, which were also seized by the police. According to investigations, Zhu Anqiao had formerly served jail sentence for espionage, and was released on parole for his good behaviour in jail. It was a surprise that he would commit a robbery so soon after his release. The prosecutor announced that such a hardened criminal must be punished severely. The suspect testified that his motive was to redeem his wife—she was forced to remarry someone else, who demanded a large ransom for her. The prosecutor believed that Zhu's explanation was ludicrous and that he was just making that up...*

Sometime later, we heard that Zhu Xiaokang escaped from the

hospital.

The prison guards interrogated all of us once again, but got no answers. I suddenly realised that Xiaokang had already predicted that it would be impossible to escape from jail. Therefore, he came up with a back-up plan, or even a back-up for the back-up, behind our backs, and used the chaos created by the group for his own escape.

But where would he go? Where could he go?

In that moment where he crushed his own arm, I saw an astounding calmness and loneliness in his eyes

* * *

Early in the morning of 19 November, 1969, the prison warden came and read out a list of names, mine and fourteen others. We were asked to pack up and get ready to leave at once. Handcuffed, we went down to the beach and waited to board the boat. Just like it was six years ago when we arrived, it was a landing craft, and once again we were put in the bottom of the boat, not knowing where we were to be transported.

Autumn had visited earlier in September to bring news from home. She told me happily that Chunshao had finished military service and was moving back home. After Daoxiong's death, she seemed to have taken Chunshao in as her only son, caring for his every need. She arranged for him to attend university, and worried for him when he was in the military. This was more than caring, I suppose; it was a more intimate love than that of a mother's. I asked her about Floral. She said that Floral was a very popular singer now, almost going to be more popular than Autumn herself. I had a feeling, when she said that, that she saw Floral as an unrelated colleague, and not her own daughter. Floral and I had exchanged letters every now and then. Although cipher songs could pass through prison inspection, we could only encode and decode a few lines of content at a time, and could not speak to our heart's desire. I really wanted to see Floral. I wondered what she looked like now.

This journey did not take very long. As the landing craft stopped and we walked up to the deck, we realised that this was not Taiwan, but an unfamiliar island.

Lamay Island. Word had it that if a convict had served his time but his mind-set was deemed to not have improved, he would be sent to Lamay Island to serve another period of labour. This labour was quite tedious, in an intriguing way. It was like in how the gods punished Sisyphus in Greek mythology. They would order you to carry rocks to the top of the hill, then carry the rocks back, over and over again, without purpose, without end, until you had become completely fed up with life.

Here I met a familiar face. It had been thirteen years. She had become very old, very haggard. But I recognised her right away. Chunhong. Or I should have said Lihong, Xie Lihong.

But not even Xie Lihong was her real name.

"My real name is Su Bilian."

She told me the truth, looking slightly apologetic. When she was in university, her parents were accused of being Communists, and her whole family was arrested. Unable to bear the cruel tortures in jail, she accepted the Investigation Bureau's conditions. After training, she was sent as a maid to the family of a specified person.

"They sent you to monitor us?"

I had some childhood memories of our home being monitored. But before this, all I could think of was how hardworking Chunhong was, how nice she was. Back then, Chunhong and I were as close as sister and brother, or mother and son. But now Chunhong admitted that it was her. I was shocked.

"Yes. Not just your family. Many other officials were under surveillance."

"But why did they have to monitor us?"

"It's complicated. At first, it was because they found out that your mother had joined a Communist unit in her student days, and did not declare that after she came to Taiwan. So, the authorities placed her in the Investigation Bureau under a certain director, so that she could redeem herself by monitoring that director. However, the director under surveillance then sent me to perform counter-surveillance on your mother..."

"My mother's charges had nothing to do with you?" I hoped Chunhong would deny it, because she was still the Chunhong I missed.

"I don't know, maybe... it had nothing to do with me. Chunhuan, I really did not mean to hurt you. You know that I quit monitoring your family after that. Many years after I had left, I heard that the director got involved in some infighting with another intelligence agency, because of his association with a political clique. He was framed for a crime and found guilty. And since your mother was a deputy director in the same division as him, she was numbered among his accomplices. Because I was the director's informant, I, too, was implicated and locked up for several years on his account..."

"That makes no sense! They had my mother monitor the director, and then they say she's his accomplice?"

"It seems to be two different groups of people involved at the beginning and later on. Two separate issues. At any rate, those people all have their own ulterior motives and the infighting is horrendous. One moment they're cooperating, and the next they're enemies."

I told her about Yao Kunming and Uncle Yao. She was astonished, "It's the Yaos who reported you? I would never have thought. Your families were so close."

"On the surface, it seemed like it was the Yaos. But given what you just said, it might not be that simple," I said.

"The timing of the Yaos' informing on you seems to coincide with the business with your mother... Perhaps it was just an excuse to incriminate your family even further? Or perhaps the Yaos were only instigated into doing it, since those people could prosecute anyone with any excuse? I don't know..."

I looked at this Su Bilian, such a familiar face, and yet such a stranger. I wanted to ask more questions, but held back.

There were some words that she had spoken to me many years back that remained an enigma to me. But I did not wish to find out anything more from this woman. Ah! She betrayed my family. Even though I believed that she loved me, that she might tell the truth, I really did not dare to ask...

"Actually, I wasn't the only one monitoring your family. But I don't know who sent the others."

These last few words from Su Bilian seemed to be an attempt at lessening her own guilt, but also seemed to a sincere revelation of a secret. Were there others? I shivered at the thought.

The world has gone mad!

Every day, I carried the rocks furiously up the hill and down the hill, until I had spent all my strength.

PART IV

14
The sacrificed ones

A part of our lives was torn apart by some inscrutable power. We were like a magnet that had lost its force, everything inside us was pouring out and away, and we had no strength to hold anything back. All of us—we all had something taken away from us.

In April of 1971, I was released and sent home. Home was no longer the mansion with the flower gardens, fish ponds, bamboo groves, and meandering paths. Father had relocated to a neighbourhood where nobody knew us. Even though it was just a small house with a small yard, it seemed empty with just three of us living in it. Except for not having any more guests and banquets, life at home remained the same: antiques and art, gardening and landscaping, and Autumn. The loyal Autumn came over all the time.

"We're just an empty shell now. We completely rely on Autumn for our livelihood," said Chunshao.

"Isn't Father still running a business?" I asked.

"He's just saying that to keep up appearances. He's been jobless for so many years. When I was in university, every time I came home I only saw him idling around, not doing anything. What could he do to earn a living? Father said that he has a joint business with someone else, and I know that's a lie. He doesn't let me share his burden, but he lets Autumn help him, just like he's still the master, accepting service from his servant."

"He still has quite a few antiques and paintings..."

"He wouldn't sell them. He'd rather hold onto them as a poor man than to sell them," said Chunshao.

"Exactly how poor are we now?" As soon as the words left my mouth, I regretted it. I was asking the obvious. Because of Mother and I, the government confiscated our house and dismissed Father from his position. Even if they did not take any more money from us afterward that, living must not have been easy at home.

Chunshao heaved a sigh, "I don't know. Only Father and Autumn would know. In all these years, they let me live a carefree life, like nothing had changed. But I know we had become poor long ago. How could we not, after everything that happened? Even though everything still looks normal, I feel that everything is fake. You can't look too closely. There's nothing beneath the surface. They've been hiding something from me all along..."

"Chunshao, that's because they love you. There are some things that you can't look too closely into. If they could tell you, why would they bother to hide things from you?"

"I think it's because Father had lived a life of ease for too long. He's too used to luxury and comfort. When disaster struck, he didn't try in the least to be prudent or to exercise restraint. Either he was oblivious to the situation he's in, or he was intentionally being insensitive."

I didn't know what to say to that. I was shocked that Chunshao actually begrudged Father. Was he truly resentful, or was he just feeling bad for Autumn? Or, was he jealous of Autumn's endless sacrifices for Father's sake? I felt, though, that his fault-finding was more like excuses for his discontent about losing everything. Chunshao was reluctant to part with the past. He sneaked back to see our old house several times. He told me that he half-intentionally let Uncle Yao see him. At first, Uncle Yao had a bit of a guilty look on his face, but later on he was downright sympathetic. As for the Zhus, who got in trouble almost the same time we did, there had been no news of them for a long time. Upon mentioning the Zhus, we started missing Xiaokang.

"Right, Zhu Xiaokang came to look for Father four years ago," said Chunshao.

"Zhu Xiaokang came to look for Father?"

"You might not know, but Uncle Zhu Anqiao went to rob a bank and was sentenced to death..."

"Oh no, Uncle Zhu died?" This should have been expected, but I would rather not have anyone tell me.

"You probably didn't read about it when you're inside. It's all over the papers."

I said I had read the papers. Chunshao fell silent, and after a while, he added, "I don't know what happened, but Zhu Xiaokang became wanted for murder. He's been on the run for a long time. That one time he came to visit Father, Father didn't tell me what they talked about..."

In August, Father arranged for me to continue my schooling. I became a mature student in a private secondary school where a diploma was guaranteed for anyone who could pay.

A few months later, I ran into Fat Cat, a former teammate. He told me surreptitiously that he was now with Zhu Xiaokang—a dozen or so teammates released from Green Island formed a gang, and Zhu Xiaokang became their leader.

"After we came out, we had no idea about what's going on in the world. We ran into snags everywhere and couldn't make a living anywhere. Good thing Xiaokang took care of us unemployed old good-for-nothings."

"I heard Xiaokang killed someone and is a wanted man?" It was an awkward question to ask, but I couldn't help myself.

"The arsehole was asking for it. Chunhuan, maybe you don't know..." he gnashed his teeth, his face flushing with anger. "The arsehole forced Xiaokang's mother to marry him, and extorted a large amount of money from Xiaokang's father as well. So his father was forced to rob a bank. The whole reason Xiaokang broke out of there was to kill him....

"And then, Xiaokang found a tonne of money from I don't know where, and gave it to his mother for her daily living. He himself went on the run, and he had to go look for his missing little brother as well. His brother, Zhu Xiaotian, is now with us... It's totally heart-breaking.

When Zhu Xiaotian was found by his big brother, he was all skin and bones, and sick as a dog. He was a beggar lying beside a ditch. The heartless arsehole—the special agent that Xiaokang killed—he'd lied about sending Zhu Xiaotian to an orphanage, but in reality he abandoned him by the roadside and let the kid fend for himself..."

I told him to take me to Zhu Xiaokang.

"Now I'm doubly a criminal. Even if I don't count as a bandit yet, I'm at least a hooligan." Zhu Xiaokang said in self-mockery as soon as we met up. As hard as he tried to put on the airs of a hooligan, there was still a babyish look in his expression.

"Likewise. I'm a Communist rebel who's done time, and now I'm in a school for delinquents. Because that's where I belong."

"Trying to one-up me in wickedness? Give it a rest. You're way behind me. I'm a rebel spy AND a murderer, you know," Xiaokang chuckled and slapped me on the shoulder.

We gazed silently at each other, taking in how ridiculous each other looked. I had an urge to burst out weeping.

"There's one thing that I... I really owe you." Xiaokang voluntarily told me that he went to see my father.

"I heard about that from Chunshao, but my father didn't tell him anything."

Xiaokang lit a cigarette and took a few laid-back puffs. His weathered voice drifted with the smoke toward a faraway place. "I'll come clean with you. Before my dad went to jail, he gave me two sealed letters. He told me that if I should run into trouble in the future, I should take these letters to Uncle Song and Uncle Yao. But soon I was arrested as well. I gave the letters to Xiaotian to bury beneath the wall of our old house. Once I escaped from jail, I dug up the letters, and went to your place first. Your father was very generous and gave me a large amount of money. Then, I went to Uncle Yao's. He didn't give me a lot, so soon after I went back again to ask for more. Uncle Yao wanted to take the letter from me. I wouldn't let him, so he snatched it from me and kicked me out the door. But I had made a copy in advance..." Zhu Xiaokang smirked slyly.

"Are the two letters from your dad the same?" I asked.

Zhu Xiaokang smiled and did not answer.

"What's in the letters?"

Zhu Xiaokang gazed at me with a rare dour look. "Don't ask. Like I promised Uncle Song, I burnt the letter. No one will ever see it again."

"I'm not allowed to know?"

"No. I promised him not to bring it up again. He gave me a lot of money. I gave it all to my mum. Sorry, Chunhuan."

* * *

After Chunshao was discharged two years ago, he had stayed home all the time. The proudest thing that he did happened when he was serving in the navy. There, they encountered a CCP fleet in international waters, and they dealt them a sound defeat, even chasing them past the Taiwan Strait Meridian. He had a long scar on his arm, a souvenir from a stray bullet then. The word "CCP" seemed to be a punching bag for him; every now and then he'd have to take a swipe at it, gesturing ostentatiously with his hands as he mentioned it. I never told him about my participation in the Naval Battle of August 6th—in stark contrast, our contingent was dealt a sound defeat by the CCP. Since childhood, Chunshao and I both dreamt of fighting a real battle, on a real battlefield, with real weapons, not just a child's game. Our wishes had both come true; the only difference was that one of us won, and the other lost.

In my mind, Chunshao was a noble prince, a courageous knight; but that never rubbed off on me. "Like elder brother, like younger brother" was a joke. When I stood next to him, I was always a baby brother, and nothing else.

But he certainly loved me as his dearest little brother. That was what I had always believed.

In the few months after I returned home, Chunshao showered me with attention, as if trying to make up for the eight years I was torn from the family. He really was the best big brother ever. I always remembered how, when we were children, he wrapped his arms around me and Anna together and shouted through his tears, "I won't let you die. Never ever." Whenever I thought of that, I would feel incredibly sentimental.

But soon I noticed that Chunshao had been in denial of the fact that there were two rebel spies in the family. Even though it was not true, he still felt embarrassed and ashamed of himself. Ever since I came home, he had not brought friends over, and would not mention Mother at all. Sometimes when he ran into friends when going out with me, it was as if he didn't know how to introduce me, an overaged secondary school student. He would just grab me by the shoulder, and, before even saying hello to the other person, drag me away quickly. Perhaps Chunshao wanted to protect me—that was how I explained it to myself. However, the look on his face could not fool me—it was the look of one who had been humiliated and had lost all self-confidence. He only wanted to escape, to hide far, far away.

Once, a friend of his came over to visit. It just happened that neither Chunshao nor Father was in, so I chatted with the visitor for a while. When I found out that he had served on the same ship as Chunshao, I brought up that battle they had with the CCP fleet in international waters. He did a double take, and suddenly burst out into laughter.

"Song Chunshao sure knows how to spin a yarn. Hah, hah, there was no fleet."

"Huh?"

"Our patrol boat encountered their speedboat at a distance. At first, a few of the windbags on our side shouted out all kinds of challenges, like we're going to declare war on them or something. I remember Song Chunshao yelled along with them as well. But what it was, was that our radar was broken and we didn't realise they were there. They're the ones who saw us first. They're just coming to remind us not to get too close."

"What about the scar on Chunshao's arm, then?" Unwilling to concede, I brought up the sole piece of evidence.

"That scar is even funnier. So we're calling out challenges to them over the loudspeaker, and the Communists also greeted us with a few words of warning through their loudspeaker. Song Chunshao thought we're about to engage, and he got so scared he jumped into the water. But he didn't really know how to swim. He was the worst swimmer on the team. Finally, when we fished him out of the water, he was almost on his last breath. He made that scar himself when he jumped. He didn't aim properly and hit something. He'd be fleeing as soon as he hears the Communists are coming. Fighting them off would be the last thing he would do."

I never knew this feeble side of Chunshao. He had always been so proud. I almost could not believe that he would be this faint-hearted. After that, whenever I heard him boast about the Communists, I would feel sad for him. Perhaps Chunshao was not feeble, but it's just that the word "Communist" was too frightening. Both his little brother and his mother were arrested because of it. And so he prated on about fighting the Communists, just as a way of whistling in the dark. He dared not let this word even come close to him, or have the slightest to do with him. It was the only possible explanation, even though it was insufficient to set my mind at rest; I too, was afraid, as my past had been a blemish in Chunshao's life. Our respective fearfulness pulled us apart, bit by bit.

I don't know what compelled me to tell him that I saw Mother's confession statement during my trial...

I told him that Mum was not his biological mother. The time and the age were not right. Someone acquainted with her knew that she was neither married nor pregnant at the time. He did not know me to tell lies. Seeing the agitation on his face, I felt gratified. But just for a fleeting moment. And then I felt insecure. What if she wasn't my biological mother either? I had enjoyed motherly love that was not mine to enjoy. I was like a thief, accusing another thief of being the guilty one.

"Did they mention Father? Did they say anything about Father's biological relationship to us?" Chunshao continued inquiring desperately.

"I don't know," I suddenly dodged the question, not daring to say anything more. I had torn a hole; I could not let this hole expand indefinitely. I just didn't want to listen to Chunshao whine about home, or watch him listless and apathetic like this. In my heart I screamed: "Song Chunshao, why are you still unsatisfied? In the eight years I was in jail, you enjoyed Father's full attention, became accustomed to the life of ease of an upper-class boy. You even had Autumn go help you do your laundry when you were in university. You scum, you who took all the good things and ended up a good-for-nothing! You always got to play with the dog's head, and I only ever got to pet the dog's bum. What right do you have to say this is unfair?"

I did not mean to create a lose-lose situation. But I had hurt Chunshao, and hurt myself in the process, too.

One day, Chunshao said to me, "I've had enough of these years. They let me live like an aristocrat, exactly like in the old days. But I'm scared that this empty shell will be shattered one day. He had Autumn earn money for my schooling, and Autumn was willing to do anything. She even went through the list of items that I had lost, and bought them back one by one for me. I never saw any business going on at home, but Autumn corroborated with Father's lies to make our family look respectable. She has been defending our family loyally, but I'm feeling very ashamed of myself."

I suddenly became angry, "Can't you go independent? As long as you're dependent on them, of course they'd do everything to protect you."

"I did go look for work, but with our family's history..."

"No one wanted to hire you? You could also do menial labour, do something that doesn't require status or a CV." Once I said that, I began to be angry with myself. Could I really tell Chunshao to go do menial labour? Father and Autumn for sure would not hear of it. Nor would I want things to end that way.

I did not know what to be angry at. I had once looked up to Chunshao, thinking that I would follow him like a knight following his king. But the king had fallen. As for Autumn, although her sacrifice looked so selfless and noble, there was something dodgy about it. She let Chunshao depend on her, let our family be in need of her. She would not let go. I felt that she was not sacrificing anything, but was just comfortably enjoying the fruits of her design. She was growing old. She was still beautiful, but the men who used to like her started going for the novel, pursuing Floral instead. Floral inherited Autumn's beauty for the most part; although she was not as gorgeous as Autumn was in her youth, Floral was more delicate and charming. Autumn had Floral take their money, and then she used that money from those men for keeping her own man. Meanwhile, poor Floral was only living a life of a supporting role. She fulfilled Autumn's loyalty, as an obedient sidekick. Even if Floral was also being loyal to Chunshao,

Chunshao only remembered Autumn's virtues. It was Floral who was the sacrificed one.

* * *

Zhu Xiaokang's power expanded rapidly. He and his gang, billing themselves as the "Gangsters of Green Island", were quite effective in intimidating those thugs who had never been on Green Island. He charged a fair rate, and businesses were willing to pay their protection fees to avoid trouble. His conquests were mostly hotels, cabarets, and dance halls. While he did not touch casinos, it was possible to find any other kind of entertainment through him. The hotel where Floral was engaged as a singer was within his area of protection.

"Anna was once my apprentice." Whenever he mentioned Floral, Zhu Xiaokang would calling her by her stage name. He said they had been friends for a few years. "Anna was quite talented at the trade," Zhu Xiaokang chuckled as he revealed Floral's secret.

It turned out that Floral, to avoid her life as a sing-song girl, had run away from home for a period of time. I had not known that before. Almost as soon as she left home, all her money was stolen. Without a penny to her name, she resorted to begging, living off other people's table scraps. One day, when she was starving and no one was giving her any money, she went and snatched a monk's alms' bowl from him. Instead of shouting after her, the monk walked away slowly, leaning on his staff. After this initial success, Floral itched for more. A few days later, she sneaked onto a train stopped at a station, intending to pick a few pockets during the hustle and bustle. Just as she was about to get off the train after a successful pick, a hand grabbed her and said, "Don't set your sights so low!" The man demonstrated several advanced methods of pickpocketing; every wallet he got his hands on was nice and plump. The train whistle blew, and the man, holding Floral's arm, alighted calmly. Floral thought he looked familiar—she recognised him as the monk from a few days ago, but also remembered that she had seen this person at my home when she was younger. That person was none other than Zhu Xiaokang. At that time, Zhu Xiaokang had returned to Taiwan from Green Island for medical treatment after maiming himself. He had just escaped from the hospital and had not yet gained his own gang and territory. He spent his days hiding from the police, sometimes disguising himself as a monk, sometimes as a hawker, and sometimes engaging in pocket-picking. For a while, Floral became Zhu Xiaokang's apprentice. As Zhu Xiaokang was used to taking cover under his disguises, it was a bit inconvenient to have Floral around; however, they made a good team, and committed all possible kinds of larceny together. On one operation they had got into a scrap of trouble and barely escaped arrest. He covered Floral to let her escape; he gave her some money and told her to run away as far as she could.... Zhu Xiaokang managed to get away at the end. When he eventually found Floral again, he found that she had turned into a nun.

"She couldn't make a living by herself, so she actually went to a Buddhist monastery to steal a set of robes. She shaved her head to disguise herself as a nun in order to beg for alms. What she earned from almsbegging was more than what she got as a thief..."

"Why did you come back? Weren't you able to get away from all this?" I asked Floral about what Xiaokang told me.

"My mother could not leave your family. I found that I was the same," was all Floral said.

Floral was a pretty decent singer. She earned a bit of fame for herself, and even got on the newspaper. Sometimes Zhu Xiaokang treated me to go to her concert for free, and sometimes I went on my own. When she saw me, Floral would hum a few bars of a melody for me that no one recognised. That was our own code.

When she hummed *re'* | *do   do mi* | *do do'   re do   do fa   do fa   re' do fa   ti* | *do   re mi   do   re sol* ("I am running away"), that was a secret message for me to meet her at the little hut.

Floral had a little hut. It was in the hills. That was her secret base. One day, she took me there.

Just like back when we were children, Floral led the way in the front, and turned around every now and then to give me a look, signalling for me to go this way or that. She was used to doing that, like Anna. But I did not dare to have a second Anna. I didn't want a loyal dog. I didn't want a faithful servant. If Anna could be resurrected, I would not let her be my faithful servant again. I would treat her as my best companion, and protect her forever.

I caught up with Floral, and walked beside her contentedly. Floral giggled and refused to let me walk with her. Like a monkey, she climbed up a cotton tree nearby, picked a couple of flowers, and tossed them down to me. I busied myself with catching the things that she was throwing down to me. When I missed something, she giggled even more gleefully.

The tree was blooming with vermilion-coloured flowers. Some had already produced a capsule, in which grew silky white fibres like cotton. When the breeze came, the cotton fluff dissipated in the sky, floating in tufts in the wind. Some spiralled onto the ground, while others were unravelled by the wind into long threads, blown into trees even farther away.

Floral spun around, looking all around her as if at a loss. But then, she started reaching her hands out to catch the cotton strands in the air. She waved her hands about wildly for a long time, catching nothing. I watched her under the tree; the silhouette of her crouching all alone on the tree appeared so distant.

I asked her what she was still doing up there. She said she was looking for her fairy wand.

A while later, she descended back to earth. Forlornly, she said, "The fairy wand flew away." She pointed around and showed me: This is it, and that is it too. The cotton strands, floating all around the forest, glittered in the sunlight, like a fairy wand that had disintegrated into millions of threads of gold.

No one had played the King and the Princess game with her for a long time. She promoted herself to the role of a fairy, and performed magic for herself here in the forest. She said that, if she held enough of this cotton fluff between her hands and tossed it hard into the air, it would have the same effect as waving a fairy wand.

I asked her what she wanted to conjure up by waving the fairy wand. This was the first time in a long while that I said something this childish.

"I want to conjure up something that I like," she said, while throwing her empty hands forcefully into the air.

Nothing appeared before our eyes. But perhaps the shiny cotton strands all around us were the miracle that she imagined.

Floral said, she most wanted to turn herself invisible. Not entirely invisible, though, but into thousands and thousands of cotton strands like these, each indistinguishable from another. "Those are all me. I am flying everywhere, but no one will recognise me."

I said, "Then you might as well be the Monkey King in the stories. He can pluck a handful of hair from his body and turn them into many, many copies of himself. But you'd have to do it backwards, and turn yourself into many, many strands of hair, and not let people realise that it's monkey hair." Catching Floral off her guard, I plucked a piece of hair from her arm, blew on it, and shouted into the sky, "Floral, where are you? Why are you everywhere?" Amused by this little game, Floral giggled. She did not know that I did not blow the piece of hair away, but instead tucked it under my fingernail.

An azure-coloured bird flew ahead of us, stopping on a branch every now and then to preen its feathers before flying ahead again. We parted with the bird at a fork in the trail, and turned into a little path. The narrow dirt path led to Floral's little hut. On either side, trees reached to the skies, their roots covered by a carpet of moss, lichen, and ferns, dotted with little pale-purple flowers.

In front of us was the little hut. A white mountain-cherry tree grew before it, standing out amidst the layers of greenery. Sunlight shone through the trees; colourful butterflies flittered to and fro in the spots of light. My eyes followed a few of the most beautiful butterflies. Dappled with the most brilliant blues and reds, they circled the snow-white mountain-cherry tree in a spiral dance... As I chased those flittering shapes, I felt an ineffable sense of beauty and of loss. It had been many years since I had seen something that stirred me so much. It was a luxury to be able to feel regret for something beautiful.

The hut was an abandoned work shed. After it had been tidied up inside, it became a rustic little nest.

"My mother and Chunshao used to come here," Floral told me.

She knew that Chunshao liked her mother. She used to follow them to the hut. Once, Floral forged Autumn's handwriting and invited

Chunshao here. As he walked into the hut and saw that it was Floral, he was not particularly surprised. Chunshao said, he knew Autumn's handwriting. Even though he could tell the handwriting was forged, he still wanted to come see what it was all about. Chunshao behaved very kindly towards Floral, which made her beside herself with joy. Floral told Chunshao that she had liked him for over a dozen years, that he could have both her and her mother at the same time, and that she would be satisfied just having a tiny little part of him... At the time, Chunshao neither rebuffed her nor accepted her proposal; but whenever he met her later, he acted more courteous and more distant, as if he was avoiding her.

"You've liked Chunshao for over a dozen years, but Chunshao has liked Autumn for even longer. He fell in love with her almost the first day she came to work for us," I told her regretfully.

Floral gaped at me, shocked. A long while later, she appeared to have come to terms with it. She only mumbled, "I only wanted a tiny little bit of him. I wasn't asking for all of him."

I wanted to say, I could give her my all. But the words never left my mouth.

I asked her what she was doing here.

She said, she came here originally only because she missed Chunshao. She felt satisfied just lying on this bed.

"Chunshao has slept on this bed." Floral stroked the wooden bed wistfully, saying that she had found a strand of hair on the bed, which must have belonged to Chunshao.

I asked, "Aren't you worried that you'd run into them here?"

"They won't come anymore. There are snakes around the house. Once when Chunshao got out of the bed he found a little snake crawling out of his shoe. I heard him tell my mother not to come here anymore. Chunshao is afraid of snakes. So they never came here anymore."

"Aren't you afraid of snakes? Why are you still coming?"

Floral smiled very innocently, "I cut up all the snakes that I saw. I used a large pair of iron scissors. I bet the other snakes don't dare to come here anymore after seeing all the cut up ones."

"You're still thinking about Chunshao? You can only think about him here?"

"Yeah, I guess I still think about him. But I can't think about him too much," Floral was probably trying to comfort me by pretending that she was not too sad about it. But that only made her look ridiculous.

"Anyway... this is a nice place," I tried to make conversation, not knowing what to say.

"Yeah!" In an about-turn from her wistfulness, she beamed with excitement. "This is a nice place. I come here whenever I want to run away. Also, no one ever comes here. It's great!" I saw the glow in her eye, and understood what she was saying. It was like when I sneaked into the sea for a swim on Green Island when the supervisor was not looking. It was one of those rare interludes of leisure in one's life.

Floral added, "Really, this is a great place. And it's got many great parts too."

She led me to the back of the hill. There was a stream there. We walked down to the water.

The stream was not wide. Above it was a thick canopy of interwoven branches, through which the sunlight sieved into flecks of golden sparkles. Some white and pink petals from unknown flowers floated down, covering the surface of the water. We sat side by side on the branch closest to the water and soaked our feet in the water, feeling a never-encountered sense of freedom.

I opened my arms wide joyfully and flapped them in the air, like a bird getting ready to take off.

Floral pointed at some black dots on my arm. "See, you got some leeches on you."

"There are leeches in the tree?"

Hastily I brushed the leeches off. But Floral caught them, one in each hand, and held them together so they would suck on each other.

"Haha, that's what they get for being suckers."

There were many other fun things besides leeches. Floral introduced them to me one by one. For example, there were some lettuce-like plants growing on the tree trunks. The leaves were filled with water. "Look carefully. There are many bugs inside." Floral flicked a few insect eggs from one side of the water to the other side, while I herded a pair of tadpoles over from the other side to eat the eggs. Floral flicked a few more over, and I sent the tadpoles after them. And so we went back and forth, back and forth...

"Like playing ping-pong," I remarked.

"No, like playing checkers. My white pieces are all taken by your black pieces."

Floral said, sometimes when it's too hot out and the water in the leaf dried up, she would use her shoe to scoop some water from the stream to fill up the leaf again, turning it into a tiny little pond. And then, if you waited patiently enough by it, you could see birds coming over to wash themselves, and frogs hopping in and out of it.

She did have her own ways to amuse herself! With all these diversions, she should be able to forget Chunshao.

No, she would never forget Chunshao. But at least she could make herself happy...

Floral reached out and picked a string of berries from somewhere nearby. The branch quavered. Suddenly a frog jumped onto my head, and then onto Floral's. It went "ribbit, ribbit", and jumped into the stream with a plop, sending ripples through the water surface, and distorting our reflections. Floral and I looked at each other and smiled. In spite of myself, I held her hand lightly. I shifted my gaze away from her, and onto the reeds hanging low on either side of the stream, watching them swaying gently in the wind.

A teal climbed ashore and disappeared into a sparse patch of reeds, leaving just one eye showing, darting to and fro in the sunlight.

Some ginger-lilies stood tall and graceful by the water's edge. The shore a bit farther away was covered with pure white blossoms. The wind was sending gentle ripples through the water. We were mesmerised by our reflections in the water, feeling that the world was vacillating in the water, that the fish were floating into the heavens. Time passed so slowly that it was impossible to tell if this was an ephemeral moment, or an eternity.

Dusk began to fall. A shroud of gloominess covered the water. Floral reached into her pocket, fished out the last of the cotton strands and sprinkled them onto the water. We watched them float away, out of our dim vision, as if we were sending them off.

She said she wanted to go to a wide, new world.

I volunteered to go with her, but she said she was going to go on her own...

The two of us gazed at the surface of the stream, dark and devoid of anything except for the reflection of the moon. All around us was silent. Once in a while, there came the slight noise of leaves falling down and falling onto each other in the air; they gently floated onto our hair, onto our shoulders, and onto the water, without a sound. I felt that an ark in my life had set sail. I knew not where it was going, only that it, without floundering, without going stray, was drifting quietly into obscurity.

Something rustled in the branches. Squirrels, maybe? I said. No, it's the birds returning to their nests, said Floral.

A few sparks of starlight slowly descended upon us, and then gently guided our sight towards the night sky. Our gaze followed them farther and farther, swimming with the fireflies towards the heavens. Floral reached out her hand and caught a speck of light, and stuck the firefly in her hair. Instantly, her face was shrouded in a veil of light green; the colour was like the moss growing beside a well, clear and refreshing.

That day, we sat like that on the branch, like two birds returning and reuniting in the night. I could remember, Floral suddenly reached out and touched my forehead... At least I can still remember that feeling. In this world, there are some lights that do not extinguish, as tiny as they are, such as starlight. And this touch was one such light that brightened up my heart.

* * *

We waded to shore under the starlight, our stomachs growling. Torches in hand, we looked for edible things along the path. Floral mischievously shone her torch into insect holes in tree trunks, saying that she was trying to get the little fellows up from bed ahead of sunrise. I replied that even if the bugs all got up they wouldn't be enough to feed the two of us, so there's no point wasting batteries. We dug for taro roots and sweet potatoes in the earth, and lifted up rocks on the river bed to harvest clams. Then, we built a fire on the muddy ground, and roasted everything until it was fragrant.

It was late at night. Floral did not want to go home yet, but eventually she had to.

That night, when I walked her to her door, Floral told me that she was trying to hide from a man. This man occasionally went to her house to wait for her.

When she pronounced the name, I felt a shudder in my heart.

Tian Lin. Captain Tian. The Captain Tian from the Green Island penal colony also returned to Taiwan. He was put in charge of the Third Division of the National Security Bureau—the internal intelligence division—thus becoming a veritable spymaster. To boost Floral's popularity, he even sent a few reporters to the hotel to cover Floral's singing. They all said this nine-fingered special agent was a monster who would kill without thinking twice. Though I had suffered under him on Green Island, it was another side of him that left the greatest impression on me. Once, Captain Tian took Jian Liangnan and me on a boat to run some errands in Taitung. After finishing our business and having had lunch, there was still time before the return journey. He told us to wait at the restaurant, while he dashed off in a hurry. Jian Liangnan, out of curiosity, dragged me along to follow him. We saw Captain Tian enter a residential house with a neon light outside. The wall was not high, and the windows inside were lit. Jian Liangnan climbed up the wall to peer inside, while I stayed below the wall to keep watch for him. A few minutes later, Jian Liangnan jumped down from the wall. He grabbed my arm and ran, chuckling as we fled.

"It's an underground brothel. The girl inside the room was only wearing a sheer camisole, and you could see her bra and her panties." Jian Liangnan was choking with laughter. "I bet Captain Tian had it pent up for too long, and we two were just being a drag and getting in his way... So he actually... hah, hah, as soon as the girl took her bra off, Captain Tian suddenly... suddenly collapsed on the bed. He had only half undone his belt when he stopped moving... Wish you could have seen how dejected he looked. It's too bad. He's been so cruel to everyone, he deserves to lose his ability to have women..."

"I had heard that Tian Lin was injured. When he was fighting on the Mainland, he was captured by the Japanese, and they did something... very inhumane to him. So I thought that's why he didn't care for women after that..."

"Oh, so he's a patriot, sacrificing himself for the nation," said Jian

Liangnan, "But he must resent being incapacitated like this. So he wanted to get a woman to prove that he could still do it..."

Tian Lin took a fancy to Floral. Sometimes he went to the hotel for her performances, and sometimes he went straight to her house to wait for her.

Autumn treated Tian Lin as an honoured guest, but Floral was afraid of him. Floral said that whenever he looked at her, it felt as if he was going to chop her up with a knife and devour her piece by piece.

"Once, he opened my purse to put a present in it. There was a photo of Chunshao in the purse. He took the photo out, looked at it and put it back. Afterwards, I found that the photo had been crumpled up...

"Another time, he picked me up in his car for a ride. He chatted with me. I didn't say a lot. He suddenly turned the steering wheel and drove straight up the hill. He took me to a platform on the hillside. On one side was a tunnel, and the other looked like an abandoned mine. He pointed at the mine and said to me, there are many people buried there. All the disobedient people are buried in there."

If Floral knew ahead of time that he was going to her house, she would evade him by asking me to go with her to the hut on the hill. But this only happened a few times. We could not keep doing that, as the spymaster could not be tricked so easily. Naturally, he had ears and eyes to keep tabs on all our movements.

After Floral discovered that someone was spying on us, she did not see me again for a long time.

"You have to stay out of his way. With Tian Lin around, you must not come meet me. The more the mouse runs, the more the cat chases it. I have to continue living normally, and not avoid or cross Tian Lin," Floral said the last time we met.

Floral and I almost cut our contact. Once in a while, she sent someone to me with a flower with words carved behind the petals, while I would send back cards with secret writings in lemon juice or rice broth. As for childish games like cipher songs, we didn't use them, fearing that someone would figure them out.

Once I questioned Autumn why she let Floral quit school to go sing.

Autumn said, "These days it's really dangerous to go to school. There are always stories in the papers about female students going to jail and male students getting arrested. Your mother, even though she was the deputy director of the Investigation Bureau, ended up dead. There is danger everywhere in our world. Sing-song girls and bargirls are looked down on, but we earn money fast, and don't run as many risks as you educated folk. We aren't educated and we don't know a lot, so we don't come under as much suspicion as you do."

"But what would Chunshao think? It's one thing for you to go into the business, but you've dragged Floral into it as well."

"Chunhuan, leave Chunshao out of it. I'm doing it for Chunshao's benefit too. We can't afford to cross people like Tian Lin. Don't forget how your family was destroyed. You should be considering how to protect your family. Director Tian is a generous man and he will help Floral become a rising star. And he will give Chunshao a future too," said Autumn.

Indeed, Tian Lin helped Floral become famous. The radio station began to broadcast her shows live, with word that an album would be released soon. Chunshao, on the other hand, was recommended to work in Tian Lin's office and became a mid-level staff. However, it was a small world, and his supervisor turned out to be Pan Baojiang.

"Pan Baojiang used his father's connection to rise through the ranks, and became a team lead at a young age. "

When Chunshao said that, he pretended to be unconcerned it. He had lost his usual dignified, reserved look. In its place was a smugness at holding such a privileged position. I did not tell him that Floral and Autumn had sold themselves for his job. I feared that it would further crush his spirit.

15
We were on the highest clouds

One day after school, just as I was approaching the school's front gate, a child ran over and handed me a flower. Behind the petals were carved several words, the name and address of a high-rise building, and a room number.

I hurried there. I knocked. The door opened. There was no Floral.

Suddenly, a sharp pain. I fell unconscious.

When I came to, a man had taken a seat in front of me—Tian Lin. He was sitting on the sofa, coolly sipping wine, holding a thick, lit cigar between his fingers. On either side of him were several men in black suits.

"What are you doing here?!" As I tried to move, I found that my hands and feet were tied up behind my back. I could only heave myself up to a kneeling position.

"What are you arresting me for?" I shouted at Tian Lin.

"You came here yourself. Perhaps it's my turn to ask why you barged in here like that?" Tian Lin chuckled duplicitously.

"Where's Floral?" I anxiously looked around the room.

"You mean Anna?" Tian Lin blew a casual smoke ring.

"What did you do to Floral?"

Tian Lin glared at me with an expression of mockery. He did not answer.

"Let me go!" I yelled again.

"Why should I?" Tian Lin made a gesture, and one of the other men immediately brought my schoolbag over. He opened the bag, took out a sheet of red paper from it, and handed it to Tian Lin.

"What is this?" Tian Lin waved the red sheet before my face.

"I don't know. How did it get in there?"

Tian Lin began to read from it.

"I never wrote that! You planted that on me!" I shouted vehemently. Tian Lin was reading a Communist pamphlet.

"You still remember how you got caught back then, don't you, little spy? This pamphlet is written in the same handwriting as yours. We've checked it against your schoolwork. This thing can send you back to jail for, at the very least, thirty years. You're going to be an old man by the time you get out." Tian Lin made another gesture. The pamphlet was put back in the schoolbag. The black suit tossed the bag onto another sofa, with an expression saying that he was ready for the show to continue.

I stared at Tian Lin desperately. My mind was completely confused. I could not think of how to—no, there was no need to—defend myself. Disconcertedly, I asked, "Where's Floral? Where's Floral?"

"You want to implicate Anna? If she's in cahoots with you, she'd get at least twenty years too and come out as an old maid. There's someone else who's involved as well: Song Chunshao. The two of you have quite similar handwriting, don't you? Who took the rap for who? Wasn't it Song Chunshao that we're supposed to arrest back then? How did it become you..."

"You scumbag! What do you want?!"

Tian Lin assumed a serious expression, and emphatically stubbed out his cigar on the coffee table. "Zhu Xiaokang, the convict on the loose. You're still in contact with him, aren't you? Where's he hiding?"

"Zhu Xiaokang? I don't know. I haven't the faintest where he is," I denied, shaking my head forcefully, as if I was indignant of being accused of something I knew nothing about. As soon as Floral had told me about Tian Lin, I reminded Xiaokang to stay low. The fact that Tian Lin asked about him showed that Xiaokang was still safe.

"I have ways to make you talk."

"Let me go. I really don't know." I bowed and begged. But I didn't dare to bring up Floral again, fearing to anger Tian Lin.

"You want to go?" Tian Lin waved, and another man in a black suit brought over a bottle of wine and a wine glass. He put them on the coffee table before me, poured out a glass, and held it up to me. "We haven't offered you a drink yet. Here, drink up."

The man in black held the glass up against my lips.

"I forgot that you don't have hands anymore for holding the glass. So we'll give you the full service. Drink up," said Tian Lin.

I held my lips together tightly and turned my head around. Not doing it.

"Hah, hah, it's not poisoned." Tian Lin, like a cat toying with a mouse, was not in a rush to finish off his prey. "If you don't drink it the nice way, you'll have to drink it the hard way." With another wave, the man holding the glass poured the wine over my head.

"What do you want anyway?"

"Speak. Where is Zhu Xiaokang?"

"I really don't know."

"Then, who would know? Give me a name."

"How would I know... Oh, God might know."

"God? Hah, hah, that counts as a name, I guess. All right, let's play a game..." Tian Lin crossed his legs, letting his back sink deep into the sofa, watching his prey comfortably.

"What if I don't want to play?"

The man in the black suit picked up the schoolbag from the sofa and smiled savagely.

"All right. Go ahead, what kind of game?"

"You'll first chug this bottle of wine, then—" Tian Lin gave an attendant a look, and the man in black walked up to the window, drew back the curtain, and opened the window. Tian Lin continued, "As you see, there are two wire poles outside. The wire's pretty taut between them. You're going to step on the wire, and walk from this pole to that one, and back. If you don't fall, you win."

"Tian Lin, you're insane," I tried hard to compose myself. "What if I win?"

"Then you can leave."

"That's not enough. Floral too. You have to let Floral go."

"How can I let her go? Did you see me lock her up? Mind yourself before worrying about other people."

"Whether or not she's in your hands now, you can't bother her anymore." As soon as the words left my mouth, I felt stupid. I knew full well that I shouldn't bring up Floral. Why did I mention her again?

"When have I ever bothered women? It disgusts me to hear you talk like that. Hrmph... Anna... all right, if you win, you get Anna as well. But if you lose..." Tian Lin made a point of leaning out the window and sizing up the height of the poles.

"I accept. Tian Lin, hurry up and untie me. How do you expect me to wire-walk tied up like this?"

"I was going to let you think it over first. But you seem quite eager to die." Tian Lin signalled to one of the suits, "Loosen his ties. Let him finish the bottle first."

I stretched out my limbs, sore from the bounds. I stood up straight, picked up the strong-smelling bottle of liquor, unsure if I could finish it in one go. "Tian Lin, you mean what you said?"

"Of course," Tian Lin chuckled, looking at me from the corner of his eye. "But don't forget about your legs. One seems a bit shorter than the other."

"Don't trouble yourself over it." I steeled my resolve, held up the bottle, and poured it down my throat. A few gulps in, and confusion started to set in. I continued drinking, feeling that my head was swimming beyond my control. When the whole bottle was emptied, my mind was similarly blank, and I was unable to focus.

"Can you still stand up straight? Song Chunhuan," Tian Lin's face swirled before me, his hand pointing somewhere, "the window is over there. It's now three-something in the middle of the night. There's no one out there. If you don't walk well, no one's going to see you, and no one's going to laugh at you either."

I went up to the window and looked out. It was dead quiet outside. Indeed, there were neither people nor cars on the streets; the only source of light in the neighbourhood was one solitary streetlamp. A few flying insects, moths and mosquitoes, flittered around the lamp. Staring at them made my eyesight swirl around the lamp along with the bugs.

I turned around and took a look at the black suits behind me, composed myself, and cleared my mind of their images. I took a few deep breaths, and attempted to focus my attention by gritting my teeth.

I took the first step out of the window, my hands holding onto the window sill.

Then my second foot stepped out. My feet both stood on the narrow eaves hanging out from under the window. I kept my body and face against the wall. I held onto the wall with my hands as well, slowly steadying myself.

The chilly air outside sobered me up a bit. I took a few deep breaths, turned my head away from the wall to the direction of the wire pole. I eyeballed the distance and made a mental note of the surroundings. I let go one hand, and, grabbing the baluster on the side of the building, slowly shifted my weight to one side. Then, I lifted one foot and reached it out towards the wire pole three feet away.

Once one foot arrived onto the pole, I pushed my body away with the hand holding onto the baluster, and gently let go. My centre of gravity shifted from the wall of the building onto the wire pole. My other foot, which was still standing on the eaves, also moved up to meet the foot on the wire pole. Finally I was standing on the pole with both my feet.

I stood steadily, eyes looking straight ahead of me. I did not look down at all. Even though from the corner of my eye I caught sight of Tian Lin and the black suits by the window, I did not think about them. My mind went back to one of those times in my childhood when I perched on my special tree. There were times when I sat there all day. Even when my legs fell asleep and I couldn't move, I wouldn't fall off.

The people inside the window made noises. It seemed that they were either hurrying me on or trying to distract me.

I ignored all of that, focusing only on reminiscing...

In my childhood I climbed around rooftops with Floral. The roofs were flat or slanted, low or high; but no matter how high they were, the sky was even higher. We lay on the rooftops, watching the birds and the clouds in the sky; we climbed about the rooftops like cats, looking at our neighbours' houses, the flower gardens all around us, the fish pond, and the bamboo grove and the stream beyond all that. Those were our happiest moments. We hummed cipher songs, exchanged sheets of paper with secret writing, revealing the hidden content by heating the paper underneath magnifying glasses in the blazing sun. There were insects chirping in the trees, and in the pond there were fish swimming up to the surface of the water, blowing bubbles...

We were on the highest clouds, in the peaceful winds, never afraid of falling, never afraid of pain. Perhaps we were the cats, the birds, the bugs, the butterflies, hopping along the narrow roof ridges. That was a game, an amusement. We were not courting danger. There was nothing to fear.

The night was dark before my eyes. Apart from a weakly-glowing streetlamp, there was nothing to guide my sight. But in this night I could daydream, be enraptured in my reverie. Dreams make one happy, make one forget about everything. There was no need to focus on anxiety. I only needed to focus on this delightful scene...

There and back, flittering joyfully as a bird playing in the sky, I felt loose and relaxed all over. I could not worry. I could not feel tense. It was as if I was walking on cotton fluff, my footsteps soft and light. There was no gravity, let alone any trembling or seizing up.

I did not know how I returned through the window. I only

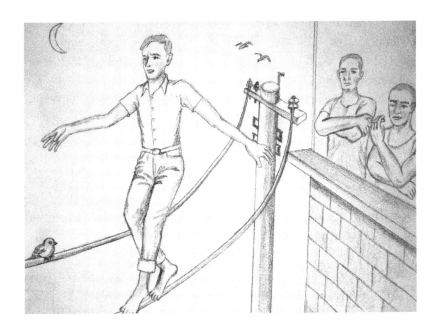

remembered myself saying to some swirling faces in front of me, "I won." And then I passed out.

The next time I felt anything, I was just regaining consciousness under the pain of hunger and thirst.

My eyes were blindfolded and my hands were tied behind me. My legs were tied together as well. I tried to move my body, feeling the objects in my surroundings with my cheeks and my bound hands.

This is a room with a table and a chair.

The four walls are not far from each other.

There is a window.

The door is locked and could not be opened...

Something stirred outside the room. People were talking.

"You locked him up in here?" It's Floral's voice.

"He's a suspect..." It's Tian Lin's voice.

Anger raged in my heart when I heard that. The scumbag didn't mean what he said. How could he still keep me locked up?

"How do you know he's a suspect?" asked Floral.

"This is his schoolbag. There is a Communist pamphlet in there," Tian Lin explained.

I shouted angrily from inside, "Floral, don't listen to him. He planted it on me to frame me!"

"You've slept really well, haven't you? What a strong voice you have."

"Tian Lin, you didn't honour your words. You kept me locked up here. Let me out."

"I always mean what I say. I let you leave that building where we were. Now, you're in a different building. I also brought you Anna."

"You're just playing with me," I yelled again.

"Director Tian, please let him go," Floral interceded for me.

"Anna, it's not good for you to be hanging out with such people. Listen to me, cut off all ties with the rebel spies," Tian Lin said.

"I already don't hang out with him anymore..." Floral said in a timid voice.

"So why do you still give him flowers, still accept cards from him?" After a brief silence, Tian Lin continued, "I sent you an invitation in his name, and you came out. Anna, you're not being honest..."

"It's true, I haven't seen him for a very long time already. I don't know what you mean by flowers and cards."

"Oh, so if you aren't involved with him anymore, it wouldn't matter to you if I let him go or keep him here."

"No, please let him go."

"Why are you pleading for him again?"

"He... really isn't a rebel spy."

"Then it's the other one. Song Chunshao is the rebel spy."

"No, neither of them are. They're both good people."

"Anna, why are you lying for a rebel spy? Back then, he was convicted after irrefutable evidence was brought against him. On top of that, he's concealing the whereabouts of another escaped convict. They are in cahoots. It's no small crime to fail to report a spy..."

"Ah! what are you going to do to him?"

"Make him reveal the location of his accomplice and I'll let him go. If he refuses, he'll stay locked up inside, with nothing to eat or drink. If he refuses for a day, he starves for a day. If he refuse for two days, he starves for two days..."

"Tian Lin, I'm not saying anything no matter who you bring here. Don't waste your time," I shouted from inside.

"Anna, you stay here and tell him to speak." Tian Lin ignored my yelling. In his usual, even voice, he continued, "I will send someone to bring you food every day. There's someone on guard outside the door around the clock. Holler if you need anything. But if you don't get anything out from him, you don't get to go either."

"Tian Lin, don't waste your time. It doesn't matter who you bring here to ask me..." I shouted again.

"Anna, do you still remember that ditch I showed you? Disobedient people end up like that. Inside the ditch are piles and piles of nameless skeletons," Tian Lin exhorted earnestly, but behind his words was death.

"You have no evidence. You can't kill me," I yelled again.

"It's true, I'll need evidence to kill you. But it won't be too late to get the evidence after I've killed you. Remember, no tricks. My men are just outside. If you try anything funny, I won't be responsible for the consequences."

Having declared these last words, Tian Lin left.

Floral was held captive next doors. Her door was locked from the outside as well. It was a very deliberate door-locking; the key turned one round and another. Even with another door in between, I could still hear it clearly.

It was quiet outside for a long, long while.

"Floral, are you there?" I asked, experimenting with speaking right up against the edge of the door.

"I'm here. I'm figuring out your lock," Floral whispered.

"Can you open it?"

"It's tough. I just tried using a bobby pin, a safety pin, and everything that I could try, but nothing worked."

"Might not do to open the lock. Do you have pen and paper on you?"

"When Tian Lin left he took away everything I had. I don't have anything to write with."

"Let's try thinking from a different angle. You have a window there, right? What's outside it?"

"It's an empty lot. There's a pile of rubbish in the corner," replied Floral.

"Are there houses on the other side?"

"No."

"What's beyond the empty lot?"

"A wall."

I was a bit crestfallen. "How many storeys is this building?"

"Fifteen," said Floral.

"Which floor are we on?"

"The thirteenth."

"Can you climb to the top of the building from the window? I'm blindfolded and my hands and feet are tied behind me. I can't climb..."

"There's no way. There's nothing to hold onto."

Floral looked for ideas around the room. A few hours passed by. There was no hope.

Someone opened the lock on the outermost door. After a while there was the sound of a door locking.

"They've brought supper. Chunhuan, how are you doing?" Floral asked quietly by the edge of the door.

"I'm weak all over from hunger. And very thirsty," I said, also very quietly.

"Yikes, this door of yours doesn't even have a gap at the bottom. Can't feed things through," said Floral.

Not long after, Floral suddenly called for the guard outside. Then came the sound of a the door being unlocked.

"I want a soft drink. Could you get me a bottle of something? And a straw as well." Floral said to the guard.

Another while later came a similar unlocking sound. "Miss Anna, here's your drink." And then came the sound of the door being locked.

All was quiet for a while. And then some light noise came through the edge of the door.

"Chunhuan, Chunhuan," Floral called to me softly, "Try to hold your face against the doorknob. There's a keyhole underneath that..."

I felt something thin poking through beneath the doorknob. It must have been pushed through the keyhole.

"Do you feel it? Suck on it," said Floral.

It was a straw. I moved my mouth to it. The refreshingly cool fizzy drink tasted like nectar from the heavens.

"Floral, I want water too. Do you have any water?" My thirst not completely quenched, I could still drink a pond of water.

"Wait," said Floral.

"Chunhuan, here's the water," she then called to me.

I moved up to the straw, drinking up all the water in big gulps. Instantly I felt almost myself again, though my stomach was still growling uncomfortably.

The straw was drawn back. "Chunhuan, wait a moment."

A few minutes later, the straw poked through again. This time, the end of the straw was flattened and folded in half, like a little scoop. My tongue felt the difference. There was also something sticky on it.

"Chunhuan, this is rice and vegetables. The hole is too small. I can only give you a tiny bit at a time."

I sucked this pea-sized morsel off the straw. The straw was retracted. When it came through again, I sucked on it again.

At one point, the guard came in to collect the dishes. Floral hid a piece of meat. She chewed it up, and fed it to me bit by bit through the keyhole.

"Floral, it's my fault."

"No, don't say that. It's not," said Floral, "Are you still hungry?"

"I'm much better now, thank you."

* * *

"Floral, I feel that you're my Anna."

That night, we leant against the door, each on one side of it, ears held up against the keyhole, feeling each other's warm and moist words flow through the ears into the heart.

"Floral, listen to me. All I want is you," I whispered these words, which I had kept to myself for over a dozen years, through the tiny hole in the door.

"What do you want me for?" Floral asked me, either not understanding or pretending to not understand.

"What do I want you for?" I was dumbfounded for a moment, then broke into a silly giggle.

"Not for anything in particular. Only... to be with you once in a while," I stuttered, not knowing what to say, "It's like... a kind of serenity, when the storm... suddenly pauses and there is a moment of serenity. Or maybe it's enough to know that you live in my heart. Really, that would be enough. It's like you're the one who's living, you're the one who lives on for me..."

There was no sound from the other side.

I continued to call to her, "Floral, I need you."

"Chunhuan..."

"Floral, you don't have to give me an answer. You also shouldn't feel I'm imposing on you. I often think, even though I need you, I don't know if you need me. I don't know..."

"Chunhuan..."

"I don't know what I am to you. But I know what you are to me. You're like my home. You're like Anna, who made me impatient to go home and see her every day..."

"Chunhuan, I'm not that good," a slightly rustling voice said. It sounded like sobbing.

"Don't cry, Floral." I could not help tearing up either, the tears rolling down my cheeks through the blindfold. "Once, that was when I first had that feeling... I was helping Autumn in the kitchen and we made a pot of the best chicken stock. The next day, the leftover stock congealed into a beautiful jelly in the pot. Autumn said she would heat it up for me. But as I looked at this pot of nutritious jelly, I could only feel my heart ache. I could not eat it, like... like I would only feel joy eating it when I am with someone I love. But I knew you couldn't share it with me... It felt so tragic. I felt like I had lost myself, not knowing where myself went. For the first time, I realised that I didn't care about myself at all. I only cared about how another person was doing."

The sobbing from the other side became gradually clearer. It did not seem completely dark before my eyes anymore. There seemed to be a subtle brightness ahead.

"Floral, don't cry. Can you see the moon from there?"

"Yeah. The moon is right outside the window."

"Is it shining in?"

"It's shining in."

Floral did not stop sobbing. I lifted my head to feel the moonshine on my face, imagining the translucent light washing over us, wrapping us closely together... The sobbing in my ear seemed to be from a distant dream, a true expression from the heart that I had yearned for.

"Floral, can I ask this of you? Maybe I'm asking too much, but can you be my Anna?"

"I... I can't be as good as Anna was."

"I think you are. In my heart, no one is as good as you."

"I... I'd like to be your Sisi. That'd be good enough."

I did not know whether to laugh or cry at her answer. She had said before too that she only wanted to be Sisi. "Why?"

Floral said, "It's because I owe you. I have to repay you."

"What do you owe me?"

"Sisi. It was me who starved him to death."

"No, my mother said it was Chunhong... even though I didn't believe it at the time."

"It wasn't Chunhong. It was me."

"How could it be?"

"At that time, my mum found that Chunhong was up to something. During those few days when your family went to Alishan, Chunhong did something at your home that my mum felt was fishy. So she kept a secret watch on Chunhong. But as you know, Sisi was very friendly with Chunhong. He thought my mum was going to do something bad to Chunhong, so he barked at my mum. In the spur of the moment, I grabbed Sisi from behind, tied his mouth shut, and locked him in the cage. He wasn't usually kept in the cage. You kept that dogcage in the backyard until it's all rusted instead of using it. I stuffed him in the cage. It was night-time then and very dark in the backyard. Chunhong didn't see me, and my mum didn't know either, because she was focusing on watching Chunhong. I used to like to sneak into your home when you're out, to watch your maid and my mum play cat-and-mouse. It was a lot of fun... That day after I locked up Sisi, I scrambled over the wall and went back to my home in a panic. I was little then. I didn't know what to do after doing something bad. All I knew was to hide at home. I only realised two days later. By the time I climbed over the wall to your backyard again, Sisi had already died. I hurried to take him out. I removed the cloth on his mouth and threw him somewhere in the bushes. For some reason, Chunhong didn't even notice that Sisi was gone. Perhaps she was too focused on doing something else... Later on, my mum told me that Chunhong looked like she was looking for something..."

"I knew. Later on, my mother found that there's something wrong with Chunhong and fired her. But why did Chunhong took the blame upon herself for starving Sisi to death when she didn't do it? She was so kind to Sisi, but she didn't defend herself."

"It's possible that Chunhong... It's complicated. She's a spy, but it seemed she liked your father as well. Even though my mum thought she was sneaky, she had no evidence to prove that she did anything. The only thing she had was a note. My mum somehow found a note that Chunhong wrote to your father. My mum threatened her, told her to claim responsibility for Sisi's death, or else she'd show the note to your mother. Because we knew how much you loved Sisi, and I starved him to death. We could not take on the responsibility for killing him, and at the same time Mum didn't like Chunhong... Anyway, this is how Chunhong was stuck with being the dog-killer."

"Your mother likes my father too, did you know?"

"I... didn't."

"On one hand, your mother was being loyal to her employer. But on the other, she was getting rid of a rival. And her rival, Chunhong, held more of a grudge against my mother, since it was my mother who sent her away..."

"Perhaps my mum hates your mother too."

"I guessed as much. She had you cut our clothesline and spit gum on my mother's wig, didn't she?"

"How did you know all that..."

"I do. But let's not talk about those ridiculous things anymore. Floral, let's not worry about the grown-ups' business. Let's just think about the two of us, about how we're going to live in the future."

"I will... try to be your Anna..."

"But you only feel that you owe me, and not that you love me?"

I should have felt content for receiving this precious promise from Floral. But that damned sensitivity just had to come out and play tricks on me, making me feel that this promise, obtained so easily, was more or less based on gratitude or pity. That was all very clear to me, and so I could not help telling myself, this was not love, but was rather the most sincere declaration of friendship.

16
As she fed me rainwater from the skull

The next day, Tian Lin came by to question Floral. Floral told him nothing.

"He didn't say anything? He must be eager to starve to death."

A moment later, the door to my room was unlocked. I knew Tian Lin was standing in front of me, examining me. I continued to pretend to be asleep, not responding to any noise from the outside world.

"Let's see how much longer he can hold out!" Tian Lin sulked and left.

I knew I could not pretend to be asleep forever. That game's going to be up in a day or two.

Floral told me that there would occasionally be a rubbish collector in the empty lot, picking through the rubbish. But we could not yell for help; the guard would certainly hear us. There was neither pen nor paper in the room, or anything we could use.

On the third day, Tian Lin came again. I heard the door open. He might have looked me up and down for a while.

"Anna, you're a bad girl. Though I don't know how you did it." Then, Tian Lin's voice said to me, "After three days of not eating or drinking, how could you have anything to excrete? The smell of pee... hrmph..."

"Anna, sorry." Tian Lin called for someone. "Tie her up. Hands behind her back. Tie her ankles as well." "From today on, you will starve along with him, until he speaks."

Then came the sound of a door locking again. The key turned once, twice. The noise was piercing, and particularly agitating to my already-strained nerves.

"Chunhuan, it's my fault. I know that even if you tell him, he wouldn't let you go," Floral's voice became frail

"I know too well that if he wants something, no one can fight him for it."

"You've been missing all these days. Your family should be out looking for you. My mother might even..."

"But we have no way of calling for help, and we can't drag our families into this either," I said.

"Do we have no way out?"

"I don't know. But I won't give up."

* * *

Some small creatures were tickling me all over. The stench of my bodily wastes over the three days attracted some bugs, maybe cockroaches. I despondently let them crawl all over me.

There must be a way. All I could think of was Floral. I could not let her die with me here.

"Floral, go look outside the window. Is that rubbish heap still there?" I said, leaning against the door.

A while later, Floral replied, "The rubbish heap is there. There's some new rubbish piled on top of it."

"Beside the rubbish heap, is there a streetlamp?"

"No. There's nothing else."

As a last resort, with my hands still tied behind me, I tore off a small piece of my shirt-tail.

Then, I used my right hand to undo the watch strap on my left wrist, then forcefully stabbed the small hook on the strap into the tip of my right index finger. I pushed the hook in to deepen the wound. Then, placing the piece of the shirt-tail on the floor behind my back, and holding it down with my left hand, I wrote on the cloth with my right index finger.

Perhaps there was not enough blood, and perhaps the piece of cloth was not big enough. I could not see behind me. I could only write as neatly as I could, judging by touch.

After the note was written, I lay on my side, bent my legs back, and held my heels to my buttocks. I bent backwards until my fingers could reach the leg of my trousers. I turned my leg slightly, and with my left hand behind me, I rolled up the right trouser leg, grabbed my right sock, and with both hands tore a notch in it. I pulled a thread out from it, a long, long thread. Then, in the same way, I used my right hand to pull up my left trouser leg, and tore a thread from my left sock.

I sat up with my legs bent. I could do nothing pant and rest, and stay still for a long, long time.

A cockroach finally climbed onto the back of my hand.

It crawled down past the bleeding index finger, and explored its environs. Its two antennae were tickling my palm, then its prickly legs crawled onto my palm as well. It was time. I made a fist and caught this long-awaited cockroach.

With touch alone, I held up the thread from the sock, and tied it around the cockroach. I wrapped it around thrice, tied a knot, and attached the rolled-up piece of cloth on the cockroach's back.

When all was ready, I shuffled over to the side of the room where I remembered the window to be, feeling for the window. Once I had found it, I hoisted myself up, turned around, and let the cockroach and

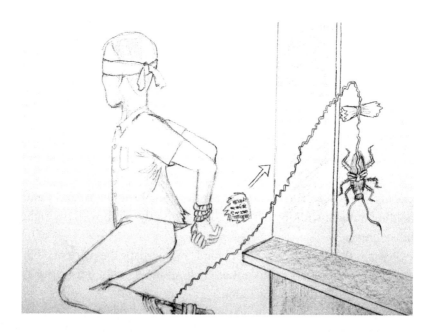

the note down the window. After letting them down for a distance, I continue unravelling the thread from my sock, longer bit by bit; and when the thread from my left foot ended I connected it to the thread on my right foot.

I estimated the length of the thread in my mind. For thirteen floors, letting the string longer, floor by floor, until it reached ground level. And I still had to estimate the length of the empty lot and the distance to the rubbish heap...

And then it was a matter of waiting, and luck. On the note I wrote down the name of a dance hall and a person, indicating that whoever handed this note to this person and brought him here would be rewarded with a thousand *yuan*. A thousand *yuan* was a great temptation. As long as the note was found, it would be reasonable to believe that the finder would be enticed by the offer. It was too bad that Tian Lin had already emptied my pockets and I had no money on me; the message would have been even more tempting if it had been writing on a bank note. I also imaged many other possibilities: the cockroach walking in the wrong direction; the note not getting picked up; the finder of the note thinking it was a prank; the note falling into the hands of the enemy...

Tian Lin came by again in the evening. I sat on my heels, leaning against the wall, so that he could not see the torn corner of my shirt.

That night, Floral told me that, since she was a child, her mother had detested her, calling her a disgusting thing. Autumn used to point to her and burst into a tirade, saying that her father was an old piece of trash, and that she had not wanted to give birth to this little piece of trash either.

"Do you know who your father is?" I asked.

"Apparently an old shaman from the hills."

"What's his name?"

"Elas Fasay."

"Who lived in Penglai Village in Nanzhuang, Miaoli?"

"How do you know?"

"My mother's people did a background check on Autumn. But the name Fasay isn't from the Highland tribes around Miaoli..."

"They weren't originally from Miaoli. They moved there and they both took different names... Once my mum drank a lot of wine. She took a straw figurine and stabbed it with needles. She pretended that the figurine was Elas. She was ranting about Elas Fasay being a beast. That day, she said many things, and for the first time—and the only time—I saw her that sad. She said Elas was her grandfather on her mother's side, but he was my father as well... Elas made her pregnant, and sold her to a veteran who didn't know what was going on..."

A long time passed. It was maybe around midnight.

I heard a noise. The ding-a-ling of a bell, very soft, very near, like it was right at the window.

I moved towards the window. Now I could hear even more clearly. There were two rings every ten seconds.

That was my secret signal.

Quickly, I moved back to the door. Floral and I had chatted up late, so she should be sleeping right by the door. I pressed against the doorknob, and said into the keyhole, "Floral, Floral."

A response from the other side.

In a low voice, I instructed her, "Floral, hurry and go wait by the window. If you see a rope hanging down, turn around and grab it with your hands and tie it around your wrists. Then lean your upper body out of the window."

Then, I shuffled back to the wall and felt for the position of the window. I stood up, leaned out of the window, and tried to find the rope. My nose felt the bell hanging on the end of the rope. Tilting my head to a side, I caught the rope in my mouth, and gingerly pulled it into the window. After that, I turned around, grabbed the rope with my hands behind me, and undid the bell.

I wrapped the rope a few times around my bound hands, and tied it tight. Then, I sat on the window sill, with my back facing out, and yanked on the rope thrice.

The rope began drawing upwards. When I felt that my upper body had cleared the window, I drew up my knees and pushed hard against the ground. Immediately I bounced out of the room.

Now, I was hanging in mid-air, face-down, hands tied behind my back and above me. My eyes were blindfolded and I could see nothing.

It was drizzling outside. The rain stroke my face. I felt a chill, and my head felt swollen and uncomfortable from the blood flowing down to it. My body rose up, bit by bit, and for some reason, I suddenly remembered that time on Green Island, when Xiaokang was hogtied, suspended on the pole, and swung around. It probably felt rather like this.

The rope stopped at some point. Two strong arms grabbed me and pulled me in forcefully. I finally returned to solid ground.

The blindfold was torn off my eyes, and my limbs were released. I saw Fat Cat and Lucky.

The rope was let down from the roof once more, but this time it was shifted over to Floral's window. Floral was hauled up the same way.

We climbed over to the roof of a neighbouring building and descended the stairs there.

There was a car on the street. We had to cross the courtyard in front of the building to meet up with the car.

Four people moving in the streetlamp in the middle of the night would be rather conspicuous. A building manager noticed us. We pretended to be a couple of drunks, staggering and stumbling, with arms on each other's shoulders, out of his sight.

With no one near, we quickly got into the car. In the driver's seat was Black Pine.

We drove for a while, and then Black Pine suddenly sped up.

"Sod it, Someone's tailing us."

In the rear-view mirror, a black car was closing in on us. Black Pine stepped on the accelerator to put some distance between us.

"What should we do? We can't go back to the hideout," said Fat Cat, looking over his shoulder again and again.

Black Pine said, "We'll go to my bird's place."

"They're following too close," said Lucky.

"Check this out!" Black Pine turned the steering wheel sharply. We turned into a street and came out of another alley. The car sped along the main roads and zigzagged through side streets. "They're for real! Not even a cat going after a mouse would go this far!" Black Pine knocked over a few hawker carts in a row, and finally shook off the pursuit.

We had barely breathed a sigh of relief when before us came two identical black cars.

"They want to play hardball, damn them!" Black Pine reversed the car hastily, and spun towards another direction.

The car drove onto the expressway. It grew darker and darker around us.

"Not going to your bird's?" asked Fat Cat.

"Nope, I don't want to make myself a widower," said Black Pine.

"This area... No one lives here," Lucky said, looking all around.

"No one lives here, but there are ghosts." Black Pine accelerated into the hills. "Apparently Military Judiciary buried a whole bunch of political prisoners here. Let's pray that the souls of the wrongfully killed will protect us."

The car drove along the hillside, going around and around the hill, going deeper and deeper in.

"We should've lost them," Fat Cat, who had been looking behind us all this time, breathed a sigh of relief.

Black Pine slowed down, and we continued quietly along this pitch-black road on the hillside.

Before us, besides the small, pale white spot illuminated by the headlamps, it was eerily dark all around, and the night fog lay heavily on the ground. We could not see the road clearly. We could only feel that there were ditches and potholes all over: the wheels shook violently. Once in a while, we would get to a vantage point where we could see the dark, phantom-like shadows of the hills; otherwise, we seemed to be driving interminably into an endless black hole.

We could not tell when it was that the hilly road suddenly opened up and became bright—a strong beam of light shone from behind. I turned around, but the light was so blinding that I could not keep my eyes open. This behemoth was charging towards us, gaining on us.

"What's a lorry doing here?!" Black Pine accelerated again. But there were fallen rocks on the road surface, and we could not go too fast.

A loud boom. The lorry crashed into our rear bumper. We were jolted up from our seats from the impact. And again, an even more forceful crash, again and again—our car was pretty much pushed along.

"Goddammit, go to hell!"

Suddenly Black Pine pulled the emergency brakes. The car did not stop, but abruptly flipped over a cliff. When all was tumbling around us, Fat Cat pushed Floral and me out of the car.

The car burst into flames. Floral grabbed my arm and ran for our lives. My leg was numb from the pain, and I was basically dragged along over the ground.

Someone was coming down the hill with hand-torches. Floral and I immediately hid ourselves in the tall grass. We saw a few men in military uniform standing next to the lorry, whose bright headlamps flooded half the cliff with light.

In the distance, Black Pine's car was still ablaze. Two soldiers climbed down and was about to approach the burning car. An explosion was heard, and the two men threw themselves to one side.

Several other people came down and carried the injured soldiers up. Following that, they inspected the car, now flipped upright. Fat Cat, Lucky, and Black Pine were dragged out, all covered with blood. The hand-torches shone all around, but did not discover anything else.

Rain began to descend from the skies. We saw someone at the top wave his hand, and the people below stopped searching. Carrying their quarry, they climbed back up the cliff and returned to the road on the hillside.

The lorry drove away. Floral and I stumbled around to find shelter.

The rain came down heavily. We slid into a ditch. When we picked ourselves up again, we sensed that there were hard and sharp things poking at us from all around. I felt them with my hands—they were human bones! The ditch, the valley was filled with human bones! There were kneecaps, leg bones, ribs, and a few round skulls rolling away beside us.

We ran further with all our strength, and finally found a tunnel that seemed to belong to an abandoned mine.

* * *

At dawn the next morning, by the weak rays of light shining in from the outside, I saw that in the tunnel were some bits and pieces of shattered human bones as well. I lay on the ground, more dead than alive, unable to move due to my injured leg. I was hungry. I was thirsty.

I was freezing all over. But the site of the injury was feverish, burning to the touch.

"Floral, is it still raining outside?" I asked.

"It is."

I examined the human remains around me, and picked up a skull whose jaw had fallen off. "Floral, take this and collect a bit of rainwater. I'm thirsty."

Floral stood by the entrance of the tunnel, washed the skull meticulously in the rain, and came back with a scoop of water.

Floral carefully helped me sit up. I rested in her arms, as she fed me rainwater from the skull, feeling a strange mix of contentedness, fear, and anguish.

The rain stopped. The sun shone intensely on the earth, quickly evaporating the moisture on the ground.

Something stirred outside. Floral went out to take a look, and ran back in a panic. "They're here. The people from yesterday are searching the hill."

"In military uniform?"

"And a few in plainclothes."

"Where?"

"On the cliff from yesterday. A similar lorry is stopped there."

"There's nowhere to go. We can only hide in here. I wonder how long this tunnel is?"

"We'll hide as deep as we can."

At once, Floral dragged me into the tunnel. The light grew dimmer and dimmer as we went, until we could see no more.

"Floral, I'm a burden to you. Leave me here and run for your life."

"I won't abandon you," Floral continued dragging me with all her might.

"Floral, we'll starve to death hiding in here. Don't mind me."

The air became worse and worse. I felt a bit suffocated. Floral continued to drag me forcefully. I could hear her panting. It was the only sign of life in the dark and sunless bowels of the earth.

"Floral, that's enough. Please leave. Don't worry about me anymore," I implored her again. This tunnel seemed to be endless. I could hear Floral's heavy breathing. She could almost drag me no more.

"Weren't you wanting me to be your Anna? Would Anna abandon you and run away by herself?" Floral actually managed to keep her light-hearted tone, even as she grabbed tighter onto me.

I said, "I don't want Anna anymore."

She replied, "You can't stop wanting Anna just whenever."

On this day, we played the game of the King and the Princess once more.

"Please grant me death, my lord," said Floral.

"How would you like to die?"

"Please hide me away in a very long tunnel, and let me die of darkness."

"Can you actually die of that?"

"Of course. It's so dark in there that you won't be able to tell life and death apart," Floral's tone was just as innocent as it was in her childhood.

* * *

The tunnel was not completely devoid of life. We listened to nameless insects chirping in the darkness, letting them roam freely all over us. Floral did not dare to move for fear of hurting me.

"Floral, you can let me lie on the ground. Aren't you tired with me leaning against you like this?"

"Of course, but now I'm numb and I don't feel a thing. If you stop leaning on me, I won't be numb anymore, and I'd feel even more tired."

"What kind of logic is that? Hah!"

"Actually, I want to go look for someone. He can definitely help us," Floral said suddenly. "In those years when you were in jail, I sneaked out to the President's house a couple of times. I wanted to tell him to let you out. But I didn't have a chance to. You know, he forgot me again. As soon as I stepped in front of his car, the guards told me to go away."

I still remembered her photo, and remembered "the one who mattered", whom I had almost forgotten.

"Tian Lin is his subordinate. All the people in jail are there because he ordered their arrests. All the special agents are sent by him. Why beg him for mercy?" I asked.

"I keep feeling he's a nice man. It's just that he doesn't know what his special agents were doing."

"We can't even get past Tian Lin. Can we really hope to go find him and beg for mercy?"

"If we manage to get out of here, I will definitely go tell him to tell his men to stop harassing you."

* * *

There was no water inside the tunnel. We did not even have any urine to drink.

Floral and I lay on the ice-cold ground, waiting for death--or, rather, no different to being dead.

The insects crawled all over us. We ate a few, but that did not quench our thirst.

"Floral, let's not play the King and the Princess anymore. Let's play the Immortal Saves the Princess instead."

"How does that go?" Floral's voice was thin and faint.

I pulled myself up into a sitting position, lifted up a leg and propped it up against the wall of the tunnel. Then, feeling around the ground, I found a large rock, which I picked up and smashed it against my leg—

"Floral, hurry, hurry and hold it!"

I pressed Floral's head against my elevated leg, insisting that she drink the fresh blood. Floral struggled, but I did not let her get away. "Hurry and drink it. You must not die!"

Floral really drank it. She sobbed as she drank.

I was in indescribable pain. The world spun around me. But my hand still held on tightly; I did not let go of Floral. I needed her to continue drinking, until she had enough to survive.

A long while later...

Floral suddenly broke out of my hold. She felt along my body, and soon she grabbed hold of my face. She put her mouth against mine—instantly my mouth was filled with blood. Mouthful by mouthful, she took the blood from my leg, and fed it into my mouth.

In the darkness, we must have looked like we were embracing and kissing incessantly, joining into one another, over and over.

17
Troops in pursuit

Faint rustling noises were heard outside the tunnel.

Floral, who was lying in my arms, suddenly sat up. She shook me and woke me.

"They're back."

We listened carefully. Dogs! They brought dogs with them!

The barking became clearer and clearer, closer and closer.

"Chunhuan, stay here. Don't make a noise. Don't go out."

As soon as she finished speaking, Floral dashed out.

"No!"

I crawled on the ground, but as hard as I climbed and crawled, I could not keep up with her.

Footsteps were echoing in the tunnel. Thud! Thud! Thud! Thud! My heart shattered with each thud.

Floral ran straight at the people outside. At once, the voices of people and dogs gathered and grew.

My mind was breaking down!

Floral, Floral, my Anna! I cried in my heart, tears rolling down my cheeks.

The sounds of dogs and people became fainter. Their voices were taken away. Floral was also taken away. Everything I had was taken away.

Hopeless. Utterly hopeless.

I turned over and lay supine on the ground. There is no breath. There is no thought. This time, I am truly dying.

I am dying. But it isn't comfortable. Something keeps scratching my ear—my tears have flooded my ear, and in it are insects, bobbing up and down, struggling to stay afloat.

I lost consciousness for a long, long time, before a noise brought me back to this world.

Footsteps were approaching in the tunnel. I knew that being captured this time meant death. The worst case scenario was death. There was nothing else.

I could not be bothered to move. Let them come take my body away.

There was a light. A hand-torch circled round and round, searching randomly. I continued to keep my eyes shut.

The footsteps stopped by my ear. The light shone back and forth on my face.

"Chunhuan! Chunhuan!"

I opened my eyes. It was Zhu Xiaokang.

Xiaokang crouched down and draped me over his shoulder. "Thank goodness you're still alive."

"How did you find me?"

"Anna told me in secret. It's such a bother to crack your cipher songs." Xiaokang said, when she was apprenticing under him, she taught him cipher singing.

"Where's Floral?"

"Anna, uh, your Floral was taken away by Tian Lin."

"Then what about Fat Cat, Lucky, and Black Pine?" I remembered how they were covered in blood on that day as they were dragged out. I expected the worst.

"Fat Cat went to meet his maker. Lucky and Black Pine didn't die, but they're in the hands of Tian Lin's people, and so they're guaranteed a rough time. But they won't give me away."

Xiaokang set me up in a basement. My leg injury was deteriorating badly, but I couldn't go to the hospital.

Not long after, Xiaokang kidnapped a doctor and brought him to me.

The doctor was blindfolded. Only when he had been brought before me did Xiaokang remove his blindfold. Xiaokang held a gun to his back with one hand, while putting down a large bag of surgery equipment with the other hand. Two of his men served as the surgeon's assistants.

He injected too much anaesthesia. My mind wandered as I listened to the clanging of the surgical instruments, and soon drifted off to sleep.

When I came to again, the doctor had been taken away.

"Even though he came in blindfolded, it's not safe here anymore. At the very least he knew this was a basement. We have to get moving." Xiaokang looked me up and down, and knitted his brows, "But look at you. You'll draw too much attention. How do we get you out of here?"

Later that day, Xiaokang came back with a pram with a large hood. He put a baby hat and a bib on me, and covered me with a baby blanket; he himself was dressed as a woman, in a long dress and a wig, and with make-up on. Leisurely, he went outside, pushing the pram.

The pram wove its way through the noise of people and cars. The hood was drawn down low. I could not see the sights on the street.

Soon, another person in a dress drew close, pushing a similar pram. This person swapped prams with Xiaokang, and pushed me away.

And once more, another person in a dress swapped for my pram.

The din of people and cars grew less and less. We suddenly turned into a quiet alley. We entered a courtyard, then turned though another doorway. The hood above me was drawn back. Greeting my eyes was a room full of coffins, and, in women's clothing, my teammate from Green Island Flathead, whom I missed greatly. "Flathead, go get changed," said Xiaokang. Flathead gave me a look, and immediately went to the back of the room.

"Is this a coffin shop?" I asked hesitantly.

"More or less. It's a funeral home, but we get more live people than dead ones. Business hasn't been that great." Xiaokang, who had already changed back to men's clothing, was sitting on a coffin. Pointing to another coffin beside him, he said, "Someone's reserved this one already. I can let you sleep in it for two days. Day after tomorrow I'll have someone take you away."

"Where to?"

Xiaokang looked as if he was racking his brains, "Anyway, we'll hide you somewhere farther away. You can't go home, but I don't know where you can go either."

"What about you? Tian Lin is after you. Where can you go?"

"I don't know. I'll deal with it one step at a time."

"They will never get off my back until they find me."

"Worst case, be a wanted man like me. Join the trade and be my second-in-command."

"I'm really worried. Floral is still in Tian Lin's hands."

"At least Tian Lin can't bring himself to off her. But he's sure to be quite eager to off you."

Laughing, Xiaokang walked over and tore off my baby hat. He then tossed a set of burial clothes to me. "You'll be wearing this day after tomorrow. We'll be sending you to paradise."

On the third day, my coffin was lifted onto a modest hearse, while another coffin was loaded into a van. I knew that this was how they ran their smuggling business—sometimes smuggling goods, sometimes smuggling people.

I was delivered to the countryside in central Taiwan to go in hiding. Xiaokang sent an associate to take care of me. While this was going on, Floral had already gone back to singing in the hotel, and occasionally the radio would broadcast her performances. I kept the radio by my ear every day. Once in a while she would hum an impromptu tune; I could tell that she was using a cipher song to ask how I was doing.

A month later, I had mostly recovered from my leg injury. Xiaokang drove over to pick me up.

"Oh, the boss himself is driving me this time? What happened to the hearse?" I joked.

"They're on our trail. We've closed the funeral home."

"Looks like Tian Lin won't ever leave us alone."

"Yeah, we're in the same boat now."

"I wonder if Tian Lin went to bother my family?"

"I heard that he sent someone once to check them out, watching them for a fortnight or so. But that's it. Obviously, Anna helped. She was very obedient to Tian Lin and did everything he wanted. Probably she pleaded with Tian Lin to spare your family. Tian Lin is a regular at that hotel now. His limo is always parked outside. I don't even dare to go collect protection money from them now. Oh, and, I sent someone to notify your family that you're still alive, but your whereabouts can't be revealed. Anyway, it's not like you can go home anymore. Might as well join up with us. I've worked it out with my men already—you'll be my right-hand man, and we'll create our future together..."

The car drove into the hills. Suddenly came a few gunshots. A bullet shot through the rear window, and Xiaokang's man sitting in the back died on the spot.

"Damn it! They've found us." Xiaokang stepped on the accelerator violently and the car lurched forward.

I looked over my shoulder and saw two black limos tailing us. Xiaokang swerved this way and that, trying all he could to shake them off. "They're sticking to us like shit on a shovel. Xiaokang, it's my fault for getting you into this mess. You shouldn't have had to worry about me."

"What's this your fault my fault? Cut this woman-talk. D'you think I'd actually kick you out of the car now?" As he spoke, Xiaokang kept his eyes fixed on the rear-view mirror. "Actually, I had wanted to quit this long ago, but the minions wouldn't let me go. They got in all sorts of trouble and expected me to clean up after them. Either way, even if I didn't get involved in your case, I have other enemies who have business to settle with me. Rather than getting killed by a bunch of thugs, I might as well do my duty to a friend, and earn a good name for dying for a good cause."

The car went around a bend in the road and drove onto a bridge over a river. With our pursuers not yet in sight yet, Xiaokang yelled, "Jump!"

We opened the doors simultaneously and rolled out of the car, which continued forward. We held each other's hand, and, with a "one, two, three!", jumped into the river together.

Xiaokang tugged me towards the only sampan in the vicinity. We swam over and hid beneath the craft. I sneaked a look up towards the bridge: a few figures in black had just stopped their car, and were peering about the river. Hurriedly I tucked my head back.

A while later, the boatman suddenly spoke, "They're gone."

Xiaokang pulled me up to the sampan. Right away the boatman handed us two bamboo hats and two old shirts. Xiaokang motioned for me to put those on. "This is Old Luo. He's our man. Handles some smuggling business for us. He usually waits for our orders here." We quickly put on our disguises, and the boatman began rowing the boat towards the shore. Before going on shore, Xiaokang turned around and said a few words to him:

"Same place. Notify Flathead to come meet us."

We slipped into the forest, and went to an abandoned work shed where we rested. About three hours went by. Xiaokang began to check his watch impatiently.

"We'll wait another hour at most. If we don't see him before dark, we'll go on ourselves."

Half an hour later, we heard a whistle outside the door, two short blasts and one long. "Here's Flathead," said Xiaokang.

Flathead poked his head in, "Boss, it's me."

We followed him to the other side of the forest. A car was parked there.

Flathead drove us towards the city. On either side of the road were nothing but bamboo fences and squalid tile-roofed houses.

Xiaokang asked, "Why are we taking this route?"

Flathead replied, "There's construction on the other road. Can't get through there."

"What rotten luck!" Xiaokang kept turning to look behind him. A few moments later, he shouted, "That car behind us is fishy. Flathead, get away from him."

Flathead spun the steering wheel, and we wove in and out of the traffic. After quite a while, the car behind us was no longer in sight. Flathead suddenly did a sharp turn, and the car drove into a narrow alley, and sped all the way to the end.

"Flathead, what are you doing?"

Xiaokang turned around and saw that the car from before was just driving into the alleyway. Flathead hurried to open the door.

"You squealed on us!" Xiaokang grabbed Flathead's arm to stop him from getting away.

"Sorry, boss. Because of him, we've already lost Fat Cat, Black Pine, and Lucky. They're so hot on your heels that we're forced to let go of the cabarets and the dance halls, and even the funeral home had to be closed down. We can't lie low with you forever. These days, it's no biggie to kill or steal, but once you get implicated in rebellion you'll never hear the end of it..."

"You!" Xiaokang's fist was about to strike while Flathead tore himself free, opened the door, and ran away. We saw him wave at the car behind us. However, a gunshot rang out, and Flathead fell on the ground, a bullet through him. Xiaokang immediately hopped into the driver's seat to get us out of there.

I looked behind me. The car was driving over Flathead's body and coming towards us. I said, "They killed Flathead."

"Stupid idiot! How could Flathead believe those sons-of-bitches? Rewarded with death for squealing."

This was a cul-de-sac with no way out. Xiaokang hastily put the gear in reverse, and drove into a house with laundry hanging outside.

All hell broke loose. The car broke through the back door of the house. On the windscreen were a pair of trousers and a bedsheet. I rolled down the window, and reached out to remove them. As I did so, I saw a black limo behind us. "Xiaokang, they're here again!"

"Still clinging on like shit to a shovel!" Xiaokang stepped on the accelerator. Suddenly, a gunshot rang out, and half the glass of the rear window shattered. Xiaokang was shot. The bullet pierced through his left shoulder blade. Instantly blood spurted out like a fountain.

The limo shot at us again, then intentionally drove into us. It hit us once, twice; the door on the driver's side was broken, and hung precariously by the side of the car.

I saw them! It was Tian Lin sitting in the limo, along with Floral.

Floral was screaming for him to stop. Tian Lin kept a hand on the steering wheel and slapped her with the other. "Stupid whore! You keep bugging me to let you come. Did you really think I didn't know what's on your mind? I'm going to let you watch me send him to his death!"

The limo drew close again, almost going shoulder to shoulder with us. All of a sudden, Xiaokang let go of the steering and jumped out, grabbing the door of the limo and threw himself in through the window. Tian Lin fired a few more shots. Xiaokang leapt onto Tian Lin. The limo began to zigzag; the wrestling inside was raging fiercely.

The limo sped along the road, completely out of control. I raced towards it from behind.

Suddenly Floral shrieked—

I abruptly stepped on the brakes. Just as I did so, I saw the limo fly off the road and fall into the sea.

A thicket of wildflowers, smashed, scattered all over.

Xiaokang! Floral!

A little flower flew in through the window of my car.

Two black limos drove up from behind. Two men in black yanked me out of the car and handcuffed me. I looked over my shoulder over and over again; the other few men in black were already standing by the edge of the cliff, scanning the land below.

One of my captors struck me with his fist, and pushed me into the limo.

After a while, all the men in black returned to the cars. The cars started, driving towards the city. Dusk was falling before us. My mind was going blank...

Xiaokang! Floral!

PART V

18
The mysterious prisoner

"Man can hardly even recognize the devils of his own creation."
— Albert Schweitzer

On the landing craft headed towards the outlying islands, someone found half a crumpled newspaper. It was apparently used to soak up the water and line the floor, when water was coming into the ship's hold, and was never cleared away. It was dark inside the hold, with only a bit of light near the deck. He read the paper by that bit of light, and when he was done, he passed it on to others. When it got passed into my hands, the largest headline on the page caught my eye—"Community and government leaders support him with one heart". It turned out to be a jointly-signed letter by some officials, recommending the "Crown Prince" to the post of Premier of the Executive Court. The letter praised the Crown Prince as one both talented and virtuous, the one who would bring about the restoration of the nation; because of that, all prominent community leaders, as well as all officials in the civil and military services, recommend him wholeheartedly to "Old Papa". In the long list of names I saw my father's name—"Song Jiafu". I remembered that, before I was sent to Green Island the last time, the Crown Prince had already taken control over all the intelligence agencies. This time, even my father, who had been dismissed from his post, had to declare loyalty to him publicly, while I was a prisoner of an agency under his command.

The year was 1974. I was sent to Green Island once more. The original building, called the "New Life Correctional Centre", was no longer in use, but had been replaced by the newly-constructed "Reform and Re-education Prison". The new prison was an even more impregnable fort; the walls were seven to eight metres tall, with high-voltage netting on top of them. There were over a dozen watchposts all around.

There were two sets of metal doors to pass through before one reached the cells. The cells were divided into eight areas. I was assigned to the ten-men room in Area 8. This was the most crowded cell; there was only a two-by-six-foot space for each man, and one had to sleep on his side. Both the toilet and the sink were in the cell. Bathing and laundry-washing had to be done in the toilet. Here, I did not have the opportunity to go outside on work detail, unlike before. Except for a thirty-to-forty-minute period of free time twice a day, we spent the entire day locked up in the cell. To prevent the inmates from colluding with each other, the prison was under even stricter control than before. For example, the odd-numbered cells and the even-numbered cells were given free time at different times, one before meals and one after. Before the inmates were let out, all windows or peepholes facing outward were covered up, so that we could not see the inmates from the other cells. And even when we were out in the courtyard, the prison officers, squadron leaders, and the political warfare officers kept a close eye on us. On top of that, surveillance cameras were installed on every watchpost along the wall; no one was free from monitoring. If a few individuals tended to gather and chat, they would have their pictures taken for further observation; if someone came under suspicion of insubordination, a video recording of his self-criticism during his trial would be broadcast in public.

I adapted to this life quickly. I knew that complaining and protesting would only serve to get myself in trouble.

Soon, they transferred me to a more spacious six-person cell. And not long after that I got the opportunity to work outside the prison.

One day, when I was sent to go purchase daily essentials, I ran into Yao Kunming. He was on work detail from another area of the prison. He looked very awkward when he saw me.

"Uncle Zhu Anqiao left behind a letter that he wrote when he was still alive, and someone sent that to the Investigation Bureau. My father had a heart attack during the trial and died. And after that our house was confiscated by the government..." Yao Kunming explained the reason for his incarceration.

"What did the letter say?" I remembered the two letters that Zhu Xiaokang mentioned.

"I don't know, except the Investigation Bureau used that letter as evidence to accuse my father as being an accomplice of Uncle Zhu, a Communist."

That meant, the content of the other letter would be similar. I remembered that Xiaokang promised my father to keep the secret. It was probably him, too, who sent that letter to the Bureau to implicate the Yaos. It had been in his hands, after all. I sighed inside, and suddenly felt sorry for Yao Kunming, even though I ought to hold a grudge against him. "Kunming, I heard that it was you who reported on me way back then?"

Yao Kunming lowered his head in admission. "Yes, it was me who told on you. Pan Baojiang made me do it. It was to get even with Chunshao, to make him pay for breaking the remote control plane. Or perhaps he had hated Chunshao all along. But I didn't know that it would end up hurting you..."

"Didn't you hate me for winning that much money from your father?"

"At first I did feel a bit indignant or angry, but it wasn't really because of that. How could I blame you if my dad lost..."

"Really?"

"Really. It's my fault. When my dad found out that I reported on you, I got in a lot of trouble."

"Why was it that even my mother was arrested?"

"I don't know. I really don't know how the matter got that big. I heard my dad say he was trying to save you, but it didn't work."

"Was there no other reason?" Of course I still did not understand how we were targeted by the Yaos for no particular reason. Unless they had played a big enough part, the government would not have bestowed our house upon them. But I did not want to point this out directly to Yao Kunming. I waited for him to volunteer the answer.

Yao Kunming thought for a bit, then said reluctantly, "Someone said, Pan Baojiang's father was in a power struggle against your mother's office. Pan Baojiang's father dug up some dirt on your mother's office, and managed to report on a few of their directors and deputy directors. A lot of people got dragged into it..."

It appeared that what Chunhong had said before was not baseless. But was it a coincidence or a plot that the two events happened so close to each other? It had looked like my family was targeted in particular, too. Also, if it was the Pans who had orchestrated this, why did the government award our house to Uncle Yao and not Pan Baojiang's father? Could it be because it was the Yaos who first stepped forward against us?

Finally I asked Yao Kunming if he managed to get this cushy job of running errands outside by making a deal with the prison authorities.

He nodded.

"So let's say we have a mutual understanding here. You tell your tales and I mine, but we'll steer clear of each other," I said.

Yao Kunming, looking at me, nodded again.

I turned around and took two steps away. Sudden I halted, turned around and asked him:

"What amperage of static do you need for the missile to launch on its own?"

Yao Kunming did a double take, and then he laughed. Laughed like he did when he was little.

I gave him a friendly look. We gazed at each other for several seconds, before walking away from each other, pretending that we were strangers.

Both he and I became snitches in the prison. We were monitored by the prison guards, but we also monitored other elements in the group; by informing of them, we gained more privileges and freedom for ourselves. I only intended to go through the motions of doing it, though, just to stay afloat by handing over some unimportant pieces of information. Power can be used both to harm others and not.

Yao Kunming and I ran into each other occasionally, but as much as possible we avoided all contact, in case we drew attention to ourselves.

I maintained distance even with the others in my cell, observing, but never joining in. I did not trust anyone. I had no friends and would be nobody's friend.

But I still had one friend on this island whom I could trust. Mr. Phantom, the big fish with the phantom-like face. To my surprise, he still remembered me. Whenever I could steal away to swim in the sea, he would still come to touch my forehead with his puckered lips, wanting me to pet him. After that, he would turn around once, twice, in the water, looking like he was as comfortable as could be.

* * *

The first typhoon of the summer arrived tumultuously. Though we were lying in the cell, we felt we were cast afloat on the ocean. We felt that everything was shaking, that the building would be uprooted and cast among the roaring beasts in the mountains.

The guards mobilised the prisoners to go out into the storm and place sandbags on the roofs to hold them down. Some of the roofs had almost been pried off by the wind, and there were not enough sandbags to go around. So the guards picked some prisoners to take turns to lie on the roof. When those inmates returned to the cell, they were invariably shivering and pallid. They all said that the waves were as tall as the hills; Heaven and earth shook as lightning and thunder clashed; it was hellish.

I could not help but worry about that man, Number 2336, that enigmatic prisoner in solitary confinement. His dungeon must have been flooded in such a storm. From what I heard, he had already been confined in the seaside dungeon for over half a year. Everyone else who was sent there for punishment stayed at most half a month. And if they were to be interrogated, they would be brought out every few of days and flogged outside the dungeon, and sent back after the interrogation. This inmate, though, was neither flogged nor interrogated. I had no idea what offence he had committed to warrant such a long stay in the dungeon.

I had been delivering water and food to him for over two months. The prisoners in the dungeon were allowed only a basin of water and a bowl of rice every day. That basin was all they had for drinking and washing. The bowl of rice came with nothing but a few dashes of salt. None of the other convicts were willing to go work at the dungeon. As there was no toilet in there, all business was done directly on the floor. When the tide came in and flooded the dungeon, each cell became a pool of sewage, and the inmate soaked in his own filth. Once the tide ebbed, the entire floor would be covered in sludge. You could smell the stench a long way away from the dungeon, and the place was infested with mosquitoes and flies. I, though, was a very obedient worker, and I would do whatever no one else was willing to do, as long as my superiors gave me more freedom to walk outside.

For some reason, I was very curious about him, and sometimes I would hide a bit of vegetables in his rice for him. However, he always kept silent and aloof, as if he had nothing to do with the rest of the world. As much as I wanted to talk to him, our interaction was limited to exchanging looks.

Once, after I had delivered water and food to him, he suddenly spoke, "Give me a toothpick." The second day I whittled a toothpick and brought it over when I delivered his meal. At once he stuck it in his mouth and dug around, looking like he was quite enjoying himself. "The greens you give me are too tough. They get stuck between my teeth," he said. I asked what his name was. Number 2336, he said, and then reverted to looking at me with the same aloof expression from before. He spoke no more.

"I came in around the same time he did. I recognise him." One day, when I mentioned the inhabitant of the dungeon to Yao Kunming, he revealed the man's identity to me, "Liang Zhibang, the president's private doctor. I'd met him before. He'd treated my father once when he was sick."

"Why is he in here?" I asked.

"I don't know, but as soon as he got here he was locked up in a solitary cell. Even when he was transferred to the dungeon later, he was locked up by himself. Some of the other cells had four or five people in them at a time."

"Are there any other inmates who know about his identity?"

"I never told anyone. There must be a special reason for anyone to be locked up in solitary confinement. If I let others find out that I know him, I'd just be inviting them to associate me with him. And if I get implicated with him, I'd be in for a lot of trouble."

The day after that that, when I went to deliver his meal, I called him "Doctor". He lifted his head and gave me a meaningful look. After that, even though I did not speak when I came in contact with him, we seemed to have come to a tacit understanding. He knew that I was aware of his identity, but since I did not reveal what I knew, he also pretended that nothing had happened.

Some days later, I was moved again. This time, it was to a solitary cell, but I did not occupy it alone. I had a cellmate, Dr. Liang. He had been released from the dungeon. To be more precise, I was ordered to be his cellmate, to monitor him, and to report everything he said to my superiors.

But he was always taciturn. I did not gain his trust. Or perhaps, he could not trust anyone.

We spent each day together silently. Besides occasionally exchanging a glance, there was nothing more.

One day, he suddenly spoke, "You talked in your sleep last night."

I asked him what he heard. He had an equivocal look on his face and, instead of answering, asked, "What were you humming?"

He hummed a snippet of a tune to me. I said it was a cipher song.

A look of wonder appeared in his eyes. I knew that his curiosity was piqued. I volunteered to decode it for him, and also taught him how to make songs with code.

"What got you in here?" He asked. This was the first time he showed interest in me.

I told him every single detail of my family background and how I ended up in jail. This was not intentionally for buying his trust, but simply spilling pent-up frustration to someone who could empathise. I guessed he was also a victim of wrongful accusations, that he suffered more than I did, that he was more resentful than I was.

"You are Song Jiafu's son?" He looked me up and down.

"You know my father?"

He nodded and smiled slightly.

"To tell you the truth, they kept me in here to monitor and report on you," I revealed my mission.

"No big deal. I'm used to it. They've tried everything in the books but they still don't know what to do with me."

This was the first time he spoke so much to me. I was elated. I did not report the actual details to my superiors—I changed the part about me talking in my sleep to him talking in his sleep, and made up some other details to give the officers a reason to keep me in this cell.

We conversed more and more frequently. To avoid drawing attention from the guards or anyone eavesdropping, we agreed to avoid speaking out loud generally, unless it was for unimportant things. He knew Morse, so we conversed by tapping out code on the floor with our fingers.

The following is the content of our conversation.

"Why did you get arrested?" I asked.

"They wanted to ask me about a secret, and they were worried about another secret leaking. So they could neither let me go nor kill me, until I have disclosed the secret."

"What kind of secret could make them not know what to do with you?"

"I'll tell you when we get out."

"If you don't tell them, how are you ever going to get out?"

"Here? I won't be let out even if I tell. Only if I don't tell would they keep me alive, until they lose their patience. If I tell you and let you know, don't imagine that you can trade it in for goodwill. They will kill you anyway."

"Then..." I gazed into his eyes, which had a slightly wistful, but inscrutably deep expression, one of boundless emptiness, as if he was awaiting death. "I'll help you get out of here. And you'll tell me the secret."

"You want to escape?" he sneered.

I made a wager with him. If we managed to get out, he had to tell me the secret.

* * *

I got a fairly good idea of the layout of the "Reform and Re-education Prison". There was approximately a whole brigade of soldiers in total guarding the prison. My cell was behind a watchpost. In front of that, at the entrance of the section, two patrols were stationed. Because surveillance was focused on the entrance area where people came and went, the rear of the prison offered more opportunities. As for the electric fence some seven or eight metres high, that was out of the question. The main thing, though, was that the island was in the middle of the sea, and one could not go anywhere even after escaping—unless there was a boat. I remembered the location where Zhu Xiaokang had hidden the boat in the past. Once, when I was sent out on work detail, I found the hidden cave in the rocks. Fortunately, the boat was still there. Even though it was covered in rust, it should still be seaworthy.

But how could one get out from the back? Besides a vent with a metal grate, a square foot big and about three or four metres up from the floor, there was nothing in the cell but a heavy metal door. There was a small hole at the bottom of the door for passing in meals. It was only opened once a day by the prison worker delivering our meals. Even if there was a way to leave through the metal door, we would be caught right away upon encountering the patrols. The vent with the grate did face outward, but it was too high, making it difficult for two people to escape at the same time. Besides, there was also the question of how to break the grate. I did not think it was a good place to start. The only remaining option, then, was the most primitive one—digging a tunnel.

The concrete at the bottom of the wall was not strong. Through years of corrosion from the salt and moisture in the sea water, it had become brittle. A simple test revealed that it would not be difficult to dig through it.

I secretly bought a small, pointy trowel from the villagers. Every day, I dug out a bit of concrete, covering the hole with my blanket. I crumbled up the concrete pieces and hid them in my clothing, disposing of them as I went out to run my errands. Thus, over the course of twenty days, I had dug a small tunnel all the way through the wall. Excitedly I peered through the hole, but was instantly chagrined—the cell was built along a cliff, a very steep cliff. It was bare as bare could be outside, with no foothold in sight.

Dr. Liang crawled over and took a look out the hole. Then, he looked at me with an expression of mockery and pity, as if saying that I had laboured in vain. "It's not just concrete. Look, there are slabs of stones lining this too. It'll be hard to remove them." He pointed at the stone showing through the concrete hole, telling me I might as well give up now.

That night, the wind howled from the sea, and the waves of the incoming tide were heard clearly. Dr. Liang lay on the bed; under the moonlight shining through the window, I saw that his eyes were glimmering—he had not shut them. He shot me a glance, as if asking me "You're awake too?"

He dragged my hand to him and tapped in my palm in code:

"What day of the lunar calendar is it?"

"I don't know," I tapped in his palm.

"Can you see the moon if you stand up?"

I stood up on my toes and lifted my head to look at the ventilation window high, high up.

"No."

"Put me on your back. Let me stand on your shoulders and see."

I crouched down and let Dr. Liang get on my shoulders. Carefully I walked to the spot he indicated. A while later, Dr. Liang got down, and tapped in my palm, "It may be full moon in a few days."

I looked at him, not knowing what he meant.

"What a mess you made. That hole you dug is going to be trouble," he tapped.

I still did not understand.

"Listen to the tide coming in. I think the tide is almost right below our wall. At the highest tide of the month, the water will surely come in," he tapped again.

"Can't undig the hole now," I looked pensively at the hole in the corner of the wall.

"Can you get us some nitric acid and some hydrochloric acid? The sooner the better."

I looked tentatively at Dr. Liang. Then I remembered that they were components of disinfectants for washing toilets and scrubbing floors. Yao Kunming was responsible for procurement, I thought. "All right, I'll try."

"Also need a few pieces of wire or thin pieces of iron, and some cotton. Don't ask why," he tapped in my palm at the end.

On the next day, Dr. Liang took out a few pills that the medical office had given him in the past for pain, and told me to soak them in half a cup of water. He did not drink it; rather, he used this colourless solution to write some lines on a sheet of paper. Then, he stuffed this blank piece of paper into a bottle. He instructed me to place it at a specific location far away, and hang a rope with two knots in it on an east-facing branch of a certain tree. I ran this errand for him when I was sent out on official business.

That evening, I asked him what he was using to write on the paper.

In my palm he wrote the word "antipyrine".

I shot an astonished glance at him, then I shut my eyes and looked at him no more.

Perhaps I should have known and not be so shocked. I was reminded of something I read in a book when I was young. This painkiller was great for secret writing. Words written in a solution of it would not be affected by UV rays, heat, or iodine; they could not be revealed through normal methods. The only way to reveal them was by using a 10% solution of ferric oxide. I should have known that Dr. Liang was no simple doctor.

Two days later, I collected everything that Dr. Liang wanted. He instructed me to make aqua regia by mixing one part of nitric acid and three parts of hydrochloric acid, and put it in a brown glass bottle. When night fell, he had put him on my shoulders. He lifted his arms up high, and, dipping a wire in the aqua regia, he began to work on corroding the bottoms of the metal bars on the ventilation window. I suddenly understood what he was aiming for.

We worked through the night, three nights in a row.

On the fourth day, Dr. Liang did nothing but crouch by the wall. From the little hole in the corner of the wall, the sky seemed especially bright orange. Half of it was clear and cloudless, while the other was covered with dense, fire-red cloud formations. "A typhoon is coming." A cryptic look flashed on Dr. Liang's face.

That night, a gale, in presage of a rainstorm, arose. The wind leaking through the walls chilled us to the bones.

Dr. Liang and I looked at each other, both with expectant and anxious looks in our eyes. The rain suddenly became heavy. The roar of the surging tides bellowed through the heavens.

The moment was at hand. I suddenly felt worried, my heart thudding loudly, my soul feeling like it was being pushed by the tide to the tip of the waves, the tip of the winds. This was an enormous gamble. But, having come so far, there was no turning back...

"The typhoon is here. All the prison guards must have gone on storm duty," I tapped in Dr. Liang's hand.

The waves crashed into the boulders with a loud boom. "The tide is rising!" Dr. Liang tapped.

The water soon came in through the hole in the wall. Instinctively I got up and avoided it.

"The more the merrier." Dr. Liang stood in the water, examining the volume of its flow.

There was more seawater than expected. It kept flowing in. Just 20 minutes later, it covered us to our necks. We lay back on the water, trying as hard as we could to stay afloat.

The water level gradually rose in this tiny cell. It did not take long for the water level to double.

We swam to the wall, and, reaching out towards the vent, we each grabbed hold of a metal bar. In the cover of the din of rain and waves,

together we kicked the metal grate outward. It snapped instantly. The metal bars that we were holding onto, which had also been corroded, could not carry our weight any longer, and broke off from our hands as well.

Dr. Liang and I fell into the water and had our noses fill up with water. We laughed heartily. Striving on, we squeezed out of the ventilation window, and swam into the sea.

Through the veil of the storm, I could vaguely make out a few landmarks--Jiangjun Rock, Niutou Hill, Mt. Huoshao, and the lighthouse; with them I charted our course. However, with the powerful tidal waves pushing against us, we were unable to stay on our planned course. We were like two cornered animals, wrestling with the sea while holding onto each other.

Suddenly, something bumped into my feet and my body. I lowered my head and saw that it was Mr. Phantom, my old friend. As I had done before, I signalled for him to go towards a certain direction, and he twisted his enormous body and began to lead the way like a pilot. Dr. Liang and I held onto him as we swam forward, and for the entire way neither wind nor wave could separate us.

We reached our destination. I patted Mr. Phantom as a signal for him to stop.

Dr. Liang and I swam single file into the sea cave and pushed from it the boat that Xiaokang had hidden. Dr. Liang climbed into it first while I stayed in the sea to keep Mr. Phantom company.

Mr. Phantom touched my forehead with his lips. Just as before, I reached out to pet him. He turned around in the water, around and around, in sheer innocent joy. It was gut-wrenching for me to watch him. I could not help but kiss his forehead as well, and flip around and around in the water along with him.

From the boat, Dr. Liang told me to hurry. Reluctantly, I gave Mr. Phantom a push to tell him to leave. He circled around me twice and rubbed against my leg. I pushed him again, and he finally swam away.

I watched as he disappeared into dark, dark sea. Heaven and Earth were blended into a boundless whole by waves that reached the skies.

* * *

The storm abated temporarily. The boat drifted about in the sea. I rowed as hard as I could.

"Where are you going?" asked Dr. Liang.

"Taiwan," I answered without thinking.

Dr. Liang snatched the oars from me. Just as I was about to protest, he looked at me inscrutably and said, "Don't ask. Just come with me." He had a commanding presence that made it impossible for one to disobey him. I held my tongue and let him row.

A while later, I opened my mouth again, "Can you tell me the secret?"

"How impatient you are."

"You promised me. You can't go back on your words."

"All right, I'll tell you." He put on a strange expression on his face. "This president of ours is sick. With a strange disease."

That night, I listened, jaw-dropped, to Dr. Liang describe the symptoms of Old Papa, doubting time and again the veracity in his words.

"He often has hallucinations. They were neither dreams or imaginings. In short, he is in full possession of his faculties, but what his eyes and ears perceive is different to what normal people see and hear. When he is face to face with you, he may not be seeing you, but rather the you in his mind. But that's not really you, but someone else. Or, he'd look at a yellow dog and call the name of a white dog. He would look at something familiar and take it to be a strange monster. He would look at something that is open, without secrets, and say that it is closed, hidden..."

"Because all that he sees are ridiculous phenomena that aren't grounded in reality, he spends all his day in anxiety. Only by destroying the strange phenomena that he sees can he be at ease..."

"So here he is, in some gigantic distortion, but not realising it. At the same time, he is an absolute controller of power, and everyone worships him. Those around him do not betray him, nor would they dare to; however, because his view of the world is so distorted, his corresponding actions are all twisted as well. And thus he commits a grave mistake. He keeps sending officials and commoners alike to jail, treating innocent people as his enemies, because he feels he is seeing betrayals and lies. And those who worship him play the role of executioner for him, using twisted methods to continue distorting the situation..."

"How did he get this disease?" I asked. Actually I was not certain what Dr. Liang was trying to say.

"I don't know," he handed the oars back to me, and took a breath. "Let me put it this way. He wants to be a hero, but he doesn't know that he has lost long ago and he is still dreaming. When he wakes up from the dream and finds that everything is wrong, he blames the world, and waves his sword at it. There's something wrong with his mind; everything he sees is altered..."

"You said that there's something wrong with his mind, but perhaps you wanted to say there's something wrong in his heart..."

Dr. Liang fell silent pensively for a while before replying, "He was a hero once. He was a patriot, and all patriots are called heroes. But once a hero becomes obsessed, he becomes the devil... He had ambitions, but he has lost. He had desires, but only failure remains in his heart. He had hope, but more than that he has fear... Anyway, he has to force himself to forget about those failures and fears, to resist the distorted realities. On top of that, I discovered that he had another symptom. For a long while, his memory remained in the time before retreating from the Mainland. He believed that he still lived in those bygone years, and was impervious to anything that was happening before his eyes. Additionally, he was in a car accident a few years ago, after which his memory became even more limited. It was frozen at specific times. When he woke up in the morning, perhaps he'd have forgotten what had happened the day before. When he had new attendants, guards, or secretaries, perhaps he'd call them by the names of his previous staff. Because he could only remember a certain moment, he was fixated on that moment, and this caused the phenomenon where he obstinately insisted on treating people and things from another moment as objects of the moment of his fixation."

"So why did they lock you up?"

"He went into a coma," said Dr. Liang. "It's a big deal for a president to fall into a coma. They're worried that anyone could use this as an excuse to rebel. They couldn't let the news out, so they resorted to secretive investigations. They asked me what medication I gave him. I said it's just sleeping pills."

"Was it really only sleeping pills?" I asked.

"Yeah. He couldn't stop worrying, and kept having insomnia. Only with sleeping pills could he get a night of peace. He had me prescribe them and he took them every night."

"Then your situation is completely undeserved."

"Not exactly," Dr. Liang grinned, "I'll let you in on this. I increased the dosage of a certain substance in his prescription. When taken over time, it accumulates in the body, and even if it doesn't kill a man outright it'd put him in a coma."

"Ah! You were out to harm him!"

"I had no choice. He was too powerful, and if everyone obeyed him, the world would be in chaos. His only way out was to realise it himself, to figure out by himself that he was sick. And then to destroy himself, before the world is destroyed by him. Sadly, he never had that self-realisation."

"So you just went ahead to murder him."

"I was only keeping him in an indeterminate coma."

"But I saw his picture in the newspaper just some time ago. He regained consciousness."

"That was only someone who looked like him. I knew him all too well. The man in the picture was missing something on his face. He was only ninety percent alike and thus was an imposter. My guess is, he's been in a coma for too long and it's impossible to keep it under wraps anymore. To stabilise their political power and to avoid unrest, his family found a fake to show his face, so as to dispel any rumours."

"Dr. Liang," I was most puzzled and disturbed by this man before my eyes. "Are you really just a doctor?"

Dr. Liang did not answer. He took the oars from me, and began rowing.

We were engulfed in endless darkness. I asked worriedly, "Where are we going?"

"Back over there."

"Over where?" My voice was almost covered by the sound of the waves.

"This secret cannot stay in Taiwan." He shot a glance at me, "I am a Communist."

"A Communist! They sent you over to get rid of him?"

"You should say, to treat him." As he said this, Dr. Liang leant over ever so slightly, his gaze sharp enough to slice a man in half.

"You..." With nothing but the raging sea around us, I was feeling desperate. "How are you going to row all the way to the Mainland? It's a long way."

"Someone will come meet us. Sit tight, don't upset the boat."

"You expect me to let you do whatever to me?"

"You can jump overboard, if you really want to go back to Taiwan. Or you can push me overboard and row back to Taiwan yourself. We only have one boat between us."

I did not know how to choose at that instant.

I took a deep breath and grew less agitated. "Let's put it this way. There's a cause for his paranoia. It's just that he had accused too many people wrongly. There really are rebel spies around him."

"Hah, hah! I don't like the term 'rebel spies'. I am neither a rebel nor a spy. I am a veritable doctor, and one that only treats leaders of nations at that. I am the most authoritative doctor around. You should have said that I cured him. Whether on Taiwan or on the Mainland, my medical skills will forever be above suspicion."

"You have been the doctor of the leader of the CCP?"

"Yes."

"What was he sick with?"

"Hah, hah, hah."

"What was it?"

"Hah, hah, that will remain a mystery."

A briny wind arose from the sea. All I could hear was the doctor's dreadful laughter.

The patient, who has lost certain neurological and psychological functions due to a disease, is locked in a particular point in time and space, with no past or future, and unable to perceive events that happen to him... These symptoms have already been described in detail in the traditional literature on neurology. But how do such impairments change a man fundamentally, and how does he interact with the world, while operating under a completely different mental model? These questions must be posed in the empirical realm of psychology...

—Liu Xukai, attending physician, Department of Neurology, National Taiwan University Hospital

Such cases of 'anosagnosia' may be of many kinds—and may arise from excesses, no less than impairments, of function...There is always a reaction, on the part of the affected organism or individual, to restore, to replace, to compensate for and to preserve its identity, however strange the means may be...

Although right-hemisphere syndromes are as common as left-hemisphere syndromes, we will find a thousand descriptions of left-hemisphere syndromes in the neurological and neuropsychological literature for every description of a right- hemisphere syndrome... So much so that they may demand a new sort of neurology, a 'personalistic' science...

—Oliver Sacks, M.D., American neurologist

The doubling of consciousness... There is the quasi-parasitical state of consciousness (dreamy state), and there are remains of normal consciousness and thus, there is double consciousness . . . a mental diplopia.

—John Hughlings Jackson, English neurologist

For what is it that constitutes a 'disease entity' or a 'new disease'? [...] The physician is concerned [...with] the human subject, striving to preserve its identity in adverse circumstances. [...T]his 'striving to preserve identity', however strange the means or effects of such striving, was recognized in psychiatry long ago—and, like so much else, is especially associated with the work of Freud. Thus, the delusions of paranoia were seen by him not as primary but as attempts (however misguided) at restitution, at reconstructing a world reduced by complete chaos... [This] organized chaos [is] a chaos induced in the first instance by destruction of important integrations, and reorganized on an unstable basis in the process of rehabilitation."

—Ivy McKenzie and Oliver Sacks

19
He left

Upon the passing of my late father, the entire nation came out in force to pay tribute and mourn. I was incredibly moved by the depth of sorrow and the sincerity of hope expressed. Afflicted and overwhelmed with grief, I am unable to personally thank everyone who has offered sympathy; I can only obey my father's last will and devote my life to the cause, to repay the hearts and hopes of the people of this nation.

—Chiang Ching-kuo, 16 April, 1975

On the matter of Party leadership, I, He Yingqin, endorse the appointment of Comrade Chiang Ching-kuo to the position of Chairman of the Party Central Standing Committee... His accomplishments over the last two years as the Premier of the Executive Court have won unanimous support from both local and overseas Chinese, and our international allies. Under Comrade Chiang Ching-kuo's leadership, the power of our party will certainly strengthen and solidify, and our mission of recovering our nation from the Communists will soon be achieved.

Comrade Chiang Ching-kuo is a man of tremendous revolutionary spirit and outstanding leadership skills. He has demonstrated the ability to handle international crises calmly. His stalwart determination in opposing Communism is approved wholeheartedly by this committee, and his down-to-earth, approachable manner is well-loved by the public. Currently, international situations are ever-changing, while the anti-Communist contingent is wavering. To carry out the Will of President Chiang and to pursue our revolution, our Party needs strong leadership and unity in order to maximise our effect as a political party of revolution and democracy... As such, Comrade Chiang Ching-kuo is truly the most suitable candidate for the position; this is also the unanimous opinion of the Members of the Party.

—Kuomintang Central Standing Committee meeting minutes
28 April, 1975

On the 5th of April, 1975, Old Papa passed away. On the 17th of April, every newspaper in Taiwan spared no effort in their coverage of the cortege and the pomp surrounding the interment. Tens of thousands of students knelt along the route of the procession; shops hung scrolls with elegiac couplets on their doors. On the front page of every paper was a photograph of Chiang Ching-kuo leading high-ranking officials of every district in kowtowing and mourning before Old Papa's hearse.

Father had been restored to his former position prior to that, in February. From a copy of Central Daily News from Taiwan, I saw that he was listed as editor-in-chief once more.

In May, "the Crown Prince" took on the position of the Chairman of the Party. Soon after that he granted a general amnesty to all political prisoners. The editor-in-chief of the Central Daily News became someone else.

In June, my work unit suddenly ordered me to go clandestinely back to Taiwan for a mission. Despite this assignment, I knew they were still uncertain about me. I had to bring back something to prove that I was worth their trust—unless I did not plan to return at all.

After arriving in Taiwan, I first took a room in a hotel and tried to contact Chunshao. Even though this could have jeopardised me, I really missed my family.

The next day, a uniformed hotel staff knocked on my door, and handed me a new set of toothbrush and toothpaste.

I examined this extra set of toiletries, and understood. I opened the toothpaste tube, squeezed a bit of toothpaste out, and there it was—a tiny scroll of paper slid out of the tube as well. On it was written a time and place to meet. The bottom of the toothbrush handle could also be opened up. In it was hidden a key.

I went to the appointed place. It was a ramshackle brick bungalow. Outside it were some scrap paper and junk for the junk collector. I opened the door with the key. The house appeared to have been vacant for a long time, but on a chair lay a straw hat and a set of old clothes. There were some stains on the clothes. They looked dirty, but it was evident that they had just been washed—they still carried the fragrance of laundry detergent. Beside them was a carrying pole with a basket on either end, filled with materials and tools—the kit of a travelling cobbler.

Ten minutes later, a man came in. He took off his hat and wig.

"Why did you come back?" Chunshao asked in a low voice.

"I've got something to do," I replied.

"Don't mess up. I can't cover you."

"I know."

"Even though there's an amnesty, you went over to the Mainland and actually got a job there. They're not going to let you off. You have to keep yourself hidden."

"I know. I only came back to see you and Father. I won't stay for long. I won't cause you any trouble, or do anything that would make things difficult for you... If you want to arrest me, that's fine too." We gazed at each other, exchanging a meaningful glance, seeing a hitherto-unknown weathered look in each other. After all, it had been many years.

Over the last few years, Chunshao had become a researcher at the Intelligence Bureau, while I did the same work on the other side of the Strait. I did not tell him about Dr. Liang, but he knew that I had escaped Green Island anyway. As for my occupation on the other side—the Taiwanese Intelligence Bureau would have had that on file long time ago.

"They wouldn't just let you come back. They told you to come back on business?"

I did not deny it.

"So you're really working for them? And you're still going to go back there?" Chunshao asked again.

"I know what you're trying to say. You want to persuade me give myself up and confess, in exchange for trust or acceptance on this side. That's impossible. You must know that the Mainland just recently released a bunch of war captives, all special agents that the KMT had sent there. After they were captured, they were sent to labour camps. There they suffered and grew old. Then, the CCP released them and allowed them to decide whether to go or to stay. They all wanted to return to Taiwan. They were sent to Hong Kong, to wait for the KMT's arrangements. But the KMT did nothing. One of them waited in Hong Kong for a long time. He renewed his visa again and again, and when he had waited so long that he was completely broke, he finally received a letter from the KMT denying him entry. So he committed suicide."

"I know about that," Chunshao's expression was grim. "But we can't be too careful."

"So, I have to go back. There's no safe haven for me in Taiwan. If I betray my mission and remain in Taiwan, I would die anyway. Your government will kill me. My organisation knows too well that I have no choice. I have to go back."

"Then I'll have to arrest you. As soon as you make a move, I'll have to bring some guys over and arrest you. If I don't, you'd be arrested by others anyway, and in the hands of other people you'd die even faster." Chunshao paused momentarily, then looked at me with regret in his eyes, "If you hadn't stepped forward back then, it would have been me who was arrested, and it would have been me in jail... Chunhuan, don't blame me..." Chunshao picked up the hat and clothes from the chair, took a look at them, and replaced them. "As soon as they decide to arrest you, they'll trump up a bunch of charges for you even if you haven't done anything wrong. This country keeps a pack of people whose jobs are to create something out of nothing..."

"Don't worry, I'll be fine. I won't be doing anything for now. All I want to do is to go home and see Father."

"Yes, you should go see him. I'm covering you up this time not because of you, but because of him. My guess is that he's holding out just to wait for you."

"What's going on with Father?"

"He's going to die soon."

Later that day, I put on the stained clothes and the straw hat; in my cobbler's disguise, I carried my equipment on a carrying pole on my shoulder, calling out my services door to door until Chunshao opened the door and invited me in.

As I turned to lift my foot to cross the threshold, I took a glance to one side. In the alleyway was a pedestrian, and a car was parked at a distance. I could not tell for sure if we were free from surveillance. I entered the house, and as I crossed from the front courtyard into the living room, I saw the calligraphy scroll hanging in the room—

O'er moonlit mountains shines a beaming shaft;
On placid waters sails a lonely raft.

After so many years, these words were still hanging in the same room. I thought of all that I had gone through these years, but said nothing.

As if he had read my mind, Chunshao said in a low voice, "He (Chunshao pointed at the door of Father's room) wouldn't have that taken down. No matter where we moved, he still hung it up."

Let's not speak of that—I waved my hand to tell him to stop. I looked around us, and gave him a teasing look—Did he not know that walls had ears?

Chunshao motioned for me to take a look. Indeed, the windows in the house had already been covered up by wooden boards. I gave him a look of approval. In recent years, Taiwan's surveillance technology had progressed beyond on-site bugging. They had a gun-shaped mic that they could install in a car. Even if the car was parked far away, a mic pointed in the right direction could pick up a conversation in a house via the vibrations transmitted through the glass of the window.

I examined the thickness of the boards, and felt a bit more at ease. Gesturing towards Father's room, I asked in a low voice, "Is he awake?"

Chunshao took me to Father's room. He was still asleep.

I ceased my conversation with Chunshao. I could sense the perils in this house. Look at Father lying on the bed, I replayed the conversation

I had had with Chunshao in the little brick house. I had asked him then what was going on with Father. He had said, "He's sick, but he wouldn't go to the hospital. He said, when his time comes, he'd put on his burial clothes by himself, and lie there until he dies."

I had asked, "What's he sick with?"

"Don't know. He had never been willing to see a doctor. He said he'd rather just take medicine himself."

"Why?"

"Perhaps... he's worried. Apparently a few high-ranking officials died abnormal deaths. They'd go to the spa, or to dinner, or to the doctor's, and then they're found dead."

But could he really just suffer like that instead of letting someone help him?

I walked up to the head of Father's bed, and crouched down before him. Ever since I had become a grown man, I had not once watched him from such a close distance. His face was clean, with balanced, handsome features. The years had only laid a layer of frost on his countenance, and nothing else. He did not grow old; he only became weakened.

His breath was slow. His eyes moved slightly beneath his eyelids, as if he was about to wake up. I called his name at his ear. The eyelids half-opened, and he fixed his sight on me, as if trying to ascertain who it was before him. After that, he pushed himself up to a sitting position, and gave Chunshao a look to tell him to leave.

He was indeed very weak. The expression in his eyes had lost its former keenness. He did not ask me why I came back, or how I came back, as if that was all immaterial. He only gestured for me to close the door and help him out of bed.

He had me support him to a bookcase. He reached out his hand and touched something, and the bookcase moved aside, revealing an opening. We stepped into the opening, and the bookcase closed behind us.

This was a secret chamber, one that was like a storage room. There was a bookcase in there too, with an assortment of books and trinkets piled up haphazardly in it. There were also a few brocade boxes of various sides, and scrolls of calligraphy and paintings. I had never seen these when I was living at home, nor did I know there was such a secret chamber in the house.

It was very stuffy in the room. The walls all around were solid, with no ventilation at all.

"We can talk here." These were the first words he said to me.

I still did not dare to be careless. I scanned the room, then told him quietly that I could not stay long this time. He nodded.

"Chunhuan, I know about everything you went through in these years. Perhaps you couldn't understand why I never got involved or asked you anything," Father's voice, though weak, still had the note of love and care as from the past. It also had a subtle charm to it. No wonder Autumn could not leave him, I thought.

"Father, you must have had your own reasons. I understand. In these times, there's often no logic to what's going on."

"That's right. When they first locked you up, that was for testing me. They held one of my sons as hostage to see if I was truly loyal to them."

"Was that from Old Papa?"

"No, it was his heir. He was watching, watching to see what I felt, what I did..." Father pulled my hand towards him and held it lightly. His palms were ice-cold, as if they were from another world. "They also told you that you are not my child, right?"

"Dad, I don't believe it. They lied." I lowered my head in anguish.

"Chunhuan, my child," Father stroked my hair, "Go to the bookcase and get me the hard-cover Keats."

I brought over the tattered anthology. Father felt around the cardboard inside the cover, and from an inconspicuous slit extracted a small photograph.

The backdrop of the picture was a hospital. In front of the hospital was a man in a long robe, with a wooden staff in hand, and beside him was a female nurse.

Father assumed a rare expression of solemnness, and held the photo before me. "I must tell you this today. Chunhuan, this is... your father."

I saw clearly. I almost stopped breathing, my mind going blank. I did not know how to react. In the photograph, the nurse was standing beside him. I could tell who he was right away.

"It's him!"

"It is... him. Yes. I wanted you to know."

My focus was forced back to this photograph. This little figure before me, not more than two inches tall, I had seen on a daily basis before. Except, in this photo he seemed a bit more haggard, and the expression in his eyes did not look as amicable as in his public appearance, but rather aggressive instead. Yes, I am referring to that portrait, the one found hung up high in every school, that of the President.

"It's the President! He didn't know about me?"

"The President..." Father looked at me, and paused awhile. "It's true... he didn't know. But I was just working for him at the time, and found out about it by chance."

"What about my mother?" I burst out without thinking. Everything in my world had been overthrown; I had to question everything.

Father pointed at the picture, "This nurse. When you were little, it was her who fed you."

Ah, my real mother? I studied the face of this unfamiliar woman. I really did not remember what she looked like.

In my memory was only the sickly sweet smell of Star brand floral water, and the soft and smooth touch of skin.

I had tugged her nipple, flicking it this way and that. She had gently moved my hand aside, and seemed to have said something to me.

As if she was saying, it's time you're weaned. The more you eat, the faster you'll grow up. Don't think about this anymore...

In fact, she had never said anything out loud. But I understood what she meant. She adjusted her bra and tucked her nipple back in. I looked longingly at the two vague, round dots in the dim light. I did not actually wanted milk; I just liked the pretty shape of her round, plump nipples, and the faint rose colour in my memory.

"She was a nurse in this hospital. When 'Old Papa' was injured in Chongqing and hospitalised, she took care of him. For a very short time," said Father. "Around then, the 'Crown Prince' had a mistress in town as well, and after she gave birth, she was done in by special agents. When the pregnant nurse heard about that, she was terrified. She hurried to me and begged me to help her. She wept and swore she would never dare to take Madame Chiang's place, and that she would never leak out this secret. By then, the child in her womb was too big.

Even if she got rid of it then, it would have been too late. I promised to protect her and her child. I took it upon myself to take care of the nurse. The nurse gave birth to you."

"Where is she?"

"I don't know. Your mother, not knowing the backstory, sent her away at some point..."

I finally understood the reason for the darkness I remembered from my childhood. I was brought up in secret. I must not be seen. I must not be heard. At that time, holding a button in my hands comforted me.

The button I plucked off the blouse of the woman smelling of Star Floral Water, when I was grasping at her nipple. She gave it to me, and I sucked on it. She warned me not to swallow it. She pried open my fingers and took the button away.

I cried. She immediately held her hand over my mouth, and spoke in my ear again to remind me, don't swallow it.

* * *

Before Chunhong left in 1956, she told me, "You're not this woman's child. Your birth mother was sent away by this woman, and she was never seen again. Perhaps she's been killed."

But we had no nurse anymore by the time Chunhong came to us. How could she have known that backstory?

Right, Mother (Li Juan) had once told me that Chunhong was sent by the authorities to monitor us. She was a plant. She knew everything about us.

Right, they had exposed each other. But they were both nice to me. I would have preferred them not to have fought each other in this way.

When I was in jail in 1964, I had a nightmare. I dreamt that Father was on his deathbed. He needed a blood transfusion. The doctor asked me to go get my blood tested. I ran away at once, crying, fearing that the blood test would reveal that I was not his son.

* * *

His determination, courage and patriotism have assured him an enduring place in the history of our times.

— Vice President Rockefeller of the United States of America
April 1975

He never admitted defeat.
— The New York Times' editorial on Chiang Kai-Shek
April 1975

*His death could hardly have been more dramatically timed. To Chiang,
the rout of anti-Communist forces in Indochina must have seemed the
inevitable continuation of the long and losing Asian struggle against
Communism, in which he was the principal casualty.*
— Time Magazine, April 1975

These editorials, clipped from newspapers and lying on my desk,
cycled through my mind one by one like a slide show. All those words,
seemingly having nothing to do with me, suddenly crashed onto me
from above, burying me as I tried to flee. All I wanted to do was to
push them aside.

"Did Old Papa know what happened to the nurse afterwards?" I
asked.

"I heard that he later sent someone to look for her in the hospital.
But she'd already resigned. I had once thought that he had forgotten
about her. However, one day, he handed me this picture, asking me to
find out about the nurse for him, in private."

"Did you tell him where the nurse was?"

"No. The nurse had already left us by then, and I didn't know where
she went. It'd be like finding a needle in a haystack. 'Old Papa' probably
knew that it was no easy task, before asking me to look for her."

"He missed her?"

"Yes. He asked me about her a few times, but I couldn't tell him
anything. At the same time, he sent trusted men from the intelligence
agencies to look for her, but none of them discovered anything. It
wouldn't have had been a difficult task had it not been impossible to
search for her openly."

"And you couldn't tell him about me either?"

"Indeed. Besides, the nurse had already left. There was no evidence.

How could I have mentioned you without any basis?"

Father put the photograph in my hand and closed my hand tightly around it. "Keep it well."

I lowered my head and looked at the photo, half clutched in my hand. On the exposed half, Old Papa looked haggard but not old. "All these years, the hounds he trained had locked me up and tortured me."

"I know you must be holding a grudge against him. It's not just you. Many others hate him as well..." Father said.

"And you bear no grudge against him?"

Father's expression was equivocal, neither confirming nor denying it. "He, well, was a man who could not rise above his limits, and one whose destiny was limited by historical realities." Father paused awhile before continuing, "He knew how he was going down in history after retreating to Taiwan. He did not want to remembered as a loser, but the times had chosen the opposing side. That did not sit well with him. He could not bear living with the reputation of being the one who lost the Mainland, and so he strove to redeem his honour. He made his own determination into the nation's determination. He continued hoping to recover the Mainland. As long as he breathed, he would do anything to reunify China. The officials around him, who depended on him, followed him in launching those unrealistic ideas. They humoured him, they urged him on, until later when everything had become distorted, when idealism had turned into purges, then they either followed him blindly or used him, at the expense of the nation's well-being."

"But what happened to him? How did he turn into a dreadful tyrant?"

"All he turned into was nothingness. Sometimes, Man cannot catch up with the vicissitudes of history, let alone turn history around... I had peeked into his diary. He actually had no intention of becoming a dictator, but he was unable to implement democracy completely either. Furthermore—" Father looked at me gently, "He was mired in the depths of heavy self-censure and self-contradiction. He told me that he was sick, that he must die..."

"He wanted... to die?" I could not imagine it.

Father continued:

"Yes. He had to put himself to death. He said his illness would bring harm to others, would kill all the good people. His eyes were sick. His brain was sick. Those who were innocent he saw as guilty. And, since his power was too great, all the officials obeyed him and worshipped him, and banded together to kill for him. One day he found out that everything had gone wrong, but he could not stop it anymore.

"He said he wanted to find a way to redeem himself, but that seemed impossible. No amount of redemption could atone for the ever-perpetuating evil... He could only stop himself, stop himself from being worshipped, being obeyed. But even more difficult was that he must stop his brain from thinking those incessant, terrible thoughts and ideas. He couldn't help himself thinking distorted thoughts, seeing distorted sights. Every now and then his mind would be clear for a short time, but he worried that he could not stay clear-minded for long. And, what if his moments of clarity were actually still moments of distortion, and the whole world would become distorted along with him..."

"He told you all that? Father, how did you know?" I tried my best not to sound shocked.

"Yes. Once, he had a meeting with me in secret to tell me all that. He told me to bring him drugs, fatal drugs that left no trace. He said once he had made all the necessary arrangements for the nation, he would die. He said, he didn't want to die like a criminal. He wanted to die with dignity, in his own way. I asked him if there was no other way out. He said no. And even if there were, he could not salvage the situation. He owed too much in blood. As he spoke, he suddenly got in a fit of anger. He was riled up like one who had just contradicted himself or shamed by something. He told me to get lost and stay out of his sight forever, or he'd have me killed first."

I said, "If he trusted you that much, how could he have dismissed you and broken up our family..."

Father replied, "He didn't know. He thought I was still in my original post. I said I hadn't held that position for a long time. He asked me why I quit. I didn't tell him. That same day, he restored me to my position. He didn't have many moments of clarity. Worse still, he seemed to be fixated on the past, forgetting about the now. His brain was in some abnormal state. He was not living in reality. He couldn't control himself, and yet he was the only one who dictated the fate of the real world. As a matter of fact, over the years, most of his power had been assumed by his heir. He was only kept like a carven idol, with his officials administering to all things in his name. And so, he lived in a fictitious world, while shouldering the responsibility of everything in the actual world. I guess I was not the only one to have sensed the strange state of the matter, but his family could not let this situation come to light... Their political life, as well as everyone who depended on his patronage, forced him to stand before the stage like a strong man. They did not understand his illness. I promised to keep that a secret for him. I didn't know if he just couldn't hold on anymore, or if he was worried that he could not stay sane for much longer. I didn't expect that he would be so anxious to stop himself that he took the drugs ahead of schedule."

I remembered the secret Dr. Liang told me. Did he really take the drugs Father mentioned? Or was he drugged even before that?

"But he didn't die. He stayed in a coma," Father added. "Many people waited anxiously, waiting for him to wake up and continue to dictate the fate of the world, or to wake up and pass the torch on explicitly. But he just lay there, unable to do anything. The nation was paralysed. It did not know what to do. And so everyone did as he had done before, like a monster out of control... He was unconscious for half a year officially, but actually it had been two years and eight months. Those photos in the newspapers were forged. It's a long story... but during this period, the entire government of Taiwan fell under the "Crown Prince's" control. Our family was watched, listened to by him all along, until he felt I was of no more use..."

"Father, were you really a threat to the 'Crown Prince'? He thought you knew his father's secret?"

"No, not that. He wouldn't even have known." Father, perhaps having said too much at once, was a bit out of breath. He stopped to catch his breath, and continued in an even weaker voice, "Actually, we were under his surveillance even before that. By then, he had already gradually gained control over the intelligence system. And the first thing he did after controlling the intelligence system was to take revenge..."

I was reminded of the scene back then when Mother whispered her admonishment to Chunshao and me in the garden.

"We were a target of his revenge too?"

"Yes. But it was a misunderstanding. In earlier years, he had found out that he was being monitored. He was angry. He put on the appearance of doing nothing, but he manoeuvred for several years until he took control of one of the intelligence agencies and bought over their chief, Director Pan. Then, he used this agency to take down competing agencies, such as your mother's bureau. After that, he either recruited their members or expelled them, until several intelligence agencies were all staffed with his own people and were completely in his power. He kept tabs on everyone he was unsure of, especially the powerful staff close to 'Old Papa'. He believed that it was them who whispered discord in his father's ears and caused him to keep his son under surveillance..."

"I understand now. At the end he still didn't understand his father's illness. The 'Crown Prince' purged the party, but he got rid of the wrong people... If this is true, then Mother was arrested during the purge back then. But he bought over Uncle Yao as well? He isolated you and locked me up as a hostage?"

Father wanted to say something but held back. He nodded silently.

"What about Chunshao? Would they let him be? Why did they still let him work in their organisation?"

"Old Papa still trusted me, after all. Though he could not even open his eyes, they knew where to stop. They knew better than to exterminate us all. They are only afraid of me, keeping an eye on me... And Chunshao works for them very honestly. They know that Chunshao knows his place. That Chunshao is completely loyal. That Chunshao will continue to be loyal."

"Dad, are you saying that Chunshao is monitoring you for them?"

"Chunshao knows what to do. I don't communicate with him very often. In this family, the more we are like strangers to each other, the less we speak with each other, the less his burden is..."

"How could our family have ended up like this?"

Father looked into my eyes, a smile hanging at the corner of his mouth. It was not a real smile; he was only letting his lips lift upward slightly, so as to not let them look lonely.

"Dad, I understand now..."

"Chunhuan, I know that you can understand. My good boy."

We fell silent again just like before, watching each other, as if wanting to speak, but not speaking. I swallowed a question—the two letters that Zhu Xiaokang's father left behind. I didn't ask about them. I didn't dare to.

A while later, Father broke the silence. He seemed too anxious to say something, but coughed up some phlegm instead. His voice shook as he said, "Chunhuan, ever since you were first sent to jail a dozen years ago, I never stopped worrying about you. At that time, I could only try to bribe the prison to not treat you too poorly. I tried everything I could, even though I knew I wouldn't have been able to get you out. But I never would have thought that they'd send you to that naval battle. I knew that I was unable to stand up against the Crown Prince's will after all... When you were sent to Green Island the second time, I would have done everything I could to protect you. But Fate sent you to the other shore..."

"I would never have imagined that I could escape, either, let alone go so far away."

I tried my best to keep a light-hearted tone in my voice—if this could console him. I saw a glimmer in his eyes, the glimmer from tears. For the first time, I felt what I had desired, what I had thirsted for earnestly. I gazed at the glimmer, but not daring to look too deeply—the light opened up the wound in my heart; it had scabbed over for a long time, and now it was suddenly peeled away, leaving the wound to bleed and expand, and expand again.

"Over there—they didn't give you any trouble?" Father's voice was barely audible.

"No, because I saved someone. He vetted me."

"Oh?"

"It's a senior cadre."

I paused hesitatingly. I did not mention Dr. Liang. I had promised him to not mention to him to anyone, even though he had vanished soon after returning to the Mainland and I had not seen him since.

"As long as you're all right, my heart can be at ease."

Father seemed to be exhausted. He closed his eyes temporarily. But

I kept imagining that he would not open them again. I was truly afraid that the light would be suddenly extinguished. I kept a close watch on his breathing, making sure that he was still breathing... For over twenty, thirty years, Father and I had never said so much to each other, nor had we been so close to one another. Even in the mansion of my childhood, this had not happened. Even back then, I had sensed danger and insecurity at home. Father seldom chatted with us; he talked to us frequently about poetry and art though—if that could be considered chatting. Our conversation topics rarely touched on real life.

"Father, no matter who my biological father is, in my heart you will always be my father..." I said emotionally, while trying to keep my voice down.

There were some noises from outside the house. It seemed to be a campaign van driving past. The vehicle was broadcasting the "Letter to Mainland Compatriots" by the new chairman of the Kuomintang:

"We must carry out the late President's will, pledging to overthrow the Communist regime and recover the Chinese Mainland..."

Father opened his eyes, and began chuckling as if he heard a joke, "Counter offensive is impossible. He's a pragmatic man. He'll give up. He only wants to defend Taiwan." As he finished speaking, he coughed up more phlegm, and I saw threads of blood in it.

Before I left, Father gave me book in a foreign language and a box, saying that I could submit the contents of the box as the results of my mission, to satisfy my superiors when I went back. As for the book, it had been given to him by a friend who mattered much to him. He wanted to leave it with me. I opened the box. In it was a fine-brush painting of a flower and a bird. "This is nothing of importance, but it can keep them busy guessing for a long time." Father did not give me the chance to inquire further. Later, when I returned to report on my mission, I did as Father told me—I gave it to my superiors, saying that I had stolen it from home and that there was a secret hidden in it...

As for the foreign language volume, it was in French, which I did not read. All I could tell was that it was Jacques Copeau's theatre theory, and on the back cover was inscribed two words: "From Fei." A page in the book was dog-eared and marked with a pencil. I had someone translate the two marked lines of French for me. The gist of that was, "Each one of you must, in your secret soul, be a hero—not just a hero, but also a saint for yourself."

* * *

A few days before the end, he did indeed dress himself in burial clothing, and lay in the prepared coffin until he breathed his last.

"I don't want any ceremony. Just close the coffin and send it to be cremated, and scatter the ashes," he told us his last will.

But Chunshao did not do as he said. He buried Father by Mother's side.

20
Under careful inspection

Next to Father's grave there appeared a new, nameless burial mound. There was no inscription on it. As I walked up the hill, I stared at this new burial mound on the left hand side, perplexed. The one on the right belongs to Li Juan—Mother, and is right beside Father. But who is the one on the left? Who would lie so close? Father had just been buried—who would be buried right next to him by chance?

The next time when I went to the cemetery, I ran into Autumn. She was dressed in in white mourning garb, as if she was in mourning for my father.

She would not betray me. I did not evade her. Ignoring the fact that I should not be revealing my tracks, I took the initiative to call out to her, "Autumn."

She looked at me with her dreamy eyes. I suddenly realised that she had grown old. In the past, she had always been so beautiful that one would forget that she would ever grow old. But on this day, she was like a flower that was watered no more, looking shrivelled and withered.

"Thank you for taking care of him all this time," I said.

She shook her head, as if she was dismissing my gratitude. Or perhaps she felt that I was only going through the niceties insincerely.

"Your dad's gone." She stared at the tombstone, her voice phantom-like.

"Thank you for looking out for him, and for taking care of our family..."

She shook her head again, and looked at me askance, with as hint of mockery in her eyes, as if I had misunderstood something.

"What would you know? You don't know him at all." Autumn's eyes glittered with tears, but soon returned to their original look of indifference and dejection. "He had been preparing all along, like he was waiting for an opportunity, to accomplish an important mission... But not even I could see through him. I lived in his riddle, fell into his bottomless pit... He didn't need me to take care of him. He was just directing me. Do you understand? He was just directing me. He had locked himself up, all by his lonely self, all this time. He had a secret and wouldn't let anyone figure it out. He didn't want anyone to figure him out at all... After twenty years, I still haven't figured him out. I will never figure him out. But one thing I knew for sure, he was waiting for you to come back, so that you would have a family, a family like before. He wanted to let you feel that you were still noble, that your family was a noble one."

Autumn, gripping my arm, enunciated each word emphatically, as if she was spitting out her grudges, bit by bit. It did not feel like she was reminding me of my father's love, but rather that I owed her something. Is a father's debt for the son to repay? But I did not want to repay anything, nor could I afford it.

I gently freed myself from her clutch, and, like I was ready to say goodbye, I made some small talk with her and hurried away. As I was walking down the hill, I turned around and saw her squatting before Father's grave, her shoulders heaving up and down. She was weeping. Her head was leaning against the tombstone, looking like she was going to dive headlong into the grave. But in between them there was the mistress of the grave beside her.

If she could really dive headlong into the grave, she would only be a slave sacrificed to accompany her deceased owners, and not the mistress of her own grave. Just like a handmaid who had come into family as her mistress's dowry.

I snickered in my heart—of course she knew that. That's why she made a grave for herself. This way, she would have her own grave too, right besides Father—that nameless burial mound was hers.

Before leaving, I had asked her, was there anything buried in the grave?

She had said: A beautiful white wedding gown was buried there. She laughed and told me, she had claimed this spot, and no one could ever make her leave. She would continue to live, and for as long as she lived she would come see him; and when the time came, she would marry him in the grave.

So—I thought—would I have to call her "mum" then?

Just as I was snickered in my heart, tears were rolling down my cheeks. I did not know if they were for her or for myself.

* * *

"What was he preparing? I don't know. I think those are all excuses. Perhaps he couldn't come to terms with his loss, thinking that he was still a noble official," Chunshao responded after I told him what Autumn said.

"I think Father did have secrets. The life he put on show was intentional. He had ulterior motives."

"I can't see any hidden reasons or meaning behind Father's life of comfort. He was only treating Autumn as his servant, ordering her about forever and ever. Everything you said was an excuse Autumn made up for him. She loved him too much. It was all her imagination... Tell me, where's Autumn?"

I said I didn't know.

Chunshao, unwilling to let the matter rest, pressed me for an answer. Unable to deflect the question further, I was forced to tell him, "A new burial mound appeared next to Father's grave. Autumn buried a wedding dress in there. She wants to marry Father."

Chunshao shook his head and staggered back into a chair. "Silly girl, go marry him then. Go marry him, marry that old aristocrat."

"Is that all you can understand of Father? I think he handled everything with dignity. Even though he lost, he lost in an elegant way."

322 AS FLOWERS BLOOM AND WITHER

"He cared about you. I know. And that's why you feel sorry for him. Of course he was very elegant," Chunshao smiled wryly. His expression seemed to be admonishing me to get my feet back on the ground, to stop worrying about thinking up reasons for Father, or seeking explanations for him. Or perhaps it was a kind of jealousy, as if Father cared more for me than for him. But I believed that Chunshao loved Father deeply too. When Father passed away, Chunshao almost had a mental breakdown.

He only cared about me, but he loved you!

I bellowed in my heart.

I wanted to tell Chunshao, he was your real father only. But the words could not leave my mouth. I must keep the secret. Even though my heart wavered and I thought perhaps Father or Autumn was really planning something, I didn't want to give Chunshao the chance to argue with me. I had never been able to win in an argument against him. I was scared that I could not hold my ground.

* * *

In a secluded location, I dug a deep hole, and buried in it the "photo in front of the hospital" and a button.

This was the joint memorial mound of my biological parents.

I kowtowed to them, racking my brains to think a scene where they were together. But I could not. All my impressions of them shattered in the air, disappearing into the wind.

* * *

Before leaving, I went to the grave again and planted a rose. With large, bright-coloured flowers. I looked at the bush contentedly, as dozens of blossoms shone radiating towards the sun. I took a pin from my coat, picked the largest flower, and began to carve words in it... I told them the plans of my journey, one from which I would perhaps not return.

* * *

I walked towards the sea.

Tears welled up in my eyes. I kept thinking about those missions, those poor, naive fathers.

I kept thinking about their unfulfilled last will—launch a counter-offensive on that large swath of lost land on the other shore? Or reclaim this shore from the other side?

Has anyone ever asked, whose lost land was it anyway?

Whence should the attack begin?

Dr. Liang's smile flashed across my mind. He said, both sides are equally mentally ill!

I continued walking towards the sea, the horizon far beyond my sight. I looked around aimlessly. Could there be enemies somewhere?

The enemies, where are they?

On which side of the sea?

A voice reminded me: You should go finish the last dreams of the fathers.

Go forth!

One man, one task!

No orders, no armies, just one man.

A sampan was tied up by the shore, bobbing up and down in the seawater.

There was no one on the shore, not even enemies.

I looked all around me again. Indeed, there was no one.

Fathers, to battle!

I roared and dashed towards the sea.

* * *

"Smuggling channels cannot be trusted. The Bureau has already been tipped-off. Tian Lin and his men will come arrest you. Remember. Nine o'clock," Chunshao made a special trip to tell me earlier that day. "Also, remember, there is no next time."

Before he finished speaking, he shot a glance to his side, as if something was wrong. He sprang towards the window and moved the curtain aside to take a look. Immediately he took off his clothes to swap for mine. "Hurry and go. There should be no ambush yet at the back door."

As soon as he said that, he put on my hat, opened the door and ran out. Hiding beside the window, I could see Chunshao running for his life. Three men almost caught up with him. As soon as they realised they had fallen for a diversion, they would definitely turn back to get me.

There was no time. I opened the back window, and stomped on the window sill to leave a footprint there. I could hear people outside breaking the lock. I hid myself in a pile of rubbish in the corner of the house.

The door was opened. I heard several people entering the house in a flurry of footsteps. A voice, from where the back window was, said, "He's gone. We let him slip again. Go get him!"

It was too familiar. It was Tian Lin's voice.

Chunshao had fallen into Tian Lin's hands!

I waited for a while, until it was completely silent outside. I crawled out of the rubbish pile and left the house.

Remember, nine o'clock. Before we parted, Chunshao had already given me clear instructions. I knew that. I also knew that Tian Lin was still alive and he probably hating my guts.

Two days after that, I did not board the boat. I had someone else board in my place, at nine o'clock. I knew that as soon as he boarded the boat, special agents would follow him on board, and the whole boat would be put under lockdown. No one would be allowed to leave; those who disobeyed would be shot on the spot.

That man was dressed up as me. Zhu Xiaotian had someone go in my disguise.

At the same time, I was passing through customs on someone else's passport. Zhu Xiaotian stood in the crowds far away to see me off. I looked over there at his face, still with adolescent features, and seeing there a trace of Xiaokang. It was Xiaotian who kept Xiaokang's gang going. He still looked a bit boyish, but he did indeed kept the operation going.

Before all this, Zhu Xiaotian had hired a Thai man and brought him to Taiwan. The man's figure and facial features resembled mine at first sight. Xiaotian gave me a wig and a set of clothes that were identical to that man's. Then, he bought a plane ticket under the Thai's name, and gave me his passport and his ticket. Ahead of my leaving home, another person pretending to be me had gone ahead to lure the police away to the port. As I could not determine if there was anyone else watching for me, I first went out under another disguise, stopped at a hotel, put on the Thai's wig and clothes before going to the airport with the fake passport. When I passed through immigration I spoke in English with a Thai accent. My disguise was complete and I left no tracks. I first flew to Thailand, and then boarded a flight from there back to the Mainland. As for the Thai, Xiaotian only said vaguely that he would pretend to have lost his passport, apply for an emergency replacement, and return to Thailand after I had gone. I had worried that if two identical-looking Thai men departed from the airport one after the other, the second one might be called out. But this worry was unfounded.

Indeed, no matter what other coincidences happened that day, they would not have managed to spare a worry. The airport was in chaos, with a large group of police chasing after a man dressed in black. The man was identified when he was going through immigration, and the police circled around him to nab him. He deftly evaded them, and what ensued was a hunt all throughout the departure area, with everyone, riveted, watching this hair-raising escape. The man ran madly, like a cornered beast, but was finally captured. His captors pinned him to the floor. He was still trying to shake them off, while a metal object struck him on his fingers. I could almost sense that his hand, already missing one finger, lost a few more fingers. Tian Lin. He lay on the floor, his eyes scanning through the crowd with despair. For a fraction of a second, his eyes seemed to have met mine, even though I stood at a distance from him.

Tian Lin was hunting me. Why did he become prey instead? I could not figure that out at the time.

* * *

A year later, through many indirect channels, I came to see these files.

Today, Mr. Chiang invited some thirty to forty comrades in the Party, as well as several Chinese and foreign Christians, for tea at the Shandong Residence. During the gathering, Mr. Chiang announced two items: 1) Madame Chiang would soon be travelling to Brazil for rest and recuperation, after which she would be visiting several friendly nations;

2) there had been rumours recently slandering against Mr. Chiang's moral character, alleging that he had been having an extramarital affair; certain individuals intended on using such rumour-mongering to undermine the trust that the comrades and the army had in him. Madame Chiang also made a speech condemning the intent behind such false claims, and reiterating her respect and trust towards Mr. Chiang.

—From the diary of Wang Shijie (Chairman of the 3rd National Political Council, Supervisor of the Central Supervisory Committee of the Three Principles of the People Youth Group), 5 July, 1944

(Speech by the Generalissimo) *On the departure of my wife to Brazil on account of her nervous exhaustion, I decided to give a farewell party for her. You are all my friends, and I think the time has come to speak on something very frankly... Recently in Chungking social circles there have been quite a few rumors, some concerning me personally. You have heard of them, but only one friend of mine besides my wife told me about them... The rumors are that in my personal life, I have not been on the level. It is reported that I had irregular relations with a woman, that I have had illicit relations with a nurse and that a son was born.*

... In the 23rd year of the republic, my wife and I started the New Life Movement. Because of this moral force, we opposed communism successfully and resisted foreign aggression... Any stain on me as a leader is a stain cast upon the nation... I am a Christian. I believe in the commandments and obey them absolutely... Between my wife and me there are only sentiments of absolute purity. There is not a single stain in our relationship. There is nothing in my life that I cannot make public... I [have called you together] to defeat the pernicious purposes of the enemy.

(Remarks by Madame Chiang Kai-shek) *The remarks that the Generalissimo mentioned have been spreading all over Chungking. I have heard of these rumors and many letters have been written to me on the subject. I felt it a duty, not as a wife, but as a true patriot, to acquaint the Generalissimo with these rumors.*

But I wish to state that never for a moment did I stoop or demean myself by believing these rumors, nor did I ask him if they were true. If I had doubted the Generalissimo, I should have insulted him. I believe so perfectly in his integrity, his personality, and his leadership that I would not insult him for anything. I have been married to him for 17 years. I have been with him through all his trials, even at Sian. Therefore I know every fact of the Generalissimo's character as no one else in the world does. Knowing his character, I have complete faith in his integrity. I hope no one has given credence to these malicious slanders.

When the Generalissimo told me yesterday that he was calling his friends together, my first reaction was: "Don't bother. Rumors die of themselves." He replied that this was not a personal slander. In slandering him they were slandering China as a moral force... China's contribution to the world, he continued, was not economic, not military, not industrial-- China's contribution was as a moral force.

—Speech by the Generalissimo to gathering of 75 guests; Joseph W. Stilwell Collection (From the Hoover Institute Archives, Stanford University)

(1943) *In July, Soong Mei-ling concluded her visit to the United States and returned to Chongqing. The couple appeared to be amicable to each other. On 12 August, Soong Mei-ling moved in with her sister and her brother-in-law, H. H. Kung, leaving Chiang Kai-shek alone in the presidential residence at Huangshan. On the 16th, Soong Mei-ling returned to the presidential residence, but soon after she moved back to H. H. Kung's house. On 14 September, an informant serving as Chiang Kai-shek's personal attendant reported that Chiang admitted in his diary entry that day that he was "feeling depressed". On 15 September, Chiang wrote in his diary: "After prayers, I went to bed quietly. I feel that I have done the utmost today in bearing my pain, holding back grief, and restraining my anger" However, he had crossed out the first five lines in that day's entry. On 19 September, Chiang crossed out the first three lines of his diary entry again. Chiang spent the next few days at Huangshan strolling and meditating.* (Internal information)

(1944) *The American government was keenly interested in Chiang Kai-shek's extramarital affair, and the media also devoted much coverage to it. Rumours of the Chiangs' divorce were already beginning to circulate in the West. Chiang declared this as a Communist ploy, and Soong Mei-ling still tried to help Chiang stabilise the political situation. However,*

*the Americans were already intending to assassinate his character and
to seize power from him. In July, Marshall advised President Roosevelt
that, since the Kuomintang had been defeated again and again in the
Anti-Japanese War and the situation in China was precarious, Chiang
Kai-shek must be forced to hand over his military command and allow
General Stilwell to lead China in this war.* (Internal information)

* * *

A year after that, I tracked down a relative of Song Jiafu, my father, in
Huang County, Shandong Province. Emotionally, I started to talk to
him about Father.

He looked at me, perplexed:

"That's impossible. Song Jiafu died some forty years ago. He died
even before Old Chiang went to Taiwan..."

He died some forty years ago?

I cross-checked many things with him.

Only then did I realise, Father had no past. The past that he had
publicised was fake; it belonged to another dead man. He used that
dead man's past to stand in for his own.

Song Jiafu of Liangjiaxiang, Huang County, Shandong Province: His
grandfather, Song Lian, was a scholar in the Qing Dynasty; his father,
Song Jitang, ran an apothecary...

The father who raised me was not Song Jiafu. I did not know who
he was.

My name, on the other hand, had long since been listed by the
Ministry of National Defence as a martyr. At that time, to keep up the
nation's appearances, they had suppressed news of my escape. Instead,
they made up a non-existent special mission, and announced that I
had already sacrificed myself for the nation. However, at the same
time, in the blacklist of the intelligence system, I was, and ever will be,
a true rebel spy, an eternally wanted man.

PART VI

21
The files

North country scene:
A hundred leagues locked in ice,
A thousand leagues of whirling snow.
Both sides of the Great Wall
One single white immensity.
The Yellow River's swift current
Is stilled from end to end.
The mountains dance like silver snakes
And the highlands charge like wax-hued elephants,
Vying with heaven in stature.
On a fine day, the land,
Clad in white, adorned in red,
Grows more enchanting.

This land so rich in beauty
Has made countless heroes bow in homage.
But alas! Qin Shihuang and Han Wudi
Were lacking in literary grace,
And Tang Taizong and Sung Taizu
Had little poetry in their souls;
And Genghis Khan, Proud Son of Heaven for a day,
Knew only shooting eagles, bow outstretched

AS FLOWERS BLOOM AND WITHER

All are past and gone!
For truly great men
Look to this age alone.

—Mao Zedong: "Snow—to the tune of Qinyuanchun"
—*Xinmin Evening News Supplement*, 14 November, 1945

The 3rd of April, 1999. Willow catkins festooned the city of Beijing; the sky was full of sand and dust. I was in the archives doing some research. The windows and doors of the large, quiet room were shut tightly. The air conditioner emitted the musty smell of old paper; dark curtains blocked all light from the outside world, as if everything in here must be kept in the dark. I chose a seat far away from other people. Under a flickering lightbulb threatening to fail at any moment, I began to read the file on Liu Yanxian:

File BF7-610:
   Liu Yanxian: Father—Liu Yinghan; mother—Li Xia. Her grandfather, Liu Fangzhen, originally a salt merchant in northern Suzhou, bought a government post during the late Qing dynasty and moved to Beijing. When the Qing was overthrown, her father, Liu Yinghan, sold the family business and started a factory. In 1937, the Japanese took control over Beijing in the Marco Polo Bridge incident. To escape from the Japanese army, Liu Yanxian fled to Chongqing in 1938. There, she was accepted into the National Drama Institute and studied under Cao Yu and Zhang Junxiang; she also performed with a theatre company. In 1939, the underground party in Yunnan began promoting anti-Japanese drama. The theatre company of Liu Yanxian's school joined forces with National Southwestern Associated University's theatre company, the Kunming Arts Institute, the National Defence Drama Society, and the Yunnan Provincial Drama Training Group to put on plays including "The People Mobilised", "The Plains", and "The Thunderstorm". It was during this time when Liu Yanxian came in contact with the underground party.
   When performing in Kunming in the January of 1945, Liu Yanxian

met Lu Kepeng, an American diplomat. The two fell in love and soon began to discuss marriage. As American law prohibited diplomatic staff from marrying non-American citizens, Lu Kepeng planned to quit the embassy and become a teacher in China. The embassy rejected his resignation, but Lu Kepeng maintained a close relationship with Liu Yanxian. Lu Kepeng was the first political consultant from the U.S. Army observation team sent to Yan'an, and was in close contact with party leaders Mao Zedong, Zhou Enlai, and Liu Shaoqi.

Later, the American political position shifted, with right-wing forces in Congress gaining prominence. In June 1945, Lu Kepeng discovered that he was under surveillance. On 2 July, the U.S. recalled him to Washington to stand trial. Before leaving, Lu gave Liu Yanxian a sum of money, and bade her to sever all ties with him for self-preservation, and to flee as soon as possible. By that time, Liu was already with child. Lu promised to go back to China one day to take her with him. On the 24 July, Lu Kepeng was charged with espionage by the FBI and imprisoned. When the leaders of the underground party got news of it, they notified Liu Yanxian to leave immediately. Liu fled Kunming with the assistance of her nanny, Ms. Li...

I then continued to read File BX2-6161 on Lu Kepeng:

Lu Kepeng: Born in Kunming to Wang Jinling, a Chinese, and Louis Horne (Chinese name: Lu Hao'en), an American missionary. Lu Kepeng grew up in China, and left for the U.S. to pursue his studies at the age of 15. At the age of 23, he returned to China to work at the U.S. Embassy. During the Sino-Japanese War, Lu Kepeng repeatedly requested the U.S. Department of State to take notice of the Chinese Communist Party's role in the war, and to provide the CCP with more military assistance. In March 1945, Lu Kepeng went to Yan'an to meet with CCP leaders Mao Zedong, Zhou Enlai, Zhu De, and Liu Shaoqi, after which he reported his observations on the meeting to the U.S. Department of State. In July of the same year, the U.S. recalled him, and, under the influence of right-wing politicians, convicted him of espionage due to his left-leaning position...

334 AS FLOWERS BLOOM AND WITHER

I was assigned by my work unit to welcome Liu Yanxian and her husband, Lu Kepeng, who were returning from the U.S. for a visit in June. I skimmed through their profiles and returned the documents. The musty smell in the room was unbearable. I could feel my allergies returning. I wanted to leave right away. I walked through two rows of tables and chairs in the reading room, planning to head towards the main corridor. But I checked myself before turning in the direction of the exit. Instead, I turned back towards the file retrieval desk, as if I was driven there by some inexplicable force. It more than simple curiosity—in Liu Yanxian's file were two yellow slips marked "AT4-1028" and "AT4-1051". They may have some connection to her.

I fished out a handkerchief from my pocket to protect my mouth and nose from the allergens. I took a retrieval form, filled in those two sets of codes, and handed it over with my identity card. Again I was given a number and told to wait. Ten minutes later, the archivist emerged, and the clerk passed the two files to me. I found a seat nearby, and impatiently opened up to the first page of File AT4-1028. There were a few words in faded blue ink: "Operation Spring Garden".

Operation Spring Garden
Agents: Butterfly, Honeybee
Decode:
   • Honeybee (15-12-1949): Chiang Kai-shek had Chen Cheng resign from the position of Governor of Taiwan, and replaced him with the U.S.-endorsed Wu Guozhen, as the condition for obtaining American support.
   • Honeybee (6-1-1950): On the 5th, Truman declared that the U.S. would not interfere with Chinese affairs or provide military aid to Taiwan. After that, Secretary of the State Acheson declared that, according to the Cairo Declaration and the Potsdam Declaration, Taiwan is a province of China, and the U.S. will not interfere with Taiwanese military affairs. Chiang Kai-shek phoned Wellington Koo, Ambassador to the U.S., to request immediate military aid from the U.S., pointing out the current personnel reform in Taiwan. The Americans demanded that Chiang grant concrete powers to Wu Guozhen and General Sun Liren.

- Honeybee (11-2-1950): McCarthy sent a plane to Taiwan to take General Sun Liren to Japan.
- Honeybee (25-2-1950): Upon his return to Taiwan, Sun Liren reported to Chen Cheng, Chief of Military and Political Affairs of the Southeast, regarding the negotiations in the U.S.. He said that McCarthy promised to provide military aid and was confident in Sun's continued defence of Taiwan. The KMT suspected that there were more to the negotiations, and conjectured that the U.S. intended to use Sun Liren to replace Chiang Kai-shek.
- Butterfly (9-3-1950): To prevent Communist infiltration, Chiang Kai-shek launched a "Counterespionage Movement". To prove their worth, every spy agencies concocted and submitted fabricated lists of enemy spies, causing widespread miscarriage of justice on the island of Taiwan. At the same time, Chiang Ching-kuo took the position of "Director of the General Political Department of the Ministry of National Defence", responsible for deploying and commanding guerrilla operations against the Mainland. Chiang Ching-kuo's household, in turn, was placed under surveillance by intelligence organisations, who reported lists of his contacts and details of his communication to Chiang Kai-shek.
- Butterfly (16-3-1950): Chiang Kai-shek instructed the Secrecy Bureau to put Sun Liren in the Tier 1 Surveillance List. Many of Sun's trusted subordinates were eliminated one by one, imprisoned under the charges of being Communist spies.
- Honeybee (27-6-1950): Today Truman expressed his view that "the status of Taiwan is not settled yet". Chiang Kai-shek, while aware that the U.S. intends to split up China, still wants to use their 7th Fleet to defend Taiwan. Therefore, he delegated Ye Gongchao, Minister of Foreign Affairs, to announce publicly: The Party accepts the American defence plan, but the U.S. must not interfere with the Party's position on maintaining the territorial integrity of the Republic of China. Taiwan is a part of the Republic of China, and the Republic of China maintains absolute sovereignty over Taiwan.
- Butterfly (11-8-1950): Wu Guozhen had long been at odds with Chiang Ching-kuo and Chen Cheng. After Chen Cheng became Premier of the Executive Court, he circumscribed the power held by

Wu's Provincial Office. The powers to enforce security under Wu's name were in essence in the control of Peng Mengji, who was loyal to Chiang Ching-kuo. All of Wu Guozhen's powers were taken away from under him. Wu Guozhen publicly broke with Chiang Ching-kuo, criticising him for letting the Island be overrun with spies. Chiang Kai-shek reproached Wu for his criticism of the "root out Communist spies" ideology.

• Honeybee (13-1-1951): In late December, Sun Liren called an "End of Year Conscience Meeting" in the Army, where he expressed that the instability and corruption in current society were due to political leaders' inability to deal with each other with openness and honesty. Chiang Ching-kuo was displeased at the statement, and indicated that Sun Liren was overstepping his authority in meddling with Chiang's Department of Political Affairs. Sun continued with suggesting nationalising the military and removing the political works unit in the military. William Chase, head of the U.S.'s Military Assistance Advisory Group, concurs with Sun and demanded Chiang Kai-shek to disband the political department in the military. Chiang Ching-kuo suspected this to be an American ploy, using Sun to challenge him. Chiang Kai-shek believed that after the Korean War, the 7th Fleet from the U.S. would be sufficient in ensuring Taiwan's stability, and thus Sun would be of no more importance.

• Honeybee (1-2-1951): The CIA's Office of Policy Coordination established Western Enterprises, Inc. (WEI) to check Chinese advances in the Korean War. Its legal representative is Frank Brick, a lawyer and a Ninetieth Division veteran, and the head of the company is an agent called Johnston. They plan to set up communications stations on Kinmen, Tachen, and Baiquan Islands, where they will train Nationalist offshore assault teams for the purpose of attacking islands in Mainland waters, and to intercept military and commercial transportation to the Mainland. WEI personnel will arrive in Taiwan in March and be headquartered on Chungshan North Road, which is run by Commander Ray Peers. The staff of 72 are skilled in areas including explosives, decryption, guerrilla warfare, psychological warfare, chemical warfare, naval warfare, and parachuting. Taiwan considers them a crucial tool in aiding its counteroffensive on the Mainland...

• Honeybee (16-9-1951): The KMT Navy intercepted a full boatload of overseas-bound mail from the Mainland. Gilbert of WEI ordered for the mail to be opened, have anti-Communist leaflets inserted, be resealed and mailed out again. When overseas Chinese saw that their relatives on the Mainland sent them anti-Communist slogans, they believed that the political situation on the Mainland to be in jeopardy. Thus disinformed, Southeast Asian newspapers reported great quantities of negative information about the Mainland.

• Butterfly (11-4-1953): Provincial Chairman Wu Guozhen's resignation was accepted.

• Honeybee (17-6-1954): Chiang Kai-shek relieved Sun Liren of his duties as the Commander-in-Chief of the Army, and reassigned him to be chief military adviser to the President. Though his rank remained the same, he was in effect prevented from controlling any troops.

• Butterfly (25-5-1955): Major Guo Tingliang, instructor at the Infantry School and subordinate of Sun Liren, was arrested by the Political Works Department, on charges of attempting rebellion.

• Butterfly (14-7-1955): After 48 days of torture and interrogation, Guo Tingliang still denied plotting insurrection. Mao Tiyuan, chief agent of the Secrecy Bureau, suggested persuading and entice him to admit to being a Communist spy.

• Butterfly (2-8-1955): Guo Tingliang agreed to confess to being a Communist spy in exchange for Sun Liren's acquittal.

• Honeybee (21-8-1955): Chiang Kai-shek announced that Sun Liren had resigned over his negligence in supervision of his subordinates. After that, Chiang accused Sun Liren of plotting revolt and handed him over to the Ministry of National Defence. Over 300 people were implicated in this case and were imprisoned or executed; over 10,000 others were affected.

• Butterfly (31-10-1955): To remain in the U.S.'s good graces and to contain the matter, the Chiangs did not kill Sun Liren. Instead, they removed him to Taichung and kept him under house arrest, where he was under round-the-clock surveillance by the Secrecy Bureau and personnel from the Intelligence Bureau of the Ministry of National Defence.

* * *

In the year of 1952, I started schooling but quit immediately after. Chunhong and Autumn came to work for us. I spent my days sitting in the tree, looking at the plants in the garden around me, the low houses in the neighbourhood, and the guests coming and going to and from the house. A gentleman with a slim but vigorous face came to visit. My parents were not in, Chunhong was busy in the house, and Autumn was nowhere to be seen. The man saw me in the tree and said hello. I lowered a basket on a rope, and brought up his gift and calling-card. Sun Liren. I could read his name, as Father had taught me to read early. The fact that he had not handed the gift to Chunhong seemed to say that he trusted me more. And so, I broke the rule and took it upon myself to accept a stranger's gift. I was quite pleased with myself as Father did not scold me for it at all. He brought the calling-card into his room casually. But Chunshao warned me, "That man is surrounded with rebel spies. They've arrested a few of them already. He's a dangerous one."

"How do you know there're many rebel spies around him?"

"Little Wang from Father's news agency told me."

But Father was not worried about Uncle Sun. I suspected that Chunshao was only bluffing me.

In 1955, Mother and Uncle Zhu Anqiao were conversing in a low voice in the garden:

"Forty-eight days of torture, plus twenty-one days of enticement."

"If he refuses to confess, they'll find someone else to spill the beans."

"But he's extremely loyal to Old Sun. He's ready to give up his life for Sun anytime."

"So they did get the right person."

In the same year, Chunshao and I saw a little beggar-child by the roadside. Chunshao grabbed my arm and ran. We ran for almost a hundred metres and hid ourselves behind a wall, looking around nervously.

"What are you looking for?"

He said, "I don't know if anyone's tailing us."

"Why would anyone tail us?"

"You just took a look at him. That means you know him. We can't be associated at all with his family."

In 1956, Chunshao took me to my skating lesson on his bicycle. When we passed by a certain building, he suddenly said to me, "There's an underground dungeon in there. They keep the Guo guy there..."

"Why didn't they execute him right away like other spies? Why are they keeping him in the dungeon instead?"

"I don't know. There must be a secret in there. There must be a reason why they can't kill him. Don't ask too much."

Boyhood chatter from forty years ago, rushing back at me like a nightmare. I closed AT4-1028, and opened up another file.

File AT4-1051:
Operation Pilgrimage
Agents: Bodhisattva of Mercy, Golden Child, Jade Maiden, The Enlightened One
Decode:

• Golden Child (23-9-1957): Golden Child has already chosen the site for building the base as per mission requirements. However, the KMT has been rigorously rooting out armed bases lately, so building progress has slowed down. The KMT recently received information on a guerrilla base concealed in the hills near Xindian, and ordered Golden Child to lead a team of military police to arrest those involved. There were only a few workhouses at the site, with no indication of it being a PLA base. It turned out that the local village head had made up a false list of rebels and betrayed the villagers, for the sake of the reward money. All those arrested were innocent. This suggests that the KMT is becoming ridiculous and inept, incapable of telling friend from foe. To maintain cover, Golden Child had no choice but to act as ordered by the KMT.

• Golden Child (14-1-1958): Golden Child has already set up four armed bases at Baimao Hill, Zhuzikeng, Shigang, and Guanyin Hill. Still in need of 60 firearms and 20 grenades. However, Bodhisattva of Mercy has a negative attitude towards building bases and did not cooperate in the operation.

• Bodhisattva of Mercy (16-4-1958): Suggest putting on hold the original plans to establish armed bases. The interior region of Taiwan is too small, fenced in with hills and forests, and transportation is too convenient. Guerrilla warfare is unsuitable here. Golden Child is too radical and may cause harm to fellow comrades.

• Bodhisattva of Mercy (7-8-1958): On the afternoon of 4 August, Chiang Kai-shek met with Ronald Smoot and emphasised that the Taiwan Strait Crisis was worsening. On the 6th, the U.S. Department of State replied that Taiwan and the U.S. may hold joint defence exercises, and that USPACOM would be transferring over 20 F-86 fighters and Sidewinder missiles...

• Jade Maiden (19-8-1958): The Taiwanese obtained intelligence that the PLA had deployed 148 MiG fighters along the coast.

• Bodhisattva of Mercy (25-8-1958): USPACOM added four destroyers to the 7th Fleet, as well as adding an extra Nike missile base and six F-100 fighters.

• The Enlightened One (10-9-1958): After the 823 Artillery Bombardment, the U.S. increased its military support to Taiwan in a bid to oppose Communist China. One of the Nike-Hercules packages destined for Alaska will be diverted to Taiwan soon, and a public statement is scheduled for release on the 19th.

• The Enlightened One (8-10-1958): The U.S. Army's 71st Artillery's 2nd Missile Battalion arrived at Taipei. It is stationed at Linkou, Taipei County, to defend the Greater Taipei area. The battalion, with over 700 personnel, coordinates with the 6987 Signal Squadron (stood up by the U.S.'s Air Defense Command in 1955) to gradually transfer the Hercules model of the Nike missile to the Taiwanese army. Taiwan selected 60 graduates from the 27th class of the ROC Military Academy to train in the U.S. The Nike-Hercules uses a command guidance system, and has a range of 96.3 miles, a speed of Mach 3.65, and an intercept point of approximately 100,000 feet.. Accuracy is approximately 65%.

• The Enlightened One (1-7-1959): The Nationalist Army will stand up a missile unit in the Army. The U.S. has transferred all Nike-Hercules missiles and associated equipment to Taiwan's use.

• The Enlightened One (8-10-1959): Maps of the Nike-Hercules hilltop Integrated Fire Control (IFC) and the Launch Area (LA) at the bottom of the hill.

• The Enlightened One (21-10-1959): Weaknesses of the Nike-Hercules missile:

(1) It can only be launched against one target at a time.

(2) Much manpower is required—at least 20 staff are needed to operate each missile: 11 in the IFC and 9 in the LA.

(3) The protective cover of the radar antenna cannot withstand strong wind or rain; maintenance is difficult during typhoon season.

(4) If static is not completely discharged during maintenance but is allowed to accumulate to a certain amperage, the missile could launch on its own.

• Jade Maiden (23-12-1959): U.S. spy satellite photographed a nuclear gaseous diffusion plant in Lanzhou on the Mainland. On 20 December, Chief Cline of CIA's Taiwan Station passed the photo to the Chiangs.

• Golden Child (2-4-1961): The Taiwanese military set up the Project National Glory Office in Three Gorges, Taipei County. Directed by Zhu Yuancong, the office comprises 207 of the top talents in the armed forces, and its goal is to develop a military plan for counter-invading the Mainland. Altogether they drafted 26 counter-invasion battle plans and 216 schemas. Those include "Plans for Landing before the Enemy", "Plans for Special Operations behind Enemy Lines", "Frontal Assault Plans", "Strategic Counterattack Plans", and "Plans for Coordinating with Uprisings" (see attachments). Separately, Yu Boquan established "Project Great Light" in Bitan in Xindian, Taipei County, a joint Taiwan-U.S. project for attacking the Mainland. This is to disguise Chiang Kai-shek's true intent, Project National Glory, and to attempt to obtain American support through appealing to the alliance. However, all military leaders were of the opinion that the nation did not possess sufficient strength for counter-invading the Mainland, though no one dares to tell Chiang.

• Golden Child (10-8-1961): The U.S. Army's advisory team suspects that the Nationalist Army has a hidden agenda, and worries that the equipment sent in military aid would be used to attack the Mainland. Therefore, they keep a close watch on every training exercise, count the number of Nationalist amphibious vehicles every week, monitor the boats sailing to and from the outlying islands, and deploy helicopters to patrol over each camp in order to collect overhead imagery and electronic signals. On 9 August, the U.S. made a forced entry to the Three Gorges Camp area of Project National Glory, which irked Chiang Kai-shek. The U.S. bought over informants in the Taiwanese military intelligence agencies, and became aware of all of Chiang Kai-shek's counter-invasion plans...

• The Enlightened One (9-1-1962): After the Cihu Residence was completed, Chiang Kai-shek frequently uses his trips between Taipei and Cihu as a cover for visiting and inspecting the "Shimen Institute of Science and Technology" (see attachment for map). Concealed within the Institute is a heavy water reactor. Taiwan is developing nuclear weapons...

• Bodhisattva of Mercy (19-3-1962): Roger Hilsman, Director of the Bureau of Intelligence and Research of the U.S. Department of State revealed that the Chiangs pressured the U.S. to support their efforts in counter-invading the Mainland, saying that the people on the Mainland would rise up in support of the Nationalist Army. On 17 March, Assistant Secretary of State for Far Eastern Affairs Averell Harriman sent Hilsman to Taiwan to probe Chiang Ching-kuo for details. Chiang Ching-kuo told him that the Nationalist Army was preparing to launch the counter-invasion in 1962, but Hilsman did not believe that they would succeed...

• Bodhisattva of Mercy (13-2-1963): The U.S., having found out that Chiang Kai-shek intended to retake the Mainland alone, began strict control of arms provided to Taiwan.

• Golden Child (9-5-1963): Chiang Kai-shek arrived at the Project National Glory Office in person to provide instructions on how the war was to be conducted. He believed that they should take advantage of the worsening Sino-Soviet relationship: "First, we'll shell the Mainland for three or four days to provoke them into a counterattack. Then we can announce to the world that the Mainland was the side that started the war. This will give us a casus belli. We will first send the air force into action; the naval forces will land after that." Someone asked what he would do about American monitoring. Chiang Kai-shek replied, "Nothing in the Mutual Defence Treaty with the U.S. prohibits us from counterattacking. Our striking back would actually be an act to preserve our national sovereignty."

- Bodhisattva of Mercy (5-8-1963): Yesterday, Chiang Kai-shek, dissatisfied with the U.S. for opposing his counterattack plan, said to United Press International President Thomason: During the Second World War, the Republic of China abided by the Sino-Soviet agreement and gave the Northeast to the CCP. After defeating the Japanese, the Republic of China lost the rest of the mainland due to the Marshall negotiations. And if the Sino-American Mutual Defence Treaty were to be upheld now, Taiwan will be lost as well.

- Bodhisattva of Mercy (16-10-1963): Golden Child and Jade Maiden were arrested, but not due to their mission being disclosed. It is suspected that they were implicated in the in-fighting among the KMT's intelligence, political, and military organisations. The matter is under investigation. Bodhisattva of Mercy has put operations on hold.

- Bodhisattva of Mercy (2-1-1964): The arrest of Golden Child and Jade Maiden were due to Chiang Ching-kuo's purging of the intelligence agencies and elimination of dissidents. The Enlightened One was the informer. According to him, Golden Child and Jade Maiden had already fallen under suspicion; therefore, to preserve himself, he catered to Chiang Ching-kuo's will by informing on them. The Enlightened One has obtained full trust from Chiang Kai-shek and Chiang Ching-kuo, and will continue to carry out the mission.

- The Enlightened One (24-10-1964): On 16 October, the Mainland succeeded in their first nuclear test. Chiang Kai-shek worried that the Mainland would turn their nuclear weapons towards Taiwan. Dr. Ray Cline suggested to Chiang yesterday that Taiwan should launch a military attack to destroy the CCP's nuclear weapon facilities. This reignited Chiang's desire to counter-invade the Mainland; this also made him order the nuclear development on the Island to be accelerated...

- The Enlightened One (6-4-1965): Taking advantage of the deteriorating situation of the Vietnam War, Chiang Kai-shek once again demanded the U.S. to support his attack on the Mainland in exchange of his support of the American army in Vietnam. The request was denied.

- The Enlightened One / Bodhisattva of Mercy (15-8-1965): Ray

Cline, Deputy Chief of the CIA, went to Taiwan on the 1st to meet with Chiang Kai-shek to discuss counter-invading the Mainland. The Naval Battle of August 6th happened soon after. After returning to the U.S., Cline provided an analysis of Taiwan's counter-invasion ability, stating that the battle showed that the CCP's naval defence capabilities had increased, while Chiang Kai-shek's counter-invasion plan was completely hopeless. Cline saw that Chiang Kai-shek counted on American forces augmenting support to Taiwan if the invasion was not proceeding smoothly; however, this move would only serve to drag the U.S. further into the conflict. At the same time, Chiang Kai-shek wanted to take advantage of the famine that recently hit China, expecting the people living along the Mainland coastline to rise up in support of the KMT in the event of a counter-invasion. Cline believed that Chiang had overestimated the level of dissatisfaction Mainlanders had with the Communist Party. Should Chiang's counter-invasion fail while being supported by the U.S., it would serve to provide Mao Zedong with a pretext to paint the U.S. as an invader, which would weaken the U.S.'s standing in the world.

• The Enlightened One (8-4-1966): Unable to secure American support, the KMT is severely lacking in armaments. In order to assemble the 100 landing crafts needed for the counter-invasion, Chiang Kai-shek demanded H. H. Kung's clan to fund the construction of amphibious assault ships and landing crafts; the codenames for the projects are "Operation Daye" and "Operation Zhongxing" respectively. The plan is to construct a total of 275 vessels, to be hidden in the Beihai Tunnel in Matsu and the Zhaishan Tunnel in Kinmen.

• Attachments: Diagram of Taiwan strategic defences; Map of Taiwanese fleet deployment; Location, serial number, and branch of Taiwanese units; List of names of personnel ranked section chief and above in key Taiwanese military organisations; Name lists of individuals ranked regiment commander and above; Deployment diagram of Nike missile bases; Plans of the Project National Glory Office; Interior map of the Shimen Institute of Science and Technology...

The attachments were kept separately. Access was forbidden. I reread the file several times, some paragraphs in particular. I had a suffocating feeling in my chest. Armed bases, Nike missiles. An unwelcome thought came into my mind. Is there more?

The thread was broken.

There were no more yellow slips.

I opened each of the catalogue drawers, searching through the index cards. Besides some meaningless serial numbers and dates at the top of the cards, there were no other words. I continued searching, knowing that it might be futile.

My unit only provided me with two serial numbers: BX2-6161 and BF7-6103. Lu Kepeng and Liu Yanxian. I studied those numbers over and over again, like a young beast, having tasted blood for the first time, thirsting for the hunt in this new-found bloodlust, thirsting to slay until it saw nothing but red in its eyes.

On the 20th of April, I got my first prey. FT9-2111 was the first serial number I chased down, even though its contents were no longer a secret to me.

File FT9-2111 on Liu Dongqing:

Liu Dongqing: Father - Liu Chuanyi; mother - Yang Qun. Joined the underground party in Changchun in 1937 and served at the Changchun Army Hospital. Later, he was sent on mission under the name Liang Zhibang. In 1943, he took a position at the 14th Route Army Hospital in Chongqing. When Chiang Kai-shek was admitted to the hospital, he gained the trust of Chiang, and was later transferred to be his personal physician. He went to Taiwan along with Chiang...

Dr. Liang. I wonder where he went. I kept my promise, though, and did not mention him to anyone.

The first time I heard the poem was from this Liang Zhibang.

That day in 1974, on that stormy sea, Dr. Liang rowed the boat. I said I couldn't see the Mainland or anyone there to connect with us. I did not believe we could get there. He laughed, however, and recited a poem out loud.

I asked him what poem it was.

"'Snow—to the tune of Qinyuanchun'. Don't you know it?"

"I've never heard it before."

"Your father never recited it to you?" Dr. Liang laughed again. "Hah, hah. Of course he couldn't read it to you. However, he knew this poem very well. He even wrote a response in the same verse form, and a very good one at that..."

* * *

Responding verses; "Snow - to the tune of Qinyuanchun". — Year: 1945. Index. Cards. I continued searching.

What was Dr. Liang trying to tell me back then?

Some of the answers appeared to be obvious. I really did not need to get to the bottom of the matter. Life would be easier if I had forgotten about it, unless I meant to torture myself or intentionally kill time.

"Those who know too much put themselves in jeopardy." This public announcement senior management made in the department one day sounded an alarm in my heart.

Before I gave up on the search, I found files FT9-4102 and FT9-4134 in turn. The contents did not surprise me. It was just that, with everything laid out before me, I felt as if someone had stuffed something into my mouth and forced me to swallow it.

File FT9-4102 on Zhu Jingquan:

Zhu Jingquan: Father - Zhu Yimin; mother - Xu Manhui. Infiltrated the Kuomintang in 1940 under the name "Zhu Anqiao". In 1944, the British and the Americans plotted to stage an aviation accident during Chiang Kai-shek's visit to India, in order to assassinate Chiang and restructure the government of China. Upon receiving the secret information, Mao Zedong ordered for Chiang to be protected and the British and American plot to be thwarted. As Chiang's campaign against the Japanese had not been going well, Zhu Jingquan suggested him to focus on the domestic conflict and cancel his trip to India. Thus, Chiang avoided being killed. On 28 August, 1945, Mao Zedong and Zhou Enlai went to Chongqing to negotiate with Chiang Kai-shek. On 8 October, Zhu secretly reported that Chiang's subordinates were plotting to assassinate Mao and Zhou. But as Mao and Zhou did not board the 18th Army Group vehicle that day, they avoided the ambush at Red Crag. However, Li Shaoshi, secretary of the 18th Army Group's

Office in Chongqing, was killed in the attack. This was the "Li Shaoshi Incident" that created a stir throughout Chongqing. When Zhu was carrying out his mission in Taiwan, he created armed bases and obtained information on Chiang's "Project National Glory Office" and the American consultants...

File FT9-4134 on Yao Mai:
Yao Mai: Father - Yao Ping; mother - Wu Qiao. Joined the Party in 1945 and infiltrated the Kuomintang under the name "Yao Tiepeng". Went to Taiwan on a mission in 1949. Had once gained trust of Chiang Kai-shek and his son, and obtained secret documents on Taiwan missile bases, Taiwan A-bomb production, and Taiwanese naval deployments...

"What amperage of static do you need for the missile to launch on its own?"
Yao Kunming's innocent voice was still echoing in my mind.
"xx tilapia, xx squids, xx cuttlefish, xx preserved eggs, xx duck eggs, xx hen's eggs, xx shrimps. Look at this! Why are they buying shrimp by the unit instead of by weight?"
At that time he convinced one of his father's subordinates to show him his father's notes for various errands. Sometimes it was a shopping list for groceries, sometimes it was an order form for stationery or gifts.
Yao Kunming, like studying an intelligence report, deliberated over every word in those few lines. He was certain that there was something funny about this shopping list, and that he could trade it for a trinket in my curio box or a vial of chemicals from my chemistry set.
Surreptitiously we kept an eye on the grown-ups, discovering fun adventures behind them, as if every bit of normalcy belied something abnormal.
If we had been perceptive enough, perhaps we would not have had to wait forty years to realise that our fun, adventurous childhood already foretold the adversity of the future.

22
The Russian Rose

Russia is a riddle wrapped in a mystery inside an enigma.
— Winston Churchill, former British Prime Minister, 1939

The 4th of May, 1999. Studencheskaya Street, Moscow. The Archives of the National Security Council.

I was brought to the reading room. The archivist had me sit at a table:

"Please have a seat. The file you asked for will be here in a few minutes."

The room was completely silent, with the exception of the occasional rustling of paper. Holding a sheet of paper in my hand, I waited in anxious anticipation. The archivist said that he would bring the file out "in a few minutes", but every minute seemed an eternity. Subconsciously I unfolded the sheet of paper in my hand, which had been folded meticulously into the size of my palm. Although I had read it many times already, in such a moment of suspense, I felt compelled to read it again.

Order 00569, signed off on 3 August, 1939 by Yezhov, head of the People's Commissar for Internal Affairs of the former USSR (as reported in the Russian Immigrant News, 1 November, 1998), was recently made public. The publication revealed that during the Soviet-

Japanese war, the KGB had in its ranks Japanese and Chinese women taken captive in North-eastern China. The more attractive ones were sent secretly to the East Asian Intelligence Department Training Camp at Kiev, and forced to undergo training as sex agents. According to primary field research in Russia, the majority of them were women of Japanese origin. Personal interviews with several surviving members revealed harrowing stories of tears and blood... (Kawachi, Harada, "Female Japanese prisoners of war in the USSR", *The International*, 10 April, 1999)

There was a photo in the article. I had clipped it out and brought it with me. In the photo were female captives in the Soviet training camp 60 years ago. The seven or eight women in the front row were Asians, and their names were printed beneath the picture. There was a woman of a very familiar face—she could be the same person as the woman in the photo that Father gave me, the photo he said was "taken in front of the hospital."

A few minutes passed. A brown document folder was placed on my desk, wrapped tightly in a red string, somewhat faded in colour. I found the end of the string and unravelled it slowly, round by round, while the constriction in my chest became tighter and tighter.

I opened it up to the first page. It was a photograph, about three inches big, but all the details I needed were there.

Her features were very clear, and there was no escape from the truth. I was forced to confront it, face to face, as if looking into a mirror.

Indeed, I looked like her.

Beneath the photo were two neatly written lines, in Chinese and Cyrillic characters. The Chinese characters read: Shizuka Sato, Enrolment date: 8 October, 1939.

The second page was a registration form with personal information, such as height, weight, age, blood type, and nationality.

The third page was a sheet from a memo pad. In Russian it was written "According to Article 58, Section 6 of the Criminal Code, Shizuka Sato is charged with conducting espionage activities for the benefit of Japan."

Following that were three slim notebooks. They were all stamped with "East Asian Intelligence Department Training Camp at Kiev" in Russian in the bottom left corner. The first one was "Trainee's personal account" (in Chinese):

I was born in Harbin, China, in 1917. My father, Eichiro Sato, Japanese, ran a Chinese antiques business. My mother, Zhang Muying, is Chinese. Her father, Zhang Boda, dealt in silks, lumber, and currency exchange in the Northeast. From a young age, my father taught me how to appraise antiques, while my mother taught me Chinese poetry, calligraphy, and painting. She gave me a hand-written poetry anthology that my grandfather compiled when he was 74 years old. In small regular script characters were written poems composed by my maternal grandfather, my maternal great-grandfather, and my maternal great-great-grandfather. By the age of 10 I was able to recite them from memory.

We lived in a large mansion, full of carved beams and painted rafters, sophisticatedly ornate, combining East and West. In the interior there were imported crystal chandeliers, European wall clocks, and modern parquet flooring. The grounds outside were groomed in the style of a Southern Chinese garden. There were small courtyards both in front of and behind the house. The front yard was filled with seasonal flowers, trees and bamboos; the backyard contained a small pond, over which was built a stone bridge. In the pond there were five stone pagodas, each with a round hole on each of the four sides. When candles were placed in the pagodas at night, the candlelight reflected through the round holes onto the water, appearing like a thousand moons floating on the water. It was a very mesmerising sight. Beyond the courtyard was built a long passageway, along which were 28 kinds of decorative windows; on each window was carved a different scene of artistic pursuits. Below the windows were planted Buddhist pines, China pinks, and crabapple trees. I often read poetry or admired paintings in the passageway or on the terrace by the pond. It was a most enjoyable and comfortable time.

When I was 12, my mother passed away. My father remarried; in the following year, my sister, Mariko Sato, was born. After that, my stepmother became intolerant of me and abused me frequently. My father could not do anything about it; only my nanny, who took care of me from when I was young, showed care for me in private. When I was 22, my father passed away, and my stepmother became even harsher on me. Exasperated, I left home.

I went to work as a nurse in the Kwantung Army Hospital, and befriended a colleague, Kikuko Shimada. Not long after, war broke out between Japan and Russia in Manchuria. The Japanese army was defeated. Hearing that the Russian army would ride on their victory and press on towards us, the hospital was evacuated. The wounded soldiers were carried out of the facility; those who were too severely injured to be moved were killed by lethal injection. Kikuko Shimada and I boarded a train, intending to take refuge with a friend of hers. However, Russian troops blocked the route mid-way, and the passengers scurried away in all directions. Shimada and I lived on the streets, hiding our Japanese identity, fleeing from the fighting. Our ears were filled with the cacophony of gunshots for most of the day. Through the cracks in the rubble behind which we were hiding, we witnessed burning and killing, raping and looting, the ground covered with corpses, broken limbs, strewn innards. Only after all noises died down did we dare crawl out to look for food.

We moved in fear and wariness. Often we could not find food. Once, in the gutter in a half-collapsed kitchen, we found a layer of congealed grease. We scooped up the grease, divided it carefully and ate it. That was the most satisfying meal we had had since we became fugitives. There was not a glimmer of lamplight at night. Amid the permeating stench of corpses, in the smoke-filled abandoned city, we held each other's hands, grateful that we were alive.

However, we could not escape the pursuit. They came after us madly; we ran away madly, stepping over cracked tiles, broken pillars, rotten corpses. Gunshots fired up in strings of light all around us. We fell. We got up. We fell again. We ran again. Until, bleeding, we fell into a ditch in the wilderness.

In that -30 degrees ditch in the wild, my blood dripped onto the snow and immediately froze. I lost consciousness in my despair. When I came to, Shimada had disappeared.

I was sent to hard labour in Siberia, to work by the railway. I lived in the barn. I had no bed, and was never full. Sometimes there was nothing to eat at all, and I had to dig through the thick snow to see if there were grains of corn left over from the harvest.

Once there was a blizzard. The barn, buried under the snow, collapsed. I crawled out of the snow, shivering all over from the cold. The houses of the village dotted the horizon sparsely. I stood up in the snowstorm, feeling like I had been completely forgotten by the world. Then, I spotted a broken rubbish bin. As if discovering a treasure, I hurried to dig out all the rubbish, and turned the bin over to cover myself. I padded my thin clothing with the old newspapers I found in the rubbish. Finally, I felt a bit of warmth. I looked out from the hole in the bin. Outside, there was not a stalk of grass, nor a piece of leaf on a branch. It was nothing but whiteness to the ends of my sight. Wind and snow whipped across the land. I could not feel my own existence.

On a clear, cold, sunny morning, under the harsh caws of crows, I was taken onto a train and sent to an unfamiliar camp. Here, I was reunited with Kikuko Shimada. She told me that this was the Soviet East Asia Intelligence Training Camp. When I found out what I was going to be trained to be, I objected vehemently. But Shimada urged me to cooperate, saying that this was the only path to survival. I knew that she was right. I was willing to obey, and to undergo any training.

Volume 2: Training summary (in Chinese)

The art of seduction we are trained in as agents goes beyond attracting men and flirting with them. We take it as a liberation of desires, a freedom with no strings attached.

1) First, we had to conquer our mental barriers. The instructor once said that performing sexual intercourse is a much easier job than facing guns and bombs on the battlefield. As we already possess this free weapon, why not use it completely liberally? The students agreed with the instructor, but were still anxious about it at first. However, through courses in human anatomy, we came to understand the functions of the human body. And after watching numerous pornographic films and writing personal reflections on them, we no longer felt ashamed when encountered with sex. After this preliminary mental barrier was overcome, the instructor had everyone sit in a circle, naked, to observe senior students demonstrate various sexual acts in the centre. By then we were able to view it as a serious study and nothing to feel awkward about. Following that, we practised touching. The instructor put us in groups of four, two males and two females, facing each other to study each other's naked body. We groped and fondled each other's genitalia, and talked about how we felt; then, we switched partners and continued the study, until each of us has touched the bodies of all the students of the opposite sex... After two months, I was able to expose my body with ease and allow others to touch it, without feeling embarrassed.

2) Drills: In this next stage of training, the instructor first paired us up, woman with woman, man with man, and observed us as we simulated copulation, while correcting our technique on the spot. After that, we were paired with the opposite sex and practised actual intercourse. Then, we had intercourse as a group. The instructor filmed us, had us watch the recording afterwards, and analysed areas where our performance could be improved. What we had to remember was that, when we were on an actual mission, we must aim all our sexual acts at the hidden camera and ensure that every detail was recorded clearly, to use as material with which to blackmail our prey in the future. We must not act under sheets or in unlit places, else the work would be in vain. After hundreds of such drills, I am now as comfortable performing sexual acts as taking off my clothes...

3) Overcoming barriers of perception: During this stage of training, we practised with all kinds of unattractive people. The most important lesson was understanding that, no matter how ugly and revolting a body was, we must think of it as the most delicious dainty, while at the same time whetting the target's appetite for us. The instructor was correct in saying that, when you pursue a prey, you must be like an animal catching the scent of meat. Spoiled, fresh, or decayed—at the end, it is just meat. Your job is to eat it. Yes, by now, I am able to accept naturally any kind of rotten meat presented to me...

4) Capturing prey effectively: Each prey has an appetite for different things. We must understand and delve into his emotions and sexual psychology, and look for his fetishes. Then, we must use that to arouse a boundless desire in him. Once you become an essential object to your target, he will do everything you say...

5) Familiarisation with all kinds of spy equipment and techniques, to avoid letting any fleeting opportunity pass by.

6) Post-training practicum: We were assigned to seduce various kinds of real-life targets. These could be young and inexperienced, middle-aged and lustful, old and impotent; they could be ugly, stupid, filthy, or disgusting. We were able to arouse them all—we, who were simultaneously the most insatiable and the most satisfied people in the world... Through this, we experienced a rebirth, and are no longer limited by our former identities. We cast away our names from our previous lives; from now on, male agents will be known as "Ravens", while female agents will be known as "Swifts".

Volume 3, "Reflections upon completion of training" (in Chinese):

I wouldn't dare to say that I have been completely reformed. As they told me, people are born not with a sense of shame, but in stark nakedness. And now, I am as one who has shed an extraneous layer of clothing. Yes, I feel I have taken it off; I feel natural about it now. From now on, I also shed the name that I had used for over twenty years. We all share a common name—Swift. I have also chosen a new name for myself in addition to that—I am now only "Rose"...

* * *

After returning from Moscow, I came across a few more pieces of information:

Kikuko Shimada: A spy sent by the Japanese School of Sex Agents to Manchuria. After being discharged for her age, she made a living as a nurse in a military hospital. In 1939, she was captured by Russian forces, and, after a short period in a labour camp, was sent to a sex agent training facility. There along with her were many female prisoners-of-war of Japanese descent who were falsely convicted of being Japanese spies. Despite having received sex agent training in Japan, Kikuko Shimada still decried the Soviet training camp to be the most brutal and inhuman hell imaginable. During the interview, she recalled a member of her cohort, a woman of dual Chinese-Japanese heritage who went by the name "Rose":

"Rose was a very accomplished student of our training camp. She

succeeded easily on her first practicum assignment. However, when she heard that the businessman whom she had successfully enticed to commit a crime was sentenced to death, she wailed, crying bitterly for having led a man to his death. She wanted to go defend him before the judge, but of course her request was denied. Our leader warned her severely that she must not become attached to her prey. It might have been the end of the story if they had just given her a beating, but they went so far as to use a candle to burn her pubic hair and her underarm hair. They also stripped her and locked her in a cage with scorpions and snakes..." (From Kawachi, Harada, "Interviews with female Japanese prisoners-of-war in the Soviet Union", *Japan-Soviet Relations Research*, 16 April, 1999)

In early 1942, the Department of East Asian Intelligence of the Kiev Training Camp of the USSR sent "Rose", a sex agent, to Zhou En-lai, to further Sino-Soviet cooperation in espionage efforts to... (from Nemtsov, Lev Grigorievich, *Files on Soviet Sex Espionage*. Moscow Literature Press, 1997)

In 1942, the Soviet Union gifted a "Rose" to Premier Zhou. She graduated from the KGB spy training camp as the most outstanding sex agent in her cohort. Premier Zhou sent her to turn several Kuomintang writers to serve the Communist Party. Not only did Rose accomplish her missions successfully, but she also acquired even more literary knowledge and flair in the process. Realising that she had great potential, Premier Zhou devoted himself to training her in all things current and historical, Chinese and foreign. In July 1943, she went to serve as a nurse in the 14th Route Army Hospital in Chongqing, under the name Sachiko Miyamoto. Through working with Dr. Liang Zhibang, she became Chiang Kai-shek's private nurse... (Excerpt from Wang, Xiangxi, "The female Russian spy at Premier Zhou's side", *Memoire of the Assistant to the late Premier Zhou Enlai*, China Social Sciences Press, 1998)

* * *

Harbin, 20th of May, 1999. I finally located Mariko Sato.

"Shizuka Sato... Yes, she's my half-sister. Shizuka left home quite early, though, and didn't really keep in touch with us." Mariko Sato seemed to have realised that she said too much in one go. The expression in her eyes became doubtful. "What are you compiling this document for?"

I replied, "I'm just doing research on the Japanese and Chinese diasporas during the 30s. I'm tasked to do this by the Social Sciences Academy. It's just for a historical reference for internal use. That's all." After I said that, Mariko Sato held out her hand to me.

"Then pay me. You can't have me speak for nothing."

I gave her money. My lie was not a sophisticated one, but she either did not see through it or did not mind it at all. She weighed the thin stack of bank notes in her hand. I posed my question once more. She said, "The last time we had news of her was when she wrote to the nurse who used to live with us. She asked to go stay in the country for a year. I only know that much. There's nothing more."

I found Shizuka Sato's nanny.

Nanny Wang Sizheng, 98 and toothless, could not articulate clearly. I showed her the photo from *The International*. She said, "Shizuka... This does look like her." She stared at the photo for a long time before lifting her head. "It is Shizuka. That's right." She stroked my hair. "Child, seeing you is like seeing her. Oh! It's been... fifty-five years, in the blink of an eye!"

I said, "Granny, I am fifty-three."

"Only fifty-three?" the old nanny batted her eyes. "Oh, how's your leg?"

"It's fixed. I had an operation when I was little," I replied.

"Shizuka had a really difficult time giving birth to you. You almost couldn't come out..."

I suddenly asked her, "Granny, you said I'm fifty-five... which year was I born in?"

She said, "In 1944? Right, it was 1944. I may be old, but I still remember that clearly. At first, she kept you in the attic for over half a year, and went up to nurse you every day. Later on, she left, and had me stay in the village to raise you for her. She only mentioned that she went to Yan'an. Sometimes she sent letters and money. I knew that she went to Chongqing afterwards, because the letter was mailed from Chongqing. But she never allowed me to write back to her. She only sent more money and asked me to find both Chinese and Western doctors for your leg. Another two or three years later, she went to Shanghai, and only then did she send a letter and someone to take you back to her."

* * *

"This is Mommy." This was how Father had me greet her that year, the mother whom I met for the first time, on that great ship laden with the secret stash of gold. My little hand shivered in Father's hand, because even he was a stranger to me, a man I'd met just a few days before.

"Mommy," I said quietly. She looked at me, smiling almost imperceptibly. Only later did I find out that her name was Li Juan.

Li Juan was carrying a child who looked smaller than I was. Father said, "That's your big brother." Obediently, I said "Hello big brother," to the chubby little boy.

After that, Big Brother did grow up faster than I did, and gradually became taller than I was. He became genuinely my big brother. I was born earlier than my older brother, in 1944, though they had registered me as being born two years later. On the books, my year of birth had always been 1946.

23
A quiet exit

Whatever one may think of him, no one can deny that he was a fighter to the end.
They knew that the end was near.

—Richard Nixon

On 5 April, 1975, Chiang Kai-shek passed away.

"Ah." Upon hearing this news, Mao Zedong mumbled on his sickbed, "Has he died? Is he dead?" Mao got up and sat on his bed, his eyelids half-closed. He faced the wall in silence for a moment, let out a long breath, and had the attendant light a cigarette for him. He only took a few puffs before putting it down. His hand, slightly trembling, grabbed a pen by the edge of the desk with difficulty.

This once-luxuriant tree is withering; the life in it is gone...
Why does the cassia waste away and perish? Why then is the wutong half dead...
Once I planted willows, and they swayed and danced in the South; Now I see their leaves fall, covering the River with sorrow.
If this is so for trees, how much more grief for man?

Mao's personal attendant later recorded in his memoirs: Chairman

Man wrote out this section from "Ode to the Barren Tree" by Yu Xin
of the Southern and Northern Dynasties, then, with a faint smile, he
said, "My days have gone, my days have gone." And then he lay back
onto his sickbed.

On 8 January, 1976, Zhou Enlai passed away.
On 9 September, 1976, Mao Zedong also passed away.

In 1976, I passed by Tiananmen Square twice. The first was in the
spring, during the Qingming Festival, the traditional day of mourning.
The square was entirely covered by wreaths and flowers brought by
the crowds, leaving not even room to stand. I took a look at Premier
Zhou's portrait raised in the middle of the square, not daring to join the
crowds in their mourning. Hastily, yet lingering deliberately, I left. The
sea of flowers was there for less than a day before Jiang Qing ordered
them removed. Then, in September, I saw the fiery Jiang Qing walk
up to the high place, leading the millions below in chanting slogans,
exhorting the people to join her in building the future of Communism.
It was as if she was to become the next leader of China. Not long after,
she was put in jail, and a new leader came on stage.

In 1980, I finally obtained full trust by my organisation. No one told
me that; there was no notice to the effect. My duties and position were
still the same. But I could sense clearly that they no longer kept such a
close eye on me.

Another ten years went by, twenty years, thirty years...

Some of the old tales were declassified before they were swept into
the dust. But most of them had been forgotten already. Not very many
still cared about those events from so long ago. Whether declassified
or not, they seemed to have already been laid in the dust and buried in
the grave. Only those few whose names were inscribed in history both
in their lives and their deaths came to own their proper page in official
history, and in those appraisals that perhaps came a few decades too
late.

*Be they winners or losers, these three men had suffered great
psychological stresses... Chiang Kai-shek's death could be traced back*

to 1971, when Kissinger visited Beijing. In the same year, Taiwan was expelled from the United Nations, and over 20 countries broke off diplomatic ties with it. Then, in 1972, President Nixon of the United States became the first American president to visit Beijing. As a result of such blows, Chiang Kai-shek fell ill and never recovered. During Chiang's most difficult days, from 1971 to 1972, Mao Zedong was severely distressed by the betrayal of his trusted comrade Lin Biao, and went into shock in 1972. Zhou Enlai, having long been tormented by the Gang of Four, was found to have cancer in 1972. All three of them fell ill at almost the same time... (Ye Yonglie, historian)

Zhou Enlai's charisma struck me at once... He was the classical prime minister, always picking up the pieces, while Mao was very much the imperial dragon, appearing and disappearing among storm clouds. (Professor John King Fairbank, Harvard University)

Chiang's deep personal commitment to Chinese unity never wavered. He chose to make his last stand on Taiwan and maintain the principle of one China... Chiang was the ultimate survivor. (Jay Taylor, Associate in Research, Fairbank Center for Chinese Studies, Harvard University)

Zhou Enlai had always been Number Three. Despite being Mao Zedong's most valuable assistant, he had never ascended to the position of Number Two... However, in the history of Communist China, no one had stayed a longer time than he in the highest echelon of party leadership. From the 30's of the Twentieth Century to his death in 1976, he witnessed the deaths and downfalls of each of his comrades of yore, but he remained standing, becoming one of the most renowned "survivors" in the history of Chinese politics. (Asia Weekly)

The story of China during the past half century is, to an extraordinary degree, the story of three men: Mao Zedong, Zhou Enlai, and Chiang Kai-shek.... Zhou was one of the most extraordinarily gifted people I have ever known, with an incandescent grasp of the realities of power.... [He was] one of the most accomplished diplomats of our time... Without Mao the Chinese Revolution would never have caught fire. Without Zhou it would have burned out and only the ashes would remain...

I detected something of the Emperor in the way Mao and Chiang spoke of their country. Their gestures and statements seemed to suggest that each man had come to identify his country's fate with his own. When two such leaders meet in history, they do not compromise, they collide. One becomes the victor, one the vanquished... More profoundly, they revered China differently. They both loved the land, but Mao sought to erase the past while Chiang sought to build upon it. In victory Mao simplified the characters of the written Chinese language, not only to facilitate his literacy campaign, but also to destroy the history that each of the complex characters encapsulated. In defeat Chiang made room in the refugee flotilla for nearly 400,000 pieces of ancient Chinese art, even as many loyal aides and soldiers remained on the mainland. (Nixon, former President of the United States)

There is a common understanding among revolutionaries, both Chinese and foreign, throughout history: They may give up their lives; their name may be tarnished; their personal values may be compromised; but their goal must be achieved... Truth and power come, together, from the top, suffering no disagreement. Those at the bottom also feign compliance, using all kinds of traditional methods. This it has always been, and not even the most powerful ruler can do anything about it. Could Chiang Kai-shek have actually been deceived? Perhaps he did not know the truth? No, in fact, he was keenly aware of all the cases of dishonesty, though he was unable to do anything about them...(Ray Huang, historian)

At the exhibition were hundreds of history books and memoires. I flipped through them casually, passing through row after row of display tables. I took a look at the end of the hall, far, far away, feeling tired. I closed the book in my hand, and instead of walking on, I straightened my back and stretched my neck side to side. The receptionist was still keeping an eye on me, while others in my delegation were spread throughout the venue, each with someone watching him also. I was relatively far away from them. Chunshao had walked up next to me. He shut the volume in his hands as well, took off the reading glasses balanced on his nose, and took a glance at those people over on the other side.

"Pleased to meet you, Mr. Song," I greeted him as if we were meeting for the first time.

"You must be Mr. Chen the General Editor. We are delighted that you could make the trip here. How was the luncheon at Yuanshan Hotel?" He took a look at the volume I had just closed, "Oh? You're interested in this book?"

"It's all right. I'm just browsing."

"Would you mind sharing your learned opinion regarding these books on display here?"

"You flatter me. I wouldn't call myself learned. But my humble opinion is this: Machiavelli had already said a few centuries ago, 'A prince need not make himself uneasy at incurring a reproach for those vices without which the state can only be saved with difficulty.' Look at all these books. They spend reams and reams of paper on what could be summarised in that one sentence..." I joked.

"That's right, they all say they did what they could in difficult positions. But were they really trying to save..." Chunshao smiled insincerely.

I stopped looking at him. "In the minds of those represented on this table, was there any vice they could not commit in the name of saving something?"

"Indeed, they would commit any vice. But it's their intention that matters." Chunshao moved a bit closer, switched to a more serious tone and said in a hush-hush voice, "Back then, the Kuomintang were listening in to all the gatherings at our house."

"Oh?"

He picked up a book and pretended to read it. "I saw the files in the bureau from decades ago. They had recorded every single word we had said in the past, and how you instructed Autumn in the culinary arts, and those poetry games... I saw that, at the bottom of every file, there would be comments from the Crown Prince."

"Oh?"

"What's funny is that they're mostly words of praise."

"Oh." Again I looked casually at the receptionist ahead of me. His eyes made contact with mine. I looked away. "He was originally trying to discover some incriminating evidence from the transcripts, but failing that, he found out that those whom he was monitoring were enjoying things he could not have enjoyed. And so he praised us."

Chunshao snickered scornfully.

I believed that his praise was sincere, but I kept that to myself.

I made some small talk with Chunshao, as if it was an ordinary social encounter, exchanging formulaic expressions. It was unwise to talk more in depth in this kind of place; I was also not planning to tell Chunshao the truth. I truly did not know if those gatherings were just for passing intelligence, or if they were for enjoyment, or if they were for enjoyment and the passing of intelligence was just something that happened conveniently. Regardless, the Crown Prince did strike, and ferociously too. After all, he had already honed in on his target. As much as I wanted to mock him as Chunshao did, I could not bring myself to do it. It was sympathy that I felt more of. It's true, that after these decades, I had let it go. I had no choice but to let it go. In it all was a complicated sense of regret, borne out of a simplistic grudge. The regret was not just for myself, either—when this sense of regret is imbued with the collective experience of our society, it became one with the times. Through commiserating with others who had survived the same experience, I found release.

In late spring of 2011, I went to Taiwan, under the cover of a publishing house, to attend a conference on publications on the "Two Shores". That was where I met Chunshao. He was no longer working for the National Security Bureau, and I had also left my original organisation. We each had new positions. After lunch, the participants were free to mingle as they browsed the exhibitions. He and I wandered around the conference hall, making small talk as if we were meeting for the first time, looking absentmindedly at each other and the books before us—and at the same time keeping an eye on our minders. On exhibit were rows and rows of new and old historical commentaries, as well as fresh-off-the-press collections of declassified Chinese and Russian files. In one of the books was an account and some photographs of the day when Chiang Kai-Shek fled in 1949. In one of the photographs, he was standing beside Uncle Zhu, Uncle Yao, and his personal physician, Dr. Liang.

Pointing at the picture, Chunshao said, "Old Chiang used to say 'Rebel spies are right beside you'. How true that is."

"Not just right beside him. Right now you've got one next to you, too," I said.

We looked at each other and laughed.

A while later, after Chunshao had unhurriedly scanned around the room, he said in a low voice,

"How about two hours?"

"Huh?"

"We'll go out. For two hours."

"From right under their noses?" I asked.

"Say that you have a stomach-ache and had to go back to your hotel to rest. Or pick something more sophisticated. You should be quite good at this. It'll be fine as long as we make it back before the meeting this afternoon."

I glanced at him hesitatingly. "All right."

We went to the toilet separately. Then, avoiding notice by both sides, we sneaked into a taxi together outside the conference centre. The taxi drove to a secluded alley and stopped. Chunshao held me by my arm and walked away, and got into a small grey sedan parked by the side of the alley.

"Chunhuan, oh, no, Mr. Chen Xisheng—I only learnt of your new name yesterday—why is everyone sent by your publishing house all from the CCP Central Committee's United Front Work Department?" Chunshao teased me as he drove.

"Then, Mr. Song Chunshao, why is that your publishing house's delegation are all people from National Security, National Defence, and the Presidential Office?" I countered.

"Hah, hah, the pen is mightier than the sword. The pot is just as black as the kettle, isn't it? Chunhuan," Chunshao assumed a serious air, "Tell me, the things you discussed in the backroom yesterday, did you really mean them?"

"Well, did you mean the ones you discussed?"

At that we both laughed.

I said, "Every man for himself."

Chunshao looked askance at me, "Every man with his own schemes."

"All you're after is an exchange of interests," I said.

"But you don't know the cards in our hand. This is only one script. We have another hundred or so scripts waiting to be played. We don't trust you."

"We've seen through this little trick of yours. But you need us more and more."

"It's true, we need you. But it depends on what you can give us."

"That depends on how you behave. In short, it's about an exchange, a compromise. It's about what we can trade from each other."

"Or, rather, it's about what we can sacrifice, what we can give up," said Chunshao.

"You say 'sacrifice', like you got the short end of the stick," I intentionally rubbed it in for once.

"I wouldn't dare say that. Who knows which of us will come off worse at the end? Anyway, it's just about carrying out the government's secret wishes. Which government in the world would tell her people or her opponents the details of all her schemes and plots? You can't speak too genuinely, not even in a secret meeting."

"Even though we call this a negotiation, we're still wary of each other. Look at those receptionists of yours. They've got their eyes fixed on our people, watching our every move, not letting us go about on our own at all either."

"It's not just us. Even your people are monitoring each other too."

"And you're any different?"

"Of course our governments have to be wary of us. We are only puppets. The show is controlled by someone else. How could we act on our own?" said Chunshao.

"I'm quite curious about this show," I answered him irreverently, "Is it going to be drama, action, or comedy? Forget about my side for now. Look at yourselves. On your tiny little island you've got more than seventy-seven hundred anti-aircraft missiles. In terms of density you're second in the world, only after Israel. With this many missiles in your pocket, you still dare to demand that we remove ours. Is that not laughable..."

"Then let's laugh together." Chunshao took a look at the rear-view mirror, and suddenly spun the steering wheel and drove onto another expressway. "Great! I have a reason to take off now. I'll tell them that I was responsible for keeping an eye on you. I saw that you left your group, so I came out to grab you and return you to the Communists. Hah, hah!"

Chunshao sped up. As he stepped on the accelerator, time slowed down.

At half past one in the afternoon, we arrived at our parents' graves. Beside them was a small mound, the memorial where I had buried Floral's personal belongings in the past. We talked, heart-to-heart, before the graves, and as we reminisced, I recalled Floral's fate after she became a sing-song girl, and blurted out:

"Floral was the fourth dog who died on Autumn's account."

I did not know if I truly believed that or why I said that. Or perhaps it was an excuse, an unreasonable complaint for having to cope with the regret that I had not been able to dispel from my heart in all these years. I kept feeling that Floral died because of me. This made me emotional and it broke my heart. But I would rather not deal with the heartbreak and the emotions. I could only concoct an artificial reason and pin the blame on Autumn. Over the decades this belief solidified in my heart, and gradually let me ignore the connection between Floral's death and myself. Occasionally I had blamed myself for being a coward—if I could not deal with emotions, then why would I keep thinking of her? And why couldn't I deal with them anyway? Cold-blooded, that's what I was! My work trained me to be indifferent. But the more I acted that way, the more guilty I felt. And this day, when I stood before her memorial mound, I felt as I was found a liar, and I was hit hard by the fact. I had no choice but to stifle the anguish in my heart. The pain was still there after all these decades!

Chunshao gave me a confused look and said nothing. He reached out and picked a dead leaf off Floral's mound, and reflexively flicked away the speck of dirt on his fingertip. Not deliberately, it seemed, but rather as a subconscious motion. I felt that he had not completely grown out of his aristocratic habits and could not tolerate a bit of dirt on his hands. Or perhaps, he had not completely grown out of his mentality from his youth either, as if he still thought of himself as Floral's master, and that what he just did was a boon that he was granting to a servant.

"Look at this flower," Chunshao pointed at a bouquet of flowers before Father's grave, lying next to Floral's.

"Hmm?" I did not understand what Chunshao was hinting at.

"It's Autumn."

"Autumn?" I was shocked. "It's been decades. Autumn... She still comes here?"

"Yes, she visits every month."

"How... how's she doing?"

"Not too well, not too badly," said Chunshao, "She's lonely, all by herself."

"She... she must be old now..." A superfluous statement. It's just that, when an image of Autumn in old age went through my mind, I felt a bit absurd at once.

"She is old," Chunshao said thoughtfully, "But she's still really pretty."

I shot a glance at Chunshao.

He could not forget her still. I knew Chunshao had never forgotten her. But she could never forget the person in the grave. Chunshao had stayed single all this time—I did not want to ask him why, nor did I want to stir up his old feelings so brusquely. "She was truly Father's 'Anna,'" was all I could remark, sighing.

"You still remember Anna? It's been decades," Chunshao said evenly, not exactly wistfully, but not exactly indifferently either.

He stooped before Mother's grave, carefully clearing the weeds on the tombstone, a glum look on his face. "To this day I can't discover how Mother died. Father never spoke of it when he was alive. I wanted to ask him, but the look in his eyes made me not dare to ask. It was one day when I was coming home from school when Father took me to kowtow before this grave. I didn't even know when she was buried. I didn't even know what she was found guilty of. I bet she died during interrogation."

"Yes," I chimed in, "I heard that her body was claimed from a formalin pool packed full of bodies, and was buried right away. Father was worried that you'd be sad if you had seen it, so he didn't let you know too much."

"But he let you know?"

"It's just hearsay. I've spent a lot of time locked up, so I've heard all kinds of things in excruciating detail. I asked Father about it afterwards and he didn't deny it."

Chunshao stroked Mother's tombstone tenderly, over and over again. "I keep thinking, Mother died just like that, without reason, without explanation, and yet I joined the ranks of her executioners, those executioners who killed our mother... But at the time, I only thought about having a good job, a safety net. It's like I was craving it and nothing else. So I joined them, without even thinking twice..."

"Yes, you became an executioner." I blurted out in spite of myself, though I had not wanted to provoke him.

Chunshao gave me an uncertain look. I continued:

"That Guo Tingliang, Sun Liren's subordinate."

"You found out about that?"

"The public here may not know about things that happened here, but over where we are we know these things. Back then, he was coerced by the Kuomintang to confess falsely to being a Communist spy. He thought that by doing so he could have saved General Sun, but it was a trap. Thirty-seven years later, he finally returned from Green Island. He went all around trying to clear General Sun's name, and that's when you started monitoring him constantly. On the 16th of November, 1992, he was thrown off a train onto the station platform..."

Chunshao stayed silent.

I continued, "He had been shot dead before then. That day you were on the same train as he."

"You're thinking that I'm shameful and cowardly."

"You could say that, being dependent on them, your will was not your own. Or you could say, you're a willing accomplice to the tigers. Regardless, they've raised you into a tiger cub now."

"My superiors once gave me a copy of an internal document, to let me know that Father had been under surveillance and suspicion for a long time..."

"So you were forced to act against your will?"

Chunshao said nothing.

"They have no shortage of henchmen. They can't be so inept as to use Father's case to pressure you. If they had the evidence, why didn't they go arrest Father directly? Why wouldn't they send other killers instead..."

"Guo Tingliang had visited Father when we were kids. I had met him a few times. He knew me, so it's easier for me to approach him..."

"And that's how you got chosen?"

"No. I disclosed this relationship to my superiors."

"I understand now. You must've been trying to clear your own name. And so, fearing what people might say of you, you thought about redeeming yourself, by cutting all ties with your family, and every by volunteering to do their work."

"Perhaps you've seen through me. But anyway, I can't really describe how I was feeling at the time."

"If you live long enough in the tiger's den, you'll become more or less like a tiger yourself. How drastically can human nature transform in there..."

"You're saying that I'm callous..."

"Chunshao, don't blame yourself. I am in no position to accuse you of anything. It's not just you. All of us have become callous to some extent.... I know you're afraid that, if you didn't act like a tiger, you'd be eaten by them. And so you did everything you could to behave like a tiger. Chunshao, you were afraid. You have always been afraid..."

Chunshao sighed. "Maybe you're right, maybe you're wrong. But I won't deny that I had once wanted to do my part as a tiger. Not just a bad tiger. I wanted to be a good tiger as well.... But who'd have thought, nowadays a tiger is no longer what he was before. His claws and teeth have been removed. He can do nothing. Such a person now cannot count as an executioner. He no longer has a sword to kill with. Hah, these days, all that a national security officer gets to wield is a flyswatter. You can't even kill a fly with it." He shook his head, and added, "A few years ago, Pan Baojiang was trying to work on a cold case involving someone taking a cut from an arms procurement deal. Only when a colonel who had the inside scoop was murdered did Pan Baojiang get a lead. But unexpectedly his boss stopped him, and instead told him to hurry up and retire. Also, there's Tian Lin—you must remember him. Thirty-six years ago, Pan Baojiang was coveting his position. Pan Baojiang had his old man unseat him, and even made up some charges to arrest him on. He fled to the airport in an attempt to leave the country, but he failed and was locked up. He was a tough one. He endured all kinds of torture and interrogation, and eventually even worked out a way to escape from jail. You'd think such a ruthless character would come back and exact revenge on Old Pan, but no, he went straight to the Mausoleum at Cihu, and took his own life before Old Chiang's sarcophagus. Tian Lin left a note. The man who collected his body gave me a sneak look at it. It said, he had spent his life in President Chiang's service, from the Mainland to Taiwan, risking life and limb for the Party and the Nation. And yet the country allowed the petty-minded to run the show... He must have been extremely disillusioned at that time. Hah, hah, if he hadn't been ousted back then, he'd be clawless and toothless now too, and he'd probably kill himself anyway..." Chunshao chuckled again dryly. It was a forced, unnatural chuckle, sounding as much as a sob as a laugh.

"I'd never have guessed that Tian Lin would end up like that." I suddenly felt that I didn't really hate him that much. "That year, to help me escape, you were caught by Tian Lin. After that I had no way of finding out what happened to you. Could it be that it was Pan Baojiang who let you go?"

"Yes, you guessed right. I had a role in Tian Lin's downfall. Pan Baojiang had me step forward and inform on Tian Lin, because when I was arrested, I claimed that Tian Lin had arrested me on trumped up charges because I knew of his secrets and he wanted to suppress me. Pan Baojiang believed me, without collecting evidence first. I'm thinking maybe it wasn't that he believed me, but rather that he wanted to use me. He was just in need of a hitman who could do this deed for him. He had me use a lame trick—forgery—and plant a forged document on Tian Lin to incriminate him. However, Tian Lin's got a pretty strong network. Pan Baojiang and his father had to work together and strike fast to get Tian Lin to jail with no opportunity for an appeal. As for your case, it had nothing to do with his position, so he didn't worry himself over it."

"And then where did you go? I couldn't get news of you over there. You disappeared suddenly for seventeen years. You weren't on any of the government staff lists in all of Taiwan."

"Pan Baojiang found me a cushy post behind the scenes. He didn't entirely trust me back then, but I had been of service to him after all. You know what happened after that. Seventeen years later, I was put back in my position, and did that thing for them. After that I served them pretty loyally, but was kept back from promotion all along... Until the last year or so—the government seemed keen to dig up survivors from the previous era—and reinstated me like I was someone important. Speaking of which, I wouldn't be where I am now without framing Tian Lin. But these days, you wouldn't find anyone else with Tian Lin's level of loyalty, and who ends up with a fate like his."

"Ah. As much as I resent Tian Lin, I can't help feeling sorry for what happened to him. Strictly speaking, he wasn't really a villain."

"He doesn't count as a villain. You can only say that he was unfortunate enough to have become the villains' henchman. Even Pan Baojiang—that rich kid whom I had every disdain for—found his conscience in his old age, and out of the blue decided to do something proper for once. But as soon as he got around to it he got fired."

"Who'd have thought that Pan would be thrown out this way?"

"And then—you'd know already, given how well-informed you are over there—Yao Kunming came onto the stage, " said Chunshao. "It was because of him that Pan Baojiang got kicked out. After all those years locked up on Green Island, Yao Kunming came to possess a double identity—victim of political persecution, and family of a victim of political persecution. The opposition party supported him; the Kuomintang repented to him. His title of a victim was like a badge of honour for his life-time achievement. Even after two changes of governments and presidents, nobody could budge him from his position... Hah, Yao Kunming is a man who has lived in both the wrong era and in the right era. Every dog has his day— if you had stayed and toughed it out at Green Island back then, you'd probably have yours too."

"You'd want me to be a dog like that?" I grinned wryly back at him. Chunshao shook his head.

We lit the fire. As the incense burnt, we gazed at the photographs of the deceased on the tombstone. But my mind wandered.

Chunshao was very quiet. While he uttered no sound, on his face there was a disturbed, unquiet look.

What did he want to say to Mother? From the corner of my eye I glanced at him, so fixated on the photographs... his hair, greyed, appeared particularly sparse when ruffled by the autumnal gusts. I really wanted to tell him something, but I held myself back...

* * *

File FT9-5187 on Zhu Zhennan:

Zhu Zhennan: Descendent of celebrated calligrapher and painter Zhu Beihong. Went on mission to Taiwan under the name "Huang Yingbi"; became art instructor to Chiang Kai-shek's wife, Soong Mei-ling. After Liu Dongqing was exposed, Zhu Zhennan terminated his mission and returned secretly back to the mainland...

File FT9-3126 on Li Juan:

Li Juan: Father - Li Xianheng; mother - Zheng Xiu. Joined the China Art and Drama Society in September 1945 and became a core member of the society. Performed in various plays including "The Taiping Heavenly Kingdom", "Rickshaw Boy", "Cai Wenji", "Mei Mengxiang", "Guan Hanqing", "The Wilderness", and "The Romance of the Qing Palace". She was best known for her role as Jinzi in "The Wilderness", Tiger Girl in "Rickshaw Boy", and Empress Cixi in "The Romance of the Qing Palace", and was highly praised by Chiang Kai-shek, who on several occasions invited her to perform at his residence... When Li Juan took the oath on being admitted to the Party, she declared, "Love the party in yourself, and not yourself in your part", which was adapted from Stanislavsky's famous line "Love the art in yourself and not yourself in the art". All were moved by her words. In 1949, Chiang Kai-shek ordered Song Jiafu to bring his family to Taiwan and report on his work. Li Juan, posing as Song Jiafu's wife, went to carry out her mission in Taiwan together with him...

On June 19, 1999, Mr. and Mrs. Lu Kepeng came to visit. I met up with Liu Yanxian.

That day, some colleagues and I were sent to welcome the American ambassador and his wife. I had read up on their files beforehand, and had a basic knowledge about their background. I had thought about what to chat about when we met, but when we actually met face to face, I was at a loss for words.

After the reception, the ambassador's wife invited me for a walk at Beihai Park, just outside the hotel. We strolled along a path lined with pagoda trees; the cool and refreshing breeze washed the air of the summer heat. Gazing at the hillock beyond the trees, the lake by the hill, the little boat and the red bridge on the water, I felt an eternity in the moment, and felt a sense of both relief and dreariness that made me not want to pursue that which was in the past.

Without a word, I looked at the ambassador's wife, once my mother, Li Juan, waiting to see if she would speak first.

"I didn't know you were still in this world." At the end I was the first one to speak.

"They traded me for arms," Liu Yanxian seemed to be dying for me to give her a conversation topic. "Jiafu and Kepeng saved me."

We exchanged a glance calmly, two wizened individuals, not easily startled by any strange or astonishing news. Liu Yanxian continued, "Jiafu informed Kepeng of my arrest. Kepeng knew that the Kuomintang were just planning to purchase arms from the U.S., so he told the U.S. about what happened to me and requested them to make the Kuomintang release me secretly as a condition for selling arms to Taiwan."

Liu Yanxian then narrated the story about her and Lu Kepeng. "At the time he was leaving China, he told me to wait for him. I promised to wait, even if it took a lifetime. After his case was redressed in the U.S., he tried everything he could to locate me, and then he started communicating with me... Jiafu knew about it. At the time, I wanted to give up on everything and go to the U.S. to be reunited with Kepeng, but Jiafu stopped me. He exhorted me to continue carrying out my mission, to not abandon my mission. Through this matter, though, Jiafu got in contact with Kepeng. They exchanged intelligence with each other, but each for his own purposes. They were only of one mind when it came to me..."

"I heard that it was the Crown Prince who had someone inform on you?"

"To be precise, there were two things at play. First, there was the infighting among the spy agencies. To curry favour with the Crown Prince or Old Chiang himself, they cooked up all these cases of wrongful accusations, by hiding facts from everyone else in the system. At the same time, the Crown Prince was just about to clean up the intelligence agencies and recruit them to his cause. So the two sides came to an agreement instantly."

"But did you know that it was Uncle Yao who turned you in? He's also done the same to Uncle Zhu."

"I know. Old Yao... perhaps he didn't want to do that, but the situation had turned on its head on him. I heard that he gained great trust with Chiang Kai-shek and his son. So, he used me and Old Zhu out of convenience to increase his own power. At the time, the Crown Prince was intending to restructure the intelligence and military organs. He sent a deputy director of the surname Pan to find out about me and Old Zhu from Old Yao, who played along and provided intelligence on us. It also was a way to show respect for the intelligence system... But he's not to blame. Perhaps we had indeed accidentally disclosed something and let others on our trail. Actually, sometimes it's necessary for an intelligence officer to give away a colleague. Not long after we arrived in Taiwan, one Deputy Minister Wu from another operational unit, then working in the MND, exposed himself. Seeing that things were going badly, Jiafu volunteered Comrade Wu's information to the Kuomintang for self-preservation and to build up the Kuomintang's trust in himself. It was a way to salvage the remaining value in the man. You remember the calligraphy hanging in the living room of our old house? *A thousand-gold sword, ten thousand words of learning—both have I squandered.* That was Comrade Wu's work. Jiafu took over his house, and made a point of keeping his calligraphy. You can imagine what was going through his mind..."

I was dumbfounded. I could only feel confused and despondent.

"Mother, what was your codename during your mission?"

"Butterfly and Jade Maiden."

Something was ascertained in my mind.

"And Father's?"

"Rose, Honeybee, Bodhisattva of Mercy..."

I recalled several old files. The image of Father I pieced together in my mind became simultaneously clearer and blurrier.

"Mother... if you don't mind, I'd like to keep calling you Mother—there's one thing I can't get out of my mind. My mother by birth—is she still alive? Did you really kick her out? Did you kill her? I have not been able to find her..." I clung on to one last thread of hope, hoping that Liu Yanxian would know the whereabouts of Shizuka Sato. Even if she was dead, please let me find her grave.

"Chunhuan, why do you ask me that? I don't know anything about her. I really don't. I haven't even met her. How could I have kicked her out or killed her?"

"That's what they told me. Both Chunhong and Father told me that."

"I don't know what stories Jiafu told about me. He could have said anything he liked. He had his mission, so perhaps he had no choice. As for Chunhong, I don't know where she would have heard this from, but perhaps it's from the same source. Chunhuan, I must tell you, back then the party put us together as a couple only because Jiafu told them that he needed a nominal wife to facilitate his work. At that time I already had a child, but no one knew about him yet. So, I took this opportunity to register Chunshao as Jiafu's child, to give Chunshao a father. Later on, Old Chiang sent Jiafu to Taiwan. Old Chiang demanded that all his closest aides bring their families to Taiwan and not leave anyone behind on the Mainland. He and I boarded the boat to Taiwan, and only on that day did he tell me that he had a son too. That was the first time I saw you. He said, his first wife disappeared soon after giving birth. To avoid difficult explanations later on, we pretended that I was the mother of his child. When we arrived at Taiwan, he registered you as his second son."

"Did he mention the name of his first wife?"

"He did, when he provided his personal information to the party, but I don't remember it."

"Was it Shizuka Sato? Or Sachiko Miyamoto?"

"I don't remember anymore. All I remember is that he had said that his first wife's identity was very sensitive, and that no one should find out about their relationship—and obviously no one should find out that he had a child by his first wife either..."

It started to drizzle. We found a gazebo and sat down in it. Gusts ruffled up the surface of the lake, raising a curtain of mist before the dusk sky. Heavy clouds veiled the darkening sun, merging into the grey-green water of the lake. My heart also felt like it was covered with cloaks of mist. I would not have thought that, after all these years, my mysterious beginnings would become even more uncertain.

"Had you never thought of leaving with Chunshao? He was your son, after all."

Liu Yanxian stared into the rain blowing towards her eyes, a look of embarrassment and regret crossing her face. "I didn't know what to tell Chunshao... I had indeed carried Kepeng's child, but I miscarried when we were on the run. Chunshao was the nurse's child. The nurse was also pregnant when she was helping me escape. All she cared about was protecting me... She died of childbirth on the road. I promised her to raise the child for her. Afterwards, we arrived in Chongqing, and I took on the nurse's name and became Li Juan. As you know, I was implicated in that business with Kepeng, so I was forced to change my name. I couldn't have explained all that to Chunshao..."

I sighed, "So, he isn't your child either." I looked at this mother of ours, who knitted me a sweater with a coded message woven in with her own hair. "But we both remembered you as our mother. We both need a mother who we can remember..."

Liu Yanxian held my hands. "Chunhuan, I am willing to be your mother, if you are willing to consider me your mother..."

"I'm willing to take you to be my mother. I'm also really happy that you're still alive."

Liu Yanxian hugged me tightly. Tears glistened in our eyes. In what I remembered of my childhood, she rarely hugged me. This was the one embrace I yearned for the most, over the decades.

The rain stopped. Several birds flew low over the water's edge; a crisp chorus of chirps rose out from the dense, verdant woods. We walked out of the gazebo and strolled onto a white stone bridge. The Buddhist temple in the distance was lit up with glass lamps, the lamplight flickering on the surface of the water. We gazed, silently, into the distant lamplight and the reflection in the water, feeling that we could hear each other's innermost thoughts. Remembering the past brings nothing except for sighs, but time is the best painkiller.

"Mother, did you and Father... ever have... the kind of feeling between husband and wife?" I thought about what Autumn and Chunhong had said.

"We... well, it's hard to say what feelings we had." As if she was reminiscing something, Liu Yanxian had half a smile on her face. "The most husband-like thing he ever did for me was helping me draw on my eyebrows and apply blush. Oh, and also, painting roses on my toenail. He liked to cover my big toenail with bright red paint and draw white roses on them... The only times he ever touched me was when he did that, touching my toes. There's nothing else."

"Nothing else..." I found it difficult to sever my memories of our happy family in my childhood, and what I had imagined of Father and Mother. In my heart, they had always been Father and Mother, they had always been at least a couple. But my memory was to be shattered from now on.

Liu Yanxian looked at me, appearing as if she understood my question. But maybe she got it wrong. "Let me put it this way... we never slept together. At first I said I didn't want to, and later on I found out that Jiafu didn't want to either. To be precise, we were only husband and wife for the purpose of the mission. I hadn't seen him take interest in any other woman either, even though many women took a fancy to him..."

"For the purpose of the mission," I repeated her words reflexively. "Was it all for the mission? Are you telling me that Father lived his whole life in his mission?"

"I cannot guess what kind of conviction allowed him to hold out for this long, to the point of giving his whole life to it. Perhaps that is an accurate reflection of the destiny of a certain group of Chinese agents at the time." Liu Yanxian's gaze moved away from my face and onto a duck that had just landed in front of us. "But that's probably not all. I also have a feeling that... perhaps he was one with no control over his life. At first, it was truly for the mission, but later on, the mission became just an excuse."

"He needed an excuse?"

"That's right. Even when he had no more mission, he spent his days like he had one."

"Mother, this is something I don't understand. When you didn't have a mission, couldn't you have spent some time for yourself?"

"You're in the same business. You should know not having a mission is harder to bear than having one. Sometimes, you go through all this effort to gain some intelligence, but don't know where to send it. And even if you send it off, you might not get a response from your organisation. But we can't become regular citizens either and pretend that we don't know anything. We are like wolves that have lost their pack. The road ahead is still long. We cannot relax. We still passed our days in waiting and watchfulness. Is the leader of the mission still there? Which link in the chain was it that went wrong? At the end, the remaining few can only monitor each other, seeing who has failed to be loyal to the post, loyal to this... this party that has already forgotten us."

"Was Father monitoring you too?"

"He was, but through that, he inadvertently shared my love and my secret. I knew he intended to let me go, that it was just a matter of time..."

"Father did indeed let you go. He made us believe that you're dead. He let everyone know that you were no longer of this world."

"I'm in Jiafu's debt for that. He probably underwent a lot of trouble for that. Indeed, it couldn't be known that I had gone to the U.S."

"Father announced the false information that you had died in prison, and even erected a burial mound for you," I said, smiling wryly.

"Yes, over the last few decades I never stopped feeling bad about him. Back then, when I said I felt I owed him something, that I worried that he was putting himself through too much trouble for me, he was unperturbed about it and only hurried me to leave. I asked him what he would do if he let me go. I told him to leave as well, but he wouldn't. I said, 'What are you waiting for? Do you really think we'll get another mission?' His reply was, 'I don't know. My life is full of setbacks.'"

"He probably couldn't set his heart at ease," I said. But another voice said in my heart: He wasn't doing that for himself, but for the two camps he served. He had originally worked to entrench each camp against the other, but eventually he realised the necessity for their mutual existence. And so at this critical juncture he had to find a way to halt the progression of things.

"My guess is that he knew too many secrets," Liu Yanxian continued. "He had hitched himself onto the chariot and could not release himself from it. His only option was to continue forward. But this only recourse for him was not necessarily a viable path."

"I felt that he was trying to contribute to, or change something."

Liu Yanxian sighed, "What would he want to change? Change the mission? Restore the things that he had broken or make them better? But if he couldn't even control his life, how could he control the situation? In this line of work, there is no greater desire than to be in control of one's life, but that is utterly impossible. We are ordered to meddle with other people's fates, but are not allowed to become masters of our own. No matter how hard you work, all you can do is push yourself ever deeper into the vortex. You can't ever be free of it."

"Mother, perhaps he wasn't trying to free himself from it, even if it's an endless vortex. He was willing. If... this was his version of loyalty."

"Loyalty? What is loyalty?" Liu Yanxian smiled. "Unconditional support and obedience? He had achieved that, but he had also gone beyond that."

"Mother, if true loyalty was merely simple-minded obedience, wouldn't that count as blind devotion? What if Father had gone beyond that because he had seen something clear on the front line... because he no longer saw just one side of the issue, but the picture as a whole. That would be an achievement, an ideal..."

"Perhaps you're right. He went beyond because of his loyalty. However, in the system, to go beyond something is to become a liability, to have violated something." Liu Yanxian sighed, "He could only continue driving his chariot, covered in all his wounds, even if it meant being swallowed up by the vortex."

"Even so, he would not abandon his conviction."

— That is keeping watch eternally.

Scenes from the past swirled in my mind confusedly, including Anna bobbing up and down in the river. I also recalled that last time I saw Father. Before we parted, I suddenly asked him what was the definition of loyalty.

"That is..." Father took a deep breath, "keeping watch eternally."

He had said that with all the strength left in him, as if those were his last words.

"He was keeping watch," I mumbled.

"Chunhuan, do you still not understand?"

I frowned, as if I was stubbornly holding onto my own opinion even though I knew it would be refuted.

"There is a kind of keeping watch, that's a bird in a long, continuous flight, unable to stop even though it has been injured; it cannot find a place to land, and can only keep flying, looking dizzily at the earth, until he falls from the sky. Because to him, the sky is in the vortex," said Liu Yanxian. "I admired Jiafu, but I tried hard to leave it."

"Leave it?" I lowered my head, feeling that I had forced her to say something she should not have said.

"That's right. I have asked myself if I was truly loyal, but I also felt unsure about the vortex which I am in. It's like, there are only three kinds of Chinese people I see—pro-Russia, pro-America, or pro-Japan. What have the past few decades been all about? It was just a long, unending proxy war. In fact, I understand less and less as time goes on. Or perhaps I have become confused. I should leave it all." Her voice lowered to a whisper. "In reality, I haven't touched a mission in a long time. I only came this time to be with Kepeng..."

"Yes, Mother." I closed my eyes and exhaled deeply. "You have indeed gone far, far away from it all. Also, I shouldn't hold you back with the past. I should stop pursuing the matter."

"Pursuit is indeed futile. What you should do is muddle through your days, living out your life in simplicity. But you cannot let matters lie either, and therefore you are in pain."

"Perhaps it's true I cannot leave it all. But Mother, I've thought it through. This shall be the last time I call you Mother. There will be no next time."

"Son, you got it wrong. Leaving does not mean severing all ties. How can a man live when his mind has nothing to hold on to? Do not empty yourself into a soulless shell, just for the sake of avoiding pain. When I said living in simplicity, I meant not manoeuvring for power, not getting bemired in the system. Else you would just be sending yourself to the grave faster. If there is anything in your mind that gives you support, gives you strength, go ahead and hold on to it."

"Mother! Mother!" I called earnestly. I was scared that she would disappear, or that she would abandon me. I called out to her, holding dearly onto this moment, feeling utterly helpless.

Liu Yanxian reached out her wrinkle-covered hand and stroked my face. In that instance, I became her little boy from the past again. "Chunhuan, in these times, we are fortunate to have survived."

The next day, the higher-ups held an official banquet, during which they presented Mr. and Mrs. Lu Kepeng with a painting.

"This is a landscape painting by the late Zhu Zhennan, the only student of the famous painter Zhu Beihong..."

Liu Yanxian and I gave each other a knowing look. She smiled gracefully. She had no way of leaving this behind, I thought.

In July, 1999, Liu Yanxian returned to the U.S., and forwarded me a letter. There was no signature on the letter, but I recognised the handwriting to be Father's. It was dated a month before he passed away.

As history goes on, injustice accumulates. There is not one period of history that was created by pure innocence.

They wanted to rebuild order in chaos. But before that, they had probably created the chaos in what was orderly. Rebuilding seems to be a necessity of every era. But, for many historical figures, the process of rebuilding necessarily include some unspeakable crimes. I do not think that they were truly insensitive; this fact surely transforms into nightmares in their souls, enough to make them repent and redress it with their lives.

For over thirty years, I had not developed any real personal relationship with others. I was like an island, separated from the rest of mankind. Over half my life was spent for the Cause. The more I did, the more I felt exhausted deep in my bones; and at the end, I broke myself into pieces and drove myself beyond hope. For the longest time I did not know what compassion and mercy were; not until I decided to redeem myself did I realise that I had lost thoroughly, that my entire life was either a story of futility, or a story of sin.

By the way, after Chiang had been lying in a coma for two and a half years, I revived him with a special drug. However, not long after that, he was made unconscious again by an alliance of officials who were content with just holding the island. Chiang's former ideology of "counter offensive" and "not coexisting with the enemy" had ceased to exist...

* * *

I was told that in the fine-brush painting Father had me bring back was hidden a microdot a millimetre big. It was taken with a reversed macro lens, which shrank the image into a microscopic size. Stuck amidst the feathers of the bird in the painting, it could not be discerned with the naked eye. They removed the dot with the tip of a needle and examined it under a microscope. It turned out to be Chiang Kai-shek's diary, all printed on one page. I did not find out what the contents were, but just that while it was a precious find, it was no longer of much use.

* * *

This was perhaps the last operation Father was involved with and recorded by the Party. I was unable to find out about his follow-up plans. Perhaps the files had not been put in order yet, or perhaps he had been hiding them from the Party all along.

File CT4-2088
Operation Nightingale
Agents: Tailor, Rose, Scholar, Gardener
Decode:

• Rose (18-3-1960): Scholar has successfully infiltrated Nightingale's residence to teach Nightingale's wife to paint. He has installed listening devices in the living room and the painting room, but Nightingale seems to have expected that already. He does not discuss important matters indoors. Additionally, "Gardener", his attendant, has been recruited as a new member. He is to monitor Nightingale's daily life and to be a reference for Tailor's prescriptions...

• Tailor (11-5-1960): Nightingale's illness is indeed a strange one. He is showing signs of serious perceptual distortions and depersonalisation...

• Rose (20-8-1961): A woman is added to the operation as Gardener's wife, to validate Gardener's dedication to this operation. Every night, before going to bed, Nightingale takes off his false teeth and gives them to Gardener for safekeeping. Gardener found an opportunity to pass the false teeth on, through his wife, to Rose. Rose has already found a way to install a miniature listening device in the false teeth.

• Rose (15-6-1962): Gardener made a mistake when attending to Nightingale, and injured his anus. Gardener was sent to jail.

• Tailor (7-4-1965): Nightingale's illness becomes stranger by the day. He is showing signs of temporary amnesia, memory lapses, and derealisation...

• Tailor (16-9-1968): Nightingale and his wife were in a motor vehicle collision today at Yangmingshan. The lady had minor injuries, while Nightingale was seriously injured. The cause of the collision has not been determined. The responsible party fled the scene...

• Rose (18-9-1968): The jeep that collided into Nightingale's vehicle belonged to a major-general of a certain army division...

• Tailor (6-11-1968): Nightingale has not recovered from his injuries yet. His power and responsibilities are gradually transferred to his eldest son...

• Rose (8-4-1972): As shown in the filmstrip, in his diary Nightingale grieves over the corruption in the KMT bureaucracy, and wishes to reform the KMT...

• Rose (3-5-1972): May I suggest greater discretion in Nightingale's diagnosis and prescription? Nightingale has already become aware of his own illness, and feels deeply contrite about it. He intends to put an end to himself. But Nightingale must not die, for the sake of preserving internal stability on the island and preventing it from being controlled by the U.S....

• Tailor (30-5-1972): Nightingale's cognitive distortions are becoming more and more serious. Tailor asks for permission to use this opportunity to provide drugs to worsen his condition. But Rose is still of the opinion that we should continue observing for now. The members of this operation cannot come to a consensus...

• Rose (23-7-1972): In the afternoon of the 22nd, Nightingale suddenly fell into a coma.

• Rose (4-9-1972): Tailor was arrested and sent to the authorities for investigation. This team is temporarily putting all operations on hold.

• Rose (6-4-1975): Nightingale passed away last night at 23:55. A few pages of his diary had been torn out and cannot be retrieved...

* * *

Ants' heads. Microdots.

Tweezers, needle points, thread...

I reached as hard as I could in memory to that earliest haze, to the origin of things that I believed I would never reach again.

They were all one millimetre in size.

Dark.

Ovoid.

They all joined together in a string.

Perhaps those random hobbies I had when I was a boy were imitations of what I saw in my childhood?

And, those stationery lists representing military units, those convoluted games of hiding things—did I come up with them on my own?

My narrative was only based on what I remembered. I cannot ascertain the accuracy of my memory.

That secret hiding game was something that I had loved from the beginning. I chose it. I cannot blame it on fate. And what about him— and them? Did they do it purely for their mission, or did they come to love it in the same way? Secret operations, secret heroes—was it because they were so secret that they would become legend?

Eternity. Keeping watch. Flying.

What if we smuggled a page of a personal legend through a thick tome of historical records? Would a solitary bird be allowed to hold up the skies by itself?

In the year of 2005, I came across this file. Though I felt that I had lost all expectations through prolonged exhaustion, or that everything would be as I expected, I still read through it carefully, dutifully poring over every character.

File FT9-7167 on Song Jiafu:

Song Jiafu: Father — Song Jitang; mother — Deng Shuangrui. Recommended by Zhu Anqiao (alias), an underground Party member who had infiltrated the KMT, to the KMT in February 1946, as a result of the "poetry response" incident. The "poetry response" incident began on 14 November, 1945, when the *Xinmin Evening News Supplement* published Mao Zedong's poem "Snow — to the tune of *Qinyuanchun*". This poem enraged Chiang Kai-Shek, who criticised Mao for harbouring imperial ambitions. He mobilised KMT-owned newspapers to attack Mao's poem, and resolved to one-up his literary flare. All KMT members were ordered to compose anti-Mao verses or poems in the *Qinyuanchun* verse style. On top of selecting some of the best works and publishing them under the name of high-ranking officials in the party, the KMT hired writers of renown to help out. Among all the entries, the *Qinyuanchun*-style poem written by Song Jiafu and submitted by Zhu Anqiao received the highest commendation. Chiang's literary advisers Chen Bulei and Yi Junzuo both praised it as rivalling Mao's original. At last, Chiang Kai-shek felt that he had turned the tables on Mao, and the "poetry response" farce came to an end.

In April 1946, Song Jiafu was appointed attending secretary to Chiang Kai-shek. He was able to set up a transmitter secretly to provide the Party with military intelligence. In June of that year, Song Jiafu obtained secret information on civil war strategies and military deployment from a high-level KMT meeting; it would prove helpful to the PLA's march southward. In 1948, he left Xikou with Chiang Kai-shek on the vessel *Taikang*, on a month-long patrol of Hainan and the Dachen Islands, during which he also transmitted military intelligence to the Party Central Committee. In 1949, Song Jiafu was given short notice by the Kuomintang to leave Shanghai for Taiwan with his family, aboard a KMT naval vessel that was secretly transporting gold. Upon learning of the departure, the PLA sent another undercover officer on board. However, after redirecting the vessel, he was discovered by the Nationalist Army personnel on board, and was captured, failing his mission. After that, Song attempted to transmit signals from the boat to coordinate with the PLA gunboat to intercept the gold.

Though ultimately unsuccessful, he avoided revealing his identity as an undercover agent. Before going to Taiwan, Song Jiafu had made an incision in the lower right abdomen to conceal a micro-camera, which he removed after arriving in Taiwan, for the purpose of taking pictures of military secrets with microfilm.

Since arriving in Taiwan in 1949, Song Jiafu continued to obtain military intelligence from the KMT, including: the U.S.'s position on Taiwan; Chiang Kai-shek's counteroffensive plan; strategic defence maps; fleet deployment maps; military diagrams; the location, serial number, and type of Taiwanese units; list of personnel ranked section chief and above in key Taiwanese military organisations; lists of individuals ranked regiment commander and above. Song Jiafu came up with an original code for passing information with his teammates, using terminology related to antiques and artwork. The dating of antique pieces corresponded with various individuals or entities. Antiques from different dynasties or reigns of emperors represented different intelligence targets:

Emperor Qianlong—code for Chiang Kai-shek

Emperor Yongzheng—code for Chen Cheng

Emperor Jiaqing—code for Sun Liren

The Han dynasty—code for Chiang Ching-kuo

The Tang, Song, and Ming dynasties—codes for the navy, army, and air force respectively

The Yuan dynasty—code for the Mainland.

Types of items passed along represented different types of military intelligence. For example: inkstones represented naval vessels; ink-sticks represented guerrillas bases; ceramic or celadon wares represented aeroplanes; brush-stands represented artillery; snuff-bottles represented firearms; statues of Buddha or human figures represented military strength; items decorated with a dragon-and-phoenix represented Chiang Kai-shek and Madame Chiang, while a double-dragon design represented Chiang Senior and Chiang Junior.

In the scrolls of calligraphy and paintings were written military diagrams, maps, or name lists. Most of the intelligence items passed through a gallery operated by Zhu Zhennan (cover name Huang Yingbi), under the cover of normal trading. A portion of the antiqueware were originals that the KMT had brought from the Mainland to Taiwan; Song Jiafu found ways to obtain them through socialising with officials. He returned some items taken from China to Taiwan back to the Mainland, while other originals he sold for funding the military. Song Jiafu used numerous pieces forged by Zhu Zhennan to pass as his own collection for the purpose of showing his guests; all the calligraphy scrolls, paintings, and antiques used to transmit intelligence were forgeries as well.

In the winter of 1955, Song Jiafu, having won even greater trust from Chiang Kai-shek, was given the role of messenger in secret Sino-American talks. In June, 1956, Chiang Kai-shek sent him to Hong Kong to contact Cao Juren, special correspondent in Hong Kong for Singapore's *Nanyang Business Daily,* and to send Cao Juren as a representative to the negotiations in Beijing in July. In 1957, Chiang Kai-shek sent Song Jiafu to Hong Kong once again, to deliver a letter to Song Yishan, Chiang's representative in Hong Kong, and to convey orally matters relating to the negotiation. After Song Jiafu returned to Taiwan, Song Yishan took the letter from Chiang to the leaders of the CCP and went to Beijing via Hong Kong to meet secretly with Li Weihan, Head of the United Front Work Department, to negotiate a KMT-CCP cooperation agreement. He brought back a report of the negotiations, and delivered it to Chiang Kai-shek through Xu Xiaoyan, the KMT's representative in Hong Kong. Chiang Kai-shek was displeased at reading it, believing that Song Yishan was siding with the CCP in the report. He thus stopped using Song Yishan as a secret emissary. In October, 1958, Song Jiafu was again sent to Hong Kong, to commission Cao Juren to participate in secret talks in Beijing under the cover of conducting a special interview for his news agency. There, Mao Zedong proposed the "One Guiding Principle and Four Items" model, emphasising:

As long as Taiwan returns to China, both sides would cease espionage and sabotage activities against each other. The guiding principle of the cooperation was to isolate the United States; as long as the Chiangs were willing to oppose the United States, we promise that the Chiangs can keep military control over Taiwan; even if the United States cuts off military support to Taiwan, the CCP will provide fully for their military needs. The people of Taiwan will maintain their current way of living.

After Song Jiafu received the contents of the negotiation from Cao Juren, he returned to Taiwan to report them to Chiang Kai-shek. He then reported back to the Party Central Committee, saying that Chiang still had doubts regarding Mao Zedong. Song also provided the United States with the results of this negotiation. After this, Taiwan sent Cao Juren on numerous occasions to Beijing as a secret emissary for negotiations, and every time Song Jiafu reported Chiang's reaction promptly back to the Party, while informing the U.S. of the same. On several occasions, Song Jiafu was suspected by Party comrades to have been bought over by the U.S.. It was later demonstrated that he passed Taiwanese intelligence to the Americans, and acquired intelligence on the U.S. for Taiwan. At the same time, he probed the Americans for what they knew about the intelligence that the Mainland had regarding Taiwan. Thus, through this exchange of intelligence, he obtained intelligence from the Mainland, the United States, and Taiwan. And through all that, he never failed to report back to the Party Central Committee on Taiwan and the U.S.'s responses.

During the Taiwanese presidential election of 1960, Mao Zedong and Zhou Enlai ordered Zhang Zhizhong, a good friend of Chiang Kai-shek's, to pass on a message. Through Song Jiafu, Zhang conveyed a message of support to Chiang, emphasising, "We would rather keep Taiwan in the hands of the Chiangs than to have it fall to the Americans." in 1961, Song Jiafu advised Chiang Kai-shek against trusting the U.S., quoting Zhang Zhizhong's words: "The ones who are against Taiwan today are the Americans, not the CCP, whereas the ones who are supporting Taiwan are the CCP and not the Americans." On a later occasion, Mao Zedong announced during a reception of foreign guests that "It's better to have Chiang Kai-shek as president in Taiwan. For everything that should not be repudiated in history, one must accord it sufficient consideration, and not repudiate everything just because he stands in opposition to it." Song Jiafu then passed those words on to Chiang Kai-shek, and reporting back that Chiang was beginning to change his mind and becoming open to negotiating mutual cooperation.

In 1963, Chiang Ching-kuo conducted a sweeping purge of the intelligence and military agencies, and Song Jiafu's operation team was affected by the politics on the Island, losing a number of members. In 1964, Song Jiafu was able to extract himself unscathed, but was dismissed from his position and placed under even greater surveillance by Chiang Ching-kuo. However, Song maintained his friendship with Chiang Kai-shek. While appearing to be spending his days idling at home, Song secretly transformed his modus operandi. In 1967, he bought a hotel frequented by high officials in the KMT, and placed it under the management of a trusted woman, using her to train attractive girls in her employment to obtain intelligence relating to party politics...

* * *

In 2008, I was transferred to the Party Literature Research Office, and assigned to a research group responsible for organising and analysing biographical information on Zhou Enlai and Deng Yingchao. Some other files of related individuals were also included in the pile. Large quantities of documents, letters, and meeting minutes had already been sorted by their importance and date of creation. I was in charge of handling unindexed files forwarded to us by other organisations, as well as determining the relevance of some less obviously relevant documents.

There was a large box of material, damaged by mildew, moisture, pests, or smoke; not apparently useful, it was stored in a corner. Like panning for gold amidst gravel, I picked up each item for closer examination. There were a few volumes of *The People's Daily Magazine*. I flipped through them to kill time, not registering a single word in my head.

There was no shortage of magazines of this sort in the library, no matter how long ago the publication date was. The addressee on the envelopes, though was perhaps the sole reason these were sent to the research office. It was just two seemingly unimportant lines:

Hu Fei, c/o Wang Shijian
No. 1, Xinhua Alley, Xi'an

The identity of Hu Fei was unknown, but Wang Shijian was of great renown. During the War of Liberation, he performed underground work for the Party in Xi'an. The "Research Bookstore" he founded, as well as the *Xinqin Daily* he started after that, were clearinghouses for intelligence. Perhaps it was due to this indirect connection that these envelopes were also taken to be literary material. But there was not much to analyse from them—at most, they demonstrated that at that time Wang Shijian was in contact with someone of the name— or pseudonym—of Hu Fei. They could possibly be in an intelligence partnership. There was no return address on the envelopes. The "c/o" might deserve looking into further. Why were the envelopes not addressed directly to Hu Fei, but were sent to Wang Shijian for forwarding? *The People's Daily Magazine* was not a rare publication, so why did Hu Fei not purchase the copies directly? Furthermore, it was not a subscription—the volumes numbers were not consecutive; in some cases there were hiatuses of over a year, and there were also duplicate copies. But I could not conjecture anything more than that.

It was unclear where those materials came from. Rumour had it that they were confiscated from cadres or commoners during the Cultural Revolution. I could only imagine how sacks and sacks of items were confiscated without rhyme or reason, with no consideration for their purpose. It would be hard to say if they would still be useful now.

But I had a feeling they could be useful. I flipped through them very slowly, sometimes letting my eyes take in a few words in spite of myself, or reading an article or two.

There were tiny markings, hidden obscurely.

I found them. It was not an illusion. But they were hidden so casually that one would mistake them for floaters in one's eyes—a mild case of myodesopsia, something that I had all along, and something that preceded macular degeneration.

It was a secret code etched in with a blade, hiding sparsely between certain words every other page. However, when put together all the marked pages formed a trove of information.

After studying them meticulously, I finally picked out some patterns. And then it took me even more time to decode the messages.

They were letters. Not really intelligence, but secrets, confidential

information nonetheless.
   The sender was signed "Rose".

(Postmarked 16 July, 1943)
The evening mist is clearing
The birds are hushed
Only bouts of quick rain are heard
drumming on the rooftop.
Bamboo shoots, green as jade, are peering
over the fence, their powdery white bloom
already washed away, their
tender tips dancing in the breeze.

The moist air weighs on the strings of the zither
The chill assails the canopy of the bed.
Swept by the wind, strands of cobweb cling
onto the bamboo screen.
—"Spring rain" by Zhou Bangyan

When I first arrived in Chongqing, I couldn't help but think about this
lyric poem of Zhou Bangyan's. Even though it's not spring, the endless
rain drizzled mistily outside the bamboo curtain, making one feel like
he's floating in a cloud of light smoke.
   Everything is refreshed by the wash of rainwater. Even the cobweb by
the eaves caught a few crystal-like beads, most beautiful to behold. Lo!
After being bathed by rain, even the birdsong outside sounds clearer.
   This house of the South is tall and deep, like a well, with a sense of
bottomless profundity. It is most suitable for thinking and contemplating.
It's like, right now I'm sitting in the room, and I can't help myself but to
think about you. Your image is projected into this deep well, creating
ripples in the water, appearing particularly real before me. I can almost
hear your breath.
   In my courtyard is a toon tree with tender branches and leaves. I often
picked them to toss with sesame oil or fry in an omelette. They are very
delicately delicious. Right now, there's nothing I want more than to bring
a plate of toon-leaf omelette before you, and feed it to you with chopsticks.

Rose

(Postmarked 24 October, 1943)

Do you remember Tchaikovsky's Nocturne Opus 19, No. 4? You gave me the record as a present. You told me that it was played on Giuseppe Guarneri's Ole Bull violin. I loved the rich tone of the G string. But one day, you broke the record in half. You said, "If you listen to Tchaikovsky's nocturnes every day, the Revolution will never succeed. You must learn to become hard-hearted."

At that time I was shocked by your sudden cruelty. But I knew that you were doing that to protect me.

We must not have true feelings for each other.

Not just for you—I must not have feelings for anyone.

This is all that I can offer to the organisation. Or perhaps I could say that this is all I can do to be loyal to us. I cannot love again, nor can I hope again to possess love—from that one moment on.

But that quote that you mentioned on the record—"J'ai fait rêve heureux dans le sommeil complète de votre ombre."—I asked someone to translate that from the French and committed it to my heart:

"I dreamt a happy dream in the slumber full of your shadow."

I believe that both you and I have dreams like that.

Rose, who hopes to appear in your dreams

(Postmarked 8 December, 1945)

I would never have thought that my "poetry response" would be so useful. Can I really be of that much help to the Party?

It was funny, though, that the Kuomintang made such a big show of "poetry responses". They spent all that money hiring well-known writers to help them, completely not realising that they were bringing members of the Communist Party to themselves.

Did I really write the best response? When they told me that, I was both shocked and glad. Chairman Mao even assigned me to infiltrate the Kuomintang. I feel so honoured.

"But it's best not to send a woman. Make it a man... The Kuomintang lacks literati. A woman could not do much by his side. With Madame Chiang around, he doesn't take interest in other women anymore. A

man, however, would be immensely helpful." Chairman Mao has a good point. I understand what he means. I will think about it. I know that you were only passing on the Chairman's words and were not coercing me; for that I am grateful. Do you wish that I agree to it? You sounded quite ambivalent in your letter, but you did pass on what he said. Did you have the same idea too? In the last few days, I kept wondering, what would you want me to do? Or what would I want myself to do? By the way, some good news—I just finished the mission the Party assigned to me. The rich merchant is willing to donate to us the food and money that he was originally going to give to the Kuomintang. I will be able to come see you soon.

Rose

(Postmarked 21 December, 1945)

Sometimes, I want to seduce you. To a female agent like me, you are the greatest challenge. I didn't actually want to seduce you with my advantages in my looks or skills. I only wanted to win your heart by pure means. This would be an even greater challenge.

You said to me, you didn't want me to continue devastating myself like that, even though the mission I accomplished was holy, my heart is holy, and all that I do for the Party is a free-will offering. You would rather that I am not a woman. You said, "I'd rather the Party not accept offerings of this kind. It is too cruel."

I said, "Would you be happier if I were not a woman?"

"Yes, I'd rather you not be one. If you weren't a woman, you wouldn't have to suffer this much."

"If I were not a woman, would you still love me?"

You did not reply. By the way you looked at me, I understood. I have kept that in my heart. That is enough.

In this era of turmoil, one's mission must be placed about one's emotions. For me to want you to love me, I must understand that. Of course, I wouldn't use my acceptance of the mission to win your respect for me. Your eyes told me that, even if I didn't do anything, you would still gaze at me just as lovingly. Because I am worthy. I am confident in myself.

If I say I agree to your request, I would make you feel guilty. So I am going to tell you, I do this willingly. It has nothing to do with anyone else. Don't feel bad for me, and please don't be shocked at my sudden decision.

Rose

(Postmarked 30 December, 1945)

I used to have this idea: As a female agent, I am a successful case story. I successfully captured many important men, controlled their sight and desires, transforming them into the desires of the Party. However, no matter how successful a woman is, she makes a living only through the desire of man—her sole value, the reward bestowed upon her by men. She relies on their rewards. They are her masters, and she their servant. As for the contributions and achievements she made for the Party—are those actually even important to her? You have never revealed the goal or the consequences of the operations; in actuality, she did not need to know either. To you, she is also a servant. She is always trying to make you happy, to please you.

But what if she isn't a woman? Such a person can succeed without relying on man's lust for her. This success will belong to her and her alone. Perhaps she doesn't want to continue living in the body of a woman. Or, to put it another way, she just wants to live her life in a legitimately-obtained identity of a man.

She can own two worlds: one living in her original body and spirit, the other living in a society with more freedom, one that can only be owned in another body. The original body dies. Another one takes her place, continues to live. Do not be harsh on yourself; I did not sacrifice anything for you. This is also what I wanted for myself.

Dr. Liang took very good care of the wounds from my surgery. I will recover quickly. Don't worry. However, even though I was masked during the surgery and every day after that, and though he never saw my face, Dr. Liang will recognise me anyway. Not that I don't trust him, but I am no longer me. I am no longer his nurse. And I should cut off all relationships with him. For the sake of full secrecy in my future mission, I should undergo plastic surgery again. Help me choose a doctor. As for a name for my new identity, I have already decided on something. It will be my decision this time.

Finally, allow me to use a poem by Fu Shan to describe my current
state:
A solitary lamp burning on, beyond sun and moon
shining on my cares, nor sleep will find
Here, lying between life and death
On what should I rest my mind?

The Masked Rose

(Postmarked 14 March, 1946)

This may be the last letter. I only ask you to let me tell you a story.
There is a Russian fairy tale called "The Frog Princess". In the story, a
father told his three sons to go out to the open field, to shoot an arrow,
and to find a wife where the arrow fell. The two older brothers both found
the wife of their dreams, while the arrow of the youngest son fell into a
pond. There, he found a frog carrying the arrow in its mouth, and thus he
had to take the frog to be his wife. The frog-wife could only throw off her
frog skin at night and become a woman, in which form she carried out
her duties as a wife with her beauty and wisdom. Once, when the couple
went to a ball, the husband slipped home and burnt his wife's frog-skin.
After that, as the frog-wife could not be parted from her skin, she left her
husband forever.

If the frog's skin is a guarantee, a secret, a necessary condition for us
to communicate, why would we despise it? It is because we often sense
its ugliness, its impediment, and the barrier that it brings; it split us up
into two worlds—one lonely, one raucous; one dark, one light. At the
same time, the loneliness and darkness make us sense the distance and
the barrier even more keenly. However, rarely do we realise the torment
we would feel if we destroyed this barrier. The torment inevitably begins
after the destruction; but, of course, we can always calm down, and put
on once more the frog skin that belongs to us.

I will never forget the words underlined in the book you gave me:
"Each one of you must, in your secret soul, be a hero—not just a hero,
but also a saint for yourself."

Yes, a hero and a saint. I believe we are of the same mind.

Rose in a frog's skin

There was a postcard clipped to a page in the magazine. On the front was printed the image of Rosa Luxemburg and Karl Liebknecht, and on the back was a line in Russian. I copied it down, and found someone to translate it for me:

The greatest happiness is to be like them in the future—to go to
our execution together, smiling, gazing at each other.

(Unsigned. Postmarked 28 April, 1944)
No matter where I hide, you manage to find me. You've guessed
correctly; I am with child. It has nothing to do with you, even though I
had once thought about it. Or perhaps it has. If you are willing to think
that way. Don't ask me if the child is his. Let's just say I was careless, but
I won't get in trouble. I went to the countryside and got rid of it. Give me
some time to rest and recuperate; think of it as a well-deserved holiday.
After getting rid of what's left of this life, there will be the beginning of
another life.
Thank you for sending me the chicken extract recipe. I will take care
of myself and get well.

The working group sorted the materials chronologically. Where there was a gap, we filled it in by interviewing those involved at the time. For example, to fill in information on the year Premier Zhou passed away and his last moments, we interviewed his doctors Wu Weiran and Zhang Zuoliang, secretaries Li Weixin and Zhou Wei, guards Gao Zhenpu, Han Fuyu, Zhang Shuying, as well as Nurses Gao, Wu, and Ye... All of them, who attended to Premier Zhou, mostly talked about how his heart was with the concerns of the nation and with his comrades during the last days of his illness.

—He called for Li Bing, and told him to pay attention to instances of lung cancer among workers in tin mines in Yunnan.

—He made an effort against his illness to deal with the Vietnamese Prime Minister Pham Van Dong, successfully rejecting his greedy demands.

—Despite his poor heath, he went up to the Babaoshan Revolutionary Cemetery, to participate in the burial ceremony of He Long's ashes.

—He wrote to Mao Zedong, recommending Deng Xiaoping as his replacement. He also advised Deng Xiaoping to bear with it.

—He had Hua Guofeng come and entrusted to him matters regarding entering Tibet and assisting the Tibetans.

—He summoned Luo Qingchang and said the word "entrust" several times. The details are unknown.

—He had Wang Yeqiu pass on a message to the revision and editorial committee of the *Cihai* encyclopaedia, that when compiling the entry on "Yang Du", they must include the details of Yang Du's joining the Communist Party of China in his old age, and his achievements for the party, lest he be forgotten by generations hence.

—When he spoke with Ye Jianying, he dismissed all of his attendants. But as soon as Ye Jianying left the room he ordered us to ready pen and paper, to record whatever the Premier had to say from then on. But the Premier did not say anything more...

—While Premier Zhou did not say anything more, he probably had a list somewhere. He had orally entrusted a few people and things to the care to Ye, presumably people whom he wanted to take care of privately. He was speaking very softly...

In this one interview transcript, the interviewee was unwilling to have her name recorded. According to my colleague, she was old and sick, and said that she just wanted to live out her days in peace, and didn't want to be disturbed by what happened in the past.

(Interview location: Room 116, Beijing Hospital, Interviewee: Anonymous, former nurse of the PLA 305th Hospital)

He once said in his sleep, "I didn't manage to protect you..." I heard him when I was keeping watch by his bed.

I don't want to get into trouble.

But... I... I don't want to... all right, if you insist, I'll tell you. That day, Ye Jianying came and left. Premier Zhou had a grave look on his face, like he wanted to do something. I thought about bringing him pen and paper or something. I asked him if he needed anything, he said no, don't bother. I kept asking him anyway, asking him to please let me do something for him. He paused for a moment, then said, if... if it's not too much of a trouble, if... it's possible to find it, go find me a foreign tune.

I asked him: You want to listen to a foreign tune? What kind of tune? Tchaikovsky... he uttered a few words slowly: Nocturne Opus 19, Number 4.

That day, I brought him a cassette tape as well as a small tape recorder to play the tape for him. The cassette wasn't of good quality. The sound was full of static. I said this was all I could find. I copied it from a friend's record. I've filled the tape for you, you can rewind and keep playing it. He thanked me, sat up, and closed his eyes in the music like he was extremely content. He had a smile across his face. I sat for a long time next to him. Seeing that he stayed silent, like he's fallen asleep to the music, I was going to leave. Suddenly I heard him speak behind me:

Snow settles on the old bridge
like powder on your radiant face
as it does every year, before
melting and joining the springtime river
carrying it far, far away.

The wildflowers in the courtyard, who
saw the wind whisk away your shadow,
remain, to lament with my memories
of you, who once stood here.

I stopped right there, and asked if the music brought out his inner muse. It's not every day that he looked so happy. I wanted to stay with him and chat a bit longer. He looked really lonely, after all. He shook his head. I asked him to recite the poem again. He dipped his fingertip in a cup of cooled tea and began writing on the desk, and that's why I still remember it. He said, it's a poem he composed on a whim some decades ago. He bought a paper fan by the banks of Fenhe River, and wrote a poem on the fan to gift to a friend. After that, he had not seen this friend again...

My colleague said, "I still wanted to ask the old nurse something, but she suddenly reached out and turned off my tape recorder. 'I said too much. Will you write all of that down?' I couldn't give her a definite answer. Neither of us spoke, as if it was time for the interview to be over. Before leaving, I thanked her for the interview. The old nurse sighed, like she wanted to say something but not say too much, 'That day, he listened to the tape until he fell asleep, I went in his room to tidy up for him. I saw that a pill bottle had fallen over on the table, and there was some half-dried tea stains, bits here and there, looking like words... or maybe... maybe like the drawing of somebody's face.'"

* * *

"A political storm is about to descend on us, and yet we are still engaged in struggling. When will this struggling end?" (Zhou Enlai, 3 December, 1975)

"I think, in this last period in life, I must still reflect, examine myself, and clarify certain things. Even though it's too late..." (Zhou Enlai, 15 November, 1975)

* * *

In his last moments, Premier Zhou Enlai said to secretary beside him, "I won't forget my old friends in Taiwan, my old friends who contributed to the cause of the revolution. Over all these years, I have not forgotten them..." (Xinhua Daily, 20 December, 1975)

In this photograph from an old newspaper cutting, I saw that on the wall behind his bed was hung a calligraphy scroll with his signature on it:

Alas! All hope has fled, from life and death.
From yonder shores your thoughts once came to me,
and dreamt of glory. Sleepless, down I lay
my greying head—A world has passed away.

I recalled that Father had also hung this calligraphy scroll in his room:

A solitary lamp burning on, beyond sun and moon
shining on my cares, nor sleep will find

Here, lying between life and death
On what should I rest my mind?

Two scrolls of words, calling out to each other through the void.
And the handwriting on the scroll on the wall...
I studied the photograph on the newspaper with a magnifying glass.
I studied it and studied it. I heaved a long sigh from the bottom of
my heart. I remembered the wooden box from my childhood. Father
forbade me from opening it, but inside it was only a yellowed sheet
of lined paper, with a recipe for chicken extract written in calligraphy
brush.

The lines of ink from decades ago matched up. The two sets of
handwriting were so incredibly similar. All I could feel was an ineffable
pain behind those words.

* * *

Chunshao, what do you want to say to Mother (Li Juan)?
I was still glancing at him from the corner of my eye, as he remained
fixated on Li Juan's grave.
He had grown old. For whatever reason, at this instant he looked
particularly old.
I turned my attention back to the photograph on Father's tombstone,
as bit by bit ashes fell from the incense stick in my hand. What should
I say to "her"? Words I had read three years ago came to mind again:

After getting rid of what's left of this life, there will be the beginning of
another life.

"She lied to him," I thought.
A crow cawed twice on a tree. It broke my train of thought. As I
lifted my head, the crow flew off.
Was the child by "Nightingale"? Or the man who she wanted to feed
toon-leaf omelette to?
"Did she lie to me as well?" I had thought more than once.
"Perhaps she wasn't sure really." The crow flew back and gave a few

caws. "Perhaps she did have expectations... but she could make her own decisions. So she only asked him to grant her a longer vacation and go give birth on her own. This was not a mission. This was the only freedom she allowed herself."

I must tell you this today. Chunhuan, this is your... father.
It's him!
It's... her. Yes. I wanted you to know.

What did he want to tell me that day? Did he mean to point at "her"? Maybe he wanted to say, "This is your father—your mother," but I was staring at another person, the President.

I picked a flower by my hand, and placed it on the tombstone of Song Jiafu, "Father". It was difficult to reconstruct "her" original looks from the photo on the tombstone. The sunlight reflected my face on the shiny, dark marble. I looked at my own face, as if looking into a mirror, "Mother, would you have looked like this?" This was the first time in sixty-seven years that I had called to her, "Mother", so intimately. I then fell silent.

Everything was passing away. Life is an eternal experience of passing away, through remembering and through forgetting.

Chunshao, apparently finished with his silent prayer, stuck his incense stick into the brazier before the grave. I did likewise. We stared at each other, as if we did not know where to begin. We had been separated for decades; there should have been endless things to talk about. It was just a moment ago that we were just chatting freely; and now we could only face each other in wordlessness.

A while later, Chunshao took the initiative to break the silence.

"It's been forty years," he sighed and said. "How fleeting and unpredictable life is."

"Isn't it so? The past has died, and who knows how long the future will live?"

"Only when I saw you did I come to the sudden realisation how the times have changed. Then, I looked at myself—I have spent decades jousting about in reality, and now that I seem to be reaching the end of my life, I realise that nothing that I had expected from life happened the way I wanted it to."

"It's not just you. How many people can get what they wish for in this life?"

I lit a cigarette for each of us. Chunshao smoked quickly, and I slowly. Over the years I perfected a special skill—keeping the ashes in one long bar at the end of the cigarette, without falling. Admiring this perfect bar of ashes, I said:

"That's life. We spend our time wearing ourselves out with work, while trying to escape from work. We're playing in the water at the same time we're drowning in it."

Chunshao flicked the ashes off his fingers. A breeze rose up. The cigarette ashes scattered in the air, reminding one of the ashes of paper money in burnt offerings to the dead. He blew a few last rings of smoke, threw the butt on the ground, and stomped it out with his heel. "Too bad. We spend so much effort in living, putting up with so much, but no one can get what he wants in life. Either you live with regrets, or you suffer setback after setback in your daily life."

"That comes with being alive. Thus it has been since the beginning of time. Whether a man has lived in joy or sorrow, he will finally fall into a void. Because death is the end. It is the absence of experience, the destruction of thought. No one has ever returned from there, to tell us what goes on over there."

I was staring at the cigarette butt Chunshao flattened on the ground. My mind wandered for a moment, and the perfect bar of ashes fell off from between my fingers. I looked regretfully at the falling ashes, as if a part of me was falling off along with them. I turned my gaze to Chunshao, who had lost much hair and his former flamboyance, thinking as if he looked not so far off from a spectre. I could not help but imagine what he would look like when lying in his grave in the future, or I myself... In the future, I would like to buried beside him, with Floral lying on the other side. A century hence, those without a burial plot will be laid on top of our graves; a few centuries later, newer graves would be piled up, layer upon layer, above us, while we shall sink deeper and deeper into the earth, until we fall out of all memory...

"For some reason, I'm thinking of Marx. I remember that he said, 'Men make their own history, but they do not make it as they please; they do not make it under self-selected circumstances, but under circumstances existing already, given and transmitted from the past. The tradition of all dead generations weighs like a nightmare on the brains of the living.' He seems to be talking about our generation," I said.

"It's not just our generation," said Chunshao. "I have a feeling, that those in our generation, and the next few generations, will finally encounter an immense upheaval. I don't know when, and I don't know how. To the individual, it could spell misfortune, but to society as a whole, it could mean an important breakthrough. Look at the world around us. Driven by profit, it has lost the distinction between socialism and capitalism, but has replaced it with a globalised wall called the System. It is indisputable that the individual's rights is being trampled upon, more and more every day. Our discussions on what we consider 'justice' seem to have been relegated to antiquated words that carry no more actual meaning..."

"Yes, everyone is caught up in the changes and transformations that are still going on. No one can stand outside of them. All along, we thought the world would change, that it would change for the better. It did indeed change, but now it has nothing to do with good or bad. It has transformed beyond what we know as common sense..."

"As I said, you can't just look at our generation. If you consider the past two millennia, we haven't progressed beyond what our forebears achieved, in terms of our attitude towards life and death, towards love and hate, towards courage, curiosity, ambition, and kindness. All we've done is to footnote this era with our names, because we are only individuals in a greater scheme of things. People are malcontent not because the lack of eternal life, but because of the eternity of incertitude. Thus, there will always be a kind of dispirited resistance. In resisting our lives, the expectations that we have will possibly or predictably come to nothing."

"Chunshao, don't worry about all that. That's just a way of comprehending and summarising the past, a way of looking back at yourself, from your own perspective. We aren't qualified to judge the rightness and wrongness of every answer—it is only a result of a particular phase. Although there is stagnation and challenges every time history moves into a new phase, it's not true that that history only ever regresses. When the past is dissolved, new trials and possibilities emerge. When the new has been put together, it awaits destruction again. I wouldn't judge it from the perspective of right or wrong. For example, is it necessarily true that during a period of repression there would be no truth? That there would be nothing but lies? Or that after democratisation truth would exist? And people would speak the truth? I don't think so. What I'm gradually sensing is an existence where joy and destruction co-exist. Does the justice we know truly represent the journey in body and spirit of people in these generations, and the possible changes that we continue to hope for? There were many things that made darkness appear to be the norm, that made courage and sacrifice appear precious. Indeed, sometimes, the more we understand something, the farther we become from the truth. More and more I do not dare to say what is absolutely correct..."

"By your reasoning, all the difficult problems we have are given to us by fate? We have no choice but to struggle futilely in our attempt to free ourselves of our bonds?"

What was Chunshao aiming at? I continue playing this game of riddles with him patiently.

"However, if one holds firm to a most divine faith in his heart, if the faith is strong enough, all of his sacrifices will prove to be meaningful at the very last moment. The Bible story of Abraham sacrificing his only, beloved son to the Lord exemplifies that..." I sad.

"In our times, even if you want to be Abraham, or even be the sacrificial Isaac, you can't be sure if the Lord would appear in the very last moment. The faith between man and the divine has already collapsed. The tests that the times impose on us may not be the tests that God intend to impose on us. Didn't Hugo say something like, 'Man is the creator, while God is the miserable one?'"

"No, rather, God is just the sacrificial lamb. Haha."

The sun became more and more piercingly bright. We walked towards the back of the cemetery. At the bottom of a slope stood a small gazebo. "Not many people come here," said Chunshao. He warned me to be careful and not to trip. I saw that there was a ditch in the earth, over which were haphazardly laid two wooden boards. They looked old and used, but they seem to have been choice building material once. Looking more carefully, I saw that there were words carved into them, though the characters were mostly covered by the dirt.

"Do you still remember this couplet?" Chunshao read from the board on the right:

Guilelessly the white clouds float
While birds flit hither and fro, fro and hither

Reflexively, I recited the second line:

Silently the clear brooks flow
As flowers wither and bloom, bloom and wither

"That's from our old house, the couplet we made together in the last spring banquet we held there. I still remember it."

"Yes, it's hard to forget it. After Yao Tiepeng took over our house, he had someone carve the couplet on these two wooden boards, and hung them on either side of that gazebo we had in the backyard. After Yao Tiepeng was brought down, the house changed hands again. The new owner overhauled the courtyard, and these boards were thrown out. I found them in a rubbish heap near our old house. I didn't know where to put them, so I placed them here. Every time I come pay respects at Mother's grave, I would go rest in this gazebo here. I don't know if I feel satisfaction or melancholy inside when I step on them," said Chunshao.

"I wonder what was going through Yao Tiepeng's mind when he had this couplet carved?"

"That I don't know. I also don't understand why he would do that to us."

Chunshao crouched down, picked up a broken twig and cleared the dirt off a part of the wooden board. He wanted to show me something—

"Someone installed something inside," I said.

"Yes, a listening device. They were pretty thorough back then."

Chunshao stood up, and rubbed that trace off with the sand under his sole.

"Looks like he was under surveillance at that time too."

"Mm-hmm. He only lived in our place for a few years before he was thrown behind bars. He was even charged as a rebel spy. But didn't he get promoted by reporting Communist spies in the first place? How ironic."

"At that time, it wasn't so ironic." I thought about Uncle Yao. He must have been trying to conceal his identity in order to continue his mission. How could he have explained everything, even to Xiaokang?

The breeze in the gazebo was cool—no, I should say it was chilly. The bones on my back were aching from the chill. We did not sit long before we walked out again, to Father and Mother's graves.

"It's time to go back," I looked at my watch.

"Back to the table again." Chunshao stopped after taking two steps. "Chunhuan, and your bottom line is..."

I glanced at him. He finally spoke of his objective. "Then, what about yours..."

A gale swept over the tombstones with sand and dirt. We both squinted.

After the wind stopped, we still squinted warily, looking at each other through the narrow slits of our eyes. Even after we opened our eyes fully, we still looked at each other, uncertain if we were supposed to be in a standoff. The sun became hot. We looked up at the same time.

It was very bright. Very hot. Something seems to have melted, dissipated.

Under the strong sunlight, everything was laid bare. Nothing would remain hidden...

After listening to all that, Chunshao took a deep breath. "Will the future be the end or the resolution?"

"There are always shadows in history. Some things will be buried in the shadows, while others will be brought out to the sunlight."

"When a people decide to walk towards their own destiny, they will not remain under the control of a political will," said Chunshao.

"What profits politics and what profits a people may join together, whether by chance or by necessity. This could either give rise to a crisis or to a chance for change."

"By the way things are going now, will it be change or will it be a crisis?"

"I'm not sure. But it will come anyway. This is fate. There is no evading it," I said.

"But we both were in it, we both caused it. Whether we did good or evil, we cannot escape the consequences."

"Before we are judged for doing good or evil, we would probably have become artefacts from a different world," I joked.

"If that is true, we won't be able to witness anything in this life, nor do we have any hope to keep watch for..."

"At any rate, after all the turmoil in this world, we are all used to being weeds growing about this wasteland, being an inseparable part from this landscape. No matter what comes, let it come. My opinion is that there will be a reform or a transformation."

"You say reform or transformation, but I feel it's going to be the end. Either way, things will change."

"Yes, they will, and it's going to be a monumental change, the change of this century. Any kind of change requires the right historical circumstance. And I feel that it is coming upon us."

"You're that sure?"

"Yes, we can't escape it during our lifetimes."

"We can escape. See, just today we escaped out here. For two hours," Chunshao grinned.

"We still have to go back."

"We should. But it's going to be different now. We got to come out and go back, but they have never even stepped outside. You see a different view from the inside and from the outside."

"We don't even count as insiders or outsiders. We are only those on the margin."

"Then we will liberate the insiders from the outside."

"Chunshao, are you joking or are you serious?"

"I'm serious. Chunhuan, tell me, what have we created in this life? Nothing. All that life has given us is an existence that we can't extricate ourselves from, just like how it was in our parents' generation. Before we return to dust, we are already dust in the eyes of history."

"You seem to think the nail's in the coffin even before we have returned to dust. But I agree with what you said."

"But I don't agree that life should pass away like this, to finish like this. Since great changes are coming anyway, why don't we join hands now to do something grand? We'll do something grand before they get a chance to act," said Chunshao.

"Do what?"

"We'll be leaders, the ones who act. We won't wait. We won't be passive."

"What will we be leaders of?"

"Salvation. To save this era."

"Salvation? Yes," I nodded. "We should save, and not conquer."

"That's right. All that went wrong was due to people only wanting to conquer, and not to save."

"Just the two of us?"

"That's right, just the two of us." Chunshao's tone was like that in our childhood when he invited me to play War with him.

"But do we still need heroes in this era?" I said in a mocking tone.

"You're right, this era does not need heroes anymore. Heroes cannot save the world. The salvation of the world rests on the collective strength of the people, and not on individual heroes. Perhaps there is no more place for a hero, no work for a hero, but we need to play the role of heroes just this once. We have never had our own time to shine."

"Stop dreaming. Neither of us can control the situation. The boat cannot be turned around."

"Chunhuan, you got it wrong," Chunshao assumed a serious expression. "The times have changed. The two sides are standing off for reasons that are different to those from before. Neither the changes and reforms you mentioned, nor the ending that I said, are at the heart of what needs to be saved. The key is, the problem now is no longer the opposition between you and us, or the contention between two political bodies. It is furthermore not a choice between peace and war. Too many people are misguided. In our world, the inhumane exploitation of the individual by the collective is no longer the prerogative of centralised societies. Haven't we witnessed many real-life examples of that in history? Any invasionary power has a scary tendency to permeate everywhere. Profit has become the 'conviction' that is held onto most dearly in every rivalry. Those governments who claim to be seekers of justice have been following an antisocial path, through all history All they do is cover up and avoid talking about the truth. Some even take it to the extreme, force-feeding a set of specious ideals to its people, until the people forget common knowledge and are completely muddled. Let me put it even more plainly. This is an era of chaos. The chaos is not the kind with armed conflicts, with burning and pillaging. The chaos of our days is more complicated than that. It's disorder, unrest, injustice, the lack of ideals, the grave divide between the rich and the poor, the depletion of social capital, the loss of discipline, morality, trust, sense of shame, and any value that is worth keeping. When the governments around the world are failing, we must find the way out for our own nation."

"Only the people are the masters of their own destiny. Besides, human society has been a history of the development of crime, be it in the name of the nation or of the nationality. What if the people have already been habituated to that?"

"That would be foolishness. The people are forgetful. They are also blind, and easily incited. The majority, what we call the ignorant masses, are the most terrifying enemy we must face in the search for justice and truth."

"Chunshao, your dreams are too lofty. We are only conveyors of the message, representatives in one negotiation out of many more to come—in what's left of our lives, which isn't much."

"But they got the direction wrong. They even got the focus wrong. But we have a clear goal."

I waited for him to continue.

"Listen well. We have enemies on three sides," said Chunshao. "Over where I am, over where you are, and, we have to join together to counter U.S. interference."

"And," I added, "the dead. We must let go of the hatred, stubbornness, and arguments of the dead."

"Deal!"

"Passcode?" I got excited by what he said.

"Conceal our secrets; reveal the spies..." he blurted out the slogan we heard the most in our childhood.

"Hah, hah, then I'll reply with 'Death to KMT agents.'"

"All right, be serious."

"The person asking would say, Abraham asked what the Lord wanted. And the reply would be, The Lord said Isaac and a lamb." I offered an alternative.

"Excellent!"

"Then what are we called?"

"We'll use the same codename. You and me both."

"You and me both?"

"Yes, to muddle the waters."

I said, "The Rose of Mercy."

"What a strange name."

"Rose for love and eternal fragrance; mercy as in the Bodhisattva of Mercy, the saviour of those in distress." I recalled the names she used.

"Fascinating. Sure, we'll use that. I'll now use it for calling you: Rose of Mercy calling Rose of Mercy..."

Chunshao suddenly leant towards my ear, "I just bought our old house. Haven't got around to renovating it yet, but guess what I found? A tunnel, like it was dug a long time ago. There are some cables in it that linked to a dedicated phone line. By the way it runs, I'm guessing that it's connected to the former Army Command HQ."

"You sure it's the kind of cable that connects to tape recorders and mics?"

"You bet. Cables for listening in. The tunnel was a bit caved in so I couldn't follow it all the way."

"Where would that kind of cable come from?" I sighed in my heart. Was it the original inhabitant, Deputy Minister Wu? Or was it Father or Uncle Yao? Or somebody else? The Kuomintang was monitoring them, but they ran cables from the tunnel to monitor the Kuomintang.

"The house really is haunted. I couldn't figure out who would have dug that kind of tunnel. After Yao Tiepeng died, the house changed hands three times. The last owner lived in the U.S., leaving the house vacant for over twenty years. It was just put on the market recently. If it was that Commie spy, Yao Tiepeng, then the Kuomintang was right to have arrested him. With a bit of fixing up the tunnel can still be used."

Chunshao looked at me. I knew what he wanted to do. But that would be a joke.

"We—we will begin with this tunnel..." He said.

"This is not a game. Wiring from decades ago. Plus, the HQ moved long ago."

"What you know over there can't be more than what I know over here..." Chunshao grinned enigmatically.

We did not get to discuss the actual plans of this operation. A dog barked as it ran towards us, wagging its tail at Chunshao.

"Sisi," Chunshao called to it. Upon that, the dog stood up on its hind legs, facing us.

"Every time I come visit the grave, it comes too. I don't know whose dog it is. It likes to hang out with me, so I treat it as mine. See how it looks just like our old Sisi? It's a carbon copy of him."

I crouched down to look at the dog. Chunshao also stooped, bending his arthritic back. Two old men looked at each other's greying, thinning hair, were suddenly reminded of something, and began laughing at once.

"Just like the old days—" said Chunshao, "I get to pet the dog's head, you pet the dog's butt."

We petted the dog, just like we did 50 years ago. When I stroked the dog's buttocks, it would turn around every now and then to lick its tail, giving me the satisfaction of getting both the head and the tail. "It really is Sisi!" I exclaimed in delight.

"Sisi, good dog, don't move, be good at let me pet your head." Chunshao actually started to beg the dog.

"Chunshao, do you remember this smell? There is a smell on the dog..." I said, "Floral water!"

"Yes, every time it comes it smells of that. You can't find this kind of kitschy perfume these days anymore. Its owner is probably some old lady."

"Old lady? As old as us?" I joked.

"Mm-hmm, must be quite old. Very old. Quite a bit older than us," said Chunshao.

Sisi turned its head around again. This time, it did not lick its tail anymore. Its two jet-black eyes shone at me, like two deep lakes of memories.

I gazed at it, and it at me, looking at each other like two old, old friends.

I looked into that pair of eyes. Between the grass and the trees, the sun looked blurry, but the reflected light shone clearly. Into this eddy of light I fell, falling endlessly. She... she must be very old now, an old lady now...

"I... I'd like to be your Sisi," a breeze whispered into my ear.

24
Relics

Chunshao's tunnel was completed. He sent me the first news of it. Apparently he didn't treat it as a game.

Call it being sensitive, but I sensed that something was wrong around me. Not that there were strangers or strange sightings. It was just that, on the wire pole outside my door, there was a piece of clear sticky tape. It did not look like it had been left behind when someone removed a poster or a bill. I kept an eye on it. Sometimes, the tape changed locations or directions, but I couldn't see who stuck it there.

Anyway, I had to be more careful than before.

It looked like it happened there naturally, like when someone had just run their hand on a wall to get rid of something they didn't want, or to rub off some dirt from their hand. But it also seemed to form a pattern, if one could decode it.

* * *

In the summer of 2011, the Beijing Capital Theatre ran a play called "The Russian Rose". On the sign posted outside the theatre, large characters proclaimed:

Adapted from *Tales of Espionage*, the memoir of Peng Yunhong, Confidential Secretary to the late Premier Zhou Enlai

A Russian rose, a Japanese-Chinese mix, a sex agent from a spy camp;
She undergoes sex change surgery for the sake of the revolution,
sacrificing herself for her intelligence mission

My eyes were fixed on the actress on stage from the beginning to the end. Continuously she changed her mask and changed her mask, and everyone around her kept their eyes on her, expecting her to change into another person, to change into someone else.

At the end of the play, the actress, now playing a ghost, tore off her last mask, and from the grave of her eternal repose, recited these words—adapted from Marx:

Men make their own history, but they do not make it as they please; they do not make it under self-selected circumstances, but under circumstances existing already, given and transmitted from the past. The tradition of all dead generations weighs like a nightmare on the brains of the living. Although we betray ourselves, we do so in order to seek salvation. We continue our endless betrayal, betraying others and ourselves. We cannot stop, unless we fall into eternity, halt our footsteps, turn around and see if the era has been saved through these betrayals...

It was like witnessing a hoax being carried out. This cannot be real, but it seems so real!

After the curtains fell, I raced to the backstage, just to see a familiar face walk away indifferently before my eyes.

Floral! I called out in my heart.

I followed her into a hutong, into a courtyard where multiple families had taken up abode...

She can't be Floral, I thought.

But then I caught sight of the photograph hanging in the main room of this house.

It was a smile full of misery, and with a tinge of mischievousness. The former I had never seen before, but the latter was extremely familiar from my childhood. These two conflicting expressions wrung twisted wrinkles into her face. Floral—ah—she grew a bit old!

An old man inside gazed at me with the same strange, twisted expression. He was in the dark and I was in the light, and so I did not notice him at first, until his husky laughter startled me. I shifted my gaze from the photograph and onto him.

"Come in!" said the old man inside. At the noise, the young girl who looked like Floral also poked her head out from her room.

"My daughter. Looks like her, right?" The old man beckoned the young girl over. The young girl approached us awkwardly. The old man slapped her on her shoulder with one hand, while gesturing towards the photograph in the room with the other.

The old hunchback sitting in the main room stared at me with a look of seriousness. His face was so thin that it appeared sunken; his gaze was like flames and ice at the same time; his expression as sharp and steady as in his youth. I recognised him. Xiaokang. Xiaokang, on the other hand, was still keen-eyed despite his age, and had recognised me at once. I almost could not believe that we would meet again in this life.

"Floral said you'd come look for her. She kept saying that when she was alive." Xiaokang pointed to a chair next to him and motioned for me to sit down.

"She really said that?" I felt guilty.

"Sometimes I felt she could sense things as accurately as a dog," Xiaokang, getting hoarse, cleared his throat. "But she said you're like a dog too, and could trace her by smell alone."

"I..." I smiled wryly, "My nose isn't good enough. I couldn't pick up her scent."

"But you still got here at the end," Xiaokang said. "I originally thought she was just making stuff up. But later on, I came to feel the same way. I'd wait for you until I'm dead! Unless you'd gone to hell first."

I glanced at Xiaokang. When he energetically pronounced each syllable just now, his emaciated body sat there as still and steady as a mountain. I softened my gaze, as if I was too ashamed to look him straight in the eyes. I had never planned to look for them. Perhaps I had woken up from a dream where I was searching for them in vain, but I had never put that into action. Back when I escaped to the Mainland with Dr. Liang, I was assigned to an intelligence agency and was kept under strict surveillance for over a dozen years. I did not do much for myself, nor did I have the desire to do much for myself. I had transitioned from a physical prison to a formless one, and all I had wanted was a tiny bit of peace. Over the decades, all I did was think about resting, or sneak in a rest in a cave I built for myself.

"So you have found me."

"No, I didn't find you. You came to my door," Xiaokang smiled, as if he was satisfied with himself.

Standing beside him, Xiaokang's daughter assumed an inscrutable look.

"I changed my name. Indeed, no one could have found me." I looked at Xiaokang's daughter. She fished for something in her pocket, took it in her hand and flashed it before my eyes. It was a picture of me in my youth. I continued, "Even if someone recognised me, they couldn't verify that it's me. But I..." Who could it be that gave me directions with sticky tape, and who was it that wanted me to see her in the play? She took out a small roll of sticky tape from another pocket. She had a mischievous, teasing look; she shot a glance at Floral's picture, as if indicating that Floral had taught her this trick. She brought me here, but she was still looking at me as if she did not trust me. "... found myself here like I was transported here by magic," I said finally.

"It was indeed magic," Xiaokang nodded.

I told him about my later adventures, but I glossed over my actual job, telling him only that I was working for a publisher. Xiaokang then told me about their escape back then.

"The moment we fell into the sea, we opened the door and jumped out, so we did not sink with the car. The only one that sank was that bastard. Me and Floral held onto a rock that was standing out of the water. When we heard voices up on the cliff, we dived under the rock and hid there... After that, we drifted for a whole day on the sea, and Floral brought me to the entrance of a strange cave. From there, we crawled into a tunnel. She said this was Old Chiang's escape route, and led to the Presidential Palace. When she was little she had snuck over the walls of the palace and explored the tunnel... At that time, she actually thought we could run into the palace and beg the old dotard to spare me. I stopped her... We hid in the tunnel for a long time. There's nothing to eat, and we were so hungry that we tore off pieces of our clothes for food... Anyway, we snuck out at the end. We hid ourselves

in a pile of dead branches and leaves that the gardener had pruned, and were carried out in a rubbish cart. At that moment, I knew we couldn't stay in Taiwan any longer. So I got an old partner in the smuggling business to send us over the sea. And before you know it, it's been forty years..." Xiaokang said toothlessly, stopping and going.

I did not tell him that Tian Lin did not actually die. This was no longer important. "Over these decades... how was Floral?" I asked impulsively and a bit timidly, but I did not have the courage to hear an answer that was worse than what I had imagined.

"She almost went completely blind."

A spasm gripped my heart.

Xiaokang looked towards Floral's picture and was silent for several seconds. Then, he said, "But she was just as pretty."

"She has always been pretty." Her face, through the years, flashed through my mind... "With the things that go on in this world... sometimes, it's better to not be able to see." I did not know what to say. I knew my words were silly, but I could not speak any words of consolation. Anything I said would seem foolish and superfluous. I did not want to think about what happened to Floral. If I had a choice in vision, I would choose not to see, like Floral.

Xiaokang's solemn expression softened into desolation. "Sometimes, when she was worried about falling or losing her way, she would tie a rope onto a pillar and onto herself, and walk around by touch, walking in circles around the pillar, like a dog. Later on, even when she ate she would crouch on the floor like a dog and refuse to sit at the table..."

She tied herself up like a dog! Ah, she did not want to be a burden to others. I glanced at Xiaokang again, and did not speak my thoughts. I kept my tone as even as possible, "How did she go blind?"

"Not sure, perhaps malnutrition," Xiaokang said. "When we first arrived as stowaways, the Communists took us to be Kuomintang spies and threw us into jail. We went through all kinds of suffering in jail. Floral grew weak. My leg was maimed and I lost my teeth. After we got out of jail, for a long time she took care of me. Neither of us got enough to eat. Whenever we ran out of food, she was always the one to find something. I've seen her fight with dogs over spoiled food in the rubbish, and steal pig swill and chicken feed. Only when she was unable to fight or steal did I realise that there's something wrong with her eyes. Later on, she could only sense a bit of light. She basically could not see anything."

In spite of myself, I shifted my gaze to that photograph, to those eyes again.

Xiaokang grinned sardonically, "She did not admit to going blind. She said she could still see. She kept saying, there's light in front of her eyes, like starlight from far, far away... She said she couldn't see near, but she could see far, as far as the sky."

As far as the sky? I mused.

Yes, starlight can never be extinguished—I remember that year when, in the tunnel, she fed me the blood from my leg. It was completely dark in the tunnel, but her eyes twinkled from afar...

I broke out of thought and continued to ask:

"Didn't the Party know about Uncle Zhu? Didn't they know you had escaped from the Kuomintang?"

"Who could prove it? Who could prove that I was Zhu Anqiao's son, or whether or not Zhu Anqiao even existed?" Xiaokang eyed me askance, "And who could prove that my dad was risking his life for them? That kind of life-and-death mission was highly classified and only a handful of people would know about it. As soon as he lost communication with his contact higher-up... can you prove the mission was still going on? Or perhaps this man had already crossed over to the other side? Anyway, all they knew was, Zhu Anqiao lived in Taiwan for decades, Zhu Anqiao had once been an official in the Kuomintang, I was the son of a high-ranking Kuomintang official, I was a hooligan who couldn't even cut it in Taiwan... Anyway, nothing in the past counts anymore. Anyway, we are spies of that ridiculous Kuomintang. Anyway, after I got out of jail, I spent over ten years looking, and I couldn't find my dad's relatives or hometown at all. Zhu Anqiao did not exist at all."

"Your father's real name was Zhu Jingquan."

Zhu Xiaokang stared at me.

"Don't ask me how I know. Soon this won't be a secret anymore." I held his hands, feeling that I could finally give something back, "I've seen his files. Next time I'll copy down his information for you."

Zhu Xiaokang shook his head and mumbled, "It's been decades. Those who should have died, have died. Even those who shouldn't have died, have also died. What would I still need that for? Who knows if the real name you said was actually real? How many more 'reals' are there behind the 'real'? I've discovered that he had other names, but each time when I thought it was the real one, it wasn't... At least I never changed my name all my life. I've always been Zhu Xiaokang. Whether alive or dead, I'm only Zhu Xiaokang." He shook his head fervidly, his body trembling unsteadily. Suddenly I felt that the mountain had crumbled into sand in an instance.

Xiaokang's daughter rubbed Xiaokang's back, and steadied him on the chair. She was still observing me with an examining look, still silent. I tried to change the subject, as I wanted to know more, "When did Floral pass away?"

"Some twenty years ago." At the mention of Floral, Xiaokang's tone softened, "For some other random reason, they came to take her to jail again. She refused to go. From her pocket she took out a black pill that she had kept for a long time, saying that it was a pill of immortality, that it was most effective when taken right before death. Not long after she swallowed it, she died. Hah, hah, she turned immortal."

The pill of immortality? Was it that one? She still had it?

I remembered the pill we created together in our childhood, the pill that her father coughed up with blood and phlegm.

"Where's she buried? I want to go see her."

"She's right here," Xiaokang slapped the table beneath Floral's portrait.

"Here?"

"She said she wanted to wait for you, here in this house." Xiaokang added emphatically, "Waiting here, with me, for you."

A corner of the curtain hanging from the table was lifted, revealing a dull-coloured cremation urn.

"She said you would not fail to come find her."

"She said that?" I lowered my head, unable to control my emotions.

"I said it for her," Xiaokang sighed. "Actually I didn't know what she was thinking. I never knew. All she said was, you would come looking for her here, make sure you find her. So, I thought I might as well let her face the front door every day and keep watch right here."

She did not have to watch. She could smell me, hear me. I recalled our conversation some fifty or sixty years ago.

If you can't see me, how will you find me?

I will be like Anna. With my good ears I'll hear you.

Then close your eyes. Listen. Where am I?

Floral really did close her eyes. She pricked up her ears, and pointed at where I was hiding.

If I go farther away, and you can't hear me?

Then I'll be like Anna. With my doggy nose I'll find you.

Close your eyes again. Sniff. Where am I?

Floral really did close her eyes, and sniffed all around like a dog.

I said, Forget it, the dog's nose is a million times more sensitive than a human nose.

But I only started being a dog today. Give me time to practise, and then I can smell you out no matter how far you go.

Then you must come find me.

You must wait for me too, and let me find you.

If you can't find me, I'll turn around and look for you.

Yes, I have come, Floral. I recalled the promises I had made to Floral, promises that have not been made good. Perhaps, between certain people, promises are not necessary, as long as there was trust.

"You both believed I wasn't dead?"

"We'd rather think that way."

"You'd rather? Sometimes that's just self-deception."

"But we were willing to wait, even if it's like looking for a grain of sand in the ocean."

"I get it, it's like seeing it as a kind of hope."

"I guess. Floral said you'd come. Every day I hoped for you to be alive, too." He sighed and continued, "There seemed to be nothing else to think about in this life, except thinking about waiting for you. After I got out of jail, I made a living cleaning toilets. For thirty years I cleaned, for thirty years I tried to get news of you. Once, in a fit of anger, I swore to Heaven, that if Heaven let you live, I would clean toilets for another thirty years willingly. Today my waiting proved to be not in vain. Ah, if I can live that long, I can probably clean for another thirty years... Daughter," Xiaokang tugged his daughter closer, and said to her—and me, "Chunhuan, perhaps only now do I understand why I had to wait for you. I waited for you because you are the only one who knows that I am really Zhu Xiaokang. Zhu Xiaokang escaped with his life from the Kuomintang. He is not a Kuomintang agent. He is not a criminal, or a real hooligan. He has never cheated anyone. He has always had a clean conscience. I can't have it that no one on this earth knows, that no one believes me. Even if it's just one person, just one person... I still waited, praying that you would live, that you wouldn't die before me... Child, your Uncle Chunhuan can prove that your father is no shameful spy. You don't have to feel you can't lift your head high. Don't be afraid anymore that anyone would find out about your dad. Don't keep avoiding dad, ignoring dad..." His daughter, who had been expressionless all along, suddenly broke down. "Dad!" she cried, and hugged Xiaokang.

"I came too late, Xiaokang," I felt as if I had been struck by lightning. Just now, I saw clearly the stub showing from the leg of his trousers. Not only did he have one leg maimed, he lost the other one as well.

I wanted to explain something to Xiaokang's daughter. Xiaokang waved his hand and stopped me, "There's no need. As long as you're here, that you're still alive, I am content." Tears glittered in his eyes.

"Oh, Floral left something behind. Daughter, go get your mum's thing." Xiaokang pretended to wipe his face casually with his sleeve; a corner of it was soaked.

His daughter brought over a small metal box. Xiaokang opened it before me.

There was a sheet of paper in there, with my handwriting from over forty years ago. There was a secret message written in rice broth on the back. I knew that she had not seen it, because the paper had not been heated.

On the sheet were two lines of a poem that I had copied down at random, to disguise the message:

"Peace, peace! he is not dead, he doth not sleep
He hath awaken'd from the dream of life"

As I read it, I turned around, letting my tears fall on the sheet. I thought I could see, vaguely, two words written as a prank in secret writing. "Silly ass"—just two words, two words that did not matter, written in secret writing as if they were of any importance. Silly ass.

Xiaokang asked, "What do they mean anyway, the lines on the paper?"

I answered without thinking, "It's a poem. Shelley."

"When she was alive, she kept asking me to read this paper out to her. She had heard it thousands of times, but she never tired of it. Because she can't read it, she felt it with her fingers, as if she could feel the words, as if she could read with her fingers," said Xiaokang.

"This was the last letter I gave her. I only wrote down two lines of poetry to amuse her," I answered Xiaokang half-heartedly, but in my heart there was only remorse.

Back then, Floral had asked me:

"Go ask Chunshao for me, how does he think of me in his heart. Then write it down for me in secret writing."

I did not go ask Chunshao, but I wrote two words on his behalf—

"silly ass"—and took it straight to Floral...

Did she not have a chance to see it, or did she not have the courage to?

I only hope she could not read it with her fingers. Was it possible to feel words written in rice broth?

Before I left, rain began to fall outside. Xiaokang and I stood at the door, watching the rain pour down. Quick-falling raindrops drummed on the roof tiles, densely, sparsely, pitter-patter; I felt I could hear a melody from the irregular pattern of the rain. Just like the codes that Floral and I used to make tunes with as a game back then.

Is that Floral? Are you talking to me?

I asked in my heart.

The raindrops continued falling, soft and heavy, heavy and soft.

I could hear her hum at me mischievously—

re' | re mi   do sol   re do   do re   fa | re'   do sol   re re   sol | re mi'   do sol | re   sol | re sol   do sol   re do   do do' | do re'   re'   do re'   re'

"I would love to... be your Sisi."

re   sol | re sol   do sol   re do   do do' | do   do fa   do fa   do

"Be your Anna."

Here is the ultimate point, the highest peak... There is no road beyond this: the path of history has come to an end. Beyond this lay a cliff and an abyss, where one must fall or fly—a supra-historical path.

— Dmitry Merezhkovsky

When a faithful pair of eyes cry along with me, the suffering in life becomes worthwhile.

— Romain Rolland

Afterword

The haunting from the past

Chang Ying-Tai

My father passed away a long, long time ago. Only in recent years did I seem to have gradually become cognizant of the fact, and then it felt as if it was not that long ago. But many days have indeed passed, though I do not know how I passed them... I remember, at that time, I walked several hours under the blazing sun until I found that police station. I requested to see the photograph of his body. On the photograph, the peeling skin appeared yellow-green, and its edges was bright green. I did not know that skin peeled off dead bodies in such large pieces. On the death certificate were only four words, indicating a most ordinary cause of death, like one of those medical conditions that were randomly applied to normal, otherwise unscathed people who die sudden deaths. I do not wish to say what it was; it does not matter whether I believed it or not. I did not. But I had no choice but to accept that death certificate.

They all said that his eyes were wide open when he died, and his fists were held tightly. I did not know who it was that closed his eyes and opened his fingers.

When I went back to my hometown to coordinate the funeral, I was

AS FLOWERS BLOOM AND WITHER

the only immediate family there. I decided on the date, and picked out the coffin, urn, and burial site; but I could not see his full body. He lay in burial clothes in the coffin, which was kept only slightly ajar. Only on the day of the cremation was he finally taken out to be put on a rack. His thawed body had shrunk considerably, appearing as if there was nothing beneath the clothes anymore. There were tiny droplets of moisture on his face; the tongue in his opened mouth was purplish-black. When the body was placed in the coffin again, I walked up to look at him one last time. For some reason, his face appeared to be white on one side and dark on the other, the division clear and abrupt. But the coffin was closed quickly once more, and was brought away and placed in the furnace.

A few days later, he came to me in a dream, still riding that ancient Fuji brand bicycle. On the rear seat was the backpack that I carried to school and to work. It was always filled with too many books; my back was hunched from its weight. The bicycle, carrying my backpack, rode into a tunnel. There was a dim yellow light emitting from the mouth of the tunnel. Before entering it, he kept turning around to look at me, until he disappeared into the darkness of the tunnel.

I felt my heart crushed by something heavy. Unable to let the matter rest, I took out his death certificate and made my way to that police station again. I accessed his photo to take one last good look at him, a good look at all of him.

When I was little I learnt a song by Dvorak called "Goin' Home". But I have to say, I hate going home. Sometimes, when I was drained in both body and spirit, I would be too tired and had no strength to think about the grudge I had borne for all this time. Later on, I discovered I had been so lazy, or perhaps I had gone through so much, that there was no room left in my heart for that grudge. All I had left were watchfulness and fear.

It was like the plot of a television serial. It started with something rather insignificant, but then snowballed into a string of misery and misfortune. If I were to tell it, it would sound like a creepy horror show, nothing at all like real life. Someone had said that all the world's a stage. A quote that's quoted too often, but I must admit that, when it actually happened to me, it did seem like a staged play, a tragedy of a grand scale.

It began with an investigation. It began with a relocation that seemed like an escape. It began with one family, but spread to friends and relatives around them, and ended up as a drawn-out nightmare of death and destruction.

To this day I do not speak of it. Or perhaps, I dare not speak of it. I can only wipe my tears.

So, let's talk about something else. We'll talk about my ignorance and naiveté.

This is a memory from the Martial Law years. I was in Primary Three. It was on the day of President Chiang's birthday, a national holiday. Bored at home, I recalled the handicraft that I had learnt in art class, and made a beautiful lantern out of a sheet of white paper. I hung it outside the house happily. When Father woke up from his afternoon nap, I made him go outside to admire my masterpiece, like one showing off a piece of treasure. To my astonishment, he gave me a harsh scolding and ordered me to take the lantern down. I was indignant and asked him why. Without another word, he dashed out and tore down the white lantern, crumpled it and threw it into the rubbish bin. Only when I was older did I understand why: If someone had seen it and reported on us, that we dared to display white, the colour of mourning, on President Chiang's birthday, we would no doubt be pinned with the label of sedition or the like.

When I was in Primary Five, one Sunday the teacher had us all gather at the school to watch a political propaganda movie. Father could not be bothered to take me to school, so he told me to stay home. At school the following day, the teacher told me to stand up before the entire class and asked me why I did not come watch the movie yesterday. I replied reverentially and honestly, "Sir, my father said, it's just some patriotic stuff. It's all right to skip it." The teacher lectured me for a whole class period on the importance of the nation and the despicability of the Communist rebels, and emphasised the wickedness of not watching the movie.

One day after class, my classmates gathered together, and, imitating the tone of the teacher from the class, began denouncing certain people as seditious elements and bad guys, as if those people were their common enemy. Who knew, I held the opposing view, even quoting the textbook to make my point: "The textbook says, Dr. Sun Yat-sen became known as the Father of the Nation because his revolution was successful. So, if those seditious elements were successful, wouldn't future textbooks call them fathers of the nation or heroes of the revolution?" Such things happened more than once. I even naively told my classmates, "I have books at home that are written by rebels!" I bragged about that like how they bragged about having posters of some movie star at home. How incredibly heedless of danger I was.

One day, out of the blue Father requested to take me out of school, and brought the entire family on a trip. Though normally thrifty to a fault, he took us all the way to Pear Mountain on a tour. After we had strolled all over the mountain, the whole family followed Father in aimless wandering. Father did not appear to be planning to go home. He bent down and asked me where else I would like to go see. This was the most generous he had ever been. I remember we went to visit a few other places. The only thing was, Father was unwilling to buy full-fare tickets; we all crammed into too few seats, like fugitives in the movies squeezing in like sardines in their escape.

However, when we ran out of places to go, we had to go home.

We found out that, during those few days, the Investigation Bureau had visited. Unable to find Father, they made inquiries around the neighbourhood, and even went to his home village in Tainan to try to track him down. My grandmother and my relatives were all questioned thoroughly. As soon as Father returned home, he was taken away by the Bureau.

Someone had told on his friend. He was brought away on account of his friend.

Apparently Father insisted on not betraying his friend. The Investigation Bureau forced a confession out of him through torture...

But Father never talked to us about that. I suppose he didn't want to look bad. He probably felt that he would lose face if his offspring knew he was tortured and forced to confess.

And then we moved away. But a new location could not guarantee

safety; a new snowball began rolling. Similarly, while it did not start
with anything out of the ordinary, it caused a huge change in our lives.
Endless catastrophes began to befall us. Bugging, surveillance, stolen
photos and mail, poison... all kinds of uncanny plot twists, one after
another. And then, my innocent girlhood terminated early.

When Father was alive, he had wished for me to apply to the
Investigation Bureau. He had insisted on that since I was in primary
school. He even had me memorise the *Six Codes* in preparation.
Perhaps this was to make up for his regret for his having succeeded
in the Investigation Bureau examinations but having his eligibility
cancelled for not joining the Party. Or perhaps, he felt that position
came with powerful privileges, such as privileges for ordering others
to one's will? Privileges for troublemaking? However, the young me
indulged only in literary and artistic pursuits, and took absolutely
no interest in the privileges or benefits he talked about. All I would
do was to obediently go visit the Investigation Bureau along with a
group of classmates who were party members, and obediently join the
political party that he did not want to join (though he always voted
for them obediently). From my second year in university onward, he
went and paid my party dues every year, letting me keep my nominal
status as a party member, so that I would not become ineligible to join
the public service in the future (that was a deep-seated thought in his
mind). Every year, he never failed to remind me in his letters to stay in
touch with that party... until he passed away. Little did he know that I
once had an award certificate signed by President Chiang Ching-kuo,
as well as a small golden medal (not having done anything of mention,
I don't remember why I received the award). He also did not manage
to find out that the times had changed. He kept worrying about me
not finding a stable job. He always said that one would starve to death
from writing and drawing. He tore down my watercolour painting
from the wall; he was uninterested in seeing the artwork for which
I won a prize; he weighed my literary trophy contemptuously in his
hand, saying, how much could you sell this to the junk-collector for?
I was furious and refused to listen to anything he said, feeling that he
was worldly and utilitarian. Only after I joined the workforce later on
could I gradually come to appreciate that, in his diffident mind, what

he desired was not any special privilege at all, but rather the guarantee of being safe, warm, and fed. He was a country boy, the son of a poor peasant. When he was still little, his father was seized by the Japanese and sent to work as a labourer in the army, and he often went hungry. He once hid in a large urn to avoid being sent away to be adopted. He was not a man without ambition; it was just that he understood pragmatism. He studied hard for his exams for pragmatic reasons. Even when he married, it was for pragmatic reasons (my mother's uncle cum adoptive father was a confidential secretary of the first independent mayor of Tainan, though he died early), because all his brothers were all child labourers. Back then, when I was sorting through my father's belongings, I discovered a "Party Member Contact Form" that he didn't get around to mailing out. It turned out that, worrying that I would not listen to him and connect with the party, he took the initiative to make the connection for me. On it he wrote, "Could you please recommend a job for me after my graduation, ideally in the public sector?" It was almost like a prayer of intention before a god. I couldn't help but laugh. Was his earnest payment of my party dues like paying one's temple dues? Whenever I remembered this in later days, my heart would ache. Indeed, he was even more naive than I was. He didn't know that the times really would change. The times will always change, though it's unclear that it's for the better. But the people always hope for change, as if change will make everything all right.

This is inevitable. People's memories invariably remain fixated on a period which they believe to be important, revisiting it time and again. When I was a child, my mother often mentioned that, during the February 28 massacre in 1947, her parents fled town in the cover of night. After that, their mansion was taken over by some general. The courtyard of their mansion was as big as the sports field at school. The wall was built very low, and the neighbours' children could climb in to pick fruit or jump into the pond in the courtyard to play with the fish. All who visited as guests were the best of society. I was once brought to the original site to commemorate my grandparents. Except for a single fruit tree, all the fish ponds, flowerbeds, gardens, and Japanese-style huts had been replaced by roads, kindergartens, and dense apartment buildings. My mother sighed as she reminisced, while I felt as if I was in a different world, listening to a fairy tale from a kingdom far, far away, the world of today and the world of the future seeming equally irrelevant and distant. My now and my future do not have to be the now and the future projected from this instance. Even though the nightmare has not dissipated, I have the right to build another dream, one of my own.

The story that I wrote here is not the story of my family. It is by and large fictional, even though the characters and their circumstances are reflections of reality. I borrowed the setting from a friend's home (combined with my maternal grandparents' house). This friend was the son of a high-ranking Kuomintang official. When he was a child, he enjoyed the privileges of an aristocrat. He had told me nonchalantly that, "it's just that" his family came to own this or that before other people did, that's all. He then reminded me in a holier-than-thou tone that I must not feel relatively deprived because of that, because you cannot truly possess a place; you are only travelling through; the house you live in was lived in by others before you, and the land you stand on, too, belonged to someone else in the past... I listened in silence, because I had never dared to think about being "relatively deprived". But that was what he projected onto me. A few years later, his father passed away, and his relatives came to claim a share of his property. He went berserk. He had forgotten what he had said to me before. He insisted on keeping, at all costs, the mansion that the Kuomintang had granted to them for a low price. I knew that it was not out of greed. He just wanted his house to continue looking intact. He missed the souls who had inhabited the house, even though they had long since departed... I then thought about the general who took over my grandparents' mansion. It was said that he did not live there for long before he was executed by his own party. Who knows how many more owners, how many more souls, have passed through that mansion? Indeed, no one can truly possess it.

No one can rest in peace, either, even after being buried in a grave. Sixty years ago, my maternal grandmother's grave was levelled to the ground, not long after her burial. This famed beauty from a high family, one-time overseas student, wife of a millionaire—short was the time she walked upon the earth, but shorter yet was the time she slept beneath it. Not even her bones could be found. She died in tragedy, but she did not know how terrifying in comparison were the things to come.

At that time I had not planned to write about my family, nor did I want to. Perhaps I was afraid, was avoiding certain fears. Or perhaps I continued to choose silence, which made me flee towards years even farther ago. Even though that era was not mine, it was just about seven or eight decades ago, which is not too far away. The living environment back then was similar to that in which I grew up. As for the psychological circumstances of that period, it is sufficient that they serve to relieve the gloominess in my heart.

The main story of this novel ended in the year President Chiang passed away. I was nine years old that year, nearing the end of the only two carefree years of my life. Even three or four decades later, I still can't help but remember those two years fondly, so long ago. President Chiang at that time seemed as remote as a mythical figure. Taipei, where he lived in the north, was like a foreign country to me, a child of Tainan in the south. To this day, I can still recite the "Will of President Chiang" from memory. It was written in the classical language. Back then, the teacher would not let us go home for lunch if we could not recite it properly. I can also recite most of the President Chiang Memorial Song from memory. It was penned by Chin Hsiao-I and the language was incredibly difficult, praising, in an ancient mode, the President's erudition and martial prowess. After all these years, I can still brag about my memory to friends five or six years older than myself. Back in that year, everyone in the nation dressed in mourning garb, and every day we observed three minutes of silence at the flag ceremony, before singing the President Chiang Memorial Song. I did as I was told, but as soon as I got home I would switch to singing love songs from romance movies in the bathroom. Though, I didn't understand what the "love" I was singing was about, nor did I understand the catastrophe that was about to descend upon us...

Three conflicting forces—the tension and changes of the period/my carefree innocence/the prison-like life in the democratic era—formed those years that wore me out, that made me continuously wanting to escape.

I never quite know how to write about home. Since I was born, I moved over forty times. It was like being a fugitive, moving from prison to prison.

I wrote the first draft of this book twenty-one years ago, using some two hundred thousand words to reminisce in great nostalgia one of the homes I had for a short time in my childhood. Twenty-one years later, I abandoned it, removing all but a mere five hundred words. I kept one of the minor characters, and started from scratch in all other aspects. I changed the protagonist, changed the setting, changed to another home, and changed the events; nonetheless, the result feels more intimate. It is closer to the pain in my heart, closer to the vanished home that I missed. I was motivated to make these changes after studying more historical materials. Those oral accounts, those files from the National Security Bureau, those victims' records and biographies (some have died in prison), as well as interviews with military camp veterans—they made me emotional, but not out of sadness. And, also, I feel very grateful that, after all these decades, there are finally people who understand and care; that we are fortunate to have survived. So, I decided to bring in all those people from that era: it is the community that made me emotional, not individuals. Though, in the story I did selfishly keep many parts of me, many secret games, many fantasies of fighting or escaping.

* * *

The illustrations scattered within the pages of this novel are mere drafts that record, in some basic visual form, certain scenes, and they helped to shape and clarify the details within my imagination. In the past, with other books of mine that have appeared in Chinese, I painted scenes with the deliberate intention of illustrating the publication. The illustrations within this book, though, are not intended to be elaborate. In fact, they should be considered akin to a film director's film "Split-mirror Sketch" draft, and are being included here in order to demonstrate a small part of my writing process.

CPSIA information can be obtained
at www.ICGtesting.com
Printed in the USA
BVOW03s1747100417

480822BV00001BA/26/P

9 781911 221043